Terri Nixon was born in Plymouth, England, in 1965. At the age of nine she moved with her family to a small village on the fringe of Bodmin Moor, where she discovered a love of writing that has stayed with her ever since.

Since publishing in paperback (through independent small press BeWrite) in 2002, Terri has appeared in both print and online fiction collections, and published *Maid of Oaklands Manor* with Piatkus in 2013.

Terri Nixon

The Watchers of Pencarrack Moor

PIATKUS

PIATKUS

First published in Great Britain in 2024 by Piatkus

1 3 5 7 9 10 8 6 4 2

A CIP catalogue record for this book
is available from the British Library.

ISBN 978-0-349-43172-7

Typeset in Caslon by M Rules

Printed and bound in Great Britain by
Clays Ltd, Elcograf S.p.A.
Papers used by Piatkus are from well-managed forests
and other responsible sources.

Piatkus
An imprint of
Little, Brown Book Group
Carmelite House
50 Victoria Embankment
London EC4Y 0DZ

An Hachette UK Company
www.hachette.co.uk

www.littlebrown.co.uk

For you, Mum. Always,
and with so much love.

DRAMATIS PERSONAE

Gwenna Rosdew: The daughter of local grocer and decorated war hero, Jonas Rosdew. In an effort to follow in her father's footsteps, she joined the flying school, but ambition made her an easy target for her unscrupulous instructor; she was drawn into a smuggling ring, and forced to transport contraband to and from the air base. She later discovered her father had also been a reluctant courier, and since his arrest she has withdrawn from almost everyone, including her former best friends.

Lynette Nicholls: Only daughter of a well-to-do Brighton family. Lynette's beloved older brother, Xander, was killed in a flight training accident at sea, and she originally came to Cornwall to find out the truth behind his death, but fell in love with Geordie Sargent and chose to stay. She discovered that her brother had died as a result of sabotage, and played her part to get those responsible arrested.

Geordie Sargent: Blacksmith. Geordie was previously a miner in Devon, but the accident that had closed down the mine also drove him down to Cornwall, away from his wife and daughter, to find work in the China clay pits. He had brought with him a reputation for stirring up labourers to fight for union rights, and this led to a march, a riot, and Geordie's eventual dismissal. Popular and charismatic, Geordie now owns a forge in Pencarrack, trading as a blacksmith and farrier.

Joe Trevellick: Former kettle boy from the South Pencarrack pit. Fourteen-year-old Joe lost his father in a landslide brought about by negligence, and was severely injured himself. He had previously looked up to Geordie as a boss and a mentor, and is now Geordie's official apprentice. With no family left, Joe also lives with Geordie in the blacksmith's cottage.

Tory Gilbert: Co-owner of Pencarrack Stables. Tory had left home at a young age, to search for her mother, and instead joined an all-female crime syndicate in Bristol. When her lover, a member of a rival gang, was killed, she re-evaluated her life and returned to her home town. She befriended Gwenna when they both took up flight training at the same time, but realised she wanted to work with animals instead. She is now half-owner of the stables, with Lynette.

Bobby Gale: Tory's regular companion. They had been childhood friends, and, since Tory's return to the area, they have become close again. Bobby had been a sapper during the war, and, following his work in the tunnels, he suffers from post-traumatic stress. Despite this, he had ventured into a disused mine tunnel to help bring Tory and her old gang leader to safety. Bobby, who has generally been known as something of a rogue since his boyhood days, takes work when and where he can, due to his inability to settle.

CHAPTER ONE

Devonport, Plymouth
26 November 1931

The Red Cow Inn was a mass of white uniforms at one end, fresh from the ship that had docked earlier that day, and, at the other, a shifting swell of off-duty matelots. It was only a matter of time before someone looked at someone else the wrong way, and then the two groups would inevitably clash, in a fury as manufactured as it was gleeful. Any bloody excuse, this lot. Daniel Pearce couldn't be doing with it, not tonight. He hadn't even wanted to come. He'd protested, argued, but finally given in, and now here he was, his head already aching, his stomach uncomfortably bloated, and his vision taking an age to catch up with each dizzying turn of his head.

He began shouldering his way to the door, but a friendly arm slung around his shoulder stopped him, and the beery breath that blew into his face made him reel back. Knowing his own would be equally foul only made it worse.

'Midshipman Pearce,' the voice bellowed, 'where'd you think you're going, lad?'

Daniel jerked his head towards the door. 'Fresh air!'

'Bit fresher out there than's good for you!' Micky Frier went off into drunken honks of laughter, and slapped Daniel on the back as he withdrew his arm. 'Good luck, mate!'

Micky wasn't wrong, Daniel reflected, as he pulled open the door and stepped out into the night; wind and rain blew down Barrack Street as if it had sought him out personally, but it felt good on his hot skin and he didn't turn away from it. He leaned against the wall, listening to the shouts from inside the pub, and wishing he'd stuck to his guns and refused to come out.

'But it's your birthday,' Micky had pointed out reasonably. He was some kind of cousin on Daniel's mother's side, so privy to the information Daniel had preferred to keep quiet, but it was out now; others had taken up the call, and there was nothing to be done but agree. He was under no illusion that it was actually a celebration for his birthday – he hadn't acknowledged one of those for seventeen years – but the B-class destroyer, *Brazen*, had docked that morning at Millbay, and it didn't take seven years of naval experience to know which way that particular wind would blow; the breeze was already stirring. The *Brazen* boys had clearly been just as keen on squaring up; otherwise they wouldn't have come down to Devonport to drink.

Daniel squinted through the rain, weighed up the options behind and ahead of him, and pushed himself away from the wall; he wasn't going to get involved in this, tonight of all nights, when he couldn't work out whether the real pain was in his head or his heart. The loss of his father, on Daniel's tenth birthday, had bitten hard, and it showed its teeth again on some birthdays more than others. He never knew when that would be, but today was one of them. He made his way up Barrack

Street, glad the dockyard was only a few streets away. Let them get on with it. He shook his head, a soft laugh escaping into the night, as his feet tangled and he almost fell over the debris that littered the road from a new building that was under way near the junction.

The rain drummed on the roofs and the pavement, running down the gutters in ever-widening rivers, and Daniel pulled his coat closer around himself, glad he was on his way back to his bed and not still stuck in that heaving mass of bravado and beer. He'd definitely made the right decision. He'd rag the other lot to shreds reporting for duty tomorrow morning, when he'd be the only one even close to sober, and hopefully not too hungover either. As he drew close to the end of the street, however, his footsteps slowed and his good feelings vanished.

A car idled at the end of the road, the back door open and the driver standing beside it, waiting for the man who'd just left the pub to finish adjusting his hat and overcoat in preparation for his brief sprint through the rain. Daniel knew that man. He'd never forget the heavily jowled face, and the small, close-set eyes that regarded everything around him with visible disdain: Alfred Dunn; owner of Dunn's Drapery and Homewares. Spreader of lies, and destroyer of lives. His mother's erstwhile employer.

Around ten years ago, Daniel had watched from his vantage point on the stairs as Dunn had fixed those mean little eyes on his bewildered and tearful mother, delivered the blow that she was dismissed, her reputation in shreds, and added that she would receive no severance pay from her job, so she needn't even ask. That same shouting bully, who was now hesitating to get his shoes wet, had been wearing a thin smile that had haunted the then sixteen-year-old Daniel since that afternoon. If it hadn't

3

been for his father's naval pension, Daniel and his mother would have lost everything. They had barely scraped through that year, and though things had improved slightly when Daniel had been old enough to join up, they still struggled on his meagre pay, and Cathy Pearce would never work in a Plymouth shop again. All thanks to Alfred bloody Dunn.

Daniel lengthened his stride, and managed to reach the car at the same time as Dunn was ducking his head to climb into the dry vehicle. As they collided, Dunn straightened and planted his walking cane between his feet.

'Watch out!' He looked Daniel up and down, scowling and impatient. 'Matelots.' The word was dense with distaste, and Daniel only just managed to resist hitting out.

'Why did you do it?' he demanded. His words ran together, and he bit back a curse and tried again. 'Why did you lie about my mother?'

Dunn evidently couldn't place him, or perhaps he simply couldn't be bothered to listen. He threw up a dismissive hand and ducked into the car again, rain streaming off his hat brim. 'Get a move on, Robertson,' he grunted at the driver, who shot Daniel a mistrustful look and shut the car door.

'Why?' Daniel raised his voice and seized the handle, yanking the door open again.

'Get away!' Dunn grabbed it from his side and pulled, but Daniel held on, feeling the metal sliding beneath his wet fingers. It ripped free from his drink-weakened grasp, and slammed shut again. All the anguish of the day, and the fury of re-surfacing memories, rose up through Daniel in a wordless shout. He slammed a hand onto the roof of the car, dimly aware that he would feel the pain of that tomorrow. As the car began to lurch away, he saw Dunn twist in the back seat to stare back at him, clearly trying to work out who he was.

'It's *Daniel Pearce*, you bastard! Remember us?'

Daniel's foot knocked something as he took an instinctive but futile step after the car, and he looked down to see a half-brick from the building works. Without a thought, he snatched it up and let it fly, not expecting to do anything more than show Dunn how he felt. But he'd thrown hard, and the car had slowed ready to ease down a side street; the brick smashed through the back window with a sound that drove away the last of Daniel's alcohol haze. His breath caught as the car veered off its intended path, and into the front yard of the house on the corner of the street, coming to a crashing halt against the door. The wood splintered, and incredulous, frightened voices came from inside the house; more came from behind Daniel, where his first, anguished shout had brought people onto the street. He knew he should run, but he was frozen where he stood.

The back door of the car was flung open and Dunn emerged, ducking low as if he thought more missiles were heading towards him. When he saw Daniel standing there, still in shock, and obviously no further threat, he grasped his cane halfway down its length, and pointed it as he advanced. But his face had lost that twisted scowl, and instead had melted into a smile that looked cold and triumphant in the thin street lighting.

'What did you say your name was?' he asked, his voice calm now, even polite.

Daniel didn't reply, but he heard his own incriminating words come back to him anyway, as the growing crowd repeated them with evident satisfaction.

'Pearce, or so he said.'

'Daniel, was it?'

'He's from the Guzz.'

'Devonport boy,' someone added helpfully, when Dunn gave them a questioning look.

'Yes, I thought so.' Dunn looked back at his car, where Robertson was gingerly pulling out the larger shards of glass from the rim of the rear window. He smiled at Daniel again. 'Go back to the barracks and sober up, Pearce.'

Daniel felt the relief start to creep through him; maybe the man had a conscience after all. He turned to leave, but Dunn called out to him and, when he looked back, gave him that chilly smile again. 'Don't worry, we'll know where to send the police in the morning.'

His Majesty's Convict Prison, Dartmoor
11 December

The Black Maria passed slowly beneath the granite archway at the entrance to the Prison, and, looking numbly up at the meaningless engraving there – *Parcere Subjectis* – Daniel felt the world shrink until there was nothing else left. There was only this bleak and remote place, looming like a scar on an expanse of moor that had once seemed the epitome of freedom to him, when he had been an adventurous boy. Now it was its opposite. At the Guildhall in Plymouth, just a few hours ago, he had looked up to see his mother, her eyes wide and horrified as the judge made his pronouncement: seven years. She had stared at the judge, disbelieving, but no less so than Daniel himself, who still could not fully understand how it had come to this.

6

That Dunn was a business-owner, Daniel had, of course, known. That he held grudges and feared for his reputation had become clear, throughout the course of Daniel's very short trial. That Dunn was also a councillor, and held so many people's jobs to ransom, was something he hadn't realised at all, until after the harsh sentence had been passed and he'd been advised to abandon any hopes of an appeal.

While he'd been awaiting trial he'd had plenty of time to think about the stupidity of his actions, and to prepare his defence: *Dunn spread lies that my mother was a thief, and fired her from her job; he made sure she'd never get work in another shop or business . . .*

But when he'd been closely questioned about why he thought a respectable man like Dunn would do such a thing, he'd had no answer. He was ashamed to admit it but, for an icy moment during the trial, he'd even been swayed into believing that Dunn might have been telling the truth after all. But the memory of his mother's bewildered dismay, on the afternoon Dunn had come to the house to inform her of the sacking, had been too real to keep that notion alive for long.

'Look sharp, Pearce.' A finger poked him between the shoulder blades, bringing him out of his thoughts, and he rose, handcuffs clanking, to disembark the van and take in his new home. He stood in the yard, awaiting the order to march, and stared up at the rows and rows of barred windows stretching into the iron-grey sky. What awaited him beyond them? He swallowed, tried not to think about what he had left behind, and when the order was given he walked, as straight and tall as he could, into the place they called 'Halfway to Hell'.

CHAPTER TWO

Cornwall
18 December

The sound of the collision was louder than she'd expected, and more prolonged. One minute Gwenna had been navigating the grocery van through misty drizzle, down familiar, twisting lanes, glad to be nearly home, and the next, a man she vaguely recognised was standing in the middle of the road. She'd uttered a short cry, jerked instinctively on the steering wheel, and ploughed the nearside wing of the van into the Cornish stone hedge. Her head connected with the steering wheel hard enough to fling it back again, and in the moment of numbness that followed, she had time to glance in the mirror to see the man still staring, horrified. But something about the sight of her broke the spell, and he turned to scramble up the hedge on the other side. At the same moment as the first trickle of blood ran into Gwenna's right eye, the skinny figure threw himself over into the field and was gone.

Gwenna fumbled for the woolly winter hat she'd discarded early on in the drive back from the warehouse. It was on the passenger seat next to her, but with one eye closed and the other one blinking to clear her rapidly blurring vision, it took longer than it should have to find it. When her hand closed on it she brought it up to her forehead and pressed it against what she fervently hoped would just prove to be a small cut.

She fumbled for the door handle with shaking fingers and got out to inspect the van, swallowing the nausea that rose in her throat, but relieved to see the damage wasn't as bad as she'd feared. The winter had stripped the hedgerow back to little more than twigs covering the stone here, otherwise there would have been hardly any marks at all. As it was, she was reasonably sure she hadn't damaged anything expensive. Hissing at the stinging cut on her head, and the soreness that was already creeping across her shoulders, she got back behind the wheel and reversed out of the hedge.

'Nigel bloody Stibson,' she muttered, throwing a black look at the place where the man had made his escape. What had he done now? People often likened Stibson to Caernoweth's resident rogue Bobby Gale, but he was far worse than Bobby had ever been, and, as far as she knew, Bobby had never actually stolen anything from her family's shop. By contrast, she had to watch Stibson from the moment he entered, to the moment the door closed behind him, and even then she couldn't be sure he hadn't pocketed something.

She put the van into gear, and quickly transferred her left hand back to her forehead, keeping the woolly hat pressed in place as she drove, and trying not to think about the fluff that would need to be pulled away as a result; it was still better than being blinded by blood. Her progress was painfully slow as she wound carefully through Pencarrack village, and she felt her neck stiffening. Her head throbbed harder than ever, and she was still feeling queasy, too, so, with a sigh, she pulled over to the side of the road outside Doctor Stuart's surgery. She got out without checking herself in the mirror; she'd look a sight anyway, whether the cut was serious or not, and it wasn't worth frightening herself over.

This was borne out by the reaction of a small boy as he skipped along the pavement beside his mother; he stopped dead still and stared, eyes like saucers, and wouldn't move until his mother seized his wrist and pulled him away, giving Gwenna a look of mingled apology and sympathy. Gwenna gave her a reassuring smile, which seemed to make matters worse, and she could only assume there was more blood on her face than she'd realised.

From the pavement she opened the front door and stepped into the hallway, the dimness of the surgery making her blink furiously after being in the bright daylight outside. Ahead of her, the stairs rose to the Stuart family's living quarters, and the clinically white-painted wooden door to her right stood half open, letting light spill from the waiting room to illuminate a slim triangle of the worn linoleum hall flooring. Her first feeling, as she pushed open that door all the way, was relief that it wasn't too busy for an early Friday afternoon, but the medicinal smell that hung over the small room brought back the faint dizziness and a fresh swell of nausea, and she took her steadying breaths through her mouth rather than make it worse.

The middle-aged woman at the reception desk glanced up briefly from her paperwork as she asked her to take a seat, then looked again, and jumped to her feet.

'Oh, my giddy aunt, what's . . . Doctor!' She bellowed this last, and Gwenna held up a hand.

'It's not as bad as—'

'*Doctor!*'

The doctor's door opened, and a strikingly attractive woman in a white coat came out, looking around in alarm. 'What is it?'

Her unusually light-blue eyes and delicate features might have seemed more suited to a Hollywood magazine cover than a busy village surgery, but Gwenna knew her to be a great deal tougher than she looked, and that her reputation was fast outpacing any doubts her new patients might have formed on first sight.

'Young lady here needs attention,' the receptionist said briskly, coming around to take Gwenna's elbow.

Doctor Stuart looked more closely, and gave Gwenna a reassuring smile. 'Come and sit down here a minute.'

'Gwenna?' A younger woman, with curly blonde hair half-wrapped in a sensible scarf, was coming through another door, one that led into the house behind the surgery. Her eyes opened wider. 'What happened?'

'Hello, Tory.' Gwenna was momentarily distracted from her various discomforts; she'd barely spoken to her old friend and fellow flying trainee in eighteen months, and this was hardly the image she'd have preferred to present. 'It's really not as bad as it looks. I hope,' she added, with a weak smile.

She groped, one-handed, for the back of a chair and the receptionist helped her sit down. Doctor Stuart sat beside her and gently peeled away the blood-soaked hat, while Gwenna kept a sharp eye on her expression. But to her relief the doctor's face registered no real worry.

'What did you do?'

'Pranged the van,' Gwenna mumbled. She felt a wash of clammy heat, and a watery sensation in the back of her mouth, which she swallowed hurriedly. 'Hit my head on the steering wheel. I'll be all right in a moment.'

'Give me two minutes, love,' Doctor Stuart said. 'I'll just finish up with my patient, and then I'm sure neither of these ladies would object to me seeing you next?' She directed this to the only other two patients, who shook their heads vehemently, and smiled at Gwenna.

'I'll sit with her, Mum,' Tory said, and took the empty seat on Gwenna's other side.

Doctor Stuart took the wad of soft cotton proffered by the receptionist, and guided Gwenna's hand to hold it against the cut. Then she gave Gwenna an encouraging smile, Tory a more familiar one, and went back into her room.

'How did it happen?' Tory asked, into the faintly awkward silence.

'I nearly knocked Nigel Stibson down in the lane,' Gwenna said. 'Hit the hedge instead.'

'Pity,' Tory said dryly. 'Look, Gwen, this is silly. We used to be the best of friends. And we went through so much together, didn't we?'

Gwenna immediately wanted to quash those memories, the way she had done so far by staying away from her old friends, but with Tory sitting beside her it wasn't so easy. She still felt the deep shame of having been so easily drawn into the gun smuggling ring her former flying instructor had been running from the air base. Her ambition, and desperation to follow in her father's footsteps, had been so transparent that she had been an easy target from the start. It was all right for Tory, who had her own shady past with the gangs of Bristol; she had made those choices herself, and had even revelled in her colourful life for a while. Gwenna

12

had allowed her pride to rule her decisions, and it had taken as much of a bruising as her conscience. She shifted away from Tory slightly, as if widening the gap between them could reinforce the barrier she had so carefully set in place. Tory saw it, and the light in her eyes faded.

'When Mum's set you right will you come back to the stables with me, so we can talk? I miss you.'

Gwenna felt a wave of unexpected emotion, but then Tory had always had a way of getting straight to the point, no sitting on her feelings, unlike Gwenna herself. 'I have to take the groceries back to the shop,' she said, 'but I can come up afterwards.'

'I'd like that. But only if you really want to.'

Doctor Stuart's patient limped from the surgery, and Gwenna accepted Tory's help to stand up, waited for the room to stop spinning, and then crossed the room. At the door, she turned back.

'Tory?'

'Yes?'

'It's Gwen-*na*.'

Tory grinned, as if she'd been waiting for this old, familiar reminder. 'So it is.'

Gwenna was surprised by how glad she was to see that Tory had waited, when she emerged with a fresh new dressing and some stern instructions from Doctor Stuart.

'I'll drive,' Tory said at once.

Gwenna shook her head, immediately wishing she hadn't, as the pain bloomed behind her eyes again. 'I think it's best if I just get back to it.'

There was a moment's silent battle between them, then Tory acquiesced. 'All right, but let me know if you want to swap.'

'I will.'

Getting back behind the wheel did give Gwenna a moment's pause, as she recalled the awful crunching sound and the moment of numb shock, but as soon as she pulled away from the kerb she settled back down. The stiffness in her neck was getting progressively worse, as Doctor Stuart had warned it might, but to her relief she was able to guide the van easily enough across the short stretch of moorland, and down to the family shop in the small town of Caernoweth.

Tory helped her unload the stock, then drove them back up to Pencarrack Stables, the business she and Irene Lewis had started after their own dramatic entanglement in the air base smuggling business. Gwenna hadn't visited recently, and she was surprised and impressed by the way it had grown. As well as the generously sized paddock and training pen, the yard had been levelled and now featured a small collection of buildings, dominated by the enormous barn that housed the stables and the dwelling. Gwenna could also see a more recently built coal shed, a smaller barn with a steeply arched roof, and a long, low building that might have been anything at all.

'I heard Irene's not coming back,' she said, as they pulled to a stop in the yard.

'No, she became engaged to her barrister in the end.' Tory smiled and shook her head. 'I can just see it, actually. They'll have very clever children.'

Gwenna had mixed feelings; Irene was the only other person who truly understood what they'd been through, no matter how friendly and understanding the others had been, and had tried to be. She and Gwenna had both been at the sharp end of it all, and both had been convinced there was no way out. They hadn't exactly bonded over their shared ordeal, but they had come to understand one another better. At the same time, however, Irene would have been a constant, unwelcome, reminder of it, so it might be a little easier to spend time with Tory now, than it would otherwise have been.

'So, she ended up selling her share to your friend Lynette?'

Tory nodded. 'You know about Lynette coming here to find out the truth about her brother's death?'

It would have been impossible not to have been aware of the result of Lynette's investigation; so much local shame, and one young man convicted of murder. 'Horrible business,' Gwenna said. 'I remember the lad they arrested, from our time at the flying school. Alec something, wasn't it?'

'Alec Damerel. Lynette would have gone back to Brighton then, I suppose, but she'd already fallen in love with this place.'

'And with a certain good-looking blacksmith,' Gwenna added, a smile finding its way back onto her face.

Tory laughed. 'And him.'

She led the way across the yard, towards the flat that sat atop the large stable building. A cat darted ahead of them and disappeared beneath a door, over which nodded a gleaming bay horse. A small, shaggy-looking pony shouted at them from the field, and Tory rolled her eyes as she fitted the key into the lock.

'Don't mind him, that's Hercules. He's cross about being separated from Mack there, but he's been disturbing the new horses with his constant grumbling, so he's staying out for a bit.'

'You've bought new horses? You must be doing well already.'

'We took them cheap from the pit, when they were replaced with lorries.' Tory led the way indoors. 'They're young though, so once they've recovered physically we'll sell them on. I think

15

Priddy Farm's looking for a horse to pull the market cart, which'll be a summer breeze compared to those clay wagons.'

It was clear to Gwenna that Tory had made the right choice when she'd given up flying to open the stables. Her friend was completely absorbed in what she was building here, and it showed. Gwenna followed her into the flat, which seemed much smaller than it had the last time she'd been here. Now, that seemingly vast empty space was taken up by a large open-plan kitchen and dining area, and a short hallway with three small bedrooms and a bathroom. She remembered the sound and smells of horses coming from below, and that hadn't changed, but none of that mattered next to the sight of plump, tatty-looking cushions strewn over sofa and floor, and a kitchen table covered with notepads, photographs, pens, and empty teacups. It felt like stepping into a world of easy-going comfort. Tory's heavy oilskin coat was draped over the back of the sofa, and she kicked her boots to one side as she closed the door behind Gwenna. It looked like a habit.

'I'm going to have to tidy this place up a bit,' she said, going to the kitchen. 'Tea?'

'Please. Why will you have to tidy? Is Lynette a stickler for that sort of thing?' Gwenna scolded herself for hoping that might be the case. It was jealousy, plain and simple. She'd felt real resentment last year, at how easily the woman who'd initially been Bertie's best friend had now also become Tory's. But it was her own fault, she knew; she was the one who had retreated even further into her own little world, and had remained there.

'A stickler? God, no,' Tory laughed. 'But we're planning to have a few guests over on Christmas Day, and at the moment there's hardly room to eat a biscuit, never mind serve dinner. Anyway, tell me about what you've been doing.' She poured hot water from the kettle into the teapot. 'Have you seen anyone since ...' She stopped, and a flush touched her skin, but she pushed on anyway. 'Since Peter?'

Gwenna stiffened at the mention of Peter Bolitho, her erstwhile fiancé. The crooked policeman who'd helped ensnare her father in the smuggling ring, who had not tried nearly hard enough to keep her out of it, and who was now serving time alongside her father in Dartmoor Prison.

'No,' she said shortly. 'And I don't want to talk about that, thanks.'

'Of course, I'm sorry.' Tory brought over the tray. 'It's just been such a long time since we've talked, and seeing you again brings up the memories.'

'For me too,' Gwenna said. 'But I don't think you understand that the memories are different for me.'

'Different?'

'My dad, Peter, all of that. It wasn't exciting, or dramatic, or ... or, *romantic* in any way.'

'Of course, I under—'

'No, you don't! You can't. It was lonely, and it was frightening.' Gwenna's voice rose; all this had been churning inside her for over a year, and she hadn't realised, until now, how desperately she'd needed to get it out. 'I was ready to leave everything behind to escape it. Absolutely *everything*.'

'Gwenna, I—'

'It was all right for you! You had your new business to think about, and Irene had that too. Bertie had Tommy, and her plane, and her new combat flying lessons ... But what did *I* have?' Gwenna shook her head, rising to her feet without realising she was going to do it. 'My father, and the man I'd once been ready

17

to marry, both thrown into prison, and a mother who couldn't face her customers, but still had to try and win them back after what Dad and I had done. Was it any wonder I'd duck back into the storeroom whenever one of you came to the shop?'

'We should have tried harder to reach you,' Tory said softly, also on her feet now. 'Gwenna, I'm so, so sorry!'

Gwenna turned towards the door, unable to bear the look of dismayed guilt on Tory's face, and to know she'd put it there. 'It's not your fault,' she mumbled, dragging her coat on as she crossed the room, almost at a run. 'We *will* talk, but ... not about that, and not today, all right? I ought to go back and help Mum with the stock we've just unloaded.'

Tory had evidently accepted the excuse, knowing it was useless to question it. 'Will you be all right to drive? You look worse now than you did before.'

Gwenna turned back to her, and emotion thickened her throat. 'I'll be fine. I'm sorry.'

She made her way down the steps and into the car before the tears came, and she let them run their course, aware of the worried face at the window above her but not daring to look up and catch Tory's eye. She supposed much of it was delayed shock, but knowing that didn't help. After a while she rubbed her sleeve across her eyes, and started the engine. She gripped the wheel, and took a deep breath, pushing it out in a short, hard sigh; it was no use weeping for what she couldn't change. Next year would see her father's release from prison, and once his life had been restored she would finally be able to begin the process of finding her own.

CHAPTER THREE

Lynette put her bag and case down on the platform, and pulled on her gloves against the biting Cornish wind. She vividly recalled the last time she'd done this, at the beginning of the year and still in turmoil over her suspicion that her brother's death had not been accidental after all. So much had happened since then, and now here she was with the last of her belongings from her old home; the final seal on her new life here in Pencarrack. While these few things had still been in Brighton it had felt as if she'd been doing little more than taking a very long holiday, but now it was finally sinking in that her life was entirely here. It was an exhilarating thought.

The excited greetings all around her cut through the sound of the steam, but were drowned out by the whistle as the train took off again on its way to Penzance. Lynette picked up her bags again, looking forward to getting her tight shoes off, settling back into her cosy room in the flat above the stables and seeing her friends again. Most of all she was looking forward to stepping into Geordie Sargent's strong embrace and hearing him breathe her name in that low, surprisingly soft way he had—

'Lynette!'

She stopped as she heard the anything-but-soft shout over the chatter of newly disembarked passengers, and, looking around she saw Tory Gilbert waving from the other side of the yard. She waved back and quickened her steps, dropping her luggage as she reached her friend, and returning Tory's hug with relief and pleasure.

'It's ridiculously good to be back,' she said, as Tory picked up the bag and led the way over to her car. 'It feels different this time. How's it all been?'

'Oh, you know.' Tory pushed the bag onto the back seat and reached for the case to do the same. 'The new horses I told you about have settled down at last, though Hercules still looks at them as if they're the devil's own fiery steeds.' She slipped in behind the wheel, and gave Lynette a sly look. 'Why don't you ask what you *really* want to ask?'

Lynette laughed. 'All right, how is he?'

The car eased out of the car park to begin the short trip to the stables, and Tory flashed a quick grin before returning her attention to the steep hill they were climbing. 'He's missing you, and being a proper bore about it, if you must know. But he's happy in his work.'

'Good.'

The final sale of James Rowe's forge had gone smoothly, once Geordie had stopped fighting Lynette's proposal that they stop leasing, and take it over as a joint enterprise. His argument – that it was entirely her money – had fallen on stony ground as she'd pointed out that, as eager as she was to learn new things, blacksmithing wasn't one of them. When she had further pointed out that the stables expected highly favourable rates from their new farrier, he had at last agreed that her money and his expertise were an equal partnership.

Injury-stricken James had been glad to sell for the price Lynette had offered, and the cottage attached to the forge was perfectly sized to accommodate Geordie and the recently orphaned Joe Trevellick. Lynette had trained herself not to look at Geordie's bedroom and imagine it with her own belongings alongside his, on the dresser and in the cupboard, though now and again she couldn't help mentally rearranging the kitchen and the sitting room to her own taste. Perhaps one day, but not yet.

'Between the forge, the stables, and the money I've set aside for a car, that's just about all my savings gone.' She smiled at Tory's suddenly worried look. 'And I have absolutely no regrets,' she added.

'I'm sure you don't,' Tory said. 'That's the fourth time since I picked you up that you've looked at your watch.'

'It isn't!' Lynette subsided and smiled. 'All right, but it's been a long time since I've seen him. You'd be the same with Bobby, you know you would.'

'I would,' Tory admitted. 'Though I still can't work out why.'

The car slowed, and stopped at the junction beside Gwinn's Copse. The clump of lime trees hid the forge from the main village road in the summer, but now the branches were bare, and Lynette saw a glimpse of smoke rising through them. Tory looked at her, with one raised eyebrow, and the moment Lynette realised they were not actually stopping to allow other traffic, as she'd thought, she was out of the car. Tory drove off, tooting the horn cheerfully.

Geordie Sargent was standing with his back to the doorway, carefully watching fourteen-year-old Joe Trevellick swinging his hammer down and sending sparks ceiling-wards. Lynette gave herself a minute to appreciate the broad, square shoulders, and the easy grace with which Geordie shifted his weight and demonstrated the correct actions for his apprentice. She enjoyed this moment of anticipation and the reward for waiting; in the months of not seeing him she had almost convinced herself that she'd somehow made more of him in her mind than the reality offered. But as his laughter rolled out over something Joe had muttered, the rich sound of it wrapped her in warm memories of the summer they had shared. She toyed with the idea of just slipping her arms around his waist from behind, surprising him that way, but reflected that it might be a bad idea, given that he was holding an enormous hammer.

'Geordie?'

He turned at once, and the laughter that had lit his face softened into a smile that drew an answering one from her. Joe raised a hand in greeting, and Lynette returned it, but then her attention was all for Geordie as he came over to where she waited. Heedless of his dirty apron, she wrapped her arms around his waist and breathed in the solid reality of him for a long, sweet moment. He'd lost weight, she could tell that at once; she must remember to give him a telling off for that later . . . but that trail of thought stopped abruptly as she felt him lower the hammer to the ground and return her embrace. Lynette tightened her hold, letting herself relax completely for the first time in weeks. She was home.

She sat by the forge, first enjoying the warmth while Joe finished the job he was doing under Geordie's supervision, and then watching them clean up and close down for the night. She felt no compulsion to offer help; they clearly had their routine refined and she'd only get in the way. It was good to see Joe moving with more ease now, too, after his horrific accident at the China clay pit earlier in the year. The loss of his father in the same landslide had naturally affected the boy deeply, and would for a long time to come, but the way he looked to Geordie for approval and advice gave Lynette real hope that he was at least settling into the new life they'd begun to build. His limp was still noticeable, but his left arm was almost as good as new now.

As Geordie's apprentice in the village forge, rather than just the kettle boy at the clay pit, Joe had found purpose and enthusiasm as his physical strength had returned. He and Geordie were their own little family now, Geordie's second family in fact, and Lynette sometimes wondered how he would feel about the possibility of starting a third; she just as quickly shied away from those thoughts, in case exploring them uncovered a truth she didn't want to know.

She waited until Joe had gone indoors to get washed and changed, then told Geordie about an extra Christmas present she'd found for the lad while she'd been in Brighton; a bottle-green woollen scarf, closely woven, and warm. As if in a direct comment, a gust of cold December rain blew in through the open front of the forge, and she shivered. 'Not going to invite me in, then?'

'Let me get changed, then we can go to the Engine House.'

Lynette laughed. 'Is that your way of saying you've still got dirty plates climbing out of the sink?' She didn't really fancy the pub, which would be busy at this time on a Friday evening, and if she couldn't be alone with Geordie she'd rather just crawl into her bed. 'I'll do them, if you like.'

'I knew you'd say that, which is why I'm taking you to the pub instead.' He must have seen her expression, and he reached out a hand. 'Or I could just walk you back to the stables,' he suggested. 'You look done in.'

'I am,' she said, not bothering to hide her relief.

'I'll just go and tell Joe.' He squeezed her hand, and left her to pull her coat closer around herself as she went to wait by the gate. She turned to look at the cottage, which was a rough place, and small, but still miles better than the dingy little attic room he'd rented at Mrs Rodda's boarding house. There had been a great deal of work to do on it to make it habitable, after James Rowe had abandoned it, but Geordie had made some good and loyal friends since he'd moved to Pencarrack, and had not been short of willing helpers.

He came out of the cottage, tugging his old leather hat snugly down over his dark hair, then put an arm around Lynette's shoulder and shone his torch ahead of them as they walked down the lane and into the village. Already they heard sounds of revelry from the Engine House Inn, and Lynette looked up at Geordie.

'If you'd really like to go in for a drink, I don't mind.'

'God, no.' He gave her a brief hug. 'There's only a week until Christmas, and I need to save my money. I haven't even thought of what I can get Tilly yet.'

'When you do, will you take it up to Devon yourself?'

He nodded. 'I've already written to tell Marion I'll be up next Thursday.'

Lynette mentally counted the dates. 'That's Christmas Eve, isn't it?'

'Tilly's favourite day,' he said with a little smile of remembrance. 'I know it means you'll miss the Caernoweth fair, but will you come?'

24

Lynette hesitated; she had gone with him to see his six-year-old daughter a few weeks before she'd left for Brighton, and the visit hadn't gone well. Goodness only knew what Geordie's wife had been telling the child; she'd looked at her father as if she'd expected him to snatch her up and throw her into the back of the car. Geordie had insisted she wasn't generally shy, but Lynette had kept her distance anyway, more to appease Marion than anything. It had been a quite excruciating few hours, and everyone had been relieved when the time had come to an end, though Geordie had been quiet and withdrawn on the drive home and for a couple of days afterwards.

He must have been recalling it too; he dropped his arm from around her shoulder and took her hand instead. 'It won't be the same this time.'

'Won't it?'

'Marion's written to me. It seems the bloke she's with had been warning Tilly not to trust me too well, because he's her dad now. Marion's sure it was nothing more sinister than him trying to win Tilly's affection, but he's been reminding her he's the one providing a home, and food, and – Christ!'

Still holding his hand, Lynette was jerked to a stop in the middle of the pavement, and, following his line of sight she picked out a tall, broadly built figure, rounding the corner and striding purposefully towards them. Her heart sank. 'Is that—'

'Jago Carne,' Geordie said grimly. 'He's out, then.'

Lynette's memory showed her a flash of the stables, early on a Sunday morning; Geordie curled up in the corner, coatless, blood-streaked, freezing cold, and in considerable pain. He'd admitted being at some fault for his cocky behaviour, and just as ready for a fight as Carne was, but he had also told her about the low-voiced taunt, meant only for his ears: *It's no wonder your missus took up*

25

with a real man, you liquor-soaked, useless excuse for a father.' Little surprise he had snapped, but in doing so he had given Carne all the excuse he needed to vent his unreasoning hatred.

Lynette threw a look of disgust at the man as he drew closer, and stepped into the road to avoid passing too closely on the narrow pavement. Carne barely glanced at them, but the way he thrust his hands deeper into his pockets and tucked his chin into his coat collar, made it obvious he'd seen and recognised them.

'How long did he get sent down for?' Lynette asked, when he'd passed them by.

'Five months for aiding the escape of a suspect, and two for affray. His part in the disturbance outside the Civic Hall. Not much, is it?'

'Not nearly enough.' Lynette began walking again. 'It's a pity no one reported him for what he did to you, as well. He didn't deserve to get away with that.'

'It was six of one and half a dozen of another,' Geordie said, and shrugged. 'We were both at fault, but I was stupid enough to use both hands to try and throttle him, and left myself open.' With his free hand he rubbed at his back, where a double-punch to his kidneys had signalled the end of the fight before it had really begun. 'Good thing they sacked him from the pit, he was always a dangerous person to be around. I wonder who'll give him work now, fresh out of prison?'

'Anyone who needs a brawny arm more than they value integrity,' Lynette said bitterly. She was livid that Carne had done so little time in prison, after helping Colin Damerel destroy the South Pencarrack clay works, and worse; helping Damerel to escape, along with his son, Alec.

Her feelings about the young man who had killed her brother

26

were still confused, and changed every day. He had tampered with the training aircraft in order to save his father's reputation, that was true enough, and it had resulted in Xander's death. But it was also true that he had been a good friend of Xander's, and had been shattered and traumatised by what he'd done. Xander should never have been in that plane, it was his own persuasive charm that had broken down his instructor's argument ... It had all been a shocking and devastating series of accidents, and executing Alec Damerel would do nothing to change any of it.

Geordie's thoughts had evidently been following a similar path, and he spoke quietly. 'I hear they're taking Alec up to Exeter on the twenty-seventh. He'll go to the rope a few days after.'

'That poor boy.' She felt a twist of profound regret, though she hated to admit that there were still times, usually on mornings when she'd awoken from another dream of her exasperating, but ebullient and beloved brother, when she would willingly have gone along to watch.

They reached the stables gate, and Geordie drew her into his arms. 'It's been a long day for you,' he said. 'You and Tory will still have a lot to talk about.' He pushed her hat back and kissed her forehead, then her lips. 'Go on inside and get dried off, and I'll see you tomorrow.'

She touched his face, her heart swelling with the relief and pleasure of being in his world again. Now her world, too. 'We can talk about going to see Tilly.'

He pulled back and studied her, and she saw rain beading on his thick eyelashes as his dark blue eyes met hers. He blinked it away, then closed his eyes and kissed her again. 'I love you, Lynette Nicholls.' His voice was almost too quiet to hear. 'Things will change, I promise.'

He waited in the rain while she climbed the steps to the flat, and when she turned to close the door behind her, she saw him lift his hand in farewell before setting off back to his new home at the far end of the village. She shucked off her drenched coat, thinking over his promise that things would change, but she still remembered the way Marion had kept sneaking glances at him, and she clearly recalled the odd, speculative expression that had flitted across the woman's face. She didn't think Geordie had seen it, and she herself had never mentioned it for fear of sounding like a paranoid 'other woman', but she couldn't help wondering what he would do if he *had* noticed. If he understood there was a possibility of being back in Tilly's life properly. Things would certainly change then.

CHAPTER FOUR

His Majesty's Convict Prison, Dartmoor

One week. That was all it had been, and Daniel's first night in Dartmoor crawled through his memory every time he closed his eyes and tried to sleep. It was worse than the Devonport Barracks at its noisiest, where the corridors had swelled and ebbed with largely good-natured jibes and mockery; in here the voices were just as loud, but they held brittle notes that lent a despairing edge to even the cockiest of shouts.

On arrival, Daniel had joined a handful of others at the reception desk, where he saw that someone had produced the brown envelopes into which all the prisoners had previously placed their belongings, back when they'd been arrested. It had given him a strange pang to see the envelope casually upended, and his things spread out in front of him; relics of a life that seemed to belong to someone else.

He agreed the amount and signed the ledger, and it all went back into the envelope ready for the day of his release. It seemed impossibly far off and he couldn't imagine now, what it would be like to clip that watch chain onto his waistcoat pocket, or to use that money to buy a train ticket to visit his mother. Yet only two weeks ago that was exactly what he had planned to do with it.

That first evening, he'd been led directly to a cell, where he was relieved to see only one bed. A single occupancy was the one hope he'd clung to throughout his trial and sentencing; he could just about manage, he thought, as long as he had the nights alone. There was even a generously sized window; barred of course, but through it he could see the rolling moorland in the distance, beyond the prison walls. A view, of sorts, even if he had to twist and strain to see it. He might survive this, yet.

The warder handed him a large white bag. 'Civilian stuff in here, then put it outside the door.' He pointed to a pile of clothes on the bed. 'Get into that lot, sharpish.'

Daniel undressed, slowly and mechanically at first, but soon felt the December chill coming off the stone walls to brush his skin into gooseflesh, and he quickly pulled on the replacement clothing: grubby trousers with broad arrows on them; a shirt that had seen better days, and delivered a strong whiff of stale sweat every time he moved; and a dull, scratchy, brown jumper. All topped off with a stiff coat, also daubed with arrows. The socks were thick and warm, however, and were a comfort on his icy feet, but when he looked around he found there were no boots. He fished his old ones out of the bag he'd just put outside the door, they were tight over the thick socks, but there was no question of discarding them, not as cold as the cell was.

He sat nervously on the bed, but gradually realised no one was coming back tonight, and although he felt lonelier than he'd ever been in his life, he was actually glad when the door clanged shut; at least he could fall into some kind of sleep now, and shut out the horrors of the day: the delivery of the verdict, the sentence, and his mother's shocked cries of denial as he'd been led down the tunnel to the cells beneath the courthouse.

But, as the night fell, and the noise from other parts of the prison gradually ceased, bar the odd, anguished cry, he lay curled on the hard bed, wide awake in the thick, heavy silence. He was too cold to sleep, the thin blanket pulled up over the lower part of his face so his breath warmed his chin at least. Now and again, he felt himself slipping into that strange, weightless state that heralded sleep, then a convulsive shiver would jerk him back, to remember where he was all over again.

The following morning, he was pulled from a shallow doze by a long-drawn out hooter that seemed to go on forever. Gritty eyed from lack of sleep, and grimly aware that he had just been introduced to what was to be the pattern of his life for the next seven years, he sat on the edge of the bunk again until it was his turn to be called to the hospital wing. There he was weighed, and had his eyes tested, and he patiently answered questions he'd been asked several times before, and to which the questioner had his previous answers in front of them. Did they expect to catch him out in some lie?

The library was a less intrusive experience. The new lags were given a Bible each, along with a prayer book and four other books, including two randomly picked novels. The thought of having time alone to read further lifted Daniel's spirits, even after the lights went out there was a chance he might catch some moonlight from the barred window, on clear nights at least.

He was at last taken to the bootmaker's store, where the warder saw him looking at the arrows carved into the soles of the sturdy boots he'd been given, and offered him a thin smile.

'Lots of outside work here,' he said, and tapped his nose. 'Muddy ground, particularly by the boundaries, if you get my meaning.'

Daniel pulled on the ill-fitting boots, wincing as his toes pinched, and hoping the leather would expand as he wore the boots in. 'What happens now?' he asked, standing aside to let the next new prisoner into the shop.

'Breakfast.'

Daniel hadn't realised how hungry he was, or how homesick, until that simple, familiar word cut through the barriers he had begun to build. Appalled, he felt a prickle at the back of his nose, and his vision blurred until he was able to force the emotion back. 'Bread and water, I suppose?'

The warder, a pleasant enough bloke with a thinning head of red hair, gave him a look of mock hurt. 'This isn't chokey, lad. You'll get porridge and tea, and since it's winter you'll get bread and marge as well. As soon as you lot are all done and dusted here, we'll get down to the canteen.'

'What're you in for?' one of the other new lags wanted to know, as they shuffled their way down the corridor a few minutes later. 'Me, I'm in for counterfeiting.'

'Money?' Daniel asked, interest pulling him out of his self-imposed mental hideaway.

'Gawd no!' The man chuckled. 'That's an art, that is. I forged medical exemption certificates in the war, but they've only just got me on it.'

'Bad luck.' Daniel realised the man was waiting for him to answer the original question, and shrugged. 'Threw a rock through a car window, and caused a smash up.'

'Deserved it, did he? The driver?'

'The passenger,' Daniel corrected. '*He* was sitting in the back letting someone else do the work, as usual.' For the first time since the whole sorry incident, and its awful consequences, he allowed himself a tiny, satisfied smile. 'And yes, he bloody well *did* deserve it.'

'Good.' The inmate put out his hand. 'Ray Beatty. Six-one-two, to everyone else. Four years.'

'Daniel Pearce. Six-one-six. Seven years.'

Ray whistled. 'That's a lot for smashing a car window.'

'Bloke was a local councillor, and the car went into the side of a house.'

'Ah.' Ray shrugged, accepting the explanation. 'Come on, then. This isn't my first time in stir, and the only thing I can say about this 'orrible stuff—' he nodded at his tray '—is that it'll fill you up.'

They ate quickly, both keen to escape the searching eyes of the old lags in the canteen, who seemed to be sizing up the new intake for God knew what purpose. The men on the table next to them wore different markings on the sleeves of their shirts; one wore a green horizontal bar, roughly an inch long, another couple had two such bars. The fourth had a green triangle. He was only around Daniel's age, and was the quietest of them, but it seemed to Daniel's curious eyes that he was the one the others turned to when they wanted their points endorsed. He was clean-shaven, which was unusual enough, and his clothes seemed to fit better than most. Ray nudged Daniel and nodded at the marking.

'Fourth stage prisoner,' he murmured. 'He'll be getting privileges. One to keep on side, I should say. You never know when he could come in useful.'

'Good for him.' Daniel shrugged, curiosity assuaged. 'You assigned work yet?'

'Not yet.' Ray looked over at the table next to them again. 'What's he in for, you reckon? Looks like butter wouldn't melt.'

'Probably murder then.'

As if his voice had carried more clearly on those words than on any previous, the stage four prisoner turned to look at him. He had a particularly unsettling and contradictory gaze; steady and appraising, yet somehow still giving off waves of bored in-difference. His black hair was neatly cut, probably due to those privileges Ray had mentioned, and his skin had the weathered look of someone who worked on outside detail, and had done so for some time.

He turned back to his meal as conversation buzzed on around him, and Daniel was left feeling oddly exposed, as if the stage four had read everything he needed to know and then dismissed him. He shook the feeling off, irritably, as he and the other new inmates were called for their induction meetings with the deputy governor.

'Fit for A1 labour?' the deputy asked him, checking his records.

Daniel nodded, hoping that meant he'd be considered for an outdoor detail. 'I am.'

'Military man, I see.'

'Royal Navy, sir. Midshipman.'

'Brought shame on it then, haven't you? Dishonourable discharge.'

Daniel's voice dropped. 'Yes, sir.'

The deputy scribbled on a card and pushed it across the desk. Daniel picked it up and saw *D Pearce* on one side, and 7, on the other. That was all he was now: an initial and a sentence. The card had a piece of string attached.

'Hang that on the nail beside your door,' the deputy said. 'B2, cell thirty.'

'I've already been assigned a cell, sir.'

The deputy shook his head. 'New convicts are kept away from the main cells to start with, until the medical officer certifies you clean. No TB, lice, what-not. The principle warder's the one who assigns you, and *he's* put you in B2, thirty. Go and pack your kit, we're going to need that cell.'

Daniel's heart sank, but he returned to pack his books, his wash kit, and his blanket, and to say goodbye to his short-lived view of the moor. He followed the warder across the yard to B hall, realising that his first room had been in the hospital wing, and therefore much closer to the gate. This brisk, rainy march took him past the admin block in the centre, and then beyond the kitchens, almost to the very rear of the prison. With every step he took, he felt more isolated from the world he knew.

Left alone, as the warder took the remainder of the shuffling group along the landing to their cells, he hung up his card as ordered, and put his bag on the empty bunk. He looked at the bed opposite, neatly made and as devoid of anything personal as his own, and wondered who he was going to be locked up with, for the foreseeable future. Most of the convicts were out on their various work details, so he stepped out onto the landing to look at the card hanging above his own. *S Sargent,* he read, and turned it over. *L.* So, he was in with a lifer. He didn't know which was worse: someone who would soon move on, leaving him as the experienced one, or a lifer who had nothing left to lose but his temper. He shook his thin blanket out over his bunk, privately vowing to agree with everything this Sargent bloke said, just in case.

35

When his cellmate returned from work, Daniel had been sitting on the edge of his bed trying to lose himself in one of the novels. He looked up as a shadow blocked the thin light from the landing, then sighed, as the newcomer moved and he saw his face.

'Oh, it's you.'

'So they tell me.' The stage four prisoner from earlier leaned back out onto the landing and flipped the new door card over, then came into the cell. 'What's the D stand for?'

Daniel told him. 'What about the S?' he asked.

'Stephen. And you were right.'

'About what?' Daniel realised what he meant, and swallowed. 'Murder?'

Stephen nodded. 'Killed my father.'

'Bloody hell,' Daniel muttered. 'Why didn't they hang you?'

'I asked them not to.'

Daniel didn't quite know how to respond to that, but Stephen grinned suddenly, and it took years off his taut, angular face. 'You've come at an interesting time, Mr Pearce,' he said, peeling off his wet coat and hooking it up behind the door.

'Interesting how?'

'This your first lagging?' Daniel nodded, and Stephen lowered his voice. 'Then you won't have anything to compare it to, but you can take it from me, something's going to happen. And soon.'

Daniel, on the alert for further teasing, didn't detect it now. 'What sort of something?'

'Officers have been turning the cells a lot more than usual, and lately they've actually been finding things.'

'Like what?'

'Coshes, shanks, even a hacksaw blade, as I hear it. They're keeping a tight watch on a few cons from other prisons, sent here to straighten out and evidently already planning an escape. Those blokes've been separated now though,' Stephen added, his words muffled as he pulled his damp jumper off over his head. 'Much good as that'll do.'

'How did they get those weapons in here?' Daniel was baffled, considering the level of security he'd personally endured over the past day and a half.

'Shanks and suchlike, the blokes make themselves. The other stuff?' Stephen shrugged 'Some reckon the screws are being paid to bring them in. Doesn't matter *how* they get in here though, it's what they plan to do with them. And who,' he added grimly. 'A lot of the men have gone quiet, and that's always something to watch out for.'

Daniel's insides rolled uncomfortably at the thought of something big in the offing, and he reminded himself he couldn't afford to let his guard down with this man either, no matter how friendly he seemed now. 'Why did you kill your dad?'

Stephen rubbed his hands through his hair, giving his head a vigorous scratch, then examined his ragged fingernails for lice. 'It wasn't deliberate,' he said, appearing satisfied he hadn't found any. 'I didn't want him dead, just wanted him to stop choking my brother.'

'That's rough. What happened?'

'I hit him with a rock, and he had a bleed on the brain a few days after. There was a witness to what he'd been doing, thank God, so at least they didn't give me the death penalty. I just got life.'

'Just?' Daniel repeated, shaking his head.

'I didn't think so, no,' Stephen deadpanned, and Daniel couldn't help smiling.

'No, I suppose it's not.'

Stephen gave him a wry smile in return. 'It was nearly six years ago. On my birthday, actually.'

Daniel started. 'So was mine!' He told Stephen what had happened, and how the whole night out had been framed as a celebration in his honour. 'I wish to God I'd stayed in the pub,' he finished. 'So much for preferring a quiet night.'

Stephen gave a short, sympathetic laugh. 'At least you'll be out in a few years to make up for it. Just think,' he added, pushing his discarded jumper aside and sitting down, 'I've already been here almost as long as your whole sentence.' He bent down to unlace his boots, and Daniel saw the purpled skin on his hands, where it had blistered, broken and reformed into hard callouses.

'Your time'll soon pass,' Stephen went on. 'Keep your head down and don't give the screws any trouble. You could be out long before your seven are up.' He gave Daniel a sombre look. 'Think yourself lucky *you* didn't kill anyone. There's a lad in E wing, the segregation block,' he clarified, 'name of Damerel. He's due to be moved out to Exeter after Christmas.'

'To be hanged?' Daniel's voice caught on the word.

Stephen nodded. 'His father's in here too, but the son's the killer. Messed with a training aeroplane, by all accounts, and the pilot ditched in the sea. Turns out the pilot was in on it and he survived, he's in Wandsworth now, but the other poor bugger's still out there in the sea somewhere. Young Damerel said he was a friend of his, too. He's proper cut up about it, tried to tell them how sorry he was, but that buttered no parsnips with the judge.'

'Why's his dad here then?'

'Helped him escape the police. Or rather, tried to.' Stephen stretched out on his bunk, his fingers laced on his stomach. 'Just sit tight and do your time,' he advised again, closing his eyes. 'You'll be out before you know it.'

CHAPTER FIVE

Geordie walked slowly back towards the village, his mind moving ahead to next Thursday and the visit to his daughter. He tried to suppress uncharitable thoughts towards Roderick Lawton; the man had actually seemed pretty decent, and he was trying to make the best of a difficult situation. But the thought of Tilly calling him 'Daddy' cut deeper than Geordie had expected it to, although he himself had to accept the blame; so much damage had been done by the way he'd left his family behind, and it was time to put things right. If it wasn't too late.

The road was deserted as he passed the church, so when he heard the slam and bounce of a wooden gate behind him he turned in surprise. He flashed his torch into the bearded face of someone he didn't recognise, an instant before the man barrelled into him and sent him staggering into the school fence. The torch flew from his hand and went out, but another light bobbed into view, and a shout from the churchyard galvanised him.

'Don't just stand there, get him!'

Geordie followed the wavering light that picked out the shape of the man, who had now scrambled over the locked school gate next door, and into the playground. The shouter was still strug-gling with the church gate, so Geordie snatched up his own torch and took off, still not knowing whether he ought to be helping the hunter or the prey. He vaulted the school gate, and in the yard he found the runner eyeing up his chances of escaping over the bicycle shed; his hands were already on top of the half-wall, ready to boost himself up.

'Get him, Geordie!' The shouter was scaling the school gate as well now, and his use of Geordie's name made the decision easier.

The runner had climbed onto the low wall, and was reaching up to grab the edge of the tin roof when Geordie reached him and seized one leg. The limb jerked violently under his hand, but Geordie hung on, and then wrapped his arms around both legs as they left the top of the wall. He pulled hard, and his captive let out a yell; both men fell backwards, and Geordie let go and managed to twist away in time to avoid the full weight of the escapee landing on him. The man grunted and lurched to his feet, but before he could take his first step, Geordie lunged after him and snagged his trouser leg again, pulling hard and spilling the man to the ground once more.

'Good job!'

Torchlight played over the felled runner, and the newcomer straddled him, pulling a set of handcuffs from his coat pocket. When he'd secured the escapee's hands, he stood up and turned, and Geordie was startled to recognise Bobby Gale. Of all the people he'd have expected to be on the right side of the law, Bobby was the last. And he hadn't joined the police, as far as anyone knew, so where had he got the handcuffs?

Bobby swiped a hand irritably through his wild mat of dark hair, and flashed his torch into his quarry's eyes. 'Lie still, Stibby, you moron. It's finished.'

Geordie had a hundred questions, but couldn't decide which one to ask, so he just accepted Bobby's thanks, and helped him pull the fugitive to his feet. 'Want any help getting him . . . wherever he's meant to be?'

'Wouldn't say no,' Bobby admitted. 'Mr Stibson here needs to go back to the police house down in Caernoweth.'

'Why were you chasing him?'

'He tried to break into the Tinner's Arms. And Brewer thinks he's the one been smashing the office windows over at the clay pit.' Stibson twisted, with a strong word of protest, but Bobby cuffed him lightly on the side of the head. 'Shut up, we're not interested.'

Geordie shook his head. 'No, I mean why were *you* chasing him?'

'Oh. I was just passing the police house after he got away from Brewer,' Bobby said. 'Brewer just asked me for help, that's all. Quite a run across the moor, he's led me, too. Now, you goin' to help, or what?'

Geordie studied him for a moment, still unsure, then nodded. 'Let's get him up to my place, we can take my van back to town.'

Half an hour later Nigel Stibson was back in custody at the Caernoweth police house, awaiting transport to the Truro station. Geordie heard Sergeant Brewer reading him the riot act, before he came back into the office and offered Geordie a cup of tea by way of thanks. Geordie declined, and, with his thoughts turning to supper he opened the door to leave, but there seemed to be a silent conversation going on between him and Bobby. Geordie watched the raised eyebrows, shrugs and nods for a moment, before losing patience and stepping out into the hall.

'Goodbye, gents.'

'Wait,' Sergeant Brewer said, and Geordie turned back, his own eyebrows exaggeratedly raised, in mockery of their theatrics.

Brewer, to his credit, gave a brief grin of acknowledgement. 'Sorry. Look, Sargent, come in for a minute. Get off home, Bobby, you've got an early start if you're on the boats.'

Bobby clapped Geordie on the arm as he passed him. 'Thanks again. I'd have lost him if you hadn't got stuck in.'

Geordie closed the main door behind him, and came back into the office. Patrick Brewer, who'd been Caernoweth's principle police officer for only a little over a year and was apparently a huge improvement on the previous incumbent, sat behind his desk and eyed Geordie with an unsettlingly direct gaze. He had that hard look about him that discouraged flippancy or over-familiarity, but thankfully he didn't appear to be about to launch into any kind of reprimand or interrogation. It took a moment for Geordie to reason that there was nothing to reprimand him for any more; his rabble-rousing days were behind him, and he was no longer automatically the one people looked at when there was any local unrest.

'Bobby tells me you didn't question anything tonight,' Brewer said. 'Just chased Stibson down. Dragged him off the roof.'

'Perhaps I should have checked,' Geordie said carefully, sensing that perhaps he was about to be reprimanded after all. 'I mean, I didn't recognise Bobby's voice from the shout, so I didn't know who was the one in the right. It might have been—'

'Instinct. Invaluable, not to be sniffed at.'

'If he hadn't used my first name, I might have assumed *he* was the one to be wary of.'

'Never mind. Once you knew, you went all-in. A man of action. To be commended.' Brewer, in his late thirties and less than ten years older than Geordie himself, gave off an air of dyed-in-the-wool authority, and Geordie accepted the compliment without further argument. In truth, the policeman's staccato manner of speech was making him tired, and it had already been a long day.

'Thank you,' he said, resisting the urge to snap off a quick, *doing my duty*, in case it sounded as if he was still mocking Brewer. 'I'm glad I could be of help.'

'A proposition,' Brewer said, holding up his hand as Geordie half-rose to leave. When Geordie had settled again, he adopted an easier, less official tone. 'Did you think it was strange that Gale was the one chasing Stibson?'

'It occurred to me,' Geordie admitted. 'Along with a lot of other questions, but it didn't seem the time to ask.'

'And now?'

'I'm assuming that's why you've called me back. And that this isn't the first time he's done it.'

'You assume correctly,' Brewer said. 'Have you heard of the Watchers?'

'No.'

'Good.' Brewer's eyes narrowed slightly. 'Unless you agree to my proposal, I'd prefer it if you went back to never having heard it.' Geordie waited for him to continue, and Brewer sat forward. 'Since that business last year, when Colin Damerel and his son nearly got away, I've taken it upon myself to … deputise, if you like, a few local men. Fit. Healthy. Prepared to do what you did tonight. Men of decent character.'

Geordie couldn't hold back a grunt of surprise. 'And you chose *Bobby Gale*?'

Brewer smiled wryly. 'Whatever else he's done, he's got a good heart.'

'That's true, I suppose.'

'And who would be less likely, if you stop to think about it? Look at the reaction you gave, just there, and you know the bloke better than most.'

Geordie conceded the point. 'He's settled a lot, from what I've heard he was like before.'

'I never knew him before, either,' Brewer said. 'But I gather the war's done as much good for him as bad. Anyway, there are currently two Watchers under my command. I'd like to make it four eventually, but three would do for now.'

'To chase thugs?' Geordie couldn't help smiling in disbelief. 'I wouldn't have thought—'

'Hear me out.' Brewer linked his hands on the desk. 'Putting aside all the trouble they've been having at South Pencarrack ... You've heard about the window-smashing?'

'Only just. Bobby mentioned it.'

'Seems every time they get new ones put in, someone puts *them* in, if you see what I mean. The sensible money's on Stibson.' He waved a hand. 'Anyway, like I said, putting that aside, think about that trouble we had with nearly losing the Damerels and others. Between the harbour and Pencarrack there are a hundred places where someone might get off the mainland and away, and the longer time goes on, the more people realise it.'

This was the longest sentence Geordie had yet heard him say, and, intrigued now, he waited for more.

'I'm undermanned,' Brewer said. 'Simple as that. So, I've hand-picked a few people to ... help me keep watch. That's all. Nothing else, just watch. A small remuneration from my own private funds, but I'm not wealthy so it'll be nothing to write home about. Completely unofficial. Are you interested or not?'

'What would I have to do, report anything suspicious to you?'

'Exactly that. Be discreet. Tell no one what you're doing. *No one*,' he stressed, looking Geordie directly in the eye. 'Not even that young lady of yours.'

'Why not Lynette? She won't say anything.'

Brewer looked slightly uncomfortable for the first time. 'She's . . . not from here,' he said at length, and held up a hand as Geordie started to protest that he wasn't, either. 'Listen, if you can't agree to that, you'll forget everything we've talked about. I'll have to put you on trust to do that.'

'Lynette's living here now,' Geordie said. 'Just as I am. She lost her brother to that same criminal that made you set this thing up, so she's not likely to be telling anyone about the best smuggling routes, is she?'

'Nevertheless,' Brewer said, 'the more people who know about it, the less effective you'll be.'

Geordie got it then, and he favoured Brewer with a faint smile. 'It's got nothing to do with her being from the wrong side of the Tamar, is it? It's because she's a woman.'

'Women gossip,' Brewer said gruffly. 'Especially small-town women. It's their nature. They can't help it. It's not their fault, but in a town like this it only takes one wrong word.' He sat up straight, dismissing any further arguments Geordie might have put forward. 'Just be my eyes and ears, that's all I ask. Now and again check in on that room under the folly, too. Most importantly, stay alert for the sound of one of these.'

Brewer reached into the drawer of his desk and pulled out a whistle on a chain. 'If you hear it, stop what you're doing and follow it. It means you're needed.'

He passed the whistle across to Geordie, who automatically

46

took it, still slightly bemused. 'What if I hear it, but can't stop what I'm doing?'

Brewer tilted his head. 'You wouldn't expect the RNLI to put anything ahead of their duty, once that siren sounds, would you?'

'No, but—'

'This is no less important. You don't blow this unless you absolutely have to, so if you hear it, you know someone *really* needs help. Bobby didn't blow his tonight, did he?'

'No.'

'There you are, then. It's not just there for an extra pair of hands if you let someone get away. It's your last resort if your life's in danger.' Brewer reached into the drawer again, and pulled out a pair of handcuffs identical to the ones Bobby had used. He put them on the desk and Geordie studied them, finally understanding the seriousness of what he was being asked to do.

'Who else is part of this?' he asked at length.

'Bobby you know. Other one's David Donithorn.'

'Donithorn? The bloke from the pub?' Geordie thought about it and applied the same logic Brewer had done to Bobby. 'I suppose it makes sense. He'd be in a good position to pass on anything he hears.'

'And you'll hear a lot too, in your job. Gossip and hearsay are part of it, but—'

'Oh, so gossip is *useful*.' Geordie couldn't resist it, and Brewer gave him a wry smile.

'I was going to say that it's what you did tonight that tells me you've got what I can really use. Instincts, speed, and strength. Now, are you with us? And can you keep it quiet?' He closed the drawer and sat back again, waiting.

Geordie was silent. He thought about how he wanted to settle here, and to be trusted; about how in the past he'd loathed people who sided with authority against their peers, and how he would find it hard to trust Bobby, or even Donithorn, again. Then he thought about how Alec Damerel had tampered with the training plane at the air base, and killed Lynette's brother. How Jago Carne had hidden him, and helped him and his father, not to mention all the other evil he'd done, and how close all three had come to escaping justice. Finally, he thought about the money Lynette had put into his livelihood, and how he intended to repay every penny of it. He picked up the handcuffs.

Back at the forge, he made sure his clothes weren't showing any signs of the tussle in the school yard, in case Joe questioned it, and then picked up the letter he'd begun reading and set aside, earlier in the day. For a minute he considered putting together something for tea, but discarded the idea; the bread was needed for Joe's crib tomorrow. He himself could always visit Lynette at the stables, where he'd be offered something to eat the minute he walked in. Pointless to waste what he had, then, when Joe could make better use of it. Instead, he made a pot of tea, then settled himself in his chair near the fire and started to read.

Dear Geordie,

Another month has passed so I thought I should write and tell you I'm still alive and in decent shape. The men tend to leave me alone, unless they want something, and then they're polite enough in asking – my time served is at long last working in my favour. Even the warders have stopped making it harder than it needs to be.

Alec Damerel is being taken up to Exeter on 27th of this month, and that will be his end. Poor kid.

*I received your letter asking for a visiting order, but I have
to tell you that, while I look forward to the day we meet again,
I'm not sure now is the time. I've tried to dissuade Gracie from
visiting for a little while, too, though she's as stubborn a girl as
she ever was (you'll remember!) and I can't be sure she won't
come anyway. This is no place for such a gem as her, at least
not at present, and nor is it the place for a man who should be
putting his family's shame behind him and getting on with his
own life.*

Geordie lowered the letter with a quiet groan. How long
would his brother feel he had to shoulder the blame for what had
happened? He took a gulp of his cooling tea, then sat forward
and read on.

*For a long while I was someone to be deeply ashamed of, but
I have settled and found a way to like myself again, and to
live with how things are now. I hope you'll continue to write,
and tell me all about your new love. Gracie tells me Marion
is well, and Tilly too. If you see my little niece in the coming
days, do tell her that her Uncle Stephen wishes her a happy
Christmas.*

*I have a new cellmate, he seems all right. He won't be in
long though, his crime wasn't serious. Then I suppose I'll have
another new face to get used to – they come and go.*

*Promise me you'll do everything in your power to make sure
you don't follow me into this place.*

*Your loving brother,
Stephen*

Geordie put the pages back in the envelope, and slid it into the drawer of the bureau along with the others. He looked at the clock on the mantle, and saw it wasn't nearly as late as it seemed. His first thought was that John Doidge might still be at the Engine House, and he'd be in time for last orders if he went now; then his attention went to the steady glow of the forge through the sitting room window.

He knocked at Joe's door. 'I'm going out to do a bit of work,' he called quietly. 'You can stay here.'

The boy murmured a sleepy response, and Geordie went to his own room and opened a small leather box he kept in the bottom of his wardrobe. Inside was a pewter drinking cup, beaten out of shape, but at least cleaner now than when he'd found it. He had dug it out of the ground next to where they'd found Al Trevellick's lifeless form after the South Pencarrack landslide, and put it in his pocket without knowing why; it had been a filthy thing, coated with dried clay and mud. He stood looking at it for a moment, remembering the man who'd either walked around with it clipped to his belt, or stood drinking out of it while he leaned in his shop doorway, watching his son learn his trade across the yard. The mug had never been far from Al's hand.

Joe's father had been a miner years before he'd been a clay worker, as had Geordie, and this mug had gone with him several hundred feet underground, and then followed him to his very last posting; at the side of his son, who had been put to work in the dark at the foot of an unstable clay face. Joe had been tearfully grateful that Geordie had retrieved it, but he couldn't use it. He could only look at it and remember. Now, though, Geordie understood what he could do with it.

Out in the forge, he heated the pewter and began re-shaping

it carefully, keeping half his attention on the house in case Joe's curiosity brought him outside after all. But the door remained closed, and as Geordie worked the metal he let his mind wander. He thought about his growing up years in Peter Tavy, running wild with Stephen, Marion, Gracie and the others, and about his betrothal to Marion, which everyone had expected since they'd been about six and five years old respectively.

He wondered, for the thousandth time, how different life might have been if he and Stephen had just stayed at the pub with their father that night on Stephen's birthday, and not been so keen to return to their own little worlds; he with Marion and new baby Tilly, and Stephen with Gracie. George senior would not have lost his temper and struck Geordie; he would not have fallen on him, winding him, and tried to choke him where he lay. Stephen would have had no need to pick up that lump of granite, and it naturally followed that he would not be where he was now.

But was that true? Geordie stopped work for a moment, his gaze fixed on the flattened pewter on the anvil. Would fate have found another way to rid them of their father? Perhaps he himself might have been the one to strike out, if the scenario had been different. What would Stephen be doing now, if that were the case? Married to Gracie, no doubt. A farmer, maybe, taking over her family's home at Cudlip Farm, and raising a family, as he was always meant to. If things had only been different that night. God, that *night* ... Geordie struck the pewter harder than he intended to, and swore as the piece warped beneath his hammer. He stopped again, forced himself to breathe more slowly, and then corrected the shape he was trying to form.

He brushed his fingers across it, remembered where it had come from, and where it was going, and felt himself grow calmer and able to think clearly again. Stephen didn't blame him for what had happened, though Geordie had only recently come to learn that, after many years. His rejection of any contact had been his way of protecting them both, of accepting his new existence, and not letting his brother see what he'd had to become in order to do it.

But Geordie knew, anyway. All he could do was be glad that his brother had found some kind of peace with the life he had made for himself, and to honour his silent promise that he would never join him in it.

CHAPTER SIX

Christmas Eve

By seven o'clock in the morning, the Caernoweth Civic Hall was already bustling with activity, ready for the annual Christmas fair. Tradesmen and business-owners, used to rising early, were today setting up their stalls beneath the high, domed ceiling, willing the first rays of daylight to filter through the dust and illuminate their wares to their best advantage. One corner was roped off and contained several tantalising closed boxes and a large iron tub, and tables were set out along three of the walls, with labels affixed so each vendor could find their allocated space.

Gwenna found the Rosdews' table, and put the first box of groceries on it, then gave herself a moment to look around before going out to the van to fetch more. The shop's stall had always been a focus for a lot of attention, with Jonas dressed like a well-heeled Victorian gentleman, doling out sweets to the children and offering, for a knock-down price, anything they'd overstocked throughout the year. Rachel had offered the same discounts last year, but without Jonas's charismatic presence it had fallen short, and would again this year, no doubt. Next year, he would be home, Gwenna reminded herself, and all would be well again.

Despite everything, however, she was glad her mother had persuaded her to take on the stall this year.

'It'll do you good,' she'd said last night, dismissing Gwenna's protests. 'The way you hide in here, it's like anything that happened was your fault.'

'That's how they see it!' Gwenna had jabbed a finger at the doorway of the shop, indicating the townspeople beyond it. 'I can read it on their faces.'

But her mother had prevailed, so Gwenna had loaded up the van first thing this morning, and driven it the short distance to the civic building in the centre of town. There was a cheerful, festive air in here already, despite the gusts of wind that blew the rain in through the propped-open double doors; the children from the two nearby schools, at Priddy Lane and Pencarrack, had spent all of yesterday hanging paper chains and sprays of holly, and setting out oranges studded with cloves on every available windowsill. The scent was just beginning to penetrate the musty smell that characterised the old building for the rest of the year, and Gwenna was reminded, with a little pang of nostalgia, of her school days in St Austell and the friends she'd left behind there.

'Well, good morning, Miss Rosdew!'

Gwenna turned to see Tory coming in with her arms full, shaking her head to try and unstick her curly hair from her rain-damp face. She immediately tensed, remembering how she'd left the stables after their meeting, but while her mind automatically searched for a way to escape, her heart gratefully accepted her friend's evident determination to forget it had ever happened.

'I saw the van outside,' Tory went on, 'but I expected to see your mum, not you.' She put the box down on a table directly opposite Rosdews'. 'I'm glad though. Does this mean you're running the stall this year?'

'Mum persuaded me.' Gwenna peeled the stable's name off the table, while Tory opened her coat and wiped her hands dry on her sweater, in readiness for handling the photographs and pamphlets she'd brought.

Tory saw her looking curiously at them. 'I've brought a sign-up sheet for riding lessons,' she explained. 'We're not expecting much there, though. From the rescue side, Lynette has put together a little pamphlet with descriptions of each of our horses, their problems, and what we're doing to rehabilitate. People often donate bits and pieces when they can, once they see the good we're trying to do.'

Gwenna peered at the doorway. 'Isn't Lynette coming, then?'

'No, she's going up to Devon with Geordie. They're visiting his little girl, so Bobby's holding the fort at the stables for us today. Right, let me empty this out, then I can return the favour and give you a hand.'

By dinner time, the town hall was a raucous den of voices and laughter. The Salvation Army band were playing carols quietly in a corner, the gentle sound of their muted trumpets wafting throughout the large hall, competing with the shrill shrieks of over-excited children and the shouts of parents, who were having their tolerance tested to the limit. Many of the children were in fancy dress costumes, with numbers pinned to their backs, and there was a jar on the end of the long jumble sale table, where people dropped in voting slips for the best costume.

The crowd ebbed and flowed, the occasional surge of customers making up for the sparser times, and Gwenna had to re-stock the stall gratifyingly often, from the boxes behind her. She had been the centre of some attention, but it wasn't the kind she had expected and dreaded, and she'd been heartened to receive pats on the arm, encouraging smiles, and also several genuinely interested questions, most of which she was able to deflect.

Tory appeared at her elbow, as she was putting out the last of the ha'penny mixed sweet bags that she and her mother had made up last night. 'See? It's not nearly as bad as you thought it would be, is it?'

Gwenna smiled. 'How are you getting on?'

'We've had some interest, some donations, and two new sign-ups for after Christmas. Gifts for the kids, so I've been sworn to secrecy.' Tory glanced back over her shoulder, to where people were looking through the photographs she had laid out, taken by Bertie Fox's brother, Ben. He was making quite a name for himself in that field now, and Gwenna had looked at them earlier, impressed with how he had captured the children's excitement, and the adults' hesitant exhilaration, as their mounts had responded to the signals Tory and Lynette had taught them. One showed the little black pony, Hercules, trotting over poles laid low to the ground, a kind of haughty dignity to the set of his head that contrasted sharply with his shabby appearance. You couldn't help but smile.

'I'm going to have to go in a minute,' Tory said with a look of regret. 'Bobby needs to get away this afternoon, so I'll need to be back at the stables in about half an hour.'

'I'll help you pack up when you do,' Gwenna offered. 'I've done my duty, so I might even pack up at the same time. Meantime, you'd better get back.' She pointed. 'That woman looks as if she might have more money than most here today, and I think she knows the people in that photograph she's looking at. Go quickly, make money!'

By the time the fair ended, it had long since turned dark outside. Gwenna had helped Tory pack up her stall, and then waved her off, but she herself waited until the very last minute. She had urged Tory to leave some of the photographs behind, offering to try and sell them for her, and Tory had done so with delight and gratitude. It really felt as if their friendship was finding some of its old easy rhythms now, helped by Tory's determination to keep the past firmly where it belonged.

Besides fulfilling her promise to Tory, Gwenna was enjoying the more relaxed atmosphere that had descended once the initial excitement had worn off. She felt no hurry to return home, where the only thing that awaited her was a solemn quiet and the feeling of guilt that managed to creep into almost every outward expression of contentment. Until now, it had felt right that she should think of her father's predicament instead of her own pleasure, but today had pricked a hole in that stifling existence, and the light was trying to push through it. The relief was surprisingly strong; she loved living here, but lately it had become so difficult she had been thinking she would have to leave as soon as her father returned. Now, perhaps, she could stop worrying about that.

The hall began to empty, and Gwenna packed away the last few unsold items into a single box, thinking about how pleased her mother would be with the profit they'd made today. She nodded her thanks to the man holding the inner hall door open for her, and as she passed through the vestibule another helpful figure pushed himself away from the wall, and offered to take the box for her.

'It's all right, thank you,' she said, her attention focused on not entangling her feet in the large door mat. 'I can manage, if you'd be kind enough to open the door for me.'

He pulled open the big door, letting in a gust of wind and a spray of refreshing drizzle; Gwenna laughed as her hair blew across her face, and she flicked her head to clear her eyes. 'Thank you,' she said, over her shoulder, and stepped out into the late evening.

The van was parked only a few feet away, and she balanced the box between the rear panel and one hip, while she wrestled with the catch. Behind her she heard cheerful voices calling good night, and the blessings of the season, to one another, and the brass band players tooting chirpy little final notes as they packed up inside the hall. Her sense of festive camaraderie grew warmer still. This really was a wonderful, forgiving town—

'That'll do, love. Thanks.'

The voice was harsh in her ear, and a moment later she felt a shove at her shoulder and the box of groceries slipped to the ground. Gwenna felt a horrible sense of déjà vu as she saw, in the thin streetlights, the wiry form of Nigel Stibson bending over by her feet. She gave a shout of dismay as she saw his scrawny hands reach for the money box nestled among the groceries, and instinctively she drew her foot up and stamped down on them, hard. She briefly mourned the loss of the rich fruit cake that was demolished as a result, but that was satisfyingly eclipsed by the howl of pain and the rush of curses.

Stibson was not easily put off, however. He pushed her again, and, with one foot still raised, she was off-balance and fell against the car. She shouted, and grabbed at Stibson's coat, but her cry was drowned in the general noise of people exiting the hall and yelling to one another. Stibson had found what he was looking for, and brought out the heavy money box with a little grunt of triumph, but Gwenna's anger took over at the sight of it disappearing into his satchel. She grabbed at the strap as he backed away from her, and hung on with grim determination as she shouted again for help.

This time someone heard her, and Stibson's straining ceased abruptly as he received a blow between his shoulder blades that dropped him to his knees.

'*This* time, you little sod ...'

The voice was familiar, and as Gwenna took a step closer, to thank the man who'd saved her takings, she saw it was Bobby Gale. He looked up at her, a little warily, and pulled the man's bleeding hands behind his back.

'Well, Stibby, that's twice you've been unlucky enough to cross my path,' he said, quite deliberately, Gwenna thought. 'And this time you've been caught in the act, so I reckon Brewer's going to want a word.'

'You reckon right,' Sergeant Brewer said, crossing the road at a run. He nodded to Bobby. 'Thank you, Mr ... Gale, is it? I'll take him now.' He pulled out a set of handcuffs and clipped them to Stibson's wrists, then checked that Gwenna was unhurt before dragging the would-be thief away up the hill.

'What was all that about?' Gwenna asked, stooping to return her spilled groceries to their box. 'I remember you had that same shifty look back when you confessed to being part of the smuggling ring at the base. When you told me it was really guns in those boxes and not aircraft parts.' Gwenna watched him carefully as she said it, hoping he hadn't fallen into that dark business again. It would be awful for Tory, apart from anything else. 'What are you up to?'

'And that's the thanks I get, is it, for saving your takings?' Bobby gave a brief, false-sounding laugh. 'You're welcome.'

'I'm grateful, I really am,' Gwenna said. 'But Tory's my friend. So, what's going on?'

Bobby picked up the grocery box and slid it into the back of the van, indicating she should get into the front. She did so, keeping the money box clutched tightly against her chest, and he climbed into the passenger seat.

'I'm not smuggling again,' he said bluntly. 'I never will. I've learned a hard lesson there. But if I tell you what I *am* doing, you're to promise me you won't tell Tory.'

'No, I won't promise that.'

He sighed. 'Look, Gwenna, it's nothing bad. But it's got to be kept secret.'

Gwenna hesitated, curiosity nibbling away at her conscience. 'You *swear* it's nothing bad?'

'I do.'

'On your grandmother's life?'

Bobby responded without hesitation. 'I swear. But for the sake of any good I might have done, or might do in the future, it's not to get out. All right?'

Gwenna studied him in the low light. He looked earnest and, for once, honest, and she thought back to the way he'd fought to help them put Barry Hocking behind bars where he belonged. 'I promise,' she said at last. 'But to be clear, if I think Tory *needs* to know, I'll tell her.'

'That's fair.' He nodded, still facing front, at the rain that smeared the windscreen. 'Have you ever heard of the Watchers?'

'No.'

'Good.'

CHAPTER SEVEN

After negotiating an extremely busy Tavistock town centre, where Lynette had stopped to buy a last-minute gift for Marion, they arrived in Peter Tavy at around midday. Geordie had felt his insides growing tighter the closer they came, despite telling himself that there was nothing to be tense about; clearly his deeper self knew better.

'That's the turning, isn't it?' Lynette was peering ahead through the quartered windscreen of her new car, her brow lowered in concentration as she tried to remember. 'Looks different without all the leaves on the trees.'

'That's it.' Geordie reached out and gently touched her shoulder. 'Like I said, it'll go better this time. I'm sure of it.'

Lynette took her eyes off the road for a moment to give him a smile. 'It couldn't go much worse,' she pointed out. 'But I'm ready.'

'I'm not sure I am,' Geordie said wryly, then pointed. 'It's in the middle of the row. See the one with the yellow curtains upstairs? That's Tilly's room.'

Geordie had been born in that house. He and his younger brother Stephen, always close, had spent their childhood united in fear and hatred of George Sargent senior, especially following the death of their mother. Still, they had managed to store up some good memories, and after George's death, and Stephen's arrest, Geordie and his young family had taken over the lease. They'd lived here until Geordie had left, less than a year ago, although it felt much longer, and he still sent the rent to Marion each week out of his earnings. Now, the house he'd lived in all his life looked as unimportant and bland as anywhere else.

It also looked deserted, he noticed with a slight frown; no lights to combat the oppressively dark December day, and all the windows tightly closed. He and Marion had always had to keep them open a crack during the day, regardless of the weather, to help dissipate the smoke that often belched back through gaps in the stone fireplace. Today though, he noticed, no smoke drifted out of the chimney either.

Lynette turned to Geordie, clearly equally puzzled. 'They knew you were coming, didn't they?'

'Maybe they're home, but haven't lit the fire.' But that was unlikely, especially on Christmas Eve. 'Wait there a minute.' He got out of the car and went up the short path to the front door, a little perturbed to note that it didn't feel odd to knock any more; he was already used to being a visitor in this house where he'd drawn his first breaths. When there was no answer he bent down to push the letter box open. There was no smell of cooking, or of the clove-studded oranges he knew Tilly would have left all over the house from the moment her mother gave her permission. The front door opened directly into the sitting room, and Geordie tilted his head as he looked through the letter box, to take in as much of the room as he could. The fire was not even laid yet.

He stood up again to see that Lynette had also left the warmth of the car, and followed him up the path. 'No one's home.'

'Well that's—'

'All right, Geordie?' The voice came from a few doors down, where Geordie saw a gloved hand raised in greeting.

'All right, Sam?'

'She an't been there for a day or two, lad. Comin' back today though, so I hear. She expectin' you?'

'Yes, I told her we'd be here today.'

'That'll be why she's coming back here, then.' Sam nodded wisely. 'Ah well, Happy Christmas to you both.'

'Hold on.' Geordie went out through the garden gate and jogged down to Sam's house. 'What do you mean? Coming back from where?'

'Well, she moved in with that Lawton fella, an't she? Up by the church.'

'By Colleybrooke Manor?'

'Not by, *in*.' Sam shrugged and offered him a rueful smile. 'Bit hard to believe, innit? You kids used to play there, so I recall, now this!'

Geordie shook his head in disbelief; the times they'd been thrown off that land as children … He turned to Lynette. 'Lawton must have inherited the place. A palace compared to this. Why the hell hasn't she told me?' He sighed. 'Come on then. Let's go and see how the other half live.'

'Is it far?'

'We can walk it in a few minutes,' Geordie said, glancing down at her smart shoes. 'It might be a bit muddy though.'

'I don't mind a bit of mud. My legs could do with a stretch anyway.'

They made their way back down the lane and up through the village, past the post house, where Geordie drew more than one curious look as well as the odd greeting. He returned the greetings, rewarded the looks with an overly friendly smile, and all the time he was wondering when Marion had planned to tell him she'd moved into Roderick Lawton's home, leaving their own house abandoned. And why was she so intent on keeping it such a secret, that she'd evidently planned to come back today, and act as if she still lived there? He was still sending her the rent money, and he didn't believe she'd be devious enough to be pocketing it for herself; if she was it would be down to Lawton, not her. She just wasn't like that.

Colleybrooke Manor wasn't enormous, by many standards, but it stood in its own generous grounds a short way past the church, and presented a well-kept, affluent face to the village. Walls made of good Dartmoor granite, like many of the houses around, but with large windows through which it was possible, even from the gateway, to see spacious rooms and delicate furnishings.

'It's quite pretty, really,' Lynette said, standing beside Geordie and peering ahead up the drive. 'Are we going in, then?'

'Why didn't she tell me things had progressed so far with Lawton?' Geordie shoved his hands into his pockets. 'No wonder she doesn't want Tilly to think about her old life.'

'Her *old life*, as you put it, is also very much her present life,' Lynette reminded him. 'You haven't disappeared.'

'No, but she has so much more now. And so quickly.'

Across the narrow road behind them, a gate squeaked open and a woman's voice called out. 'Geordie Sargent? Well there's a happy sight! Marion never said you'd be coming.'

Geordie turned, and smiled at the elderly woman who'd come

to stand at the end of her path; outwardly strict, even sour sometimes, Ivy Bellowes had, in Geordie's childhood, been gleefully assigned the label of 'tyrant'. In reality she'd been just as quick with a slice of pie or an apple as she had been with a cuff around the ear, and he and Stephen had often been on the receiving end of both.

'Happy Christmas, Mrs Bellowes.' Geordie raised a hand in greeting. 'I'll come over in a bit, but I have a gift for Tilly first.'

Mrs Bellowes blinked. 'You'd not have heard, then.'

'Heard?' Geordie's stomach knotted. 'What?'

'Well ... Tilly's here!' Mrs Bellowes turned to go back into her house, calling back over her shoulder, 'She's upstairs, I'll fetch her.'

Geordie and Lynette looked at one another in surprise, and followed her into the house. But the questions ceased to matter when Geordie heard the light sound of his daughter's feet, pattering across the floor above his head in pursuit of Mrs Bellowes's heavier tread.

'Daddy?' Her voice floated down the stairs, and before Geordie had time to wonder where Marion was, he saw Tilly at the top, wearing a red wool dress, and hugging her old favourite stuffed lamb, Barney. Geordie remembered the way Tilly had immediately, delightedly, accepted his suggestion for the name, and her giggles when he'd explained: *Ba-a-a-rney*.

'Aren't you coming down then, girl?' Mrs Bellowes called back up the stairs.

Tilly's dark-brown eyes were wide, but her expression remained solemn as she played with the yellow ribbon that held the bell tied around Barney's woolly neck. For a second Geordie had the horrible feeling that today's visit would go the way of the last one after all, but he swallowed the stinging disappointment and gave her a wide smile.

'There she is!' He held out his arms, and to his relief she broke into a dimpled smile of her own, and ran down the stairs to hug him, only drawing back when she caught sight of Lynette over his shoulder.

Geordie twisted to beckon Lynette forward, and turned back to Tilly. 'You remember my friend, Lynette, don't you? We came to see you in the summer.'

Tilly nodded, but shrank back a little more as Lynette held out her hand.

'Come on, love,' Mrs Bellowes said briskly. 'Say hello to the nice lady.'

'Where's Mummy?' Tilly said, looking up at her. 'You said she'd be home soon.'

'She will be.' Mrs Bellowes gestured to Lynette. 'Now remember your manners, Miss Sargent, or Father Christmas will know you to be a rude little thing.'

The tyrant side of her was still there then, Geordie reflected with an inner smile. Tilly shook Lynette's outstretched hand, but as briefly as she could get away with, then she went into the sitting room and sat down by the window. She peered out and up at the sky, and the pose was so familiar it hurt Geordie's heart a little.

'When will Father Christmas come?' she asked, still looking up at the thick grey clouds.

'After you're fast asleep tonight,' Geordie said. He turned to Mrs Bellowes. 'Where's Marion? Visiting the Martyns?'

Mrs Bellowes looked past him at Tilly. 'Stay put, child, and tell Miss Lynette all about your school. Daddy and I are going to have a chat.'

Once in the kitchen she turned to Geordie, looking worried now. 'She's not visiting, no. She knocked on, about two this morning, and told me she was going to Tavistock hospital with Mr Lawton, and could I please look after Tilly until she got back.'

'I hope it's not serious,' Geordie said. He did mean it, though he was aware that his frowning distraction made it sounded a little insincere. 'It's good of you to take Tilly in,' he added, returning the focus to his reason for visiting.

Mrs Bellowes gave him an embarrassed look. 'Thing is, I'm going away at teatime, to stay with my son and his family for Christmas. He's picking me up at about four o'clock.' When Geordie didn't answer, she jerked her head towards the sitting room. 'So, you see I can't—'

'Oh!' He realised what she was trying to say. 'I'm sure Marion will be back by then, won't she?'

'Impossible to say. They've already let the staff go for the holiday, but you can take Tilly back to your old house tonight and stay with her, can't you?'

He shook his head. 'I can't stay away all night, I've sort of adopted a lad who lost his dad recently and he has no one else. He lives with me now.'

'How old is he?'

'Fourteen.'

Mrs Bellowes waved a hand. 'Well then, he'll be—'

'I'm not leaving him on his own,' Geordie said firmly. 'This is his first Christmas with no family.' He thought for a moment. 'Lynette and I can drive into Tavistock and find Marion, so we can discuss what's to be done.'

'What will I do if you're not back before I have to go?'

'You could take her to the Martyns for a couple of hours.'

Gracie was still Marion's closest friend and regularly stepped in to help with Tilly, particularly after the Wheal Peter disaster.

'There's a nasty outbreak of 'flu at the farm,' Mrs Bellowes fretted. 'That's why Marion didn't turn there first.'

Geordie looked at her a little helplessly. 'Well ... What would you have done if I hadn't arrived?

Mrs Bellowes shrugged. 'I'd have to drop her in at the vicarage, I suppose. But I wouldn't have wanted to, not when the vicar and his wife got midnight mass to attend.'

'We could take Tilly to Tavistock with us, I suppose.'

Mrs Bellowes frowned. 'A hospital's no place for a little one like that. Marion told me what she was like when she came to see—'

'Geordie can go in and find Marion,' Lynette said, appearing in the doorway. 'Tilly and I can wait outside. It'll give us a chance to get to know one another. How far is it?'

'A bit under five miles,' Geordie said. 'I expect Tilly's used to travelling by car now.'

'She's done it,' Mrs Bellowes said, 'but only once or twice. Mr Lawton doesn't like to drive much, and he only has the car for urgent matters. Why don't you stay and have a cup of tea, and explain to Tilly what's what? Maybe Marion will get back before you've finished.'

'That would be lovely, thank you.'

While Mrs Bellowes busied herself in the kitchen, with Lynette's help, Geordie engaged Tilly in talk of very important Christmas matters.

'What if Father Christmas can't find me?' she asked solemnly, her gaze once more going to the window. 'Last year he came to the old house, but he doesn't know we moved.'

Geordie thought for a moment. 'Lynette left the car at the old house,' he said, hiding another flash of annoyance that he'd been paying, and money he could ill afford, for that house to stand empty all this time. 'We'll have to go back there to pick it up, so that we can go to Tavistock and find Mummy, so I'll help you to write a note for Father Christmas and you can post it through the door. Then he can see you've gone to Colleybrooke. Shall we do that?'

She nodded, satisfied with the solution, and he sat at the table with her and helped her to print the letters carefully onto the back of an envelope Mrs Bellowes had found. Then, with Tilly wrapped warmly in her best green coat, they walked back through the village and she put the note through the letter box of Geordie's lifelong home. No doubt Roderick Lawton never had to leave a window open to let out chimney smoke, so Geordie couldn't blame anyone for moving on from here, but it still hurt, and rankled quite a lot. He would have to discuss the rent with Marion at some point, but probably not today if she was worried about Lawton.

Tilly put up no argument or resistance to getting into Lynette's car, but gave Geordie a look of surprise as he settled himself into the back seat with her, instead of behind the wheel. She leaned forward to tap Lynette on the shoulder.

'Are *you* going to drive?'

'I am. Why?'

'The daddy's supposed to drive,' Tilly said. 'Roderick does.'

Geordie felt pain shoot through him at this reminder that Lawton had now fashioned himself in that role. 'Well, this car belongs to Lynette,' he said, forcing a smile, 'so we're going to let her take us to Tavistock.'

'Oh, I don't *mind*,' Tilly said earnestly. 'It's a nice car. I like the colour.'

'Thank you,' Lynette said, smiling over her shoulder at her. 'So do I. Now, sit tight, look out of the window, and the first one to see a field of sheep wins a prize.'

The trip to Tavistock Hospital was too short; Geordie felt his remaining time with his daughter slipping away far too quickly. They drove through to the far side of town, and Geordie leaned forward to direct Lynette to the right, up a steep, winding hill. She drew into the car park not much more than ten minutes after leaving Peter Tavy, and Geordie left her and Tilly sitting in the car while he went to find Marion. Even as he passed through the door he felt his gut tighten; the memories of this place were strong and unpleasant, and it wasn't likely that today's encounter would improve them.

A brief query at the desk guided him into a busy waiting room, where he was told that someone would find Mrs Sargent and tell her he was there. He sat down, trying not to look directly at anything that would spark a clear recollection, but still his mind took him back to the hours he'd spent here awaiting news of every member of his family at some point: his mother, who succumbed to Spanish 'flu when he was eighteen; his younger brother Stephen, who'd gone to bed on Christmas night a few years later with a griping pain in his side, and had woken in the early hours feverish and screaming. Farmer Martyn had driven him here, where he'd been operated on for a ruptured appendix, and Geordie still recalled Stephen's dough-white face on the pillow, and the horror he'd felt when the nurse told him how they'd nearly lost him.

71

And two years after that, of course, their father.

He and Stephen had waited in this very room in taut silence that night, only to be told by the expectantly hovering police officer that Stephen would indeed be charged with murder now. Such a cold, frightening way to find out they were now orphans. Geordie's throat had still been burning then, and the bruised and abused muscles throbbed where his father had tried to choke the life out of him, but despite his relief that George was gone he had still felt a sinking sense of dismay; Stephen was all he had left. He had saved Geordie's life, but now he faced hanging.

Stephen had pleaded guilty, there was nothing else he could do, so there had been no trial at first, just the icy pronouncement that Stephen must forfeit his life. It had been the worst few days of Geordie's life, let alone Stephen's, but, to everyone's surprise and relief, a witness had emerged and spoken up. Someone had been there and seen Stephen's frantic attempts to break George senior's chokehold on Geordie – attempts which had proved futile, until he had finally swept up a small lump of granite and smashed it on the back of his father's head.

The revised sentence took the witness's statement into account, and was commuted to life, but Stephen had already withdrawn entirely, and refused to answer any of Geordie's letters or allow him to visit. It was as if he blamed Geordie for what he'd had to do, and its consequences, and deep down Geordie believed he was right to do so. Gracie Martyn, Stephen's radiant new love, had told Geordie that every letter she sent was ignored, too, which was less easy to forgive, but Geordie now understood that Stephen had become what he'd needed to, in order to survive. The sweet-natured boy he and Gracie had both known was gone.

'Mr Sargent?'

Geordie, jerked back into the present, looked up to see a nurse in the doorway. She stepped aside to admit an exhausted-looking Marion, whose hair was unkempt, as if she'd been pushing her hands through it constantly, and whose eyes were darkly shadowed. Marion looked bemused at seeing him there, as if she'd thought the nurse must have misunderstood who was asking for her. He stood up, his hat in his hands, unsure how to begin, then, understanding where her focus would be, he started there.

'How is he?'

Marion looked around at the people who had raised their heads expectantly, perhaps hoping to absorb someone else's good news to ease their own misery. 'Come with me,' she said, and indicated with her head towards the corridor.

Outside, he asked her again and she leaned against the wall, her head bowed. 'He's had a stroke,' she said quietly. 'No one knows how serious yet.' She looked up suddenly. 'How did you know where to find me?'

'I went to . . . to the old house first. Sam told me you'd moved in with Mr Lawton.' He bit back the questions that resurfaced, not wanting to sound accusatory. 'I spoke to Mrs Bellowes while I was at Colleybrooke,' he went on instead. 'I didn't know Tilly would be with her.'

Marion flushed slightly. 'You've seen Tilly, then?'

'She's out in the car.'

'What?' Marion pushed herself away from the wall and started in the direction of the exit, but Geordie caught her arm.

'It's all right, she's not on her own.'

'Oh. Yes, of course, I suppose that Linda woman's with her?'

He didn't correct the name. 'I wasn't sure whether to bring her in,' he said. 'I didn't know how things lay with Mr Lawton, and I know she . . . didn't like it here before.'

Their eyes met and the shared memories flew between them; Marion subsided. 'They only let her in to see you because you're her father. I wish they hadn't.'

He understood that, much as it hurt to think about. He'd been a poor and shocking sight for a good long while after the Wheal Peter disaster; his face swollen in places, bruised and cut, and his upper body swathed in tight bandages to prevent movement; while every instinct had made him want to gather his daughter close and tell her she mustn't worry, the physical pain had stopped him. Tilly had run from the room, crying, Marion had told him the next day, as if she'd never stop.

Marion herself had lost two of her young cousins in the disaster, but from the moment Geordie had returned home she had tended and cared for him, working double shifts to make up for his lost wage, and had never once laid the blame at his feet where he'd always felt it belonged. Their parting had been bitter though, for all that; her declaration that Tilly deserved a better father had cut deep, and believing she was right had kept him away for months. Now he knew better.

'I brought her a gift,' he said, steering the conversation away from what might have otherwise become a pointless picking-apart of all that had happened. 'Mrs Bellowes is going away to—'

'To her son's, yes.' Marion sighed. 'I don't want to leave Roderick,' she said in a low voice. 'Can you stay with Tilly tonight?'

'I can't. Joe lives with me; he shouldn't be left alone tonight.'

Marion's jaw tensed. 'You care more about someone else's child than your own?'

74

'Don't,' Geordie said tiredly. He'd expected that response. 'You know it's not like that.'

For a moment Marion's eyes battled with his, deep brown like Tilly's, but filled with a fire that abruptly stuttered and went out. 'No.' She bowed her head again. 'I know.'

She chewed at her knuckle, her attention drawn inexorably back to Roderick's ward. 'He's really ill, Geordie.' Her voice was thick again and he squeezed her shoulder, recognising the genuine worry and grief in her voice. She cared for Roderick Lawton, that much was obvious, and he was evidently more to her than just a step up to a better life. Geordie was, however, aware of time ticking by, and of the length of the drive home. They both knew what the solution was, but after his last visit he held out little hope of her agreement. Still, he had to try.

'She's got the overnight bag that you packed for her,' he ventured. 'If you give me the key to Lawton's . . . to your new house, I can fetch more clothes for her. But we'll have to go soon.' She raised her eyes again, and he read the answer there. Relief swept through him, but, mindful of her situation, he tried hard not to show it. 'Come on then,' he said gently, 'she'd better hear it from you.'

CHAPTER EIGHT

Lynette and Tilly had watched Geordie walk briskly across the car park to the hospital entrance and then disappear inside. It felt oddly lonely once he was out of sight, he'd been the presence that had linked them together in an otherwise awkward situation, and now the atmosphere was strained again. Lynette turned in her seat, and gave the solemn little girl her friendliest smile.

'Have you been helping Mummy stir the Christmas pudding?'

Tilly nodded, twisting her lower lip tightly in her fingers, but didn't answer.

'How about paper chains? Have you made some of those at school?'

Another nod. Then the twisting fingers dropped away. 'I like the yellow ones.'

'Oh, yellow's such a pretty colour,' Lynette agreed, remembering the bedroom curtains. 'Do you like daffodils?'

'No. They smell like cat wee.'

Lynette had to bite her own lip then, and turn back to the front so Tilly didn't think she was laughing at her. 'You *have* got a point there,' she admitted. 'Look, it's stopped raining, would you like to go for a little walk while we're waiting for Daddy?'

Tilly nodded with surprising eagerness, and scrambled across to open the door. Lynette joined her, relieved; Tilly was like a different child now, she clearly loved the outdoors, just as her father did, and probably wouldn't have cared if it *had* still been raining. She scampered off happily, heedless of the puddles that splashed up her socks, and not bothering to button her coat against the stiff wind.

They wandered around the outside of the building for a little while, pointing to things they could see from their vantage point on the hill overlooking the town, and pretending they could even see Peter Tavy and the smoke coming from the chimney of Colleybrooke. Rounding the corner of the hospital again, Lynette looked across the car park and saw Geordie beside the car, spinning on his heel and staring around him. Beside him, a woman in a brown coat clutched at his arm and said something anxiously up at him, and Lynette gave an un-ladylike shout.

'We're here!'

They both turned, relief on their faces, and Tilly broke away from Lynette to run across the car park and hug her mother. Lynette followed, and slipped her hand into Geordie's. 'We fancied a bit of fresh air,' she said, then turned to Marion. 'I'm so sorry to hear about Mr Lawton. How is he?'

Marion looked as if she knew she was supposed to say something at this point, but only managed a tight shrug, a watery smile, and a quick, hopeful glance at Geordie.

'Marion wondered if we might like to spend a bit more time with Tilly,' Geordie said, pressing her arm. 'I said we'd be very happy to have her in Pencarrack for Christmas, if she'd like that.' He squatted in front of the little girl. 'Would you?'

Tilly looked up at her mother. 'Why can't I stay with you?'

Marion found her voice, in the face of her daughter's appeal. 'Roderick needs a little bit of nursing,' she said, and Lynette only then noticed her reddened eyes. 'Remember when Daddy needed that too? You didn't like being in the hospital then, did you?' Tilly shook her head firmly, and Marion hugged her again. 'Well then, I'm not going to make you do it again. Instead, you'll spend a few days at Daddy's house in Cornwall, all right?'

'But it's Christmas!'

'I know, my bird.' Marion touched the girl's cheek gently. 'But I can't be away from the hospital just now. Daddy will bring you back home just as soon as I can look after you properly.'

Tilly immediately looked up at the sky; Lynette saw the question on her face and answered it quickly. 'We'll need to go back to the village for more clothes,' she said, 'so we can find the note you wrote for Father Christmas, and give him Daddy's address instead.'

Tilly nodded slowly. 'Will we still have Christmas pudding?'

'My friend Tory has been making a really big one,' Lynette assured her. 'There's even a shiny sixpence in it for one lucky person, so maybe on the drive down, you could think about what you'll wish for if you find it.'

With heads full of instructions and requests, the three of them said their goodbyes to Marion and drove back to Peter Tavy, where Geordie let them in to Colleybrooke Manor and Tilly ran upstairs to her room. The house was impeccably tidy, and Geordie gave a low whistle as he looked around the hall.

'I just can't imagine Marion living here.'

A photograph hung in the hall: the man who could only be Roderick Lawton, at least ten years older than the woman beside him, who looked both bemused at her good fortune and happy with it. The little girl she held in her arms was staring boldly into the camera with familiar curiosity. A family in all but name, and Lynette suspected it would only be a matter of time before Marion began talking about a legal solution to that as well, but she didn't voice that thought. She and Geordie went upstairs to Tilly's large, comfortingly messy bedroom and collected as many clothes as they thought she might need.

'She's got a lot more than she had before,' Geordie murmured. 'And none of them are held together with darning thread, either, so I can't complain about her living here, can I?'

'But what about the other house?' Lynette said, checking Tilly was out of earshot. 'Marion must still be paying the rent you're sending her, or someone else would be living there by now.'

'That's what I wondered.'

'She can't be absolutely certain of this new life of hers then, can she?'

'I hope she is though, for Tilly's sake.' A sudden, unexpected smile lit his face, as the reality seemed to have only just hit him. 'She's coming for Christmas!' He kissed Lynette's cheek, then caught her up in a tight hug, spinning her around and making her yelp in surprised laughter. 'Lynette, she's *coming for Christmas!*'

They stopped off at the old house, where Lynette amended the note Tilly and Geordie had written for Father Christmas. She added that Tilly was staying with her daddy, crossed out Colleybrooke, and carefully printed the address of the Pencarrack forge instead. Then, as the afternoon light waned, they finally left Dartmoor behind them and began the long drive back home towards the dipping sun.

They arrived back in Pencarrack after dark. Lynette saw Gwinn's Copse ahead as they descended the hill towards the village, and slowed – not just because she would have to negotiate a fairly sharp left to get to the forge, but because she didn't want the day to end yet. Christmas Eve might have begun oddly, and taken a turn none of them had expected, but the drive home had been joyous.

Geordie, still sitting in the back with Tilly, had coaxed the girl into singing all the carols she knew, and he'd helped her with the words when she got stuck, sometimes sneaking in a clearly unrelated word to see if she noticed. When she did, her aggrieved tones had echoed around the car, making both adults laugh. They had laughed harder when she began doing the same thing, and the originally sweet Christmas singsong had soon descended into a raucous competition to see which of the three of them could come up with the silliest words.

Eventually Tilly, lulled by the movement of the car and her long, long day, had fallen asleep snuggled into Geordie's side. His arm was around her and Lynette glanced back now and again to see him staring down at her as if he thought she might disappear if he looked away. Lynette's heart filled at the sight, and she didn't speak for fear of breaking the spell.

But now the forge lay ahead, and there were lights in the cottage windows, through which Lynette could see paper chains strung across the ceiling. A face appeared as the car lights swept into the yard, and bobbed out of sight again, and Tilly stirred, looking momentarily lost, then sat forward for a better look.

'Is this your house?' she asked Geordie.

'It is. And that—' he pointed as the door opened and Joe appeared '—is the boy I was telling you about.'

'The 'prentice,' Tilly said doubtfully, trying out the word.

'And friend,' he reminded her. 'In fact he's like family now, so he'll be your family too.'

Mild puzzlement had crossed Joe's face as he saw that the seat next to Lynette was empty, and then he gave a relieved smile when he saw Geordie in the back. 'What are you doing there?' he called out, coming closer. Then he stopped, and Lynette realised he'd only just noticed Tilly, shrinking back shyly against the seat. A shadow crossed his face, which gave Lynette a twist of unease, but it vanished almost immediately, and a quick look at Geordie revealed he hadn't seen it; he'd been bending over to pick up Tilly's small suitcase from between his feet.

'This must be Tilly,' Joe said, and his smile seemed forced, though in fairness perhaps it wouldn't have, Lynette admitted, if she hadn't seen that initial flicker of displeasure.

Geordie climbed out and gave a luxurious stretch, grunting in relief. 'That's better. Come on out, Tilly, and meet Joe.' He opened Lynette's door for her and gave her his hand. 'Thank you,' he murmured quietly in her ear as he helped her from behind the wheel. 'You've been wonderful today.'

Lynette kissed him lightly, and turned to look at the two youngsters. Joe was still smiling, but Tilly looked uncertain and crowded close to Geordie's side. Lynette took the suitcase so Geordie could lift his daughter up.

'Where will she sleep?' Joe asked, quite bluntly. 'There's no spare room.'

'She can have my room,' Geordie said. 'I'll sleep on the settee. It's only for a day or two.'

'We haven't got enough food.'

'Of course we have!' Geordie forced a smile of his own. 'There's plenty for three of us.'

Tilly wriggled to be set down, and then held out her hand for her suitcase. Lynette gave it to her, but the little girl marched back to the car. 'I'm going home,' she declared, and pushed the bag ahead of her onto the back seat before climbing in after it. Lynette and Geordie exchanged astonished looks, but Joe turned away and went back into the house without comment.

'I think his nose might just have been put out of joint,' Lynette murmured. 'This *is* his first—'

'I know.' Geordie sighed. 'But once I explain, he'll realise there wasn't anything else I could do.'

'I'm sure he will.' Lynette looked into the back of the car where Tilly's frozen expression was all too easy to read. She hesitated. 'Would it be better for her to come home with me?' She saw his face cloud over. 'It's the best thing for both of them,' she said gently. 'You and Joe can come over and spend the day tomorrow, as planned, and we have a spare room now Irene's not coming back. Together we can give Tilly and Joe the Christmas they both deserve, before we take her home.'

Geordie was clearly torn, but the good sense was impossible to deny, provided Tilly could be persuaded. 'All right.'

Lynette stood back and gestured at the car. 'I'll go in and say good night to Joe.'

Inside the cottage it was easier to see the special effort Joe had made in Geordie's absence; the table was already laid ready for breakfast for two, and a hand-drawn card stood open at Geordie's place. The paper chains, which had been building into a rustling, colourful pile in Joe's bedroom ever since she and Tory had presented him with the strips of paper and the pot of glue, were now strung from corner to corner. Joe had caught them up in the middle over the centre of the table, with all the leftover circlets in a bunch. The boy was now nudging his work boots into a corner, and he looked up as Lynette came in, his expression troubled.

'I don't really mind,' he began, but Lynette shook her head.

'I know, love. But you're right, there really isn't room. Geordie's just asking Tilly if she'd like to come back with me to the stables for the night, instead.'

Joe's lip trembled a little, but he caught himself and nodded. 'She'll be more comfortable,' he said, and cleared his throat. 'Can we still come over after breakfast?'

'I should hope so!' Lynette gave him a smile. 'We'll all be disappointed if you don't.'

Joe smiled back, but the smile soon faded as he looked out through the window. 'Is Geordie angry with me?'

'Of course he isn't.' Lynette gave him a hug. 'It's been a very long day for all of us, and after we've had a good night's sleep we'll all feel much better. Happy Christmas Eve, Joe. Don't forget to hang your stocking.'

A brief grin touched his face. 'I do know Father Christmas isn't real.' But he'd lowered his voice and looked around, almost as if he thought someone might yet be making a note and selecting a lump of coal.

Lynette affected a shocked look, but ruffled his hair and said good night, then went back out to see that Tilly had readily agreed to spend the night at the stables. The girl sat in the car looking out at them expectantly, having already said her goodbyes to her father, and Lynette raised a finger to indicate she wouldn't be long, then turned to Geordie.

'Joe's worried you're angry,' she said quietly. 'I said we're all just tired.'

'Thanks, I'll talk to him.' He drew her close and kissed her. 'Just a minute, I want to show you something before you go.'

He threw a quick look towards the house to ensure Joe hadn't come back out, then reached to the back of a shelf and passed Lynette something small, wrapped in a piece of soft leather. She folded back the edges and found a flat, western-style belt buckle inside. 'Oh, this is beautiful!'

'It's made from Al's old pewter drinking mug,' he explained. 'I'm not sure I did the right thing, but it just felt like it would be a way for Joe to keep his dad close. I've made him a new belt, too.'

Lynette turned the buckle over in her hand, marvelling at the smoothness, and running her finger over the Blacksmiths' crossed hammers symbol etched into its surface. She looked up again to see that Geordie was watching her uncharacteristically anxiously.

'What do you think?' he asked. 'Will it upset him?'

'God, no.' She passed the buckle back. 'He might be emotional at first, but he'll love it.' She looked at his still worried expression and felt her heart move, compelling her to take his face in her hands and kiss him. 'It's a beautiful thing, Geordie. And a wonderful thought.'

'Good.' He relaxed and tucked the buckle away again. 'And now I think you've got some explaining to do to Tory.'

'I'm half-owner now,' Lynette pointed out. 'I've got just as much say in who stays in the flat.'

'I don't doubt it.' Geordie grinned suddenly. 'But *I* know how early Tilly gets up on Christmas morning. *And* she's slept for at least an hour in the car.' He turned away and sauntered back to the cottage, calling back over his shoulder, 'Good luck!'

CHAPTER NINE

Christmas dinner was exactly as Gwenna had expected it to be: quiet, pleasant and peaceful, but melancholy too. It was easier than it had been last year, the first year her father had been at Dartmoor, when they had returned from the Christmas Day chapel service, and set straight to work preparing the vegetables for the chicken that Rachel had set to slow roast before they'd left. Talk then, as today, had been light, aimless, and they had both been determined not to touch on the subject that had been haunting them both. However, once the meal was over, Gwenna had decided it was time.

'What's Christmas going to be like for Dad in . . . there?' she'd asked, picking up the tea towel as her mother placed the first clean plate on the drainer. 'Is it just like any other day?'

Rachel had swished the next plate slowly in the water, her brows drawn down in a slight frown. 'From what he said, it's apparently quite a special day,' she'd said at length. 'They're allowed to get up when they like, and they have a good dinner of roast beef, with baked potatoes and plenty of greens. Pudding for afters, of course.'

'And what do they do?' Gwenna had persisted. 'Do they have to work?'

'Oh, no.' Rachel had sounded more confident now, and given Gwenna a smile. 'Work is something they can choose, anyway. They're not made to do anything if they don't want to, but they can earn a good wage and buy little luxuries, and it passes the time. And they learn new skills while they're at it. There's a concert today, too,' she went on. 'Christmas songs, and such. He'll be fine.'

'Would he let me go to see him now, do you think?'

'I don't know.' It was the same reply every time she asked that question, along with the reminder that, should Jonas put a new name on his list it would have to go to the local constabulary to be approved, and might take months. 'The police will have to come and interview you as well, and that won't be nice for anyone. But yes, of course I'll ask.'

Now they were washing up together again, a whole year further on, but no new visiting order had come. Instead, Gwenna had to take comfort from all her mother had told her before. 'You did pass on my love, didn't you, when you went up?' she said, anxious her father shouldn't think she'd brushed him from her mind.

'Of course. But don't worry about him, it's not nearly so bad as you've been imagining.'

Gwenna nodded. 'You hear awful things.'

'Well, I'm here to tell you what I see with my own eyes.' Rachel began scrubbing at the roasting tin, putting a great deal of effort in and splashing slimy, black-flecked water up over the clean plates she'd set on the drainer. She glanced at them and clicked her tongue in irritation, waving Gwenna's hand back. 'I'll do them again in a minute. Anyway, like I was saying, the men I see in the visitors' hall are all very polite, the place looks and smells nice and clean, and there are no punishments except for those who break the rules. Which your father would never do,' she added, unnecessarily.

'And the cells?' Gwenna had asked many times before, but she needed to be reassured all over again, and Rachel smiled.

'Comfortable and clean,' she said for the hundredth time. 'They're not animals in a zoo, love. The prison's on a very exposed part of the moor, so the, the conv ... prisoners have plenty of blankets and warm clothes. The governors have to give them the right food, too, they're allocated a budget per prisoner. They can't have them falling ill now, can they? Imagine the scandal.' She nudged Gwenna's arm with her own. 'Go on now, I've got to re-wash those plates anyway, but I'll leave them to drain after. Go for your walk while it's still dry out.'

Gwenna hung the wet tea towel over the rail of the range to dry, and went to fetch her shoes. When she looked back into the kitchen she saw her mother pick up the first of the re-dirtied plates, look at it blankly for a moment, then drop it into the sink, sending more greasy water splashing up. Rachel bowed her head for a moment, fetched a heavy sigh up from somewhere near her feet, and picked up the washcloth.

Gwenna went out through the empty shop instead of back through the kitchen, leaving her mother with her thoughts. Her parents had gone through a difficult time, when Rachel had believed Jonas's frequent absences and secretive manner were due to him setting his cap at Doctor Stuart, but when the truth about his smuggling had come out it had hardly made things better. He'd tried to make up for it, and Rachel had forgiven him, but

Gwenna couldn't help wondering what it would be like when he finally came home.

The air outside was cool and fresh, after the stifling, smoky atmosphere in the kitchen, and Gwenna automatically turned to face uphill so she'd be coming down on the way home, though she had no planned walk in mind. For a moment she toyed with the idea of dropping in at the stables after all, but although she knew Joe Trevellick quite well, and had done since he'd been little, she didn't know Geordie or Lynette well enough to go intruding into such a cosy Christmas afternoon.

So instead, once she reached the top of town, she crossed the moor and took the cliff path down to Fortress cove, below the Cliffside Fort Hotel. The tide would be on its way in by now, but there would still be enough beach to walk on, and it was usually quite a solitary place, thanks to the difficulty of the single path in and out. It could be a dangerous beach, too, given the speed with which the tide came in and cut off anyone unwary enough to have ventured too far out onto the rocks; there were safer places nearby, where children could be allowed to run off their energy, so it wasn't surprising that there were only three other people there today.

Gwenna removed her shoes and stockings, and let her feet curl into the cold, damp sand for a minute, before crossing the small cove to the rocks that sprawled at the foot of the cliff face on the far side. Just above where she sat down was the hole in the cliff face, which Tory had explained had been the main overflow for the now defunct Wheal Furzy mine. More importantly, it had also turned out to be the secret route from the hidden room beneath Tyndall's Folly, through which Tory had helped her old gang leader to escape the man who had wanted to kill her.

Gwenna looked up at the innocuous-looking gap, remembering the terror of that time and the relief when it had all ended. Back then she had shied away from discussing it, but now she found herself wanting, for the first time, to talk to someone who understood how it had been. She made up her mind to find Tory again soon.

When she turned back to look at the sea again, her gaze skimmed the beach and stopped on a tall, broad figure just coming off the path and stepping onto the beach. Her instincts recognised him before she did, and she felt herself tense without fully knowing why; then she realised it was Jago Carne, who'd been arrested earlier in the year for helping the Damerels escape. She also heard how he'd fought Geordie Sargent outside the pub one night, and won quite decisively. He had a mean temper, and there were plenty of stories about him that she could dwell on, but for some reason the sight of him made her think of her mother, believing she was alone and giving in to a moment that could only be described as despair.

Gwenna frowned, trying to make the connection, and found her thoughts wandering back over their conversation. The too-hard scrubbing of the roasting pan. The tightening of the lips, and the insistence that Gwenna go her own way for a while. A suspicion flickered at the edges of her thoughts, but she sat quietly and let it simmer, while she watched Carne make his way down to the water's edge.

He stood there, just staring out at the rolling grey sea, not moving back as it washed over his boots, and Gwenna wondered if there would ever be a better opportunity. Before she had time to talk herself out of it, she got to her feet, picked up her shoes and stockings, and clambered carefully over the seaweed-slippery rocks to the sand. Then she took a steadying breath, and walked down to stand a short distance away from Carne, wincing as the cold water washed over her bare feet. His height was hard to gauge against the open water, but she knew him to stand well over six feet, and with that burly frame he made an imposing figure. Her resolve wavered; she personally had no issue with him, and she was a tall girl, but he had a reputation that went beyond the fight with Geordie and the arrest back in the spring. People said he'd been Colin Damerel's paid thug when he worked at the South Pencarrack clay pit, and that he'd been the one who'd broken Les Trethewey's arm; Gwenna didn't know how much of that was true, but just at this moment she didn't care.

'Mr Carne?' She hadn't known for sure she'd been going to speak at all, and her voice was small, and almost torn away by the coastal wind. But he heard it, and twisted his head to look at her. Gwenna studied his face, all but hidden behind the bushy beard, but too pale for a man who'd spent much time outside.

'That's me,' he grunted. 'You're Rosdew's girl.'

'I am, yes.'

'Been in your shop a few times,' he said, turning away again. 'Better than the Pencarrack one.'

'Oh. Um, thank you.' Gwenna took another breath, a quick one this time, and pushed ahead. 'Can I talk to you about my father?'

'Talk about what you like, I can't stop you.'

You probably could, actually . . . 'Did you see him much?'

'Once in a blue moon.'

'Oh.' Gwenna faced out to sea again. It was easier than looking up at those muddy brown eyes. 'But you'll know how he's doing in . . . in there, won't you?'

'Prison? You're allowed to say it, maid.'

'Yes, in prison.' Gwenna looked up at him again, this time hopefully. She felt like a child again; scared, but curious. 'What's it really like?'

Carne huffed a soft laugh, and shook his head. 'Haven't you been to visit him?'

'No, he hasn't put me on his list. My mother's been, though.'

'Ask her then.'

'I have. She's told me what she thinks I should know.' Now that she heard herself say it aloud Gwenna felt a slow roll of apprehension inside her. 'I think I want to know what it's really like.'

'You *think* you do?'

Gwenna linked her thumbs together through her shoelaces, and thought for a moment, no longer sure.

'Thought not,' Carne said, his voice gruff and dismissive as he turned to walk away. 'Don't spoil your mother's pretty pictures, maid. You can't do anything about it.'

'No, I *do* want to know!' She ran a few steps to catch up with him. 'Please.'

'What's your mum told you then?'

Gwenna heard the flare of a match, and looked up to see him lighting a hand-rolled cigarette, cupping the match flame to keep the wind from blowing it out. She shrugged, not wanting to display her naivety. 'It doesn't matter what she said. Why don't you tell me what it was like for you?'

'That won't tell you what it's like for your old man,' Carne pointed out. 'It's not the same for everyone, and I wasn't in there near as long.'

Gwenna picked on the one thing that had worried her the most: her father's wartime back and neck injury. 'Has he decided to work? Because—'

'Decided?' Carne nearly choked on his cigarette. His short laugh wasn't of the pleasant or sympathetic type. 'No one gets to choose whether they work or not, maid. Not even special stagers. All right then,' he said, his exaggeratedly amicable tone belying the gleam in his eyes, as he bent slightly so his face was on a level with hers. 'You wanted to know what it's really like in there, little girl, I'll tell you.'

He stood up straight again, and went on to describe a reality that Gwenna had thought herself braced for, but which she hadn't even imagined in the darkest hollows of the night. Picturing her father in that environment was close to impossible; no wonder her mother had tried to shield her from it, and no wonder she always returned from those visits smiling and talking of warm blankets and fair wages; a deflection Gwenna had chosen to believe, because anything else would have pushed her own guilt just that bit too far to bear.

'New governor didn't help,' Carne was saying now. 'They say that before he arrived, the men was allowed to change jobs every few months. Keeps interest fresh, you know? Especially for the long-term lags. But—' he threw up the hand that held his cigarette, sending ash floating into Gwenna's face '—Governor Roberts decides it affects productivity, having to keep re-training us, so now you can't change jobs for about a year. Bastard.' He spat onto the sand. 'The screws seem to like him well enough, but the convicts don't.' He drew deeply on his cigarette again, and spoke flatly on an outrush of smoke. 'He'd better watch his back, that's all I can say.'

'And what job was my dad doing?' Gwenna asked. Quarry working, wall-building and stone-crushing couldn't be the only kind of jobs there were, though, due to his size and strength

Carne would have been put to work in them for sure. Her father though, slighter of build and with little strength in his shoulders any more, must surely have been found something lighter.

'No idea,' Carne said. 'I told you, I hardly saw him. We weren't in the same block.'

'But his war injuries,' she persisted. 'Wouldn't they go some way to making sure he wasn't put to work outside, doing the same jobs you were?'

Carne plucked a piece of loose tobacco from his tongue, and shrugged. 'Maybe. Maybe not. Seen plenty of blokes with bad backs, out fixin' the warders' homes in the village. I will say this, though.' He gave her another one of those tight, meaningless smiles. 'Jonas Rosdew's no special case. Plenty of us behind those bars have seen military action, and a lot of the convicts have got the scars, the bad-set bones and the burns to prove it. Just before I got out,' he went on, in more conversational tones, 'I was working with a new lag, kicked out of the navy. He's a decent lad, just unlucky. But at least one of them warders has been gunnin' for him from the start, so if you're thinkin' your old man's gettin' special treatment thanks to a bit of metal he got given by the war office, you can think again. If there's a job needs doing, and he's in the working party, he'll do it. And if he knows what's good for him he won't complain about it.'

Gwenna swallowed hard, trying not to let a tremor into her voice as she pushed the subject in another direction. 'What's the food like?'

'If you can call it that.' Carne described bread by the ounce and tea by the pint, all of it a poor approximation of the food Gwenna knew, and although he corroborated her mother's reports of roast beef for Christmas dinner, he'd not been there at Christmas himself, so it was as much rumour from him as from her. He sounded neither convinced nor convincing.

She could hardly bring herself to ask the next question. 'What about punishments?'

'What about them?' Carne looked at the soggy remains of his cigarette, then pitched it away into the sand. 'Leave it be, for crying out loud.'

'I need to know!'

Gwenna took a startled step back as Carne rounded on her, his eyes flashing, both hands tugging hard at his thick beard as if restraining himself from lashing out.

'You do *not*! Nothing I've told you is even halfway to explaining what it's like in there, so for the sake of your everlasting soul, girl, *leave it be*!' He showed no remorse for frightening her, he just kept staring. Gwenna stared back, relieved to feel anger beginning to overpower everything else.

'It's my father,' she said, letting that anger show. 'I *do* need to know.' A silence simmered between them, and neither backed away for what felt like minutes but couldn't have been. Gwenna's eyes started to burn, but she held on.

'When's he out?' Carne asked at length, looking back out over the sea, and his voice had lowered to its normal volume again.

'In the spring.'

'Is that early, or will he have done his full sentence?'

'A bit early. Why?'

Carne shrugged. 'Fair chance he's not spent a lot of time on the punishment block, then.'

'Is that supposed to make me feel better?' Gwenna's own voice was still hard, and he looked back at her with a scowl.

'I'm not here to make you feel better, I'm just minding my

own beeswax and getting some fresh air. You came over to *me*, remember? Wishing you hadn't, are you?'

Gwenna didn't reply. She just shook her head slightly, turned away from him, and set off back up the beach towards the cliff path; tomorrow would be back to work from dawn until evening, but she and her mother still had some time left to talk today. Gwenna wanted to make sure they used every minute of it while Jago Carne's words were fresh in her mind, and she knew where she wanted to start.

She slipped out of her outdoor shoes by the front door, although all the sand had been kicked off them during the walk home, then sat down in the armchair chair opposite her mother, tucked her damp-stockinged feet beneath her, and once again brought up the subject of the visiting order.

'I've been thinking about what you said, and if the men are all so polite and it's such a clean visiting hall, I don't see any reason why I shouldn't go.'

'Oh, love. Haven't you understood it yet?' Rachel put down her glass of Christmas port. 'Your dad doesn't *want* you to see him in there. He'd have arranged it by now if he did.'

'He needn't try to protect me, and you needn't either. I want to see him.'

'But it's been nearly two years, what's the point now?' Her mother picked up her drink again and took a sip, but it looked to Gwenna rather like a delaying tactic, giving herself time to think. 'You know how guilty he feels about how he helped pull you into it all. It's best if you just let him serve what's left of his time, and then come home knowing he's paid the price for what he did and that you haven't been dirtied by it all.'

'When are you going to see him again?'

'He'll have earned another visit in the new year, I think. I'll be sure to tell him you send your love, as always.' Rachel was clearly hoping this would signal the end of the conversation, but Gwenna wasn't ready yet.

'I saw someone when I was out walking,' she said, playing idly with the antimacassar on the arm of the chair. 'Jago Carne.'

Rachel's head came up, and she looked at Gwenna warily. 'I heard he was out.'

Gwenna could tell she was dying to ask whether they'd spoken. 'I was on the beach at Fortress Cove,' she said, 'and he was just standing there looking out to sea. He seemed ... approachable, so I went over.'

'To ask after your father, I assume. And what did he say? Put the fear of God into you with lies, I suppose?'

For a moment Gwenna almost doubted herself, but the way her mother looked anywhere but at her, was enough to tell her she was right to believe Carne's version. For the best possible reasons, her mother had been lying to her from the first.

'Would you please ask Dad if I can come with you next time?' she said, instead of answering.

'Of course I'll *ask* him,' Rachel said. 'But don't be disappointed if he refuses again. Now, are you ready for a bit of leftover chicken in a sandwich? That walk must have given you an appetite.'

Without waiting for an answer, she rose and went to the kitchen, leaving Gwenna staring into the fire and thinking over everything Jago Carne had told her. And all he had hinted at but not actually said. She looked at the door through which her mother had gone, and knew she'd never see her name on any visiting order; not because her father would refuse, but because her mother wouldn't even bring it up. She believed her lies were protecting her daughter from the brutal reality of a Dartmoor prisoner's existence, but the fact that she needed to do so meant that Gwenna's imagination was running amok, and was probably painting an even worse picture than the truth.

Gwenna had to see for herself. She unfolded herself from her chair and went upstairs to her bedroom, where she closed the door against unwanted interruption, and took out her writing pad and pen.

CHAPTER TEN

By the time evening fell over Pencarrack Stables on Christmas Day, Tilly was fast asleep on the rug in front of the fire, one arm curled around Barney, the other hand still clutching a crumbling piece of Christmas cake. Joe was reading his new *Boy's Own Annual*, his head jerking now and again as his eyes kept closing, and Lynette was listening to carols on the wireless and writing in her diary. It all looked so peaceful, Geordie thought; a picture straight off a Christmas card, with the decorations hanging low over the still-cluttered table where they'd eaten so well just a couple of hours ago – all of them had been wearing paper hats, from the crackers Lynette had bought as a surprise, and had taken turns reading out the love poems the crackers had yielded. Such a calm, cosy scene. Deceptively so.

Geordie and Joe had breakfasted early, and exchanged gifts. Joe had clearly sweated long and hard over a new pocket knife for Geordie, the wooden handle having been applied by John Doidge in secret, and had even made a simple leather sheath from leather, riveted by his own hand. Geordie had been deeply touched at seeing the hard work that had gone into every part of it, and in turn he handed Joe his own package. He watched, nervously tapping his fingers on his new knife, while Joe unwrapped it to find the hand-tooled belt inside, and then raised it to study the buckle. Joe was clearly delighted, but it wasn't until Geordie explained where the pewter had come from that he knew he hadn't made a mistake after all. The lad's face had first lit up, then crumpled, and Geordie wordlessly held the boy while he wept.

As he and Joe cleared away the breakfast things, he felt a strong urge to be at the stables, to witness Tilly's joy as she realised Father Christmas had known where to find her after all. He looked at his pocket watch, and after a glance out through the rain-streaked window he picked up his hat.

'Best get over and help Lynette and Tory with the horses,' he said. 'Leave the plates, we can do them later.'

'Aren't they going to church?'

'The plates?' Geordie asked innocently, then grinned at the long-suffering look on Joe's face. 'No, not this year.' He lifted their coats from the pegs by the door, and threw Joe's to him. 'Too much work to do.'

'The plates?' Joe asked, in the same innocent tone Geordie had used, and Geordie gave a soft snort of approval.

'Come on.'

'Is that kid going to be there?' Joe asked, and Geordie was glad he'd turned away to open the door so Joe wouldn't see the way he'd flinched.

'My daughter, you mean?' he said pointedly. 'She is. Now mind, you don't have to be her big brother, but you don't have to be a crosspatch either.'

'Crosspatch?' Joe was surprised into a laugh. 'I'm not an old woman.'

'Young men can be crosspatches too,' Geordie told him. 'I should know.'

Joe looked at him curiously, as they locked up and started walking. 'Were you one?'

'The worst kind,' Geordie confided. 'When my brother got sent away you couldn't talk to me for fear of getting your head bitten off. Tilly's mother had a lot to put up with.' He shoved his hands deep into his coat pockets and picked up his pace, and they arrived at the stables just as Tory was opening up the stable door.

'Happy Christmas, boys!' she called out cheerfully. She had apparently not been fazed by Tilly's unexpected arrival last night, and told them how the girl had settled down happily, and without question, in Irene's old room. She explained they had given her one of Tory's own long woollen socks to hang by the chimney, but Geordie didn't want to make Tilly his first topic of conversation, not in front of Joe. He nodded his thanks briefly, then, pushing aside his impatience to first see his daughter, and then to kiss Lynette breathless, he gestured to Joe.

'Come on, lad, make yourself useful and grab that pitchfork.'

Things had gone well, for most of the day, at least. Between the three of them the horses were quickly done, Tory turned Mack and Hercules out into the field, and Geordie finally allowed himself to go up into the flat.

'Daddy!' Tilly jumped up from where she was playing on the rug, her face alight with smiles.

Lynette told Geordie, in a low murmur, how she and Tory had re-wrapped some of the gifts by the tree, in order to share them more evenly among everyone who was going to be there; she herself had put Tilly's name on the scarf she had bought for Joe, and Tory had re-labelled some strawberry sherbet she had wrapped up as an additional present for Bobby. Geordie's gift to her was a stack of colouring books and some wax crayons, which was received with gratifying pleasure and put to immediate use, and his relief was enormous; he'd had very little money to spend on presents.

Bobby Gale arrived soon afterwards, to complete the group, and the noise and activity levels went up yet again; Joe and Bobby had always got on well, and Bobby had a knack of making Joe laugh, for which Geordie was particularly grateful today. Bobby had never worked at the clay pit, but he had known Joe's father during happier times, when Al had been running the Tin Streamer's Arms in town, and his stories brought the lad's father alive again for a little while.

Later they had played hunt the thimble, and pinned a fluffy tail on a very disgruntled-looking donkey Bobby had painted, and then they'd sat down to dinner, where, for the first time all day, things had turned faintly sour. Tilly had been so delighted with her scarf that she'd not taken it off, despite the warmth in the room. She carefully pushed the ends of it under the table as she ate, and when she dripped gravy on it and grew distressed, Geordie and Lynette, who sat on either side of her, mopped it up quickly with their napkins.

Geordie had looked across the table to ask Joe to fetch a dab of soap from the kitchen, and saw Joe's eyes locked on the scarf, his face betraying a mixture of envy and misery. The boy obediently went to fetch the soap, but Geordie handed it to Lynette and jerked his head towards at the door; Joe rolled his eyes and went outside, and after a moment Geordie joined him. 'What was that look for?'

'What look?'

'Come on, Joe! You're not a fool, and neither am I.' Geordie put his hands on Joe's shoulders. 'You knew about the scarf, didn't you?'

Joe looked down. 'The night Lynette got back I opened the kitchen window to let the steam out, and I heard her telling you about it.'

'Then I'm sorry. But she was only trying to even things out, and you still had more presents than Tilly did.'

'But it's not . . .' Joe shook his head. 'It doesn't matter.'

'I'm sure Lynette will be able to find you another scarf,' Geordie said, his patience straining a little. He was battling disappointment as well as a flicker of guilt; he and Joe had been through such a lot together, he'd thought better of the boy than this. 'Let's not get all het up over it.'

Joe turned away and pushed his way back into the flat without replying, and Geordie bit back the shout that would have brought him back out to finish the discussion; it wouldn't achieve anything, and the last thing he wanted was to upset the boy today. He sighed and followed, pasting a smile onto his face as he rejoined the dinner table. For the rest of the time Joe kept his distance from Tilly, which made it hard for Geordie to share his attention equally between them, but Bobby and Tory helped, albeit unknowingly, by arranging a strenuous game of hide-and-seek out in the yard, which tired out both children.

Evening had been creeping in as the game finished and they all made their way back upstairs again. Tilly had lain on the rug, playing with Barney until sleep claimed her where she lay, and

Tory had been about to enlist Bobby's help with the evening feed when telephone rang. Tilly twitched but did not wake, and Tory held the receiver out to Geordie. 'It's for you.'

Geordie tensed. 'Marion?'

'How did you know?'

'She's the only person I told I'd be spending the day here. She hates to use the telephone, so it must be important.' He took the receiver, and as Tory and Bobby went outside Lynette briefly looked up from her diary, before returning to it rather than intrude.

'Marion?' Geordie said again, this time into the telephone. 'How is he?'

Marion's voice was broken, and lost sounding. 'He's gone.' She hiccupped a stifled sob, and then tried again. 'Around lunchtime. He just … He's gone,' she repeated. 'Oh, Geordie, what am I going to do?'

'I'm sorry, love,' Geordie said quietly. Lynette looked up again, and now her eyes were wide, questioning. He shook his head, and her face paled. She looked at the sleeping Tilly, clearly already thinking about how they would break the news.

Geordie spoke again, into the sceptical silence at the other end of the phone. 'You might not believe me, Marion, but I *am* sorry. Truly.' He paused. 'What do you want to do about you-know-who?'

Across the room, Joe's eyes were on him. Narrowed, suspicious. Geordie fought the urge to snap at him, and kept his voice low when he spoke to Marion again. 'Do you want me to tell her?'

'No. I'll do it.' Marion sighed; a ragged, hopeless sound. 'But not over the telephone. Just give her a happy Christmas time with you. Can you do that?'

'Of course. What will you do?'

'I don't know. I have to talk to Roderick's … other family. His children. They're already on their way down, so I can't reach them.'

'Where are they coming from?'

'His daughter moved to … I don't know, somewhere up north. His son lives in Somerset now. They don't know he's gone, just that he'd had that first stroke.' Her voice caught again, and Geordie waited, his eyes on his sleeping daughter. 'I don't know how to tell them,' Marion said at length. 'Or Tilly. I know you didn't approve of him but—'

'I honestly had no feelings about him,' Geordie broke in. 'I was angry that he was trying to be her dad, yes, but I can't blame him for it.'

'Well, anyway,' Marion said, and he could picture her shaking her hair back and pulling herself upright; her way of pushing aside anything she no longer wished to discuss. 'The fact is I've got a lot to organise now. Funeral and suchlike. I hope his family can help with that, but can you keep Tilly until she has to come back for school?'

He'd promised to do his best, and had sat watching the sleeping girl ever since, wondering how he was going to amuse her and keep her safe while he was supposed to be working. He looked across at Joe, and saw with a sinking feeling that there was more than jealousy on the boy's face now; there was real anger, and the kind of intense dislike Geordie had previously only ever seen aimed at the likes of Colin Damerel and Jago Carne. He felt sick to see it, and saw that Lynette had noticed it too.

She put down her pen and spoke brightly. 'Come on, Joe, let's get these plates and things cleared away before Tory and Bobby get back. Will you help too, Geordie?'

104

Geordie rose and feigned enthusiasm for the task, but he was shaken by the revelation of this side of the boy's character. In all the time Joe had been Geordie's apprentice at the China clay works, and then as they'd both recovered from their various injuries over the summer, Geordie had seen only the gradually emerging strength and confidence he'd always suspected had been there. Joe's sharp grief at the loss of his father had become muted in his struggle to recover, and then softened by the warmth of his welcome into Geordie's life and home. Now this. It was unsettling and worrying.

Tilly stirred, as Geordie bent to pick up Barney and set the bell around its neck jingling. She sat up looking disorientated. 'Mummy?'

'No, love,' Geordie said gently, squatting beside her. 'It's me, remember?'

She blinked and looked around her at the Christmas decorations, and then saw Joe, and her expression surprisingly calmed as she nodded. 'Where's Tory?'

'Gone to settle the horses for the night.' Geordie sat down, cross-legged, and lifted her into his lap. 'Would you like to see them tomorrow?'

'Aren't I going home?'

Geordie shook his head. 'Not for a few more days, yet. Your mummy telephoned while you were asleep, and asked if you'd mind staying here a bit longer.'

'How long?'

'Until it's time to go back to school. So maybe a week.' He didn't look at Joe, but didn't need to; he could hear the movements becoming sharper and more deliberate as Joe moved around the kitchen.

Tilly considered, then nodded slowly. 'Can Mummy visit?'

'If she wants to. The thing is, she's . . . she's going to be very busy for a little while, and is worried you might get bored.' He didn't want to tell the outright lie that she'd still be caring for Roderick; Tilly was no fool, and once she learned the truth she'd never trust him again. 'So, would you like to stay for a few days?'

She looked over again at Joe, who was studiously ignoring her. 'Would I stay at your house?'

'There's no extra bedroom,' Geordie reminded her. 'But I'll come here as often as I can, and you can come to tea sometimes too, if Lynette doesn't mind bringing you.'

'Will Joe be there?'

Geordie and Lynette exchanged a quick glance, but there was no sense in lying to the girl about that, either. 'Yes,' Geordie said carefully. 'He will. But you don't—'

'Good!' Tilly climbed out of his lap and picked up her lamb, flicking the little bell around its neck to make it ring loudly, then skipped off to help Joe in the kitchen.

CHAPTER ELEVEN

His Majesty's Convict Prison, Dartmoor
27 December

Stephen Sargent had proved an unexpectedly staunch ally since Daniel's arrival on the moor, but there was only so much even he could do. Daniel felt anger flicker like flames through his blood, as he sat waiting for the siren that would drive the prisoners out of the shelter of sleep, and into the bleak reality of a new day. Seven o'clock on a Sunday: a generous half hour later than the weekday hooter.

Sit tight and do your time. Don't give the screws any trouble ...

Well, Daniel had done exactly that. Worked where he was told to work, and done it willingly; spoken when and where it was permitted, and nowhere else; and he'd been diffident almost to the point of submissiveness. It hadn't worked.

They'd taken the kid out first thing this morning. At least, Daniel thought of Alec Damerel as a kid, and everyone who was awake had heard him sobbing as he crossed the yard to the waiting prison transport van. But it had turned out the condemned man was just two years younger than himself. Twenty-five, and soon to be snuffed into a bitter memory for everyone who'd known him, reduced to a note in a prison record book for everyone else. Gone to the mercy of Pierrepoint, or one of his assistant executioners, and he wouldn't be the last from this place, either.

Daniel had watched the kid's father over the past week, full of bluff and bluster, decrying the system as unfair and barbaric ... until they'd actually taken his son away, whereupon he'd become abruptly ghost-like, as if the reality had finally hit him. There was nothing he could do or say now. He'd fallen silent, faded into the background and there, Daniel guessed, he would remain until the date of his release. Or his death, whichever occurred first.

Daniel grasped the underside of his bunk as he sat in the darkness. That tight atmosphere that Stephen had mentioned on his first day had become apparent once Daniel knew to look out for it, but nothing big had so far come of it, and he had avoided being caught up in even the regular, smaller releases of tension. So far, so good. Except for exercise.

Exercise was the one thing he'd looked forward to since his conviction. In his former life in the navy, he'd excelled at PT, and whenever they were stood down he'd loved nothing better than setting out on his own, running across the city and then walking along the cliffs, on the other side of Mountbatten. But his illusions had been shattered the first time he'd gone out into the yard here. Half an hour twice a day, plodding in circles with the guard shouting constantly: 'Open out!' or, 'Close up!' when the men fell foul of the strict three-feet distance between them. There were other 'witty' taunts, generally uttered for the amusement of the warder in charge, and barely a breath between the shouts, so they all mingled together in a meaningless string of noise.

The men themselves were kept moving in strict silence, so there was no distraction from it, and one warder, Ned Newbury, had clearly taken a dislike to Daniel for some reason no one could fathom. Almost all the man's shouting was directed at him, and he'd been pushed to the ground twice within ten minutes of joining B group on the parade ground. He'd been puzzled, then angry, and a snapped demand for reasoning had earned him nothing but a whack on the elbow from Newbury's stick. The officer hadn't even bothered to hide his intention to stir Daniel up, and it hadn't let up for the duration of that first torturous half hour.

There had been some respite during the week just gone, when a different guard had taken over and exercise had felt almost pleasant by comparison, despite the biting cold and still constant shouting. At least this time others had borne the brunt as well. But yesterday Newbury had returned, and had once more kept pace with Daniel all the way around, alternately berating him for being too close to the man in front, then too far back.

A shove with his stick in the small of Daniel's back had sent him stumbling forwards, whereupon a hand on his collar immediately yanked him back a half-step. By the time the whistle had blown, Daniel had been the closest he'd ever come, while sober, to wishing the worst imaginable harm on a fellow human being. And, even more alarmingly, the closest to tears.

Stephen had said nothing, and Daniel had first been stung, then churned with quiet resentment at his apparently careless attitude, but it turned out that his cellmate had not been as idle as he'd seemed; a few discreet, but well-placed questions of his own had revealed the answer. Last night, as the lights went out, he'd spoken quietly.

'What was the name of that bloke whose car you smashed up?'

'Alfred Dunn.'

'Owns the shops?'

'Dunn's Drapery.' Daniel had risen onto one elbow, though it was hard to pick out Stephen in the damp darkness. 'He's a councillor, too, apparently. Why?'

'Thought so. He's got a daughter.'

'Yes. My mum worked for him, and she mentioned she'd met her. Alice, I think?'

'Alison.' Daniel had heard the rustle as Stephen's head twisted on his pillow. 'Married name, Alison Newbury.'

Daniel had lain back down, his pulse hammering against his temples. 'So, you reckon Dunn's getting his revenge by making his son-in-law give me a hard time, then.'

'Certain of it.'

'As if I'm not already taking my punishment.' He'd felt sick; another seven years of this would make an already miserable existence intolerable. 'I hope it makes him happy.'

'Could be worse than that,' Stephen had warned. He'd sat up and swung his legs off the bed, lowering his voice as he went on, 'He could be trying to goad you into something.'

'Like what?'

'An escape attempt, maybe. You'll have seen up behind A Hall, where the outer wall lines up with the row of screws' houses?'

Daniel had, as he was certain every convict had since the housing had been built. All would have just as quickly dismissed it. 'It's heavily guarded though, you'd never get that far.'

'Exactly. It's not worth the risk, and the punishment block isn't somewhere you want to spend any more time than you have to.' Stephen had leaned forward. 'The slightest hint that you're heading for that spot, even just the inner wall, and they'll have you down there on number one diet before you can turn around. That means bread and water twice a day for the duration, which isn't half as much fun as it sounds.'

Daniel had given him a brief, wry smile. 'Have you been there yourself, then?'

'Now and again,' Stephen had confessed. 'When I first came here and couldn't keep a lid on my temper. Fifteen days of number one ration's the usual,' he'd gone on, 'but if you try to escape you're more likely to get forty-two, and a flogging with the cat to go with it. *And* you'll be put on special watch. So my advice to you is to put it from your mind, no matter how much Newbury pushes you to it.'

'He won't,' Daniel had said, more firmly than he felt; he'd come so close to losing his mind earlier that day, that he couldn't be sure of himself any more. His throat had tightened with remembered rage, and the base of his spine still throbbed where Newbury's stick had constantly dug at him.

But, he reflected now, as he waited for the morning alarm, at least he knew the reason behind it, which made it easier to shake off the bewilderment and concentrate on the anger. At least in his cell. Daniel was desperate to escape the stale indoor air, but if exercise went the same way as last time—

'Don't go today.' Stephen opened his eyes in the darkness; Daniel saw the thin moonlight gleam in them. 'You don't have to on Sundays, so just don't. Give yourself the chance to think through what I told you last night.'

The hooter sounded, and the gas lights flared along the landing. Doors began clanging, and Daniel silently unclenched his fingers from the metal bunk and stood up, ready to be counted for the first of what would be roughly thirty times that day alone.

*

In chapel, he moved to the bench next to Ray Beatty, who greeted him with a nod.

'How's things?'

'Stephen's found out a bit about Newbury,' Daniel said, and he outlined what he'd been told.

Ray didn't look convinced, however. 'Why the hell would he bother with all that, for a broken window?'

'No idea, but it's the only thing that makes sense.'

'Will you face him with it?' Ray asked. 'Tell him you know what he's up to?'

'And end up on punishment?' Daniel shook his head, embarrassed not to be standing up for himself, but knowing there was no point. 'There's nothing I can do, except hope he gets bored.'

'Or someone takes a cosh to him,' Ray muttered, drawing a sharp look from Daniel.

'What makes you say that?'

Ray looked around him. 'You must know something's brewing. If you don't, you can bet Sargent does. All I'm saying is that . . . well, maybe Newbury'll find himself in the way when it does.'

Something about his tone fuelled Daniel's suspicions further, but the church army chaplain chose that moment to make his entrance, and there was no chance to talk further until they filed out at the end of the short service. But Daniel stopped Ray as they were about to part ways and return to their different halls.

'Tell me you're not part of what's coming,' he murmured, low, so that only Ray could hear. 'Stephen's been saying—'

'I'm not telling you anything.' Ray's usual genial smile grew fixed. 'You just push on through, lad. Pay no mind, and ask no questions.'

'Ray—'

'No questions,' Ray repeated firmly, and clapped Daniel on the upper arm. 'Mind how you go. Don't give that Newbury bloke any excuses, all right?'

'I never do.'

Daniel rejoined the rest of B hall, and Stephen came in soon afterwards from his own exercise, where, as a stage four prisoner he was permitted to smoke and socialise with other special-stagers. He offered a murmured greeting and lay on his bunk in his usual sleeping position; flat on his back, with his fingers linked and resting on his stomach.

He did not sleep, however, and every time Daniel glanced over at him there was a light frown puckering his brow. Now and again he would meet Daniel's eyes, but Daniel cut away quickly each time, fearing that a conversation would only confirm his fears about what Ray was involved in. He had enough to worry over, without that, and although part of him felt a stinging guilt for burying his head in the sand, a bigger part, much concerned with self-preservation, knew that there was a time to speak up, and a time to lie low. He was in no doubt which one it was now.

Four days later, Stephen's warning about Newbury returned, harsh and urgent in his mind, but by then it was too late.

It was New Year's Eve, afternoon exercise, and the rain was coming down in sheets. Boots splashed through ever-deepening puddles, heels dragged as trousers pulled, and coats grew heavier. Wind was howling off the moor across the exercise yard, cutting through wet clothing like a steel blade, stinging the skin beneath; time had slowed to a crawl as the prisoners waited for the year to turn.

For lifers it would just be another year gone, wasted. For

others, the lucky ones at least, 1932 was the year they would leave this hellhole and return to family and real life. It was still very early in Daniel's sentence, but it still felt as if he was moving a whole year closer to release; he'd been arrested in 1931, and soon it would be 1932 … It was all in the interpretation, and he'd joined the exercise group with a quietly optimistic feeling lurking beneath his breastbone, almost a kind of lightness. A determination to battle through whatever came next.

This feeling had intensified when he'd seen that Warder Newbury was not taking today's exercise; instead, one of the quieter, more approachable warders was ushering them into their familiar routine. Finegan was well respected, among prisoners and warders alike; a genial man, old enough to have fought in the war, and had likely done so, soft-spoken for the most part, and always ready to listen when a lag had something they wanted to sound off about. He could be firm, true enough, but apparently never vindictive.

The thing that boosted Daniel the most, today, was knowing that on Saturday he'd finally be seeing his mother again. That last look she had thrown him as he'd been ushered from the court had stayed with him ever since, and he had been distraught, but not surprised, to have received no response to the visiting orders he'd sent. Until association two nights ago, when the post had been handed out, he'd been resigned to her no longer being part of his life, and since she was all he'd had, even getting out had begun to seem almost pointless. But now there would be a chance to talk to her, to plead for her understanding, and to tell her he was going to do everything he could to ensure she wasn't left without help. Seeing her would remind him that there was life beyond these grey walls, and where there was life there was something to live for.

Finegan pulled his own hat lower to let the rain drip off the shiny peak, and his expression was one of sympathy as he urged the men into a brisk walk. 'Come on, lads,' he called. 'Soon be over, and time to see off thirty-one eh? Pick it up there, Greenhow, you'll trip Cosgrave up otherwise.'

Daniel felt the icy needling of the rain as it worked its way down his upturned collar, and between his clothes and the back of his neck, but he just kept thinking about midnight, the hours between then and now, and the minutes. He began counting off in bursts of sixty, not keeping a total, just silently rejoicing that another minute had gone by. Another minute closer, too, to being able to look his mother in the eyes and tell her—

'Pearce, how nice to see you!'

Daniel's head jerked up, and he recoiled when he saw Warder Newbury's face barely inches from his own, dripping rain and eyes flashing with dark glee. He looked around to see Finegan disappearing into B Block, pulling his hat off and pushing a hand through his sopping hair as he stepped into the enviable dry.

Newbury was still keeping step, walking backwards in order to keep his eyes locked onto Daniel's. 'Don't go worryin' about him, lad. He was just getting you started. I had a bit of business to attend to.' He leaned closer and lowered his voice. 'In-laws, eh?' He backed off before Daniel could respond, and thankfully turned his attention to Charlie Sparks, better known as Ruby, who was slacking in order to mutter something to the man behind him. Davis, Daniel remembered idly, then abruptly looked away again; these two were both members of the Elephant and Castle mob, transferred from London a year or more ago, and he was reasonably sure they were among the originators of the 'atmosphere' that Stephen had talked about. Let Newbury draw the ire of those men if he wanted to; Daniel wanted nothing to do with it.

'Want to know why I was late?' Newbury asked, predictably returning to Daniel's side.

Daniel didn't respond. He wiped rain from his face and kept walking, his eyes and attention fixed on the slouched back of the man in front: Edward James, another Elephant and Castle member, but more peaceable.

'I said,' Newbury repeated, leaning in close, 'do you want to know why I was late?'

'In-laws, you said,' Daniel muttered, and was rewarded with a hearty clap on the soaked back of his coat, which sent him stumbling forward, almost colliding with James. He righted himself, and felt the anger bubbling up from the pit of his stomach; sour and searching for release. He swallowed it down again. Kept walking.

'Speaking of family.' Newbury's voice was almost friendly now, but Daniel wasn't fooled. 'Isn't your dear old mummy coming to visit on Saturday?'

Daniel said nothing, just kept walking.

'Cathy Pearce,' Newbury mused, walking companionably alongside him now, instead of backwards where he could sneer in Daniel's face. 'I always thought she'd be older. Fatter, maybe. But she's really quite trim. Takes care of herself since your dad blew himself up.'

Daniel's whole body tensed, but he kept walking.

'You're not wondering where I've seen her?' Newbury patted him on the shoulder again, pressing the wet material firmly against his skin. 'We had a mutual friend at one time. My father-in-law, Alfred Dunn. Oh!' Newbury grinned. 'But you know *him*, don't you? He's the one you almost killed back in November.' He shook his head gravely. 'And he's the one your mother stole from, when he'd been good enough to give her a job. Between you and her, you really seem to have it in for Mr Dunn, don't you?'

Daniel kept walking.

'Still, it's nice to know your mother's finally going to come and see you. Probably just wants to take a last look at the son who left her without a wage coming in. She'll probably be thrown out of her house now.' He gave a heavy sigh. 'And in January too, poor woman. Still, if she will go stealing from her employer, eh?'

Daniel stopped. The man behind him uttered a curse and went to step around him, but Newbury grasped Daniel's coat and dragged him forward, and back into the endless, plodding circle. Daniel's hands were clenched, but he couldn't feel them for the combination of the cold and his growing anger. When he finally found his voice it was strangled-sounding from the effort of control.

'She didn't.'

Newbury raised his voice, for the benefit of the others, no doubt, since he was still keeping pace with Daniel. 'Your mother *didn't* steal from Counsellor Dunn? But why else would he have sacked her? Why will no other shops give her work? Come on, Pearce, answer me that.'

'Why should I? It's none of your business.'

'Beg pardon?' Newbury leaned in again, one hand cupping his ear. 'Speak up, lad.'

Daniel kept walking.

The downpour eased, but boots swished on through the puddles, flicking up water onto the men behind while a pale December sun struggled to pierce the dense cloud. Newbury broke away to shout at someone else for a minute, but Daniel didn't care enough to turn and see who it was, though he hoped it was Davis again; enough riling, and that man might well put Newbury out of Daniel's misery. He thought about Ray, and his oblique muttering about coshes. He wondered how much he should offer, and if he could live with himself if he did. More seconds ticked into minutes, and now the goal was just the end of exercise, never mind midnight ushering in the new year.

At last the circle broke, and the prisoners made their way back across the yard to the B block door. Daniel was near the back of the parade ground when Newbury blew his whistle, and later he understood that it had been no accident that he would have been one of the last through the door. Newbury stopped him with a hand placed firmly in the centre of his chest, before he was half-way across the yard.

'Where d'you think you're going?'

'Exercise is over,' Daniel said stiffly. He caught a few faces turned his way, the initial curiosity fading quickly into relief that it was him stuck out there, and not them. They turned away again and he was left alone with Newbury, who shook his head.

'Not for you, lad. You're getting an extra half hour.'

Which would mean a missed dinner, and he was already feeling nauseous with hunger and exertion. 'Why?' he managed.

'For insubordination. Go on, get walking.' Newbury stood back and gestured with his stick, which then inexplicably slipped from his grasp and landed half in a puddle a few feet away. 'Oh no,' he intoned in a wholly unsurprised voice. 'Pick that up, would you?'

Daniel hesitated, then, deliberately resurrecting the hope-ful feelings he'd had at the start of the session, he obediently retrieved the stick and handed it to Newbury. But the half-buried, childishly furious part of him made him pass it over wet end first, and, as he released it into Newbury's hand the warder's fingers splayed wide and the stick fell again. Daniel stood for a moment, looking at it lying near his feet. He breathed slowly a couple of times, fighting back the urge to kick it away, then felt Newbury's hard fingers tapping his shoulder.

'Sorry, prisoner. Would you mind?' Newbury nodded at the stick again, and the false politeness in his voice and manner made Daniel's anger flare again. Still, he bent and lifted it up, and this time when he handed it over he was sure to hand the dryer end. Newbury took it.

'Thank you. Now, off you go.'

Daniel walked. For thirty minutes, watched keenly by Newbury who stood beneath the shallow overhang by the door to B block, he responded to the shouts to *pick it up!* and to *wake up and stop sleepwalking!* His rough clothing dragged and pulled, rubbing his skin raw while his boots chafed the backs of his heels, and he counted, counted, counted. Another minute.

When the whistle went again, he braced himself for further punishment, but Newbury made no protest as he walked towards the door, his head down against the wind that cut across the parade ground. He could feel his legs quivering, the closer he came to be able to take his weight off them, and to stripping the sodden clothing off. As he drew level with Newbury, the hated voice stopped him again.

'By the way, Pearce, your mother's not coming.'

'What?' Daniel looked up, ignoring the icy rain that drove into his face. 'What do you mean?'

'Saturday,' Newbury said helpfully. He grinned, showing too

many teeth by far. 'The reason I was late, as I was trying to tell you. I was having a chat with my father-in-law and happened to mention you sent your visiting order. He made it quite clear you're to have no visitors while you're here.'

'What ...' Daniel shook his head, feeling the rain fly off his nose and chin. His mind was turning in circles now, while his breath was growing shorter and tighter. 'Not for my whole sentence?'

'I'll be monitoring all your incoming and outgoing mail personally,' Newbury said. 'The order from Counsellor Dunn is clear. No visitors,' he repeated. 'It's going to be a long seven years, Prisoner six-one-six.' He looked out with a mock pensive air, at the rain streaming off the roofs of the nearby buildings, and the desolate, rolling moorland in the distance, and Daniel realised the threat was not merely an empty show of power; he could actually enforce it.

Fury swept over him, and as Newbury's hand came down on his shoulder again he whirled and shoved, one fist came up, and he brought it around in a wide arc, feeling it connect with the side of Newbury's head.

The shock of impact ran up his arm, but he'd been in brawls before, plenty of them, and he was immediately ready to back up the first blow with another. It took a moment for him to realise that his cocked fist had nowhere to go, that Newbury was no longer within reach, and for a split second he felt a bolt of savage satisfaction go through him.

He heard a shrill whistle, cutting through the howl of the wind as it bounced around the buildings, then there were raised voices, and someone grabbed him from behind, forcing his hands up behind his back and sending a flare of pain from shoulder to neck.

He tilted forwards, thrust by unseen hands, saw the parade ground rising to meet him, and jerked his head back to narrowly avoid his face hitting it first. The breath was knocked out of him as he landed, and as he lay stunned he saw Warder Newbury, crumpled against the wall of B block, thick, sticky blood coursing down his face from a deep gash in his cheek, and he heard a bitter voice above him.

'Get him to chokey. Now.'

CHAPTER TWELVE

The afternoon had ground along so slowly that, on at least two occasions, Gwenna had stared fixedly at the clock, certain it had stopped. The one here in the shop had no second hand, like the others, and she'd only been convinced of the passage of time when the minute hand had finally, laboriously ticked onward. They were usually fairly busy on New Year's Eve, but this year things had slowed down alarmingly; the bite of the depression, no doubt. And the impact of the growth of Pencarrack hadn't helped, with its new shops springing up, seemingly from nowhere; it made Gwenna wonder, a little uneasily, what would be left for her father when he was released.

The thought led, naturally enough, on to the letter she'd posted to the prison on Boxing Day morning. As soon as it had vanished into the post box she'd regretted it; if she heard nothing back she'd know her mother had been right after all, though it hurt to think her father might have been keeping her away deliberately. But since her meeting with Jago Carne, everything he'd told her had been building in her mind, creating an ugly, terrifying image. It couldn't be true. Not all of it. On the other hand, why would he have bothered to make it up? And what good would it do to find out it was just as he'd described? She couldn't change anything, after all. But she had to dispel the endless questions, and it was clear now that she could only trust the evidence of her own eyes. It was the waiting that was so hard.

Her mother came in from the house, and began walking around the shop and straightening everything that had been knocked out of place by customers. It was her way of signalling the start of closing up, and Gwenna puffed out a sigh of relief and opened the till to remove the day's takings.

'What time are you going up to Tory's?' Rachel asked, turning the door sign to 'closed'.

'I'm not,' Gwenna said. 'I'm staying home tonight.' In answer to her mother's surprised look, she shrugged. 'They've still got Geordie's little girl up there, and the atmosphere's a bit ... difficult, what with Joe resenting her so much. And I still think Lynette blames me for getting her friends pulled into everything that happened last year,' she added. 'She never says anything, but she's so good at all that *silent reproach* stuff. I don't think she even knows she's doing it.'

'I'm sure she's perfectly nice,' Rachel said mildly, and Gwenna could see her looking around for a way to shift the subject away from the smuggling ring. She herself had been exactly the same for a long time, and she understood the need to push it all away – at least until it must be faced, and that wasn't tonight.

'Anyway, it's just going to be Tory and Bobby, Lynette and Geordie, and Bertie and Tommy,' she said. 'I'd be the odd one out, and probably stuck refereeing Joe and Tilly.'

'Well then, why don't you come with me down to the Penhaligons for the evening? There'll be a few people you

123

know there.' Rachel paused, and Gwenna knew exactly what was coming. 'Maybe they'll have invited some of the lads from Matthew's crew, or—'

'Mum, I'm not looking for a replacement for Peter,' Gwenna said. She couldn't help smiling at Rachel's hopeful look. 'I'll come though, if you'll promise not to leave me talking to Benjy Stocker or any of his friends.'

'Good!' Rachel beamed. 'Now, I'm going to get changed, so you finish up here and then find something pretty to wear.'

Pretty! Gwenna stifled a snort as she began piling up the coins into denominations ready for counting. She'd felt quite good about herself since she'd parted from Peter Bolitho and emerged from his rather stern shadow; her hair was still long, straight, and glossy, and her figure neat, considering her above average height. But she'd seen Lynette and Bertie a couple of days ago, on their way to visit Bertie's family in Fox Bay, and had immediately felt shabby and tired next to them.

They had stopped in the village to buy some wine to take with them, and they'd waved cheerfully and smiled at Gwenna, who'd just come out of the post office, hurried and distracted, and probably appearing grumpy as a result. Bertie, with her sleek dark bob, had always been effortlessly chic, even in her overalls, and Gwenna had never harboured any particular envy; it was just the way Bertie was. But Lynette, it seemed, was the same, and that day she had thrown aside her work clothes and pulled out all the stops for Bertie's family. Her blonde curls were held in place with a green velvet band that matched the colour of her close-fitting blouse perfectly, and she wore white, wide-legged sailor trousers and T-strap shoes, and carried an impractically small bag in exactly the same colour as her blouse and head band.

Gwenna had fought the urge to check the state of her hurriedly-tied-back hair, but was acutely aware of the stray bits blowing around her face in the stiff December wind, and blew them irritably away. Both girls were perfectly friendly, but as they'd driven away Gwenna imagined them being glad they were off to have fun somewhere else, and without her. She'd berated herself for that thought by the time she got home; Bertie was a good friend, and Lynette seemed down-to-earth and actually quite nice. Envy was a heavy, ugly thing, and Gwenna was determined not be dragged down by it; she had enough to think about without that.

So tonight, when she and her mother were welcomed into the home of Anna and Matthew Penhaligon, she forced herself to relax and not to spend her time wondering what was going on up at the stables, or whether she should have accepted the invitation after all. The Penhaligons had only invited a few of the other locals, and thankfully there was no sign of a man even close to Gwenna's age, so she was spared any gentle encouragement towards anyone in particular, and just sat quietly, letting the cheerful atmosphere push all Jago Carne's horror stories out of her head. After a while, however, it grew very warm in the Penhaligons' converted front room, so she went to stand outside the front door for a while, letting the cool, drizzly air brush her skin into pleasant goosebumps. She leaned against the wall, listening to the voices drifting down the hall, and smiling as she heard Anna's cousin Keir attempting a somewhat drunken song at the little piano in the corner.

Her smile faltered as she saw an irritatingly familiar figure on the other side of the road: wiry, and not overly tall, but visibly tense, and poised as if he were about to run, either straight at her, or away up the hill. Nigel Stibson. Gwenna felt a curling dislike in the pit of her stomach, and a little flicker of anger. He must have only been detained for a few days, since he hadn't managed to make off with her takings, and they couldn't even prove he'd intended to. Damned if she'd let him stare her down though; she levered herself off the wall so she could draw herself upright, and stared back. To her annoyance his tension dissipated, and he gave her a slow, mocking smile. Then he shoved his hands into his pockets and strode away, whistling a poor and wobbling rendition of 'Auld Lang Syne'.

Gwenna scowled, and went back indoors, where she found her mother and Anna in the kitchen, heads suspiciously close together like schoolgirls with a secret. She groaned, knowing what was coming.

'We were just talking about you,' Anna said, pushing her silver-streaked dark hair back behind her ears. Her Irish accent had become broader tonight, under the influence of her cousin.

'Of course you were.' Gwenna gave her mother a look of re-proach, and Rachel smiled.

'We worry,' she said. 'You're such a pretty girl, and—'

'Please don't,' Gwenna said, holding up her hand. 'I'm honestly not in the mood.'

'Why? What's happened?' Anna frowned. 'You look as if you've just dropped your wages down a drain.'

'Nigel Stibson,' Gwenna said. 'Out and about, as cocky as you like.'

'Honestly!' Anna shook her head sympathetically. 'I heard about what happened on Christmas Eve; how can Sergeant Brewer just let him go like that?'

'It wouldn't be his fault, I'm sure,' Gwenna said. A burst of laughter from the other room, raised a smile of her own. 'This is supposed to be celebration, so don't mind me.'

'We're about to play charades,' her mother said, her own smile returning. She linked her arm through Gwenna's, and turned her about to face the kitchen door. 'Come on, time to show them all how to play.'

Midnight came soon afterwards, and with it snifters of Anna's very best Irish whiskey. Matthew didn't touch it, Gwenna noticed, but he raised a tumblerful of freshly squeezed orange juice as Big Ben's chimes rang from the radio, and the old year flowed into the new on a wave of good companionship.

Gwenna and her mother walked back up the hill together a little later. The rain had stopped, though there was still a brisk wind, and the clouds scurried across a sky thinly lit by a waning gibbous moon. Gwenna remembered Tory once telling her that this phase symbolised a time of letting go, and of giving thanks for what you have learned. Determination lifted her as she looked upwards; both of those things held a strong appeal tonight. It was 1932: the year her father would come home, and her mother would be set free from all the worry she'd shouldered. The year she herself would discover what she was supposed to do with her life. Perhaps she would discover who would be at her side while she did so, but that was in the lap of the gods. Everything else was hers to decide.

Gwenna stopped to re-fasten the outside toilet door, which was standing open, and she was just hanging up her coat on the kitchen hook when a cry from the hallway gave her a nasty jolt. Rachel reappeared in the kitchen, her face white.

'We've been robbed.'

Gwenna's heart lurched, and she put a hand to her chest,

as if she could calm the sickeningly uneven thump that way. 'Robbed ...' But the instant she repeated the word, in a bewildered whisper, she knew who it had been. That smile. The casual hands-in-pockets attitude as he'd walked away. 'Auld Lang Syne'.

Her mother turned back to the telephone in the hallway. 'I'm going to call the police.'

'Tell them who it was, too,' Gwenna said, her voice hard. 'Nigel Stibson.'

'You don't know that,' Rachel pointed out, but her expression said she believed Gwenna without question. 'Where are you going?'

Gwenna had shoved her arms back into her coat sleeves and turned to the back door. 'To find him.'

'No!' Rachel sounded panicked. 'It's too dangerous. Gwenna, please—'

'What's he taken?' Gwenna stopped abruptly and spun back. 'What's missing?'

'I ... I don't know yet. Why?'

Gwenna dragged open the squeaky kitchen drawer and took out a key, then she went to the tall cupboard and reached into the back, finding and lifting out the box in which the takings were kept. She didn't need to unlock it, however, there was enough weight to reassure her that their money was safe.

'He didn't find this,' she said, and saw her mother's taut expression melt into one of relief. 'We're still telling the police though.'

Rachel nodded, and went to use the telephone while Gwenna once more slipped off her coat and hung it on the back of her chair. She sat down, tapping out an increasingly agitated rhythm on the table to get all the tension out, and finally got up and went into the shop. After a quick search she ascertained that only two bottles of cooking sherry were missing, but the shelves were a mess; all her mother's careful straightening and positioning had been pushed into disarray, products deliberately mixed up, and two bags of flour opened and upended all over the open till. A petty act of revenge, if ever there was one.

Gwenna felt quite ill. Not just at the damage, but at what it meant. For the shop, for her mother, and for their peace of mind. No wonder Stibson had thrown that smile at her when he'd seen she was occupied for the evening; he'd have known they were both at Penhaligon's Attic tonight, and their own shop was easy-pickings nowadays, without Jonas around.

Gwenna's anger returned, white-hot now, and edged with the kind of frustration that sharpened everything. So much for the moon's promise of letting go of the past, being thankful for lessons learned, and moving on. She stepped back out of the shop and turned off the light. Stibson would likely be lurking, and watching the shop from across the way, enjoying the thought of all the work the two women would have to do to clean up his mess. And they would, but not tonight.

'Sergeant Brewer will come up and talk to us tomorrow,' Rachel said. She sounded as if she was trying her hardest to remain calm and not break down in front of her daughter. 'In the meantime he said not to worry, that he'd make sure we were safe for the night. Whatever that means.'

Gwenna nodded. She thought of Bobby; would he be called away from the stables tonight, or would Brewer call on someone else to watch over the shop? She went to the window and peered up at that moon, riding over the town, mysterious and distant, and realised that she *was* actually ready to give thanks for her hard-learned lessons and move on. But that didn't mean she had to let go of what drove her, and tonight she had been reminded of what that was. Ever since she had fallen into that dreadful cycle of theft and lies, she had been compelled to repay the debt she had incurred, and the answer was clear now; it was in that shop, in the shape of spilled flour, stolen groceries, and jumbled shelves. Her future lay along the path of law and order.

CHAPTER THIRTEEN

2 January

Lynette blinked against the brightness of the electric light, as she came into the stable from the early morning greyness outside. She shielded her eyes, and Tory, who was collecting tack together for a potential new addition to the stables later today, nodded at Hercules's stall and put her finger to her lips.

Lynette blew out an exasperated breath, and reflected how quickly little miss butter-wouldn't-melt Tilly had shown her true colours. It wasn't as if she was actually rude, or sulky, and she was really no naughtier than any other six-year-old, in Lynette's limited experience, but she could try the patience of a saint. What she was doing to Lynette, who was certainly no saint, fell only slightly short of demonic.

Lynette liked to think the girl was hiding now because she couldn't bear to leave Pencarrack, and her father, but the more re-alistic side of her knew otherwise; the girl's powers of concealment had been much praised during their Christmas Day hide-and-seek games, and, fuelled by the approval of her new grown-up friends, she had only become more adventurous over the past week or so. Unfortunately, the stables and its surrounds provided ample opportunity, and Lynette had been trying to get ready to leave for over an hour now. They planned to stop off at the forge on the way, where Geordie was up to his neck in additional work he'd taken on for the clay pit, and they were running out of time.

'Tilly,' she called, keeping her voice as light as she could, 'if we don't leave soon you'll only have five minutes with your father and Joe. Tory's already hitched up the horse box ...' She looked enquiringly at Tory, who nodded. 'So we're all just waiting for you now!'

A rustle sounded in the corner of the stall, and Tilly emerged, brushing straw off her clothes. Lynette sighed; she had dressed the girl in her nicest outfit that morning, wanting to prove to Marion that they had taken good care of her and not let her run riot, and here she was back in her dungarees and boots, a wide grin on her face, and not a shred of remorse for the state of her hair.

'In the car, Miss Sargent,' Lynette said, pointing, but Tilly had other matters to attend to first, and Lynette and Tory waited with as much patience as they could muster while the girl went around saying leisurely goodbyes to Mack, Hercules, and the two newer horses. She then found Boots, the cat, who eyed her approach with deep suspicion and flattened ears, but who surrendered to the inevitable embrace with an audible sigh. Only then did Tilly pronounce herself ready, and the three of them were finally able to set off on the short but slow drive to the village, pulling the horse box in their wake.

Tilly's stay at the stables had been an eye-opening experience for them all. Once all her shyness had worn off, the little girl had proved she possessed a stubborn streak, and was quite used to getting her own way. A lot of that was probably due to Roderick Lawton doing his very best to make himself part of her life, and Lynette could only guess how she would feel when she discovered he had died. But that was in the future. For now, it had been a pleasure to see Geordie spending time with his daughter, and it shone a new light onto the way he must have been feeling this past year since he'd left her behind; they were clearly closer than even Lynette had realised.

The only fly in the ointment had been Joc. The boy had not softened or warmed towards Tilly at all, during her stay, and the looks he had sent Geordie's way whenever he mentioned his daughter were far worse than merely fed up, or even jealous. They bordered on betrayal. He would probably be the happiest person she would meet today.

Tory pulled the van into the yard at Pencarrack Forge, and Lynette waved at Geordie through the window.

'Do you want to drop me off at Peter Tavy while you look at the pony?' she asked Tory. 'Or shall I come too?'

'You'd better come too.' Tory gave her a rueful look. 'You know me, one sad look from a pair of big brown eyes, and I'll be handing over all our money and not even thinking about whether we can really help the poor thing.'

'I know the feeling,' Lynette looked into the back seat, at another pair of big brown eyes. These, though, had a glint of mischief in them that belied their innocence. 'Come on then, miss, let's go and say goodbye to Daddy and Joe.'

Geordie had already taken off his apron, having heard their arrival, and plunged his dirty hands into the bucket of water near the door before drying them on his shirt. He scooped Tilly up and planted a kiss on her cheek, but despite his cheerful greeting, there was an air of sadness about him this early morning. Lynette left them alone while she went into the cottage in search of Joe, who was finishing his breakfast.

She'd been right about his relief that Tilly was leaving; he gave her a bright smile as he picked up his empty plate and took it to the sink. 'Getting a nice early start, then?'

'We can't drive very fast on these roads with a horse box.' Lynette looked out of the window to see that Geordie was now sitting on the wall with Tilly beside him, and was talking seriously to her. She turned back to Joe. 'You haven't liked Tilly from the moment you saw her, have you?'

'It's not that I don't like her.' Joe shrugged. 'She's all right.'

'But you resented her being here for your first Christmas without . . . without your dad.'

Joe visibly flinched at that. 'I'm not jealous,' he asserted, picking up his gloves and pushing them into his pocket. 'Got nothing to be jealous about anyway, have I? I live here, she don't.'

'I'm sorry about the scarf,' Lynette said, and saw his eyes widen slightly. 'Geordie said you'd overheard me telling him I'd bought it for you.'

'I never complained,' he said at once.

'No, which was very adult of you.' Lynette stood up as Joe pulled his coat on. 'I can see you're ready to go to work, so I'll let you get on.'

'I don't mean to be a brat,' Joe said, his voice lower now, 'and I'm really *not* jealous.'

'But you're happier now she's going.'

He hesitated, then nodded. He looked a little shamefaced, however, which gave Lynette some small hope that he would come around eventually, should Tilly come to stay again. Looking out of the window once more, she reasoned that it was very likely she would; the girl had been at home here from the first, and even now she was delaying her leaving again, walking too fast along the yard wall, and giggling as a visibly worried Geordie hurried along at her side, his hands poised to catch her if she should fall.

The final goodbyes were more subdued, and there was a moment when Lynette believed Tilly was going to remain clinging to her father's waist until she was pulled away, but she abruptly let go and ran to the car. Geordie's face was set into a smile as he waved, but it was a thin veneer, and as she drove away Lynette wondered how soon he would propose another visit to Dartmoor. Another, quieter, thought crept in, and it sat uneasily in her mind: what if he decided that a visit wasn't enough any more?

Lynette made sure Tilly's coat was buttoned right up, and her new scarf tucked neatly into it, before they made their way up through the narrow roads to Colleybrooke Manor. They had parked in the square, where there was a spot large enough for the van and horse box without blocking the road, and Tilly skipped ahead of them up the lane, clearly eager to see her mother again. Lynette's heart contracted, as she remembered the child would soon have to learn that someone she'd been coming to accept as family was no longer with them. She pushed open the gate, but before they'd taken more than a few steps towards the front door, it opened and someone Lynette didn't recognise stood there: a woman, not too far off her own age, and very smartly dressed.

'Can I help you?' she called, her clear voice carrying easily to where the three of them stood. Her gaze fell on Tilly. 'Are you collecting for a children's charity?'

Tory leaned in to speak to Lynette in a low voice. 'That's not Marion, then, I take it?'

'No.'

'Who is it?' Tilly asked, looking up at Lynette.

'I don't know, love, I thought it was the housekeeper.'

'No, the housekeeper's Mrs Bradbury,' Tilly said, holding back as Lynette tried to take another step forward. 'She's old.'

'This is Tilly,' Lynette called. 'I'm just dropping her home to Mrs Sargent.'

The woman's eyes travelled from her to Tory, then back to Tilly. 'Mrs Sargent doesn't live here.' She pointed towards the gate. 'She lives in the miners' cottages on the other side of the village.'

'But . . . Oh.' Lynette belatedly put the pieces together. 'Are you Mr Lawton's daughter?' The woman nodded, and Lynette offered her a nod of condolence. 'I'm so sorry,' she said, not wanting to elaborate and give Tilly too much of a shock. 'I don't understand though, Mrs Sargent was—'

'*Mrs* Sargent has no right to live in this house,' Lawton's daughter said, her tone leaving no room for argument. 'You'll find her at her old address. I'm sure the child will be able to show you where that is. Good day to you, please shut the gate on your way out.' She turned away, and the door closed hard enough to rattle the panes of glass in their frames.

Lynette turned to Tory, dismayed. 'Why didn't Marion say something about this?'

'Don't I live here now?' Tilly asked, sounding very small as her voice was whipped away by the strengthening wind.

Lynette took her gloved hand and squeezed it. 'Not at the moment. But you'll have your old bedroom back instead, with

136

the lovely yellow curtains. Won't that be nice?' She wished she didn't sound so falsely cheerful, but for a wonder it seemed to work, and Tilly threw only a quick look back at the house she'd lived in for almost a year, before allowing Lynette to draw her back down the path and out onto the road. She must be getting used to turmoil already, with all the changes she'd had in her short life.

The door across the road opened and Mrs Bellowes poked her head out. 'Miss Nicholls?'

Lynette found a smile. 'Mrs Bellowes. I hope you enjoyed your stay with your family?'

'Oh, call me Ivy. Please.' The older woman gestured her closer, but with a pointed look at Tilly, and Lynette left the girl with Tory while she crossed the road.

'I came home on Thursday, to find poor Mrs Sargent had been hounded out of the house, and back to her old place. Cold and full of damp as it is.'

'So I've discovered,' Lynette said. 'I was there just before Christmas, and it smelled damp, but it can't be that bad, surely? They were living there not that long ago.'

Ivy shook her head. 'It's a roof over their heads, fair enough, but after that place?' She nodded at Colleybrooke Manor. 'It don't take long to get used to something like that, and the way she was pushed out was humiliating for the poor maid. She was proper cut up about Mr Lawton, too.'

'Have his children moved in then?'

'Putting it up for sale, so I hear. Anyway, the reason I called you over . . .' Ivy lowered her voice and looked past Lynette, to where Tilly and Tory waited hand in hand. 'You'll work it out for yourself, I reckon, but I b'lieve Marion Sargent's in the family way. Not that she's said anything,' she hurried on, 'and she's not pushing out her apron yet, but . . . well. That's my thinking.'

'Then surely she should be allowed to stay in Lawton's house.' But Lynette recognised the reality, even as she said it. It would actually make things a hundred times worse.

Ivy shrugged. 'Maybe she plans to wait, then make her claim later. When it's certain.'

'You don't believe Lawton's daughter will allow that, do you?'

'No.' Ivy sighed. 'Anyway, that's what I wanted to tell you, but I didn't want Tilly to hear it. She's got enough on her little plate as it is.'

'Yes. She doesn't know Roderick's died, either.'

'Poor mite. She's got a double shock coming then, on top of everything else.'

Lynette rejoined the others, and they walked back through the village again, past the van and the horse box, and up the little row of miners' cottages where Tilly had been born. And her father before her, she remembered. Knowing Geordie had spent his childhood here too somehow gave the house something of a warmer feeling.

She raised her hand to knock, but Tilly beat her to it, pushing open the door and shouting for her mother. Marion appeared from the kitchen at the end of the passage, her taut expression relaxing as she opened her arms to accept the human cannonball that crashed into her. Another woman stood just behind her, clutching a cup of something hot, and smiling as she watched the reunion.

Marion looked less comfortable at the sight of Lynette and Tory, but gestured them towards the sitting room. 'Go on in,' she said. 'I'll fetch some tea.'

'Oh, please don't worry on our account,' Lynette said, sensing the reluctance behind the polite offer. She would secretly have loved a cup, but Marion might feel obliged to also provide cake, if she had it, or biscuits, and if Ivy's suspicions were true, she was going to need to save her money; it was highly unlikely there would be any forthcoming for this child from its father's estate.

The other woman tweaked Tilly's hair in a familiar, easy fashion, as she stepped past her to introduce herself to the visitors. 'I'm Gracie Martyn,' she said. 'Which one of you is Lynette?'

'I am, why?' Lynette wondered if she was about to get the sharp end of this stranger's tongue, and readied herself for it.

But Gracie smiled. 'Because Stephen wants me to report back when I next see him.'

'You're visiting Geordie's brother?'

'I am. Finally.'

Gracie was a slightly built redhead, with pale freckles across her nose, and eyes of the brightest blue Lynette had ever seen. Her smile produced deep dimples on either side of her mouth, and the hand she held out to shake Lynette's was slender but strong; the skin rough and reddened, and the nails cut very short. A hard worker, then; Lynette remembered hearing that she lived on a farm nearby.

Gracie led the way into the dimly lit sitting room, and opened the window a little further before poking at the smouldering coals in the grate. 'Sorry about the draught, but it's better than the smoke.'

Marion didn't seem to mind at all that Gracie was taking over as hostess, and even apologising for the failings of the little house. She sat down with Tilly on her lap, and began asking the girl about her stay in Cornwall, and if Father Christmas had found her to bring her presents.

'We left him a letter with Daddy's address on,' Tilly said, looking around for it.

'Yes, I saw that. I put it in your bedroom. Did you like what he brought you?'

'This scarf,' Tilly said proudly, pulling it out of her still-buttoned coat. 'And some sherbet, and Daddy gave me a colouring book.'

'Don't you want to take your coat off, love?' Lynette asked her, without thinking, then caught Marion's expression. 'Sorry. I was forgetting myself.'

'She can leave it on for a bit,' Marion said, glancing at the open window and clearly embarrassed by the need for it.

Lynette was equally uncomfortable, and knew she'd already outstayed her welcome. 'Well, Tilly,' she said brightly, 'we have a pony to look at, in Tavistock, so we'd better set off back that way now.'

'Oh, don't go yet,' Gracie said. 'Please, I'd love to talk to you for a few minutes. It feels like we have a bit in common, both stepping out with the Sargent lads. Well,' she amended with a little laugh, 'Stephen's not doing a lot of stepping out anywhere.'

Lynette saw the sadness behind the young woman's too-wide smile, and, despite her wish to be out and on the road, away from the scrutiny of these two women who knew each other so well, she gave in. She turned to Tory.

'Have we got a few minutes spare?'

Tory nodded. 'But I'd better to go back and wait by the van, in case I need to move it. I don't want to cause a traffic blockage.'

She said her hasty goodbyes, closed the door behind her, and hurried off down the path, leaving Lynette looking after her with growing envy.

'So,' Marion said tightly, as Tilly slipped off her lap and went up the narrow stairs to reacquaint herself with her old bedroom. 'You're buying a horse?'

'A pony, yes.' Lynette looked expectantly at Gracie, hoping she would bring the conversation back. But Marion hadn't finished.

'Geordie's landed on his feet, then,' she said. 'You must have plenty of money.'

The tone was flat, accusatory, and Lynette turned back, folded her hands in her lap, and forced a smile. This could prove to be a very long few minutes after all.

CHAPTER FOURTEEN

Geordie and Joe worked steadily through the first half of their Saturday task sheet, and by dinner time they were both ready for a helping from the stew pot in their cramped kitchen. Geordie had noted a real change in the boy today, from the almost surly youth he'd been living with since Christmas Eve, and although it was good to see the old Joe back, the reason for it sat sourly in his stomach. He sat opposite him now, at the table, and watched him spooning up vegetables and thick chunks of beef as if he hadn't eaten in a week.

'Good to see your appetite's back.'

Joe flashed him the old, sweet, younger-than-fourteen smile, which had lately been replaced with the tight, forced thing that had sat so awkwardly on his face. 'Been a busy day,' he said, hunting in his bowl for a piece of dumpling. 'You didn't have much, though.' He looked up, frowning. 'You never do these days.'

'Your need's greater than mine,' Geordie said, surprised and a little troubled that the boy had noticed. 'Eat up, then. I need you to go across to South Pencarrack this afternoon.' He tore a chunk of bread to mop his bowl. 'Got a few things that need taking to the office, and the cycling'll help with exercising that leg.'

Joe didn't respond immediately, either to agree or to argue, which made Geordie look at him again, more closely. Joe was concentrating on spooning up the last of his stew, and the smile had faded; he replaced his spoon in his empty bowl and only then looked up to see Geordie watching him.

He shrugged. 'My leg's playing a bit of a merry tune today,' he said, which made Geordie bite back a laugh; it was something he himself sometimes said about his own recently healed bones, but it sounded funny coming from such a young mouth. It also rang decidedly false.

'All right,' he said, deciding it wasn't worth arguing. 'You stay here and mind the place, I'll go over to the pit myself.'

Joe nodded in relief. 'I'll get on with those nails for Farmer Garvey.' He'd evidently realised it would keep him in Geordie's good books to take on the least favourite of their jobs.

'Good lad.' Geordie stood up to clear the bowls away, and nodded towards the door. 'Off you go, then.'

He took his time tidying the kitchen before rejoining Joe out in the forge. He knew there would be no time to do it later, and although Lynette never came out with it, he felt sure she must compare this cottage, which he hoped she might share with him one day, to the house and lifestyle she'd left behind in Brighton. He had no intention of giving her any reason to think twice, when he eventually felt ready to broach the question they both knew was on the horizon. But it was a long way off yet, and lay on the other side of a lot of work.

When he was satisfied the kitchen was fit to be seen, and still with Lynette in mind, he hitched up his trousers, which had recently begun to sag while he worked. Nothing would be less appealing to a returning lover than to find her man with his backside to the wind. But he was on the last hole of his belt, so he dug out the knife Joe had given him for Christmas and turned it over in his hand, smiling as he recalled the pride with which Joe had presented it. He used its tip to pierce the leather, then tossed the knife onto the table and finished fastening the belt, reminding himself that he must be more tolerant of the lad's insecurity, and remember where it came from. He could hardly be blamed, after all he'd been through.

He snatched up his coat and went out to the forge. Joe was cheerfully working through the batch of nails Keir Garvey had ordered, but stopped to help Geordie put the few tools he had mended into his bag. The blacksmith they'd taken on at Pencarrack was keen, but inexperienced, and John Doidge, the new captain, now and again lessened his burden by sending work Geordie's way. The additional income was more welcome now than it had ever been, and Geordie rarely turned it down, but he didn't like the time it took to deliver the completed orders. He wished he'd been firmer with Joe, but it was too late now.

'Are you going to walk over, then?' Joe asked, looking doubtfully at the sky as Geordie slipped the bag over his shoulder. 'It's going to rain again soon.'

'A bit of rain won't hurt.'

Geordie didn't add that he was trying to cut down on petrol, and was squirrelling away every spare penny; it wouldn't be fair for Joe to think he was a burden of any kind. He set off through the village, the bag of tools bouncing against his hip, feeling his muscles stretch as he lengthened his stride. Despite knowing he should have sent Joe instead, he was glad to be out; it felt good, after bending over the anvil for most of the morning, and seeing little other than flame, sparks, and the head of his hammer flashing up and down. He let his eyes wander to the horizon, which, from here included only the tops of the trees by the stables, and the spire of St Gwineer's church, and let the first drops of rain cool his skin. By the time he arrived at the clay pit he was feeling refreshed, and in good spirits.

John Doidge, who'd been at his side throughout the industrial uprising of last year, and who now ran the clay pit for Polworra Consols, was just coming down the slope from the pit itself, and Geordie waited for him instead of crossing to the store.

'All right, lad?' John said, extending a hand. 'Good to see you.'

'You too.'

'Good Christmas?'

'Very. Yourself?'

They swapped a few anecdotes, and conversation naturally touched on the fate of Alec Damerel, before Geordie moved it swiftly on. 'They get whoever did that, yet?' He gestured to the boarded-up office window. 'How many times is it now?'

'That one makes four.' John sighed and pulled his hat lower. 'Costin' us a bloody fortune. They thought it was Nigel Stibson, but he was locked up when that was done, for tryin' to pinch the Rosdews' Christmas fair takings.'

'I reckon it's Carne,' Geordie said sourly. 'He's bound to have a grudge.'

'Me and all.' John kicked at the ground near his feet. 'He dug up the stone he used from here. Big bugger, too.'

Geordie looked, and saw a neat hole, now half-filled with rainwater. He sighed and shifted the bag across his shoulder. 'Well,

I'd best get on, I said I'd give Bobby a hand over at the stables later. Tory and Lynette are out.'

'They're takin' young Tilly back today, aren't they?'

Geordie nodded. 'I'm going to miss that monkey.'

John gave him a sympathetic smile. 'I'll bet. She's quite the character, that one. Get on, then, lad.' He clapped Geordie on the shoulder. 'Those tools'll be needed. Come and see me after, I'll get your money ready.'

Geordie tramped across the yard and spent a few minutes talking to Les Trethewey, who now ran the store. Then, mindful of all he still had to do before he went to the stables, he slung his now-empty bag across his shoulder again, and went to the office to collect the payment John had prepared. As he pulled the ledger towards himself, to sign for it, Geordie saw the rock that had come through the window, now placed on the desk almost like a trophy. John had been right; it was a big bugger. If anyone had been in the office at the time, and had been standing in its path, they'd have been in serious trouble.

John saw him looking, and nodded. 'See what I mean?'

'What's this?' Geordie pointed his pen at a small triangular piece of metal that sat near the rock. He bent towards it for a closer look. 'Tip of a knife?'

'Found it next to that hole in the yard,' John said. 'Reckon Carne used his knife to prise the rock out of the ground, and was so keen to get the job done he didn't realise he'd broken it.'

'So, if you could prove it came from Carne's knife,' Geordie said, his mind turning over the possibilities even as he spoke, 'you could get him sent down for criminal damage.'

'And endangering life, so Brewer says,' John agreed. 'Tobias Able was standing right over there when it came through.' He indicated a spot just to the right of the covered window. 'He might have caught the sod red-handed if he'd not been so shook up. As it was, by the time he opened the door there weren't no one anywhere near.'

'Carne's probably seen by now that he's broken his knife, and ditched it.'

'More'n likely.' John sighed again. 'Not to worry, we'll get him eventually. Tobias is talkin' about setting up someone to watch the place after the day shift goes home, and the office is shut. Not just because of this, but because of how things are generally now. The likes of Stibson and so on trying their luck more and more. What we'd pay out in earnings, we'd save on new window glass.'

'Bloke Carne's size can't stay hidden for long,' Geordie said. He finished scribbling his signature, then picked up the money John pushed across the table to him. 'I'll be seeing you soon. And any more work you can pass my way, I'll take it.'

John gave him a quizzical look. 'You preparin' for a wedding, by chance?'

Geordie smiled. 'Nothing so romantic. I'm saving up to pay Lynette back for my share of the forge.'

'When does she want payin' then?'

'She doesn't. But I won't have her out of pocket for my decisions, it's not fair.'

'She's got a bit put away though, hasn't she?'

'Not any more. She spent almost all of it on moving here, and getting me set up at Rowe's forge. That's why . . .' He patted his pocket. 'So, shout if you have anything for me.'

'Will do.' John held out his hand again. 'You're sorely missed here, lad. If you ever change your mind about the forge, there's always a job for you here.'

'Security guard?' Geordie grinned. 'I'm not working nights, thanks.'

John shrugged. 'Can't say I blame you. But I can always use a good smith, don't forget that.'

Geordie shook the hand, and left, throwing a last look behind him at the planks nailed across the office window. How typical of Carne to do something so petty, yet with such potential for danger. It seemed prison hadn't improved his character one bit.

Back at the forge he found Joe still in good spirits, having completed the task for Keir Garvey in good time and already packaged up the nails. He'd spent the extra time cleaning his bicycle and oiling the chain, and when Geordie arrived back, he presented it with visible pride.

'I can take the nails down to Mr Garvey, if you like.'

'I thought your leg was giving you problems?'

'It's loosened up now,' Joe assured him. 'I can go now, and be back before you have to go to the stables.'

'It's a long-ish way, time you get across the moor and down through town,' Geordie said, not certain he liked the idea. But he already knew that, as ever, he would give in to Joe's wishes. 'Go on, then. But don't hang around.'

'I won't.' Joe went to swap his apron for his coat and scarf, and Geordie remembered how they'd promised to replace the one they'd instead given to Tilly for Christmas. He almost reiterated that promise now, but he didn't want to bring up any subject that would remind Joe of the bitter disappointment, and spoil the cheerful atmosphere. It was a rare enough occurrence, that he wanted to hold onto for as long as possible.

'Go careful over the moor,' he said, as Joe spun the pedal up, ready to push off. 'The rain's eased, but it's misty out there.'

'Always is this time of year.' Joe checked his pockets once again for the boxes of nails, then threw Geordie a quick wave, and was off out of the gate before Geordie could think of anything else to say to stop him.

Geordie checked the time, and calculated that he had around an hour before he needed to give Bobby a hand with the evening feed, and settle the horses for the night. The list nailed to the roof beam by the door had had most of the day's tasks crossed off, but there were still a couple of small jobs that he could probably finish before Joe returned.

As he settled into his work again, he turned his mind towards how Tilly's reunion with her mother might be going, wondering whether they'd broken the news yet about Roderick Lawton. Would Tilly be deeply upset, or was Lawton less of a presence in her life than Marion had made him seem? They'd surely rattle around that big house on their own, the two of them, even if there were staff, and it was as hard to imagine Marion commanding such a staff as it had been to imagine her living there at all. If it wasn't for the circumstances it might actually have been quite funny.

Geordie checked the time again, and saw that Joe had already been gone for forty minutes, so he wouldn't be much longer now. He looked around for his knife, to begin scraping the soot from the inside of the cooled oven, but after a few minutes fruitless hunting he remembered he'd left it in the house when he'd punched an extra hole in his belt. He could even visualise it lying on the table, and he muttered an irritated oath and looked over at where Joe kept his own things, on the other side of the fire,

The boy's apron was thrown over the chair there, and Geordie reached into the big pocket at the front and found Joe's knife. He took it from the sheath and lifted it to begin work, then stopped and stared at the blade, and, more crucially, its squared-off end. He heard bicycle wheels on the wet road, and a cheerful but tuneless whistling, and, his head and heart at war with one other, he quietly slipped the knife back into Joe's apron pocket. He'd already sent one child away today; it was not the time for truths and confrontation.

CHAPTER FIFTEEN

The question hung in the air, and Lynette wished Tory hadn't left so quickly. Or perhaps Marion had purposely waited until she'd gone.

'The stables? A lot of money?' she repeated, as if it the very idea was ludicrous, when in fact, not that long ago it would have been true. 'No,' she said, 'we don't have a lot. It's cost me almost everything to set Geordie up in his new forge.' She watched Marion flush faintly, and felt bad for saying it. But it was true, and Marion had benefited from it too, since it had allowed Geordie to continue paying her rent. Lynette wasn't going to sit quietly and be made to feel somehow less of a person for being fortunate by birth.

She caught the flicker of a sympathetic smile on Gracie's face, and it helped. 'The horse we're buying isn't for pleasure,' she explained, less tartly. 'Tory rehabilitates traumatised horses and ponies. This one we're looking at worked at the foundry out on the Princetown road. She was caught up in a gas explosion, and is too skittish to work.'

'So, what'll you do with it when it's better?'

'If they want her back, and she's fit to work, she'll go back.

Other than that, we'll sell her on, or keep her for the riding school, depending on how she goes on.'

'I've got a pony now,' Tilly announced, coming back into the room, now coatless and clutching a ragged-looking knitted rabbit, while Barney was still in her other hand.

Marion looked at Lynette, deep consternation on her face, and Lynette quickly shook her head.

'Remember what we said, Tilly? Hercules belongs to everyone.' She shot Marion an apologetic look. 'He's this tatty little pony with a sweet temper; all the little ones love him. Tilly made friends with him very quickly.'

'Has she been riding, then?' Marion drew her daughter closer.

'No,' Lynette assured her. 'Just helping out with the feeds and suchlike. She's been working very hard.'

Gracie stood up. 'I'll fetch Tilly a drink.'

She and Tilly went out to the kitchen, and Lynette spent an awkward five minutes alone with Marion, trying not to either stare at her aproned midriff, or give the impression she was eager to make an escape. The chimney belched out the occasional gust of black smoke when the wind blew, and Lynette saw Marion's eyes stray in that direction every time, and her features tighten, whether with embarrassment or annoyance it was impossible to say. But Lynette felt desperately sorry for her situation anyway, and, making sure Tilly was out of earshot, she offered her condolences for the loss of Mr Lawton. Marion's eyes immediately filled with tears, and she fumbled an evidently much-used handkerchief from her pocket.

'Thank you,' she mumbled.

'We haven't told Tilly,' Lynette went on. 'I think you said you preferred to tell her yourself?'

Marion nodded and blew her reddened nose. 'I'll tell her later. I'm sorry I didn't think to tell Geordie we've been moved on from Colleybrooke, I lost track of the days.'

'That daughter of Mr Lawton's is a bit of a tartar, isn't she?' Lynette had hoped for some kind of wry agreement, something to give them a shared viewpoint, but Marion's eyebrows drew down in disapproval.

'She's just lost her father, Miss Nicholls. She's got a lot to sort out. Of course she needed the house to herself.'

'Of course.' Lynette cleared her throat, and listened, hopefully, for Gracie's return. 'It's good you have a friend close by,' she ventured after another moment's silence. 'Gracie seems very much at home here.'

'I've known her all my life. Used to help out at Cudlip Farm, sometimes. We all did.' Marion looked up as Gracie and Tilly reappeared. 'In and out of each other's houses since we were kids, all of us.'

It had the ring of someone warning an interloper off her property, and Lynette felt very much the stranger as she sat in this house in which Geordie had grown up, with two women he'd known all his life. She tried not to let it show in her face, though, and adopted a politely curious look.

'I'll have to ask him to tell me all about it when we're both home.' It was childish, she could admit, but she felt justified in the retaliation.

'Now,' Gracie said, sitting down and passing Tilly her cup, 'I want to hear all about how Geordie's getting on. Stephen's told me some of it, but you'll be able to tell us everything Geordie's kept to himself, won't you?'

Lynette gave her an uncomfortable look. 'I don't think I should—'

153

'Don't worry!' Gracie grinned. 'I'm only teasing. It'll just be nice to be able to tell Stephen I've met you at last.'

'And it'll be good to let Geordie know how Stephen is,' Lynette agreed.

'He's a bit low, to be truthful.' Gracie's smile faded. 'He wrote to me about some young-ish lad who got taken up to Exeter just after Christmas. Nice kid, by all accounts, Stephen liked him a lot. They all did, apparently. Everyone was hoping his sentence would be commuted at the last minute, but no luck.'

Lynette's own interested look froze; she could feel it still on her face, yet she knew her eyes would have gone distant. 'Why would it have been commuted? Wasn't he guilty?'

'I don't know the details. I just heard he never meant to kill anyone.'

'But he *did* kill someone,' Lynette said sharply. 'Someone died who didn't deserve to die.' Part of her recoiled at the harshness of her own words, but hearing someone defend Xander's killer, someone unconnected to her brother, who'd never known him or even met him, had awoken her anger again. That Damerel boy had people advocating for him, hoping for the best for him, but Xander had no one except her.

Gracie blinked. 'Well, yes,' she said carefully, 'and that's proper sad. But what I meant was that it wasn't deliberate, so he should have been given life in prison. Like Stephen.'

'That's different. Stephen's father was trying to strangle—'

'Would you two mind going somewhere else to talk about this?' Marion broke in, nodding pointedly at Tilly, and Lynette took the opportunity offered to her, with relief.

'I ought to be going anyway,' she said, and stood up. 'Tilly, it's been lovely having you to stay, and I hope we come to visit you again soon.'

To her discomfiture Tilly crossed the room to give her a long hug, and, looking over the little girl's head, Lynette saw a stricken look come and go on Marion's face. She eased Tilly away with a promise to come again soon, and was surprised at the depth of the sadness she felt.

'I'll walk you to the van,' Gracie said, also rising. 'I have to get back to the farm, anyway.'

As they walked back up to the centre of the village, Gracie picked up her original thread of conversation, much to Lynette's discomfort. It was hard to hear how Alec Damerel had arrived at Dartmoor a ghost of a boy, and been picked out as weak and in need of 'toughening up' by both inmates and warders. His life had been miserable, Gracie told her. The conditions within the prison were well known to be among the worst in the country, and while the diet was on a par throughout the prison system, the budget per prisoner was so small as to make the food barely edible. Enough to keep them alive, but nothing more.

Lynette tried to reignite that flash of anger she'd felt earlier; the man had killed Xander, after all, but all she felt now was the deep sadness at another wasted young life, and the realisation and acceptance that Alec had been no more guilty than Stephen.

Gracie seemed to realise she was the one doing all the talking, and she stopped and raised her hands. 'Hark at me! I wanted to hear about Geordie so I could tell his brother, not heap all this misery on you.' She touched Lynette's arm. 'I'm sorry. Tell me how your Christmas was, Stephen'll want to hear about that. He's not seen his niece since she was newborn.'

There wasn't enough time left to tell Gracie much, but it was good to turn her mind back to happier things, and Lynette described Tilly's gradually emerging fascination for hide and seek, and discovered that the child's more wilful side was already well known.

'She can be a handful,' Gracie said as they came within sight of the van and horse box. 'Marion's let her run wild a bit, but that was all starting to change.' She sobered. 'Marion truly loved Roderick, you know. It wasn't all about the money.'

'I can tell.' Lynette hesitated, then pushed on. 'I was talking to Mrs Bellowes, and she said that she thought maybe Marion was expecting—'

'Ivy Bellowes wants her mouth sewn shut,' Gracie grumbled, then sighed. 'It's true, though. Marion hopes that when it becomes clear she's carrying Roderick's child, she'll have a claim on the house.'

'And what do you think?'

Gracie snorted. 'There's no chance his snobby daughter will accept it's her father's, but you can't convince Marion of that.'

'So, she'll be stuck in that damp, smoky place—' Lynette jerked a thumb over her shoulder '—with two small children, and no wage coming in.' She didn't want to think about how Geordie would react to that, but she had a horrible, crawling feeling that she knew.

'It won't be so damp once the fires have been lit for a while, and the place is more lived in.' Gracie shrugged. 'Marion will carry on taking in mending work when she can. She's lucky that house has been rented by Sargents for as long as it has, and they weren't moved out when the mine closed down. We've been expecting it since Geordie left, though, to be honest.'

'Geordie's been paying the rent,' Lynette said. 'Didn't you know? He was pretty shocked to find out there's been no one living in it.'

'I did know,' Gracie confessed, but she looked embarrassed about it. 'Thing is, Marion didn't want to give it up. You know, just in case things broke down with Roderick. She needed a bolthole.' Gracie stopped again, this time to admire the horse box. 'That's a beauty, better than anything we've got at the farm.'

'It wasn't anything like that when we got it,' Lynette said. 'Tory found it at St Austell market.'

The box had been sitting plaintively in a corner of the market, not even for sale, the paint flaking, metal rusted through in parts, and with a decidedly unsafe floor. But Tory had pounced on it, and together she and Bobby Gale had patched it up; then Bobby had painted the name of the stables on the side, and it looked almost new now, especially against this thin, grey afternoon light.

Tory opened the van door and leaned out. 'Are you ready?'

'Wait.' Gracie caught at Lynette's sleeve. 'I'd like to talk you again, about Stephen and Geordie. Will you be back to visit Tilly?'

'I'm sure we will,' Lynette said, privately suspecting Geordie would likely be up here within two hours of finding out what had happened to his family. 'It's been lovely to meet you, Gracie. Please do give mine and Geordie's regards to Stephen when you next visit him.'

'It won't be for a while,' Gracie said. 'Stephen's convinced trouble's brewing in there, and has been since before Christmas. He doesn't want me near the place until it's blown over.' She sounded tense for the first time, and her eyes had lost the soft look they'd had before when she'd spoken of Stephen. Lynette tried to imagine how she'd feel if it were Geordie locked up, but he'd so often made that scenario all too likely, that she shook the thought hurriedly away.

'What's the name of your farm again?' she asked instead. 'We'll be sure to visit you when we come back.'

'Cudlip Farm. It's out on the west side of the village near ...' Gracie's words faltered and she gave a little shudder, then sighed. 'Near Stephens' Grave,' she finished, and smiled a little as she saw Lynette's raised eyebrows. 'It's an old marker by the crossways,' she explained. 'I just get superstitious over it, that's all.'

'Who was that Stephen, then?'

'Stephens was the last name. George Stephens. They say he killed himself over an unfaithful lover, so they buried him at the crossways. I hate that place, but *my* Stephen used to laugh at me for it. I always ran past it, while he would dance around the bloody thing and whistle a tune.'

Lynette smiled at the thought, but it was followed by a pang of regret for the loss of Stephen's youthful freedom. 'Geordie will know where the farm is, anyway.'

Gracie nodded. 'Best you go on, then, your friend's waiting. Good luck with the horse.'

She stood back and waved as Lynette joined Tory in the van, and as they pulled away Lynette looked back, and saw her throwing a savage glare towards Colleybrooke Manor. She sat back, easier in her mind now, and pushed away that niggling worry that Geordie might feel guilty enough to move back. Gracie would look out for Marion and Tilly, and whoever came along in seven or eight months' time to change the shape of their little family.

*

Lynette stayed in the van and watched, while Tory examined the pony and then passed over the money, but climbed out to help load the skittish creature into the horse box. All the way home she thought about what had happened in Peter Tavy, and all the revelations she would have to tell Geordie, but every time, her mind kept coming back to her earlier suspicion; that he would be up here the moment he learned what had happened. And then what? He would feel compelled to do more, she knew it. Maybe even to move back, to provide for the woman who was still his wife, and to be a father to the child who would otherwise be known as a bastard.

She felt cold at the thought, and, as Tory chattered about the horse, and her plans for it, she let the words fade into the background while she pondered what she should do. If she could find some way of persuading Lawton's children that Marion deserved to live at Colleybrooke, Geordie would accept that Marion and Tilly no longer needed him. He would surely realise that if he moved back he would actually be preventing them from claiming what was rightfully theirs, forcing them to stay in their little miner's cottage on the edge of the village.

By the time they reached Pencarrack, she had made up her mind. She would write to Lawton's offspring and, using all her persuasive skills she would make them understand that Marion was carrying their own half-sibling and deserved to be cared for in the family home. The pregnancy was only a few weeks along so there was plenty of time – there was no need for Geordie to know for a while. She would tell him, of course she would. But not yet.

CHAPTER SIXTEEN

Ever since Gwenna had posted the letter to the prison she'd driven herself almost mad wondering whether she was doing the right thing. She needed to talk to someone who had no reason to try and persuade her either way, so the moment her mother turned the sign around on the shop door she was pulling her coat off the hook.

'I'm going out to see Tory,' she called over her shoulder. 'I'll be back to help with tea, though.'

'Don't be late,' her mother called back.

Her voice was calm enough, but it had only been a couple of days since the robbery, and they were both still a little nervous though neither liked to admit it. Brewer had been comforting in his assessment that it was nothing more serious than an opportunistic break-in, which, since it was largely unsuccessful, given the takings were safe, was unlikely to happen again. He advised them to buy new, stronger, locks, and Gwenna intended to do that first thing on Monday morning. Brewer's reaction to her assertion that it had been Nigel Stibson had been predictably wary, considering her lack of proof, but at least he had promised to keep an eye out.

As Gwenna drove into the stable yard she saw two male figures through the open barn door, forking hay and yelling to one another, and belatedly remembered Tory and Lynette were going to be out all day, taking Geordie's daughter back home. She almost started the engine again, but recognised Bobby's voice and instead climbed out of the van. The horse box hadn't yet returned, but perhaps he would have an idea how long Tory would be; if it would be too long a wait she would just try again tomorrow. Sundays were always a little bit easier for her anyway.

'Bobby!' she called, as she approached the stable, and he popped up from where he'd been bending over by the door of an empty stall.

'Gwen!' He lowered his voice slightly. 'Look, I hope you're all right after that . . . well, that horrible stuff that's happened lately.'

'Gwen-*na*. And we're being very careful,' Gwenna assured him, certain now that he would have been the one called to keep a watch on Stibson.

'Good.' He called across to his companion, who was in the stall with one of the clay pit ponies. 'Geordie, come and say hello.'

While Gwenna knew Bobby quite well now, Geordie Sargent was another matter. He was a relative latecomer to the area, with a reputation for trouble that went before him, though he was said to have settled down since he'd taken on Al Trevellick's boy as his live-in apprentice. Nevertheless, she couldn't help feeling a little uneasy as he put out a hand. He didn't look particularly friendly.

'Pleased to meet you,' he said, quite mechanically, then seemed to catch himself, and made more of an effort. 'Tory talks about you a lot.'

'Nice to meet you too,' Gwenna said. 'I won't keep you, you look busy. I was just hoping to have a word with Tory.'

'About what?' Bobby said at once, presumably expecting the worst, but she tried to ease his fears. She had no intention of telling Tory about the Watchers, and hadn't even mentioned the robbery to her.

'It's all right,' she said, giving him a pointed look. 'I can try again tomorrow.'

'Just a minute,' Bobby said, peering out across the dark yard, 'looks like she's back.' The pleasure in his voice was impossible to miss, as was the way he smoothed his wayward hair flat and straightened his waistcoat. Gwenna caught Geordie's eye, and she warmed to him a little as they shared a private smile. She went out to help with the gate, and watched while Tory and Lynette let down the ramp and began coaxing a clearly terrified pony out of the box.

Geordie and Bobby wisely kept their distance, Gwenna noted, knowing Tory would give short shrift to anyone who presumed to know her job better than she did. They had evidently been readying the stall, however, and soon enough the traumatised animal was left alone again, to pull hay from a net hanging on the wall.

'We'll let her settle,' Tory said, brushing hay off her trousers, and it was only then that her eyes found Gwenna, hovering in the shadows. 'Why are you hiding back there? Come upstairs. All of you, I mean,' she added, looking around at them.

Geordie and Lynette had moved to embrace, and Gwenna felt a surprising pang of envy at the way Geordie's arms closed about Lynette and he pulled her against him. It wasn't anything to do with Geordie himself, it was the look of contentment on his face as his shoulders relaxed, and he rested his chin on Lynette's rain-damp hat. As Gwenna passed them on her way to the stairs, she sneaked a look at Lynette, expecting to see the same expression there too, but it was startlingly different. Gwenna couldn't read it, but although Lynette's eyes were closed, there was no peaceful smile there; her brow was furrowed, and her fingers gripped the back of Geordie's coat as if she was frightened he was going to disappear. Gwenna looked away quickly before Lynette could open her eyes again and catch her staring.

Tory left them to discuss how Tilly had settled back in at home, and took Bobby and Gwenna up to the flat with her. 'What brings you all the way up here tonight then?' she asked Gwenna, perching comfortably on the arm of the chair in which Bobby had chosen to sit.

Gwenna started to tell her about the Christmas Day conversation with her mother, but was interrupted by the arrival of Lynette.

'Geordie's just checking over the new pony's shoes,' she said to Tory, then turned to Gwenna. 'I don't mean to be rude, but were you just talking about Dartmoor?'

Gwenna nodded. 'My dad's in there ... well, you probably know that.'

Lynette gave Gwenna a sympathetic look. 'Horrible place, from what I've heard.'

'You wouldn't think so from listening to my mother.' Gwenna frowned. 'But at least I know the truth now.'

'From who?' Tory asked.

'Jago Carne. I saw him on the beach on Christmas Day.' Gwenna saw the look that flew between them. 'I know he's not a nice person,' she added quickly, 'but at least he's got no reason to lie. My mother's been to the prison, too,' she said, 'and *she's* come back talking about soft beds, and good food. And voluntary work, for those who choose to earn money.' She gave a short laugh. 'I believed her for all this time, but only because I wanted to. I should have realised.'

'She'd have done it for your own good,' Tory said, ever the diplomat. 'Don't be hard on her for that.'

'I'm not. I understand why she's done it, but I need to see for myself. So I've written to Dad to ask him to send a visiting order for both of us, not just Mum.'

'I don't think it's a good idea for you to go yet,' Lynette said, and Gwenna turned to her in surprise, and not a little irritation. What could it possibly have to do with her?

'Why not? You weren't even here when he was arrested, you have no—'

'It's not that. Or anything to do with you at all. It's just something Gracie Martyn told me.'

'Who?' Gwenna was unable to keep the impatience from her voice.

'Marion Sargent's friend from Peter Tavy. She's been seeing Geordie's brother in there, and she says he thinks something's . . . well, *brewing*, she called it.'

'What sort of something?' Gwenna asked, tightening up. 'Dangerous something?'

'I don't know, I'm assuming so. She just said Stephen doesn't want her visiting again until it's blown over.'

'Is my dad in danger then?'

'I told you, I don't know.'

'Then I'm definitely going,' Gwenna said, sounding more determined than she felt. After what Jago had told her, she had a better idea of the kind of place her father was in, and it had stolen hours of sleep on several nights. At the same time, she couldn't help trembling at the thought of stepping into somewhere so potentially explosive, which made her wonder if she was making the right choice for her future, after all. She would know soon enough.

'One of us could come with you,' Tory offered. 'Depending on when it is, of course.' She didn't have to remind either of them that she was no stranger to unpredictable violence, they had both heard her Bristol gang stories.

'Actually,' Lynette said hesitantly, 'I have a better idea. Stephen's put Geordie on his visiting list now, but Geordie's been putting it off. I think he just needs a bit of persuasion, and accompanying you might be the push he needs.'

'That would put my mind at rest anyway,' Tory said. 'If he'll do it, of course.'

'I'm sure he will, if he knows the alternative is that Gwenna goes in there alone.' Lynette squeezed Gwenna's arm. 'I'd be much happier if you were together, and it's a long drive by yourself as well. Let me go down and talk to him on his own, so he doesn't feel put on the spot.'

'I don't even know if Dad's going to send me a visiting order yet,' Gwenna pointed out. 'And I'd need to be cleared to visit by the police, too. Don't go making any firm arrangements.'

'I won't, but it'll be good to test the water, just in case. I'll do it now.'

She went out into the night again, and Tory got up to pour hot water into the teapot. She looked uncomfortable when she returned. 'Look, Gwenna, I know you're dead set on visiting your dad, but what if you see . . . ' She was clearly uncomfortable bringing the subject up again, but Gwenna had already thought of it.

'Peter?' She shook her head. 'Don't worry, I won't.'

'How can you be sure?'

'He's being kept away from the other prisoners, for his own safety,' Gwenna said. 'Because of his job.' She didn't want to think how he would be when he came out; she had enough on her mind for now.

'What happens if you get the visiting order, but your mum sees it first?' Tory asked, addressing one of those things without realising it.

Gwenna gave a short laugh. 'You wouldn't believe the lengths I'm going to, to make sure I get to the post before she does! I'm getting *very* good at distraction now.'

'You said something about being cleared by the police, too?'

'Prisoners have to put a request in,' Gwenna said, 'and that's if they're even due a visit. They have to say who it's for, and since former convicts aren't allowed, the prison sends any new names to the nearest police station, and an officer comes to the visitor's house to interview them.' She grimaced. 'That's the bit I'm most worried about. I've no idea how I'd explain that away.'

'Would it help things for you to go and talk to Sergeant Brewer first, so he doesn't have to come to your house? Then he can clear you right away, and save time, too.'

'I could,' Gwenna mused, thinking it over. She came to a decision quickly. 'I'll do it first thing on Monday.'

Lynette came back, this time bringing Geordie with her. 'Good news!'

'Are you sure?' Gwenna asked Geordie, who nodded.

'Of course.' But he didn't look as certain as Lynette, and Gwenna felt faintly awkward as she offered her thanks. She sought to dismiss any obligation on his part.

'Like I keep saying, I don't even know if Dad will want me there.'

'Well, just let me know,' Lynette said. 'And if the two of you want company on the drive, I'll come too. I'll just go for a walk, or something.'

'On Dartmoor, in this weather?' Geordie grinned down at her. 'Rather you than me.'

'Well, I'll sit in the van, then,' Lynette amended. She seemed stubbornly determined to help either way.

Gwenna smiled. 'I'll let you know, but, Geordie, if you want to visit your brother before I hear anything you mustn't wait. I'll be fine on my own, I'm sure.'

He shook his head. 'If Stephen doesn't think it's right for Gracie, you shouldn't be going up there alone either. Why don't you and your mother go together?'

'She wants me to believe what she's told me about the place, and it'll only upset her if she knows I've found out the truth.'

'We'll be finding that out together, then.'

She looked at him in surprise. 'Have you *never* been?'

'Stephen wouldn't let me at first.' Geordie shrugged. 'It's different for him. What he did was . . . It wasn't like what your dad did. And prison's changed him. He didn't want me to see how, not until recently. Right, then.' He dropped a kiss on Lynette's forehead, and started towards the door. 'I'd better get back for Joe's tea.' He stopped and looked back at Gwenna, and there was a solemnity once more in his expression. 'Don't let your mother talk you out of going,' he said. 'Believe me, you'll regret it.'

The visiting order arrived on Monday morning, around twenty minutes after Gwenna had returned from talking to Sergeant Brewer. The policeman had told her that, as Jonas's daughter, she'd be approved automatically, as her mother had, which meant she'd lied about that, as well. Gwenna had gone back to the shop bristling with renewed resentment, but that had dissolved into a swell of nervous anticipation as she stared at the letter, her heart beating fast and hard, and her palms suddenly damp. She heard footsteps, and shoved the envelope into the pocket of her apron, before handing the rest of the post over to her mother.

'Nothing for you from Dad,' she said, trying to sound casual. 'When are you next seeing him?'

'Whenever he sends me the order. I'm not certain when he'll have earned the next visit, but it should be around the week of the eighteenth.'

She looked at the few letters, which Gwenna had already seen; an advertising leaflet from a new warehouse in Truro, an envelope with a Birmingham post mark, and something with the Cornish Trade Group printed on the back. She sighed and plucked out the Birmingham letter, dropping the other two in the bin.

'Did you ask him if I could be put on the request this time?' Gwenna persisted.

'Of course.'

'And didn't you say they would have to clear it with the local police, like they did with you?' It was hateful having to force her mother to lie again, but Gwenna hoped that this time Rachel would tell the truth; it might mean that she was being honest about the request as well. But she was disappointed.

'Yes. So don't be too upset if Sergeant Brewer can't approve you. Based on . . . what happened. You know.'

She looked so evasive, that any guilt Gwenna had felt about her next question instantly melted away. 'I've told Tory I'd spend the day up at the stables one day that week, actually. Lynette's going to be away and she'll need the help. Will you mind being on your own in the shop?'

Rachel blinked in surprise. 'Oh. No, I suppose that's fine. It's nice that you and she are friends again.'

'We might need to go out and look at a horse, at some point,' Gwenna added, 'so I won't just be able to come back on a moment's notice if you need me.'

Rachel waved a hand as she went back into the shop. 'I've managed often enough in the past, love.' She didn't have to add that most of those times had been when Jonas was off collecting illegal imports for Barry Hocking, and Gwenna had been living in the dorm on the training base. 'You go up and help Tory, and enjoy yourself.'

That night Gwenna found her dreams taking her to a castle on a night-shrouded, unfamiliar moor, and into a richly furnished and deeply comfortable room; it was only when she pulled open the pretty lace curtains, to let in the morning light, that she saw the bars on the windows.

CHAPTER SEVENTEEN

5 January

Daniel huddled in his thin blanket, listening to the activity beyond his solitary cell. The misery that had descended on him when he'd been brought to the punishment block had been replaced by a sickening fear at the discovery that he had been recommended for fifteen strokes with the cat o'nine tails. Ned Newbury was one of their own, who'd been assaulted in the course of doing his duty and knocked unconscious; of course an example would be made of the prisoner who'd attacked him. A lesson to everyone in what would happen if anyone else tried it.

At this point, simply adding months onto Daniel's sentence would not seem much of a punishment, given he'd only just begun his stretch, so the magistrates had immediately sent the recommendation for the flogging to the Home Secretary. The confirmation had been delayed by a backlog build-up over Christmas, and Daniel still waited, in a state of gnawing tension, for his fate to be confirmed. Popular opinion seemed to be that the recommendation would be reduced to ten, maybe even refused altogether and replaced with a different punishment. All he could do was wait, and hope.

Even this was thankfully pushed to the back of his mind now, and replaced for the time being by curiosity. The disruption to the oppressive silence had begun hours ago, roughly when visiting time should have kept many prisoners occupied, and the shouting had continued since then. One voice in particular drew his attention as it neared his cell, and Daniel threw off the blanket and went to the door to peer through the tiny rectangle. The view was limited, but showed him a section of the hallway beyond, and he saw he was right.

'Ray? What's happened?'

'Back to your bunk, Pearce!' a voice barked, and the guard escorting Ray Beatty came into view and slammed his stick against the door of Daniel's cell. Daniel jumped back, and Ray squinted through the slot and grinned at him.

'Bit of a lively inspection today,' he said, also ignoring the guard's growled order to quiet down. 'Few of us'll be in here for a night or two.'

'What happened?'

'Cells got turned over. They found—'

'Move it!'

Ray stumbled forward a step, on the urging of the warder's stick, but his cheeriness seemed unaffected as he disappeared from view, and a moment later a door slammed.

'Pearce, you'd better get some sleep,' the warder said, as he passed Daniel's cell again. 'Governor wants to see you first thing, and I guarantee you won't be gettin' much sleep after that.'

'Shut yer hole!' Ray bellowed at him. 'Let him alone.'

'Know what happens, Pearce, at a flogging?' the guard said,

stopping to peer in. 'There's a big old A-shaped frame, and they tie your hands—'

'I said shut up,' Ray snapped. 'Unless you want to find Davis and his mates waiting around the corner of the twine shed one day.'

The guard glared at him for a moment; Daniel could only guess he'd been met with the same belligerent look from Ray. He backed off, muttering something about birch twigs, and the damage they do to a man's skin. Ray fell silent and wouldn't be drawn any further on what had been recovered from his cell, so Daniel retreated to his bunk and pulled the blanket up around his shoulders again. At least by tomorrow he would know when the flogging was to take place, and the sooner it was over, the better. Then he would set to work on the governor, with Stephen's help, to try and overturn the decision not to allow visitors.

He lay down, hoping for one of the sporadic bouts of sleep that he'd become accustomed to, but it didn't come. So he just lay on his side staring at the wall, and at the tiny sliver of light from the high, barred window as evening crept across the prison grounds. Another day done.

He was awoken shortly after six o'clock, before the hooter that would drive the rest of the convicts from their beds and into another grey morning. The warder unlocked the door and shoved it open, and Daniel hunched up beneath his blanket, trying to hold on to the flimsy fragments of his dream. But they scattered as he heard his name barked into the chilly air, and he sat up, blinking. It couldn't be time for a meeting with the governor yet, surely?

'Time to go, Pearce,' the warder said. An ominous clanking

sound followed the words, and Daniel twisted to look at him. His blood chilled.

'Why do I need handcuffs?' he croaked. He cleared his throat and tried again. 'I'm not going to run, am I?'

'You might. Nasty business, the cat.' The warder, who was still the night shift man, shot a look in the direction of Ray's cell. 'I don't think much of your mate, either. Who knows what ideas he's put in your head?'

'You'll be all right, lad!' Ray shouted, as Daniel surrendered to the cuffs that slipped over his wrists. 'Just don't let 'em think they've got you beat.'

'Come on,' the warder said. 'Governor Roberts has come in early, special.'

Daniel was back within the hour, feeling sicker than ever. Ray must have heard the door clang shut; he was immediately calling across the corridor.

'What did Roberts say? What've you got?'

'The fifteen,' Daniel managed, through lips tightened with fear. 'And nine days bread and water.'

'Back in here?'

'Yes.'

'That's best. At least you won't have to go to work right after. Pity the rest of us, eh?'

Daniel was sure Ray was trying to be optimistic, but just now he'd have been glad to be going back to work. He'd have gone to the quarry and broken rocks from dawn until dusk, or built a wall the length of the village, and he'd have done it with a song in his heart.

He sank onto his bed and heard the key turn in the lock, and he realised he couldn't feel a single part of his own body. His feet were on the floor, but there was no sensation of it; his fingertips were blue and shaking, but they might as well have belonged to someone else; his face was numb, the split and chapped lips no longer part of him.

'Look, lad, it'll be all right,' Ray said, sounding less cheerful now. 'One thing to remember, is to make a lot of noise, right? Don't be all strong and stoic, that's a fool's game. You shout, and you might upset the governor enough to make him stop after a few. Lesson learned, and all that, right? The cat's man might—'

'Enough, Beatty!' the warder snapped.

'He might go easy,' Ray persisted. 'So you howl, lad. You howl just so loud as you like.'

'He's not going to go easy,' Daniel said, his voice low. 'The new cat's man is Ned Newbury.'

A long silence greeted this, and, to his credit, Ray did not try to disguise his dismay behind more encouraging words. He simply sighed. 'God go with you, boy.'

They came for Daniel later that same afternoon. He had spent the day trying not to think about the sealed paper package he'd seen on the governor's desk, stamped by the Prison Commissioner's office, and which he knew had contained the cat. He had known it simply by the way Roberts's eye had strayed to it whenever he'd mentioned the confirmation, and the sentence, but the image was so strong he had half convinced himself he could see through the package, to the knot-laced bundle of whipcord inside.

He was led, once more in cuffs, down the stairs to where the large A-shaped frame waited. There was a medical officer standing to one side, who would not look directly at him, and a

174

white-overalled nurse from the hospital, holding a tray on which Daniel could see a couple of small bottles and a cloth. His gut twisted in renewed fear as he was urged forward and instructed to remove his shirt; his skin rose into gooseflesh at the touch of the icy air, but he could feel sweat prickling along his hairline. Once his shirt was off, it was taken from him, and he felt hands grasping his wrists and ankles to tie them to the posts of the frame.

A wide leather strap was passed around his waist and secured, to protect his kidney area, and then the preparations were done; nothing now stood between Daniel and his punishment. All sound momentarily ceased, and he felt the withdrawal of the medical staff and the warder from immediately behind him. He heard a door open at the far end of the room, but remained facing forward, his muscles tense to the point of screaming, his legs shaking, but his position held firm by the straps at wrist and ankle. Footsteps, slow and deliberate; the sinister rattling sound of the cat being lifted from its position on the nearby table; the heavy, guttural breathing of a man who has recently taken a powerful blow to the face . . .

'Do your duty,' the governor said quietly, the official signal to his cat's man. 'Show no quarter.'

The rod came down.

Later, Daniel stood in the open doorway to his cell, supporting his own weight, but just barely. The muscles in his arms and legs throbbed, his breath burned in his chest and throat, and his stomach clenched painfully tight against the urge to vomit. But his back was on fire. Still shirtless, and with rivulets of blood streaming down to soak the waistband of his trousers, he felt distantly sure that he would never be able to draw clothing on again.

He didn't want to think too hard about how his back looked now. He had been aware of Newbury pausing during the flogging to flick the cat clean, and the first time that had happened he had almost thrown up there and then. But by the third and fourth time he lacked the energy even for that. He had learned that one of the bottles on the nurse's tray was ammonia, only when he'd drifted into black relief and was brought back, choking, by the pungent wafting of it beneath his nose.

'Go on, lad,' the warder said now, and for once he sounded gentle. 'Lie down while the medic tends you.'

Daniel shuffled into his cell, feeling an odd, but strong sense of relief to be back there, and eased himself face down onto his bunk. Behind him he heard murmuring, and the sound of a bottle being opened. He folded his arms into a pillow and pressed his hot, sweating face into them, and after a moment he felt something wet and sticky brushing across his upper back. He jerked up onto his elbows and twisted to see what was happening.

'Just a bit of collodion,' the medic soothed. 'Leave it be, it'll help.'

Daniel lowered himself to his bunk again, trying to push all thoughts from his mind and accept the darkness that pressed in. But that relief danced just out of reach; he kept hearing Newbury's stertorous breathing, the grunts of exertion, and the small, satisfied sounds he'd made whenever Daniel had screamed. The hatred and anger formed a hard knot in his belly that he couldn't shift, and the tension in his body stopped him from relaxing enough to sink into much-needed oblivion. He was acutely aware of every sound, both in his cell and beyond it, and he could hear Ray's voice demanding to know how he was, first addressing the warder, and then, getting no response, Daniel himself. But Daniel couldn't answer.

Eventually the medic declared him safe to be left, and he and the warder retreated and slammed the door shut. Daniel jumped as the iron clanged into place, but the sense of relief that he would now be left alone, even if it was just for a few short hours, was overwhelming. He welcomed the chilly air that numbed his skin, finally let his shoulders slump, and wept silently into the shelter of his own arms.

CHAPTER EIGHTEEN

19 January

The drive up to Princetown was completed in near silence. Geordie had been trying not to think about what he'd learned about Joe; he had said nothing about it to anyone in the days since the discovery, not even Lynette. He knew what she would say: *the boy needs a father figure, not a friend ... you* have *to discipline him.* She was right, of course, but he was still convinced that coming down too hard on the still grieving boy would mean losing him. He couldn't risk it.

Gwenna had been chewing her already ragged nails, staring out of the window as they came through Plymouth and out onto the moor; such a familiar place to him, and he was surprised when she told him she'd never been out here. He pointed in the direction of Peter Tavy, explaining he planned to stop in on his way back, to visit his daughter, if she had no objections.

'Of course I don't mind, but won't she be at school?' Gwenna asked, making him feel foolish for not realising, but he was damned if he'd come all this way, be this close, and not see her.

'It's all right, I know where the school is,' he said, 'I went to the same one myself.'

'I look forward to meeting her,' Gwenna said. She sat up straighter as they approached the entrance to the prison and the huge granite archway that marked it. Geordie read the words inscribed on it, but didn't understand them: *Parcere Subjectis*. Whatever it meant, it couldn't be anything remotely hopeful, and he was reasonably sure he was happier not knowing.

He drove in slowly, sensing Gwenna's tension climbing and feeling some sympathy for her; his own was making his heart race. He had no idea what to expect once he walked behind those imposing granite walls. The Stephen he'd known had been the gentlest of lads, smitten with his new love, Gracie, and all he'd wanted then, at the age of twenty-three, was to make a living that would allow them to marry. Where Geordie's natural tendency had always been to stir things into changing, Stephen's was to please everyone, and his temperament had always been diffident and malleable … until the night he'd killed their father.

The few letters he'd written since his incarceration had been full of anger and bitterness, telling Geordie he would never allow him to visit. He wrote that he refused to be seen caged and helpless, that he'd had to change or die, and that he'd now spent so much time in solitary confinement that he hardly knew how to speak to anyone any more. He'd cursed Geordie for putting him in this situation, knowing Geordie's inability to pass up the chance to needle their father. He'd even thrown the blame for his life-threatening appendicitis into it, which had finally made Geordie retreat, in bewildered anger of his own.

He had remained away until Lynette, still reeling from the

loss of her own brother, had convinced him that he should keep trying. So, he'd written again, and, to his relief he'd discovered Stephen had somehow, finally, found his peace as a blend of the two people he'd once been. Now here the two brothers were, within a few hundred yards of one another for the first time in over six years, and the knot in Geordie's stomach was tightening with every footstep.

Gwenna met his eyes, as they joined the queue to be given a cursory pat-down before being allowed into the visitors' hall. She looked terrified, and he gave her what he hoped was an encouraging smile.

'If you want to leave at any time, just go,' he said. 'I'll keep an eye on you, and follow you out, I promise.'

She nodded, swallowed, and then they were shown into the hall and her focus was immediately taken up by searching for her father. He saw her give a start, then walk hesitantly towards a table at the far end, and, satisfied that he'd know if she left, he turned his own attention to scanning the room for Stephen. He found him by the wall, an empty chair opposite him, and his face turned down to stare at the scarred wooden tabletop. But, as Gwenna had, Geordie hesitated for a moment. Six years could pass in a flash in the outside world, but for Stephen they would have been long, painful, and filled with regrets and recriminations. How much would he have changed as a result? The question arose for the first time; had Stephen simply allowed him to visit just so he could level more accusations at him, and tell him more forcefully to stay away? There was only one way to find out.

He made his way over and pulled the chair out, the scraping noise of the legs on the stone floor almost lost in the rising racket of greetings and other chairs being dragged. Stephen looked up at last, and Geordie felt his heart expand at the familiar, faint grin that touched his brother's face. It whisked him straight back to the simpler days, when they'd laboured in the mine together, gone drinking together on pay days, and talked about Marion, Tilly, and Gracie as if they were going to be within reach forever.

Stephen was just two years his junior, but looked much older now; his face was thinner, his hair greying in patches, though neatly cut, and his skin was more healthy-looking than Geordie had expected, but tight on his bones. He placed his hands flat on the table and nodded for Geordie to do the same; a quick look around the room showed everyone was doing it, and Geordie complied without question as the silence between them grew heavier. It was hard to know how to begin, but the visit would only last half an hour, and there was too much to say to pluck out just one thing.

'Thank you,' Stephen said at last. 'For coming, I mean.'

'How are you?' It sounded stupid, and Geordie shook his head. 'I mean—'

'I know what you mean.' Stephen fixed him with an unsettlingly direct stare. That was new, too. 'I'm still a stage four, I haven't been knocked back down, so I'm still doing all right. More importantly, how are *you*?'

'Me? I'm fine.' Geordie frowned. 'Why do you ask?'

'Gracie told me what happened at Wheal Peter. She reckons you were lucky to get out alive.'

'Yeah, well. No one else did, did they?' Geordie shifted uncomfortably. 'Look, we're all a bit worried about what you told Gracie. That something's—'

'Hush,' Stephen said in a low but mild voice. He let his gaze roam briefly around the room, then returned to fix it on Geordie. 'I'm not stupid enough to get involved in anything, but there've been some ... developments. My cellmate among them.'

'What happened?'

'New lad I told you about in my letter. He fell foul of one of our warders, and knocked him unconscious, but everyone could see how the bloke had been goading him for weeks. You know what that's like, so I've heard,' he added. 'Had a taste of your own medicine now, haven't you?'

Geordie's eyes narrowed. 'Jago Carne been boasting, has he?'

'Said he got a few good kicks in.' Stephen sighed. 'Let him alone, Geordie, in case he decides to finish the job next time.'

'Don't worry, I've changed my ways. Mostly.' Geordie cocked an eyebrow. 'As have you, I gather?'

'Model prisoner,' Stephen said, with a return of that slight grin. People around the room were already starting to relax away from the hands-flat-on-the-table rule now, and the guards weren't enforcing it; Stephen linked his fingers on the table in front of him. 'Anyway, the thing is, we've all felt the change in here lately, and the new kid getting dragged to chokey has just made things worse. Poor bugger already had a seven-year sentence for a stupid, drunken show of temper. On his birthday, would you believe?'

'Dangerous times, clearly, birthdays,' Geordie said wryly. 'I've decided not to have any more.'

Stephen gave a short laugh. 'You always were the smart one. Worst thing is, the new bloke's just been flogged. Fifteen lashes, I heard.'

Geordie winced. 'Christ, that's awful.'

'His original crime was against someone very influential though, in here *and* out there.' Stephen nodded at the wall to his left. 'And the warder in question is that man's son-in-law. In his pay, if you see what I mean.'

Geordie scowled. 'I do. So that's what's pushing things towards trouble in here?'

'No. That's been on the cards a lot longer, but it's not helping.' Stephen checked the proximity and identity of the nearest guard, and seemed satisfied. 'The thing is, Daniel's too new to have made many friends, but one of them's Ray Beatty, who's in with a crowd from London. New kind of lag; the Elephant and Castle Gang. They call them motor car bandits.' Stephen's voice was now almost too low to hear, and Geordie guessed some of those men were nearby. He followed Stephen's eyeline to one prisoner, with 341 on his jumper, and looked away quickly.

'Davis,' Stephen murmured. 'In for an acid attack on a prostitute. One of his own, actually,' he added with a grimace. 'He works in the twine shed, and he's a dab hand with a chiv.'

Geordie's stomach rolled at the thought of Stephen being so familiar with men like that, and rubbing shoulders with them every day. He was beginning to understand more about his brother's personality change, and his new calm, assured and taut persona. He didn't like it.

'You're keeping your distance, I hope?'

'I'm doing what I need to do,' Stephen said blandly. 'And I'm being who I need to be.' He sat forward. 'There's no getting-out date for me, you know that. It's not as if I just need to hold my nerve and grit my teeth for a few more months, or even a few more years. This is *it*. My whole life.'

'I still think we should be able to appeal the sentence,' Geordie said, trying not to let his dismay at the reality of it all show in his face. He was sure it must though, because Stephen's expression softened.

'I killed him, Geordie. Even the witness who saved me knows it. There's no denying it, and I didn't try. I'm lucky I didn't go the same way as Alec Damerel.'

'What *he* did was deliberate,' Geordie pointed out. 'And the person he killed was Lynette's brother, so if you think I'm going to shed any tears over him you can think again.'

Stephen's lips thinned, but he didn't argue, and Geordie was relieved. He didn't want to spend this visit fighting over someone he'd never known, even if Stephen had spent the man's last, impossibly difficult days with him.

'I went out to Lynher Mill,' he said, in an attempt to divert the conversation on to less intense subjects. 'You know the ancestor you're named for? He was supposed to have had some strong connection to the place. I felt it too.'

Stephen shook his head. 'It never had that effect on me. Besides, Stephen Penhaligon wasn't from Lynher anywhere, he was from a place called Caernoweth.'

Geordie blinked. 'That's the nearest town to me. And there's a shop called Penhaligon's Attic there.'

'I don't know about a shop, but back in the civil war, his family owned a farm near the sea.' Stephen smiled. 'They did say he was a bit of a wild one, which never described me, did it?'

'Not then,' Geordie admitted.

'And not now.' Stephen shrugged. 'But yeah, for a time in between.' His mouth drew down in a smile that was laced with regret. 'I might have been named after him, but *you*? It looks as if you're the one whose carrying him in there.' He leaned forward and tapped Geordie's chest. 'You've got a lit fuse in you, and it'll only take a breath from someone like Jago Carne to set it burning too fast to stamp out. Be careful.'

Geordie nodded slowly. Despite his determination to put that part of him in the past, it seemed his brother still saw him clearly. 'What happened to him?'

'Who, Carne?'

'Penhaligon.'

'Lost in the civil war, at Stamford Hill, so I understand. One of General Hopton's Royalist lot.'

'I'll make a note to steer clear,' Geordie promised. 'Of Carne, that is, not Stamford Hill,' he added, with a forced little smile.

Stephen didn't return it, he just kept his eyes fixed on Geordie's for a moment, then relaxed. 'Good.' He looked around the room, and when his attention returned he seemed determined to push away the tension.

'How's Tilly?'

Geordie felt the smile fade into something more natural. 'She's a devil,' he said. 'I miss her.'

'What about Marion? How is she now?'

'I haven't spoken to her since Christmas, but I suppose she must be doing all right. Hard to lose someone you love, though, she'll still be reeling from it.'

'No, well, yes, but I mean after the accident.'

Geordie, who had been glancing across at Gwenna to make sure she was all right, came back to his brother with a slight frown. 'What accident?'

'The ice,' Stephen said. 'The . . . you know, the slip.'

'I didn't know about it. What happened, was it bad?' Geordie stiffened. 'What about Tilly?'

185

'Tilly's fine; she's with Gracie. That's how I know about it.'

Geordie felt tension crawling through him again; there was something about Stephen's expression that said there was more. 'What happened?' he repeated.

'Marion went out to get coal, so Gracie wrote. It was early, still dark. There was black ice on the path and she went down awkward. Broke her leg.' Stephen shook his head sadly. 'And she lost the baby.'

'*Baby?*' Geordie stared. 'Christ. She never told me.'

'She would have done, when she was ready. It explains why Lawton's daughter was so keen to get her out of the house though. They won't want that kind of scandal.'

Geordie's hand curled into a fist on the table. 'If Marion hadn't been thrown out, she'd not have been out fetching coal in the dark. That baby would still—'

'You can't blame the Lawtons,' Stephen cautioned. 'Stamp out that fuse, Geordie.' He sat back. 'Tilly wanted to come to you, but Marion said she had to stay at school, so Gracie's took her in at the farm instead.'

Geordie was about to reply when he saw Stephen's eyes once more steal across to where the convict, Davis, was talking to his visitor. There was visible strain there now; the visitor, a man of a similar age, was becoming agitated, and Davis was reacting in kind, leaning forward, hard grey eyes glinting.

Geordie looked over his shoulder to where the guard was standing, and saw he'd noted the change in Davis's demeanour and his stance had become less relaxed, though he made no move yet. He became aware that others had noted the tightening atmosphere, and his own heartbeat quickened without any real reason. Nothing had happened, but he suddenly understood

Stephen's description of *something brewing*. It was a feeling. Based on little evidence, but impossible to ignore.

He looked across the room again, to where Gwenna sat with her father; a pleasant looking man with grey streaks in his dark hair, and an alert manner, his hand stretching across the table to cover his daughter's. He too was looking nervously at Davis, and then at various other tables dotted around the room. Many of the visitors were wives, girlfriends, or mothers, but each one that Rosdew's gaze fell on, Geordie noted, was male; some older than the person they were visiting, some much younger, but none of them behaving as if they cared for that person, and all of them were flicking glances left and right. Geordie's instincts were shouting now. He half-rose, but felt Stephen's fingers twist savagely in his sleeve, urging him to sit. To be still. Unnoticed.

The natural ripple of conversation across the room became fractured; the comfortable, level hum replaced by protracted silences from some areas, and sharp retorts from others. Always from those troublesome tables. The words themselves were indecipherable to Geordie, and were no doubt innocuous anyway, or the guards would have intervened. But there was no denying that those guards were alerted by the sudden movements, tight whispers, and the same low buzz of urgency that Geordie could feel like a physical thing, deep in the pit of his stomach. He had to get Gwenna out. Now.

Too late: Davis was out of his chair, leaning across his table and grasping his visitor's coat collar. A few tables away a chair fell heavily, the sound cutting through the sudden hush and setting already simmering nerves alight. A heavy-set guard took a few steps towards Davis's table, and Davis lashed out, catching him on the side of the head and sending him staggering sideways into the table immediately alongside Stephen's.

Geordie leaned sideways to avoid being struck as the man fell, and felt Stephen's hand yanked away from his coat sleeve with some force; he looked up to see his brother being pulled away by another guard, who was hissing something into his ear as he twisted Stephen's hands up behind his back. Stephen shook his head at Geordie, and gave him an apologetic look, as he acquiesced without a struggle. Geordie pushed himself to his feet, seeking out Gwenna in the far corner; she too was up, and looking towards the door, and her father was holding her arm to stop her from bolting while he scanned the room for the safest route.

Prisoners and visitors alike had taken advantage of the scuffle, and the room now erupted into what could only be described as a brawl. Guards moved among the tables and upturned chairs, wielding sticks and delivering sharp, controlled blows upon those in prison clothing, pushing others away with bellowed orders. Most of the women visitors had been corralled into a little group by two guards, who were ushering them towards the door. Geordie saw that Jonas had made his decision, and was urging Gwenna to keep behind him as he made his way along the room, hugging the wall as they went. They made it just under halfway before a knot of men staggered into them, and when Jonas thrust them angrily away he was rewarded with a fist in the side that sent him to the floor.

Geordie gave a shout that was swallowed up in the general rising racket, and pushed his way through, trying to get to them both before Jonas was trampled under the boots of the struggling men. As he reached them, and dropped to a crouch to help lift the gasping Jonas to his feet, he realised this particular brawling group was not as it seemed.

From his vantage point, on the ground and looking up, he saw a very calm and deliberate exchange taking place only a few feet away between a visitor and a prisoner. While shouting and shoving at shoulder level were doing their work of distraction, a small, wrapped package was being carefully transferred from the visitor to the prisoner, who bent his leg without betraying the movement with his upper body, and pushed the package down into his boot. Some kind of blade; short but deadly, and easily concealed. Geordie realised this must have been happening all over the room, and had been planned from the start. He felt cold at the thought that Stephen was in the presence of something so potentially deadly, from which he couldn't possibly distance himself.

He pulled Jonas upright. 'I was the one who brought Gwenna here. Are you all right?'

Jonas nodded, still looking slightly dazed. Then he blinked himself back to reality, grabbed Gwenna's shoulders and planted a kiss on her temple before pushing her towards Geordie. 'Get her out, for God's sake. Go on!'

Geordie looked around for his brother and found him being held firmly, at arm's length and against the wall, by the same guard who'd pulled him back from the fray. It didn't appear that he was being ill-treated, and Geordie breathed a little more freely and turned his mind to his own situation. He had to get Gwenna out, but he couldn't let what he'd seen go unreported; there were new weapons in the prison now, and while he was sure that this wasn't whatever Stephen had said was brewing, it was undoubtedly part of it. He started towards a warder who had just broken apart a tussling pair of convicts, but who hadn't yet launched himself back into the thick of things.

'Geordie!'

Stephen was looking at him over the guard's shoulder, fixing him with a look of desperation, and he shook his head minutely. Geordie understood what he was saying; if the guards were alerted to what was really going on, anyone not involved would come under fire from those who were. And what brutal fire that would be, especially now. It sat uneasily with him, but for Stephen's sake there was no other option. He gave a brief, reluctant nod, and put a hand on Gwenna's back, keeping her between himself and the wall as he followed Jonas's intended path to the door.

When they emerged into the yard they were assaulted by icy, lashing rain, which instantly plastered their hair to their heads and brought them both out of their respective dazes. Other visitors who'd been unceremoniously ejected from the building were huddled beneath the granite archway, waiting to see if they could go back in once the disturbance had been dealt with, but Geordie couldn't see there was any hope of that. The visit was over, and the prison would more than likely be locked down now. He battled with his conscience again, but only for a second; everyone had seen him sitting with Stephen, he couldn't risk the reprisals, and it wasn't his risk to take in any case. All this would happen whether he called attention to it or not, and even if every weapon was seized now, many more would still find their way into this hellish place.

He led the way to the van at a run, and he and Gwenna sat for a while, watching the rain bounce off the windscreen and the bonnet and turn the grey façade of the prison into something blurred and indistinct. Harmless.

'Did you manage to talk much?' Geordie asked.

'Some.' Gwenna squeezed rainwater from her hair. 'Enough to know that only one person's been telling me the truth about that place, and it wasn't my mother.'

Geordie digested this, and how it must feel. He felt a surge of sympathy for the girl. 'Will he tell her you've visited, do you think?'

'I didn't have time to tell him not to. Or to ask him not to tell her what happened.'

'I wouldn't think he'd tell her about that, if he didn't have to.' Geordie started the engine. 'But it might be best if you come clean about the visit, at least.'

'I think I might have to,' she agreed, but her voice sounded distant, as if her thoughts were taking her on a journey beyond that confession. He glanced at her again, before he put the car into gear and pulled away. She wasn't staring out of the side window, as he'd expected; she was looking at the prison. There was an oddly speculative look on her face, which vanished as she shook her head in a seemingly unconscious gesture and made some bland comment about the rain easing up.

Swallowing his curiosity, he murmured an equally noncommittal response, and guided the van through the yard, past the many disconsolate, and visibly shaken, friends and relatives. When he drove past the school at Peter Tavy, Gwenna spoke up again.

'I thought you were going to see Tilly.'

'I'll still try, but it's Marion I need to see now.' He ignored her slight frown, and was glad when, instead of questioning him further, she stared out of the window at the hills that hid the quarry on their other side. His chest tightened at memory of his younger brother, then aged around twelve, standing atop Foggintor and declaring himself *King of the Moor*, while Geordie, Gracie and Marion had looked on, laughing and out of breath after the chase. He stared fixedly ahead, willing away the unfamiliar sting of tears. Stephen might have been the King of the Moor when he was twelve, and not one of them would have argued it, but he would never be anything but its captive now.

CHAPTER NINETEEN

Lynette took Mack out for a gentle hack across Pencarrack Moor, once the rain had passed on its way eastwards. Much as she enjoyed Tory's company, it was good to get away for an hour or two, and give herself time to think. Ever since her decision to delay telling Geordie about Marion's pregnancy, she had been feeling the guilt chewing away at her. She had written to Lawton's son and daughter, sending both letters to Colleybrooke Manor, on the assumption that they would eventually reach both parties, and had used every reasoned persuasion tactic she could think of. First appealing to their emotions, and then to the legalities, of which she was completely in the dark, but she felt certain something must surely be due to the common-law widow with a child on the way.

Despite telling herself as much, she was wholly unsurprised to find she'd had no replies after over two weeks, and now, she had to admit, it was probably time to tell Geordie. She quailed inside at the thought of it. Both admitting she'd known all this time, and then discovering what he was likely to do about it. She had the awful, sinking feeling that she knew exactly what he'd do, and worst of all that she wouldn't be able to talk him out of it because it was, without doubt, the only thing he could do. The only thing he *should* do.

Feeling tired and disheartened, and with darkness approaching, she turned Mack towards home, but couldn't even take pleasure from giving him his head along the moor. Feeling the vibrations thundering up through her was just making her head hurt, and she quickly reined him in and completed the remaining distance at a walk. She had just finished cleaning him down when she heard the van out in the yard, and she glanced out through the stable's half door to see Geordie getting out of the driver's seat and stretching out his limbs after the long drive.

It was impossible to read his expression in the thin light from the outside lamp, so she had no idea how the visit had gone, and she carried on brushing Mack's glossy bay coat, murmuring to him, and hoping Geordie had found something today to ease his worries about his brother. Particularly after what Gracie had said. It helped to distract her from what was to come, and from trying to work out how to word it.

'Are you sure you won't take a lift home?' Geordie called, and looking again, Lynette saw Gwenna getting out of the passenger seat. 'I can put your bicycle in the back.'

'No, but thanks. I don't want Mum to ask any questions.'

'Sorry we're a bit later than we planned.'

Gwenna shook her head. 'It's kind of you to have taken me. And—' she hesitated with one hand on the van door '—thank you for . . . you know. Everything. And for agreeing not to tell Mum.'

'I still think you should at least tell her where you've been,' Geordie said, but Gwenna shook her head.

'I will, but not today. Good luck,' she added, nodding towards the flat. She untied her bicycle from the iron ring in the wall, and then she was gone, while Lynette stood still, trying to calm the unease that was curling through her. What did Gwenna mean by *good luck*? And what exactly was she thanking him for?

Mack stamped impatiently as she stopped mid-stroke, and she completed the brushing, listening to Geordie climbing the steps to the flat above her, and knocking at the door. There was no reply, since Tory was at her mother's surgery helping to move some furniture around, but Lynette didn't want to step out and announce her presence just a few feet from where that odd little conversation had taken place; the moment for that had passed. She would have to pretend now, that she hadn't known he was even back, so she moved across to Hercules's stall and busied herself near the back.

Geordie's footsteps came closer to the stable, and stopped by Mack's door. 'Look at you, handsome lad,' he said. His voice was soft, low, but a little broken. 'Want to go for a ride tomorrow?' He let out a sigh. 'I think I need it as much as you do.'

Lynette stepped back into Mack's stall and saw Geordie had his forehead pressed against Mack's long nose and he was smoothing the horse's neck with long, slow strokes; the kind that always comforted the giver as much as the receiver. Her heart sank. She moved into his line of vision, and he immediately straightened and gave her a perfunctory smile. A greeting, nothing more.

'How was Stephen?' she asked, hoping she'd imagined the coolness.

Geordie looked steadily at her, and she felt another tremor of unease. Had he come to tell her he'd fallen for Gwenna? That over their difficult day together he'd discovered she had more depth than Lynette could ever possess? They were both aware that his initial reaction to Lynette had been an instinctive attraction to something pretty but shallow, and although he'd quickly learned his mistake, the memory of that was still there. Still niggling.

'I need to talk to you,' he said at length. 'Where's Tory?'

She told him. 'The flat'll be empty for a couple of hours yet,' she added, not sure whether that was a good thing. His eyes held hers for a moment longer, and she tried to remember how beautiful she usually found them, but today they were clouded with mistrust.

'What's wrong?' she asked, coming out through the half door and patting Mack as she passed. 'Is . . . is it Gwenna?'

'What? No, nothing to do with her.' He did look gratifyingly surprised by the notion, which helped a little, but he still held himself distant as she turned off the outside light, and Lynette was hit by another wave of dismay. It was hard to be so close to him, and to know that if she tried to touch him he would more than likely pull away.

They went into the flat, where he shrugged out of his wet coat and threw it across the back of the sofa. He pulled his hat off and twisted it in his hands, evidently not sure how to say what had soured his mind against her. He'd clearly been caught in a downpour at some point; his hair had curled in all directions as it had dried, and it was sticking to his forehead, making him look youthful, but still tired and unhappy.

'Come on then,' she said, affecting a brisk tone to hide her fears. 'Out with it, I'm not a child.' He flinched visibly at that, and she drew a quick breath. 'Is Tilly all right?'

'Tilly's fine. I saw her at school.'

'Oh, good.' She sat on the arm of the sofa and stared up at him. 'What, then?'

'Why didn't you tell me Marion was pregnant?'

Lynette froze. After all her agonising, it was too late. 'Because . . .' She stopped. 'Because it was none of our business,' she finished. It sounded weak, but it was better than the real reason.

'What the hell do you mean, *none of our business?*' Geordie's eyes glinted with an anger she hadn't seen directed at her since the night of the landslide at the clay pit – but this time it wasn't fear that was driving it, and, worse, she knew she was in the wrong. Still, she felt a stirring of her own annoyance.

'I only heard it from your friend Mrs Bellowes,' she said tightly. 'If Marion had wanted to tell me I'm sure she would have. And asked me to pass it on. Since she didn't, I can only assume she didn't want us to know.'

'You didn't tell me *any* of it, though,' Geordie pointed out. 'Not that she'd been thrown out of Colleybrooke, or that our old house was in such poor condition it's dangerous for them to live in now.'

'It was a bit damp,' Lynette protested, 'but Gracie said it would start to dry out once the fires were lit again.'

'It's a death trap,' Geordie said shortly. 'And it's already proved it.'

Lynette stared in horror, her anger vanished. 'What? Who?'

'Marion slipped on the ice, and lost the baby. Tilly's staying at the Martyns' farm for a few days, until she's able to look after her again.'

'Oh.' Lynette slid off the arm of the sofa, onto the cushions. 'Oh, poor Marion.' She looked up at Geordie, and saw that he still hadn't softened. But there was a distance to his anger now, as if it wasn't really directed at her. At fate, perhaps? She hoped so.

'I'm sorry I didn't tell you,' she said, 'but really, it wasn't my news to break.' She put a conciliatory hand out, but he ignored it.

'If I'd known about it, I might have been able to do something about the house for her before she moved back into it.'

'I see that now, but honestly, at the time I thought it would be all right. I've written to Lawton's son and daughter, to see if there was any—'

'You should have said something.' Geordie stepped away. 'I'd have fetched the bloody coal myself. Salted the path . . . *Something!*'

'Or everything?' Lynette stood up, unable to stop herself now. 'Be honest, Geordie, please. You'd have given everything up and gone back there because, when all's said and done, she's still your wife!'

'What?' He looked at her blankly, then his expression closed down. 'So you didn't tell me she was expecting Lawton's child because . . . you were *jealous?*'

'No,' Lynette said, on a heavy sigh, aware of the irony that she was even now turning her own fears into the reality she'd dreaded. 'Because I know you, Geordie Sargent. I know your sense of duty. You'd have worried about Marion's reputation, her money troubles. You're already paying her rent. Which I understand, of course,' she hurried on, seeing his expression darken further. 'You didn't know she'd moved. But you'd have gone back to your family because that's where you belong.'

'Thanks for telling me what I would have done. Maybe you could also tell me how I'd have supported them, if I had? If I leave everything behind here, I'm right back where I was when I left them.' Geordie's voice was cold, and Lynette drew on everything she could to avoid letting her tears fall as she fumbled her way through her reasoning.

'You'd sell the forge. You know you'd get a buyer, now it's a decent business again, and you've re-built its reputation. And the money would be all yours, I wouldn't try to claim any back.' She lifted her head, but was still unable to look him in the eye. Instead, she focused on the dark rectangle of the windowpane, seeing only her own ghostly reflection against the darkness. 'You've got a trade, you've got skills, and you'd have the money to buy another business.'

'Well, you've really thought all this through carefully, haven't you?' Geordie turned away and braced his knuckles on the table. She could see, in the reflection, the tension across his shoulders.

'You'd be nearer Stephen too,' she went on, unable to stop digging their grave with every word. 'Tilly would be thrilled to have you home, and Marion would be spared the embarrassment. I know she still cares for you. You could have passed the baby off as your own, without too many questions.'

There was a long pause. Geordie remained facing away. 'And you wouldn't be asking me to return *any* of the money you put into the forge?'

Lynette felt the first tear trickle onto her cheek. 'No,' she managed. 'I did it for you, not to . . . to keep you here.'

'And how would you feel, if I did go back to Marion? Whether or not she was pregnant?'

Lynette couldn't speak. She wanted to say she would be happy for Geordie, as long as she knew he was where he truly wanted to be. Wasn't that supposed to be the ultimate proof of love? But the words died in her tightened throat and wouldn't come. She went to the window, closing her eyes and pressing her forehead against the cold glass, as if it could freeze the thoughts in her head so she wouldn't have to endure them any more.

She heard him cross the room, and then the rustle as he picked up his coat, and her heart fell heavily at the realisation that he would soon be gone. From this room, certainly, and maybe soon from Pencarrack itself. She jumped as she felt a hand on her arm, and he turned her gently to face him.

'Very well put,' he said, gesturing at the breath that fogged the window, and a faint smile finally touched his eyes. 'I'd feel the same.' He dropped his coat again, and lifted his hands to her face, his thumbs brushing her cheeks. A press of his lips on her forehead removed the lingering doubt, and she sagged against him in relief.

'I'm sorry,' she mumbled against his waistcoat front, feeling his arms go around her. 'I should have told you.'

'You should,' he agreed. 'But Marion's not your responsibility. Nor mine. Tilly is, though, and I'd have wanted to know that she was back in that house.'

Lynette nodded. 'I know. I'm glad she has Gracie to take care of her for a while. I liked her.' She wasn't yet ready to let him go, not after this awful row. 'Will you stay here for a while and tell me about Stephen?'

He sighed. 'I can't. I need to get back to Joe.'

It was perfectly reasonable, but Lynette caught a glimpse of that same bleak expression as she pulled back and looked up at him. 'What's happened?' she asked quietly.

'Nothing, yet. Not really.'

'Not really? What does that mean?' Lynette hated the feeling that he was mentally pulling away from her again, and realised that worry was making her sound shrill. She hoped he didn't hear it as nagging, and was relieved to see nothing but understanding in his eyes.

'Don't worry. Please.' He lowered his lips to hers, and kept her there with the gentlest of touches on her jaw, and as she focused on his slow, steady breathing she drew on the strength and re-assurance his presence always gave her. Gradually the tension began to melt away, replaced by a richer, deeper feeling. A stirring ache that reached for him with blind instinct.

She broke their kiss, and pressed her lips to his throat instead, feeling the pulse there quicken, and the smooth movement of muscle as he lifted his chin to invite her mouth on his skin. She kissed him again, on the clean edge of his jaw, and let her hands slide up across his shoulders to link at the back of his neck. His breathing was becoming shorter now and lighter now. She could feel the rapid rise and fall of his chest against hers, and as her fingers snaked into his hair he gave a soft groan that reached down inside her and flooded her with a fierce and sweet urgency.

He murmured one word. 'Lynette . . .'

She felt the vibration of his voice in every part of her, and every part of her answered it, voiced on a tiny, regret-filled sigh, as she drew on the last ounce of willpower she possessed and stepped back. Her eyes fixed on his, and she saw the flashing desire beneath the half-lowered lids, before the thick dark lashes swept down and hid it a second later.

When he opened his eyes again she could see the flickering remnants of the same passion that still coursed through her own blood, but there was also a wry smile now, which was echoed in the curve of his lips. 'You'll be the death of me,' he said, and the break in his voice very nearly drove her back into his arms.

'That'd be a bit of a shame,' she murmured, and was rewarded by a low, throaty laugh as he held out his hands.

'Come here, and stop misbehaving.'

'You started it,' she reminded him, but she took his hands and allowed him to pull her close again. This time she resisted the urge to bury her face in his shoulder, and instead looked up at him. 'Is Stephen all right?'

Geordie hesitated, then nodded, though his brow was creased and his eyes clouded again. 'I think he's making the right choices in there. I just hope it's enough, when the time comes.'

Lynette wanted to press him on that comment, but knew it was pointless. 'I understand why you have to go,' she said softly, 'but I wish you didn't.'

'So do I.' He squeezed her hands, as if he couldn't trust himself to do anything more, then stepped back with a look of regret that matched her own. 'I'll see you tomorrow.'

She followed his progress across the yard to his van, and then watched the lights until they'd disappeared down the lane and everything was dark again. The memory of the intense longing between them remained, but so too, did the memory of the fearful look in his eyes and while the first had eased her heart more than she'd dared to hope, the second left a chill at the base of her spine that wouldn't go away.

CHAPTER TWENTY

Sunday 24 January

Shouting was commonplace here on E Block, despite the rules; there was always someone being brought in yelling about the injustice of it, or someone being gleefully let out, and determined to let everyone know. Everything had to happen at volume. Daniel clenched his fists tightly and pushed them against his ears, trying to block it out, and, along with it, the forceful acceptance of where he was. Though he freely admitted he would have preferred to stay here rather than go back onto B Block, where Newbury was said to be awaiting his return with something rather more disturbing than just glee.

Ray Beatty had passed along the dark news that Newbury was looking for someone to carry out his revenge, and that Daniel would be lucky to finish his seven years at all; there was no shortage of men who'd be willing to do Newbury's dirty work, in exchange for a recommendation for early release. Now that Daniel's time on segregation was coming to an end he was feeling sicker by the hour, wondering who Newbury had found, whether it was someone he knew and trusted, and how it would happen. In the dark, one night with a chiv, his cell door having been left helpfully open? Or in full view of everyone, tossed over the landing and labelled a suicide? He wouldn't be the first. The pain in his back would be nothing compared to what might be coming; it was almost worth assaulting another officer just to be kept down here. Even another flogging would be the least of his worries . . . He shuddered. No, it wouldn't. He had never known pain like that, and in the days that had followed he'd been convinced he would never heal.

But he was young, and despite the poor diet that delayed healing, his skin had gradually begun to forgive the torture inflicted upon it. Waking in the early hours of that first night he had been so cold he had been certain he would die; his muscles locked, his breathing tight and shallow, and since he had been too cold to feel much of anything he had dragged his blanket over himself, breathing out slowly beneath its shelter to warm his icy skin. He had regretted it for many reasons, but he was able to keep the scratchy material from too much contact with his shredded back, and the jelly-like collodion had begun to do its work.

Today, on what Daniel worked out was a Sunday, the usual shouting had become louder, and of a different kind. There was a heightened intensity about it; doors being kicked and hammered with the flats of hands, and attempts at authoritative bellowing from Warder Tucker and his men that were roundly ignored. It wasn't until Daniel's own door came under the same kind of onslaught that he realised the blows were coming from outside in the corridor, not within the cells.

His heartbeat speeded up and he pressed his face to the gap

that allowed the limited view into the corridor beyond. There were men he recognised from B Hall being brought into the separate cells, and those escorting them were looking boot-faced and grim as they fought to get the prisoners back into line and away from the doors, with shoves and the occasional blow with their batons. These men were not the ones Daniel would have expected to see here; not the known trouble-seekers and agitators, but they were certainly vociferous today.

Two days ago, Thomas Davis, who was currently occupying a cell just down the row from Daniel, had attacked Officer Birch with a razor blade attached to a piece of wood. The place had been in a similar uproar then, and it seemed something else had happened now. Whatever it was, it had resulted in the loudest protestors being brought to the separate cells in order to avoid infecting the rest of the prison population.

The visiting-time disturbance several days ago had seen Ray Beatty down here again for a night. He'd pulled himself to a stop outside Daniel's cell to give him the news. 'Few people got a bit . . . uppity, shall we say.'

'Anyone hurt?'

'One or two. No one badly.' Ray was jerked forward by the chain on his cuffs, and still managed to shoot Daniel another grin. 'Don't worry though, lad, your cellmate was well taken care of.'

Something about his grin had become hard then, and Daniel's heartbeat had snagged as he watched Beatty being pushed towards an empty cell; there was a new coldness there that he didn't like.

Whatever had happened back then had clearly not dissipated the tension, Daniel could feel it still thrumming in the air like unspent electricity. He didn't retreat to his bunk, but paced his cell, trying to walk off the sudden energy that was radiating through his limbs. He picked up word that, for some reason, the officers had recommended exercise be cancelled for that day, but that Governor Roberts had decreed it should go ahead. As Daniel's pacing brought him up against the wall, he struck the concrete in envy and frustration; he would have welcomed the opportunity to get outside, especially now that there was no Newbury to sour the air.

Despite his desire to drive away the building pressure, he soon tired. He'd been nearly three weeks in chokey now, and moved onto number two diet, but eight ounces of bread twice a day, porridge, and a pound of potatoes, was bloating, draining, and debilitating. He'd felt ill and listless for days, and although his heart and mind were racing at full speed, he lacked the energy to work it off. He sank down onto his bunk, let his head fall forward, his wrists hanging limp and lifeless between his knees, and willed his mind into a state of blank darkness.

It took a moment, therefore, to realise that the new voice he was hearing, through those fuzzy shadows, was coming directly into his cell from a mouth pressed right against the letter-box shape in the door. It was murmuring his name, and because it was pitched low, beneath the general racket, it finally filtered through and brought Daniel to his feet again.

'Stephen?' He went to the door, on legs that felt unsteady and disconnected from the rest of him. 'Why are *you* here? What did you do?'

'Nothing. Warder Tucker's ... distracted. Listen.' There was a brief moment of silence, during which Daniel questioned his own senses; was Stephen actually there? Then his cellmate spoke again. 'I have to ask you this, and think before you answer. Really *think*.' Another pause. 'Do you want to get out?'

Daniel almost laughed at the absurdity of the question, but forced himself to heed Stephen's caution. 'Yes. Why?'

'Because in there you're safe. And I don't just mean from what's going on, I mean from what comes after.'

'What *is* going on?'

'Mutiny,' Stephen said shortly. 'The prisoners are running the place. Warder Tucker and his lot have run for it. I can unlock this door, and let you take your chances, but if you're caught I can't help you. And I won't try,' he added, his tone leaving no room for question.

A giddy relief swamped Daniel, and now he did laugh. 'Yes, I want you to let me out. I mean, what can they do to me that they're not already planning?'

'That's the only reason I'm here. But you have to swear you won't give up my name if you don't make it all the way out.'

'Of course I won't. You have my word.'

'Good. Now listen. Remember what we discussed, about the warders' housing behind A block? Well, right now there's no one guarding it; the warders are all trying to save themselves. Well, most of them,' he amended. 'A few are at the gate, and a few others trying to put out the fire in the admin block, but someone's wrecked the fire engine so I don't hold out a lot of hope for that. With any luck, your records'll be so much ash by now.'

Daniel placed both shaking hands on the cold iron door. 'Are you coming too?'

'No. And if you weren't facing Newbury's goons I wouldn't let you out, either. It's too risky.'

'How did you get that key?'

'Just be glad I did.' There was the blessed sound of the key in the lock, and the door shifted in its frame, but only a fraction, and Stephen didn't open it. 'Wait until after I'm gone,' he muttered, 'and take this.' He pushed a piece of paper through the slit in the door. 'Head for Foggintor Quarry, if you can. Lie low there for the day, then get yourself to Peter Tavy after dark. It's all on the note. Don't speak to anyone, don't come looking for me, and . . .' he gave a short laugh, '*don't* get caught. Good luck.'

'Wait!' Daniel fought the urge to pull open the door as Stephen started away. 'If you're not there to boost me up, where do I get a ladder?'

A quick, impatient sigh came from the other side of the door. 'Try the fire station. I don't care how many of you use it to get out, but you're better off alone once you are, so shake off anyone who latches on. Look,' he went on, urgently now, 'Ruby Sparks and his mob have already let Davis out, and they'll be back looking for more to join them. You need to be gone by the time they remember the rest of you, or you'll be dragged into whatever they do next.'

Then he really was gone, and Daniel stood in bemused disbelief, halfway back to believing he'd imagined the whole thing. He stayed pressed against the door, not wanting to draw attention to it until he was ready, then, as he heard voices in the outer office, he realised he was in danger of missing his chance. He stooped to pick up Stephen's note and shoved it into his pocket, then eased the door open, immediately drawing a shout from the man in the cell opposite, who'd evidently had his eye glued to his own window on the world. Daniel ignored him and allowed the shout to simply blend in with all the others. A few moments later, when Sparks and his swelling gang came in, he was already poised behind the door. Conning, who'd managed to get hold of a trilby from somewhere and looked like a spiv of the lowest order, tossed the keys to Sparks and pointed at the still-occupied separate cells.

'Get cracking then!'

Daniel's heart was hammering too fast, making him feel light-headed, and he prayed none of the mob would turn and see him, but to his relief they were all focused entirely on the rows of rooms in front of them. He slipped around the door, finding the office thankfully empty, and made his escape out into the yard. He blinked at the unexpectedly bright sun, which was then momentarily blocked by a cloud of greasy-looking black smoke that belched from the administration block. His mind shifted, and clicked into a place where he could think more clearly. Where there was fire, there would be reinforcements – this new disturbance was a full-blown riot, one that could no longer be contained and dealt with by the officers here.

He tried to remember where the fire station was situated within the prison grounds; it wasn't anything he'd concerned himself with before. Men were running in all directions, many seemed to be heading towards the kitchens, and for a minute Daniel was tempted to follow; the thought of food made his hollowed-out belly growl and ache. But there was no time. He stood still and closed his eyes, trying to picture the day he'd come in, where he'd been taken, what he'd seen. He'd seen precious little since, except B Hall, the parade ground, and now the fabled chokey.

He thought the fire station might be beyond the administration block, and had just set off quickly in that direction when he saw a ladder up against the wall, below where he knew Governor Roberts's office to be. He slowed, looking around to see if it was in use; the last thing he needed now was to be beaten up by a fellow convict. His heart speeded up as he recognised Ray Beatty in a throng of men coming out of the block, and he put two fingers into his mouth and whistled to get his attention.

The whole group turned to look, but only Ray broke away and came over. His face was red, and he was panting, but his eyes were alight. 'All right, lad? Sparks get you out, then?'

Daniel was about to correct him, then nodded instead. 'Yeah. How did all this start?'

'If I said porridge, would you believe me?'

Daniel wanted to laugh, but he was too tense and just shook his head. 'Come on.'

'I'm not joking,' Ray said. 'Believe me, porridge *was* part of it. It'll all come out in the news.'

'But you got weapons smuggled in?'

Ray shrugged. 'All part of that visiting time shenanigans. Worth every minute spent on the block.'

Daniel remembered his disquiet about that day. 'What did you mean about Stephen Sargent being taken care of?'

'Nothing much.' Ray shrugged, his expression cagey again. 'Just that Finegan made sure he wasn't dragged into anything. But his brother got well stuck in, from what I could see. Pulled a girl out. Rosdew's visitor.' This time his grunt was more appreciative. 'Pretty piece, an' all. Lovely long dark hair.'

'Never mind that. You looked like you meant—'

'Forget it.' Ray turned away, and followed Daniel's sightline. 'You going over?'

'Worth a try.'

'Good. I'll come with you.'

'If you get caught you'll get years added on,' Daniel reminded him. 'Is it worth the risk?'

'Can you carry that ladder by yourself?' Ray ducked out of the way as a missile of some kind flew past them. It looked like a dinner bowl, and the absurdity of it all struck Daniel once again. From brawling with matelots in Devonport, to standing here ducking flying crockery ... Madness.

'Well?' Ray demanded. He strode over to the ladder and shook it. 'Come on. You take this end.'

'Which way do we go?' Daniel seized the bottom of the ladder and pulled it so it slid down the wall.

Ray grabbed the top before it hit the ground. 'C Parade,' he said. 'There's a gate between inner and outer walls, and better to only poke our heads up the once, don't you think? Don't want to push our luck.' He jerked his head towards the wall. 'Well, come on then, don't be all day!'

They jogged back past the admin block, and through the exercise yard by C Hall, where they found the now-unmanned gate between the two walls. Daniel's spirits lifted, and he began to allow himself to hope this might work, after all. They located the spot beyond which lay the warders' houses, then lifted the ladder together and let it drop back against the wall, still unable to believe they had come this far unchallenged. But they knew the really dangerous part was still to come.

Down here, between the perimeter walls, they had been just another two scurrying figures taking advantage of the lack of guards – albeit with the means of escape slung between them. But they were far from the only ones. Once they were on the ladder, however, they would be exposed, and clearly making an escape attempt, which gave officers the right to shoot. It was a sobering thought, and Daniel's courage almost failed him, until he remembered what awaited him should he stay.

'Last chance to change your mind,' he said, his feet itching to set themselves on the rungs. 'I've got nothing to lose. You've got everything.'

'Get up that bloody ladder, boy,' Ray grinned. He looked younger than Daniel had ever seen him; fired with determination and the thrill of the adventure to come. 'Unless you want me to go first?'

Daniel grasped the sides of the ladder, took the deepest breath he could manage, and put his foot on the first rung. After that he had no idea how long it actually took, just that it felt like hours. But as he crawled onto the top of the narrow outer perimeter wall he felt a wild sense of freedom that threatened to derail his common sense; he wasn't even halfway there yet, what was he thinking? The warders' housing ran at a right angle off the outer wall, and from where he lay he saw they'd come up several feet short of the end house.

He turned back to see that Ray had begun his ascent, and a second later both of them cried out in shock as a section of the wall a few feet away exploded into dust and stone chips. Daniel jerked his head around and saw an armed officer on a building roof taking aim again; the gun was a short-barrelled Snider carbine, one of those which Stephen had told him were used to guard the men on outside duty. He'd also said they were notoriously inaccurate, but that wouldn't stop the guard from being lucky.

He leaned down to call to an equally startled-looking Ray. 'Guard's on the roof of the French Prison. Hurry it up!'

Ray began to climb faster, and another shot rang out, sounding clearly over the roar of the admin block fire – now only one of several – and the incongruously light, tinkling sound of smashing glass. The wall right beside Ray splintered again, and Ray's

212

hand came off the ladder in shock; for a moment Daniel was sure he'd been hit, but his friend recovered himself and resumed his panicky journey.

'Get gone!' he shouted as he climbed. 'Don't hang about waiting for me!'

'Give me your hand.' Daniel leaned down and stretched out his arm. He realised his hand was damp with sweat, and he quickly pulled it back up again and blotted it on his jacket before reaching out again. If he hadn't done so, his hand would have been blown off by a third shot, but, as it was, that bullet came so close to Ray's head that the older man jerked, slipped, and lost his grip on the ladder. He swung one-handed for a moment, with Daniel grunting in dismay and stretching down even further, in an attempt to snag his coat. The fourth shot struck true. Daniel saw Ray's trouser leg jump and twitch, and blood began to seep through the rough material, midway down his calf. Ray gave Daniel one last, shocked and pleading look, and then he was plummeting the last few feet to the ground.

His cry came to an abrupt halt as he landed on his back between the walls, and his expression lost its shock and collapsed instead into a grimace of pain. 'Get gone,' he said again, pulling himself to a sitting position and clutching at his calf. 'I'll be all right.'

Daniel battled with his conscience, but only for a moment. If he stayed, he would die. It was that simple. 'I'm sorry,' he called down, hoping Ray understood how deeply he meant it. 'I hope you—'

'Go!'

Daniel saw the officer readying his carbine again and spun away, wriggling snake-like to present a harder target. The wall seemed narrower than ever, and it was taking a great deal of concentration not to roll off; no matter which side he landed, he'd be killed. His heart sank, as he sized up the jump between the wall and the house and realised he'd underestimated it badly. He'd have to get a good run-up, which meant he would be outlined against this unseasonably bright sky for a crucial few seconds, long enough for the guard to draw a bead on him. He might have been good at PT once, and well trained by the navy, but that wasn't what would decide his fate now; malnutrition, muscle-wastage, lack of exercise, and most of all fear, were the things he was fighting. Guilt, too, for leaving Ray, but he had to put that aside for now and trust in his survival instinct to do the rest.

He crawled back to the ladder and cast a look down at Ray, who stared up at him in horror, as if he thought Daniel had returned for him after all. But Daniel just sent him a quick, tight smile and grunted, 'Wish me luck,' then pushed himself upright.

A quick look at the officer on the roof confirmed his fears, and then he could spare no further time or thought for them. He ran, not daring to look down at the impossible feat of balance he was asking of his instincts; propelling himself as fast as he could for the short distance, and then he twisted and launched himself towards the roof. A bullet whined off the wall admirably close to the point he'd jumped from, but a surge of white-hot triumph lit him even as he slammed painfully into the roof and scrabbled for handholds.

The chimney was tantalisingly close, and as his foot found the gutter at the corner, he prayed it would hold long enough for him to inch along until he could grasp the brick column and steady himself. After a breath-stealing crawl, and with both arms now wrapped around the chimney, he risked another glance over his shoulder, and saw the armed officer had gone from the rooftop; he couldn't see down into the space between the two perimeter walls, but he hoped Ray had got himself to where some of the other convicts could help him, before the officer could reach him.

He knew he should have moved off right away, but it was hard to tear himself away from this view over the parade grounds. It was unrecognisable from the regimented, largely silent place he'd come to know over the past two months. There was the fire, of course, and then there were so many men, some dragging ladders, others brandishing iron bars taken from God alone knew where, and some of the convicts were even setting upon fellow prisoners; whether through some long-held grudges, or because some of them were clearly intent on actually helping the officers, it was impossible to tell.

But Daniel didn't have time to think about it. He scrambled, as quickly as he dared, across three roofs before finding a safe place to climb down, and jumped the last few feet to land in a neatly tended garden. His hands stung where he'd scraped the skin off them clinging to the brick work and the roof slates, and his weakened legs almost pitched him to the ground, but a couple of stumbling steps brought him to the wall, where he rested a moment, breathing hard and trying to ignore the raw scraping of his shirt across his back.

He threw a look towards the window of the house, saw no movement inside, and judged it safe to leave by the gate, but after that he found himself stumped. Where was it that Stephen had directed him? He had minutes, perhaps, before someone came after him, and he had no idea which way to go that wouldn't deliver him straight back to the entrance in his distinctive, arrow-covered coat and trousers. First things first, then.

He ducked down behind the garden wall, peeled off his coat and turned it inside out, then did the same with his trousers; it wouldn't fool anyone for more than a moment, but at least he wouldn't stand out quite so much. There was nothing he could do about his boots, and he wasn't going to give those up. As he pulled his reversed coat more tightly about himself he heard the crackle of paper in the pocket, and, still crouching behind the wall, he fished for Stephen's note. It was scribbled and rough, obviously written in a hurry, on headed paper taken from Warden Tucker's desk, but he was able to read it well enough.

> Quarry. West, straight across moor. When dark go NW to Peter Tavy. Cudlip Frm. Show this ltr to Gracie. Will help you.

A quick outline sketch with a clearly marked X, showed the position of the farm, and below it was another message, still hurriedly scrawled but with more care taken over the words.

> Please help Daniel to reach Geordie, his life depends on it, and we depend on you. Forgive me for taking the coward's path in this. My heart is yours. S.

Daniel rose slowly from the shelter of wall and looked around, his chest tight with trepidation, his hand shaking as it pushed the letter back into his pocket. The day was bright, there would soon be constabulary arriving from Tavistock, maybe even Plymouth, and likely military assistance from Crownhill. The whole area would soon be teeming with armed officers of one kind or another, and the opportunities for getting far enough across the moor to evade those trained to search were fast running out; there would be dogs, men on horseback, police cars, and, he reminded himself, plenty of civilians too, keen to do their bit to keep their homes safe. There was no way of knowing how many other prisoners had breached the wall before Daniel had done so, or how many would come after, and every one of them would be desperate enough to give up a fellow prisoner, in pursuit of their own freedom.

Daniel looked up at the wintry sun, and found himself grateful for it after all, as he took his bearings from it. He would have to cross the main road to get onto the right stretch of moor, and to avoid going through the village of Princetown itself he would first have to retreat to the northeast for a distance. Only then would it be safe to venture close to the road, seize his chance, and strike out west. He sent yet another silent apology to Ray, and his thanks to Stephen, and then he turned his back on Princetown and began to run.

CHAPTER TWENTY-ONE

Gwenna had been constantly turning over in her mind the notion that had been growing there ever since New Year's Eve, and which she was relieved to find had only been slightly shaken by her visit to the prison. She was still almost certain it was the right one, but first she had to be sure she'd thought of everything, because she knew that as soon as she mentioned it to her mother she'd have to prove she'd done so. She'd sat slumped at the counter each day, resting her chin on one hand, the other hand doodling across the shop's order pad and turning it into a mass of swirls that spread across the page while she'd taken stock of things as they stood.

She had no skill she could readily turn into a wage; her sewing was average at best; her cleaning, the same; her baking . . . better not discussed. She wasn't skilled with horses, like Tory, or a trained telephonist, as Bertie had once been. She could apply for work at the hotel, she supposed, but she knew she wouldn't last more than a week of being shouted at and blamed for things, before walking out. Better to save herself, and the hotel staff, the trouble. Farming held no interest for her, and they were family-run anyway – around here, that left very little beyond mending nets in Porthstennack, or gutting fish.

She remembered the terror that had taken over her life as she'd been pulled deeper and deeper into Barry Hocking's ever-tightening smuggling ring; how there had been no hope for her, at the end, but to disappear from England altogether and to take her chances wherever her running feet took her. Only her friends had been able, and willing, to put their own safety at risk and save her, and it was only thanks to them that she was free and not locked away up in Holloway. Yes, she decided, she'd come to the right conclusion, and now it was time to talk to her mother. Which meant she would have to start by coming clean about the prison visit.

She'd chosen her moment on Thursday evening, knowing she wouldn't sleep until her mind had been emptied of all the possible ways she might broach the subject. It was almost bedtime however, before she had summoned the courage, partly because her mother was clearly already on edge over something, and had been all day. But it had to be done, and just as Gwenna had shifted forward in her chair, ready to tell the truth, Rachel had produced an envelope from inside the book she'd been reading, and held it up to show her.

Gwenna had stared at it in dismay as she sat back again. Her father was probably only checking she hadn't suffered from her short, violent introduction to his circumstances, but he had certainly wasted no time, and now Rachel would think Gwenna had intended to keep it a secret forever. She'd eyed the envelope as if she could read the handwriting through it, and waited for the axe to fall.

Rachel drew out the letter but didn't unfold it. 'You remember when we lived in St Austell, I had a very good friend who moved away?'

Gwenna had been momentarily thrown, and then nodded. 'Glenys?'

'Gladys.' Rachel had fidgeted with the letter. 'The thing is, she's getting married, and I've been invited to the wedding. I'd really like to go.'

Gwenna had still been trying to adjust to this out-of-the-blue conversational turn. 'Of course you should go.' Then she'd felt a rush of relief. 'Oh, *that's* who the letter is from!'

'Did you think it was from your father?' Rachel had smiled gently. 'I know I've been waiting for a visiting order, and maybe your name *will* be on it too, but he hasn't sent it yet. Don't worry, he'll do it soon.'

No, he won't. Gwenna had hoped the guilt didn't show on her face; Jonas wouldn't be due another visit for weeks now. But at least there was something here to distract Rachel from wondering about it, at least for a little while.

'It'll be nice for you to see your friend again. When's the wedding?'

'Monday afternoon.' Rachel had given her an apologetic look. 'In Birmingham. I'll be gone for several days, and it would mean leaving you with the shop to look after on your own.' That explained the tension, at least.

'It's very short notice for you,' Gwenna had said, 'but of course you should go.'

'I've been putting off asking you,' Rachel confessed. 'The letter actually came two weeks ago. Gladys has sent me the train fare, too.'

Gwenna remembered seeing the letter, and had smiled at her

mother's nervousness. 'If Gladys is paying for it, you can't possibly refuse. I'll manage perfectly well, don't worry.' It would actually be a welcome stretch for her, taking over the running of the shop for a few days instead of just plodding around doing as she was told. And woe betide Nigel Stibson if he came within ten feet of the place, with her in charge.

Gwenna had wondered if now was the perfect time to break her own bit of news, but seeing the new glow in her mother's eyes had made her think again; there would be time enough when this wedding and the accompanying, much-deserved little holiday was over. In the meantime it wouldn't hurt to go and see Sergeant Brewer, and see what he had to say on the subject, and ask him to direct her to where she might enquire about training. As relieved as she was that his lazy, disinterested predecessor, Sergeant Couch, had moved on, she had no idea whether Brewer's mind was closed to idea that women might serve the law. She was ready with her reasons, whichever way he responded.

She had taken her mother to the station in time to catch the train to Plymouth on Saturday night, and it was mid-morning on Sunday before she was able to get up to see the police sergeant. As she walked up the hill she rehearsed what she would say, but by the time she pushed open the door to the police house she was a bundle of nerves, already anticipating an incredulous response; a dry pointing-out that she had come close to being arrested herself, not so long ago, so what hope might she have of being selected for such a role? She had all her arguments and reasons rehearsed and ready, having written them out and read through them over and over again, until they sounded both natural and logical, and she was sure that even the most sceptical audience would be unable to deny the sense of it.

She was dressed in her most business-like clothing; practical and not overly feminine, and had tied her hair back in a tight knot, hidden beneath a plain hat. Even her gloves were plain black, and she pulled one of them off, as she marched up the pathway to the front door. She rapped her bare knuckles on the door to the inner office, and Sergeant Brewer barked an instruction to come in. He was seated at his desk, tapping a pen irritably against an open ledger. 'Morning, Miss . . . Rosdew?'

'Yes,' Gwenna confirmed. 'I was wondering if I might—'

'More trouble?' He half-rose.

'No, I just—'

'Shop all right?'

'The shop is perfectly all right, thank you. Could I please ask you something?'

Brewer re-seated himself and gestured to the chair opposite, and Gwenna sat down, a little rattled by the policeman's abrupt manner, and almost all her carefully prepared notes collapsed as she struggled to picture the notebook where she'd written them.

'I know at first glance I probably don't seem the ideal candidate,' she began, 'but maybe that's actually a good thing. I mean, who better?' She saw his blank look, and tried again. 'Sorry, I was wondering if you could direct me towards the right way of applying to become a—'

The telephone blared, and Brewer held up a hand to Gwenna before snatching the receiver off the hook. 'Brewer. Caernoweth.'

He listened, while Gwenna played over what she'd just said, feeling her insides cringe as she heard the mess again. Then she realised that Brewer had been looking at her oddly and had quickly re-focused his attention on the telephone. He barked a couple of questions, thanked the caller, then replaced the receiver and linked his hands on the desk.

'Your father is currently serving his sentence in Dartmoor, correct?'

Gwenna nodded, unnerved by the look on his face, which was hard to decipher. Part tension, perhaps, and part uncertainty. 'Why?'

'That was Crownhill Barracks. A friend of mine ...' He seemed poised to say more, then shook his head and stood up. 'I need you to leave, Miss Rosdew.' He gestured, politely open-handed, to the door. 'Someone will be in touch in due course.'

'What?' Gwenna's heart gave a painful twist. 'What's going on?'

'Can't say too much,' Brewer said, then he relented. 'Bit of trouble at the prison.'

'Again?'

'Beg pardon?'

'There was a fight during visiting last week.'

'Oh. Well then yes, again.'

'Is my father all right, do you know?' Even as she asked it, she realised it was a foolish question; how would he know that?

'Someone will be in touch with you or your mother, if necessary. Now please ...' He gestured again, this time with more urgency. 'If you wouldn't mind?'

'Why are they calling you?'

'*Please*, Miss Rosdew!'

Gwenna hurried from the room, driven by Brewer's rising voice. As she stood in the hallway, pulling her glove back on, she heard him again, but this time he was the one making the telephone call.

'Miss Gilbert, this is Sergeant Brewer. I'm sorry to trouble you, but is Mr Gale with you, by chance?'

His voice dropped to a low murmur, as if he'd just realised he hadn't heard the outer door closing, and Gwenna couldn't make out anything he was saying. But if he was asking for Bobby it was Watcher business, for sure, and connected to the phone call from his friend at the barracks. There must have been escapes involved then, so presumably constabularies all across the southwest would be alerted.

She stepped out of the police house, fighting a rising fear: what if her father had been one of those foolish enough to try to escape? Or had just been drawn into it somehow, against his will? No one was going to tell her anything, Brewer's reaction had already shown her that much. With that in mind, there was only one thing she could do.

Within ten minutes she had run home, thrown together in an overnight bag everything she thought she might possibly need, and written an apology to tack onto the 'closed' sign for the shop doorway. She thought about that for a moment; her mother wouldn't be happy to return to a whole day's inexplicably lost profits, but a slow day would raise no awkward questions. So Gwenna wrote another note, and wrapped it around the spare key of her new lock.

Dear Tory and Lynette. If either of you has an hour or so to spare tomorrow, please open up the shop for me? I'll be home by teatime. G.

There was no one at the stables, so she posted the note and the key through the door of the flat, and in another five minutes she was driving, as fast as she dared, towards the Devon border.

CHAPTER TWENTY-TWO

Sunday was the only day there was no work done at South Pencarrack Pit. Joe waited until Geordie had left to visit Lynette, then checked the tyres on his bicycle and set off on the back road which led to the north pit; the entrance that had fallen out of use as the workings had begun to spread to the east across the moor. The hills this way were punishing, and Joe's newly healed leg was protesting loudly by the time he arrived, but finally the tall iron gate came into sight. He grunted in relief and pushed the bike out of sight into the hedgerow a short distance away; nobody had ever said they'd seen it there, in all the discussions about who'd been causing the damage, so it was safe to assume the hiding spot was still a good one.

Joe climbed the chained-up gate and braced himself for the pain that would strike when he landed, but as he straddled the top and looked down over the workings, the usual deep well of anger opened up and swamped everything else. He swallowed hard, slid down as far as he could, and when he landed he uttered a low growl that was only part pain.

From the north pit he could see the whole workings: the steeply cut sides, with their deep ledges which would be swarming with workers this time tomorrow; the huge open pits where the clay was left to settle, the long huts that contained the channels where the wet clay was dried and cut. And there, the now-shallow slope where he and his father had been working that night.

The memory of the initially faint, but ominous, rumble would never leave him, and nor would the horrified cries of his father as he'd realised what was happening. Joe had been slower to understand, but every time he came here he relived the unearthly terror he'd felt, as the land itself had begun its unstoppable slide towards them, imprisoning their feet before they'd had chance to move. A split second later they'd been slammed by God knew how many tons of washed-out granite, and although his father had been sheltered by the corrugated tin hut in which he'd stood, his heart and weakened lungs had failed him.

If they'd been able to see where they were working, Joe was certain that his father, an ex-miner, would have recognised the danger before it was too late, but they'd been left without lights, and both new to the job; unaware of the brittle nature of the clay face where they'd been directing the hose. It was all down to the management and their skinflint ways, and every time Joe heard the smashing of newly installed glass he'd felt the savage satisfaction of knowing he'd cost them. Never as dearly as they'd cost him, of course, but maybe when he was older, if the anger kept growing like this, he'd be able to do more. Make them pay more. Maybe that would satisfy his thirst for vengeance, but he doubted it.

He was already looking around for likely stones to stash in his pockets, as he began walking, and he fished in his pocket for his knife, ready to prise any good ones loose. He'd spent some time re-shaping the tip into a shorter, but more functional, shape after he'd discovered the broken tip a couple of weeks ago, hoping Geordie wouldn't see and ask him what had happened to it, and he was glad he'd taken the time now, as he pulled it loose from its sheath and scanned the ground. He passed the settling pits, and had picked up several good-sized rocks by the time he reached the long, low, flat-rod tunnel that would bring him out just above the main yard. He remembered a time when he hadn't had to duck to walk through here, and how he had looked up at his tall, skinny father, who'd had to almost double over, and giggled at the sight.

If he closed his eyes he could imagine being back there again, in those long ago days, and he did so now, but only for a moment, as he felt a tear leak onto his eyelid. He dashed it away in an angry gesture, and passed through the tunnel as quickly as possible. He straightened at the other end, and started towards the office, but his heart leapt in shock when a hard hand closed over his arm and yanked him off the path, and a voice growled in his ear.

'What the bloody hell do you think you're doing?'

The figure was tall, broad-shouldered and dark-haired, and for a second he thought it was Geordie, but the voice was rougher, and as the face swam into view he recognised Bobby Gale. He relaxed, but only a fraction, as Bobby shook him.

'Come on, out with it.'

'I . . . was looking for John Doidge.'

'It's Sunday morning, lad. He'll be at chapel.' Bobby gave him a bright, sunny smile, behind which Joe could see an unusual hardness as the man's gaze dropped to Joe's bulging pockets. 'Try again.'

'I'm . . .' Joe gave up. 'I'm sorry.'

'That's better.' Bobby looked both ways, then gestured into the tunnel. 'Come on, we're going to have a little chat. But not here.'

Joe shuffled miserably back into the tunnel, and he and Bobby made their way up through the site again, where Bobby climbed the gate first and waited on the other side to help Joe down. His hands were gentle as he did so, and one of them rested on Joe's shoulder as he looked down at him. Now his smile was less falsely bright, and there was an emotion there that Joe couldn't interpret, but it was comforting.

'Come on, boy,' Bobby said, and gave him a gentle shove. 'Get your bike and let's go for a walk, shall we?'

Joe pushed his bicycle alongside Bobby as they made their way back towards Pencarrack, though neither spoke for a while; Bobby seemed to be giving Joe time to think about what it would mean, now he'd been found out, and Joe was trying not to. When they came to a recessed gateway he wheeled his bicycle into it and leaned it against the gate.

'Can we get this over and done with?'

Bobby's expression darkened again as his brows came down. 'Over and *done with*?'

'I mean ... you said you wanted to talk,' Joe said. 'And it's pretty chilly out.'

Bobby folded his arms and studied him. 'You want to be somewhere warm and cosy, do you?' Joe sensed a trap and said nothing. 'Somewhere with walls?' Bobby went on. 'Doors? *Windows?*'

Joe sighed. There it was, at last. 'I said I'm sorry.'

Bobby climbed up onto the gate, and patted the top rung beside him. 'Come on.'

Joe scrambled up to perch beside him. Bobby had always been kind to him, and Joe liked spending time with him; he'd been particularly nice at Christmas, when Joe had been so muddled up about Geordie's little girl. He'd understood. Besides, he'd done some things himself that should have got him into hot water but rarely seemed to, so surely he'd understand.

'It's not right that they got away with what they did,' he said quietly. It was easier not having to look Bobby in the eyes; they were a sort of sludgy hazel, but they could still look hard. Or betrayed.

'Nobody got away with anything,' Bobby said, his voice equally soft. 'Don't you go thinking they did. The ones who made those decisions, the ones that got people hurt, and ... and killed,' he said hesitantly, 'they're the ones who went to prison. John Doidge and the others had no part in it, but they're the ones getting into trouble over it all.'

'But the company, Polworra, they—'

'Polworra Consols know they put their trust in the wrong man,' Bobby said. He slipped an arm across Joe's shoulders. ''T'wasn't their fault. They came good in the end, didn't they?'

'When it was too late!'

'Yes, when it was too late.' Bobby squeezed the back of his neck, and shook him gently. 'Life in't fair, lad. You know that better than most. But punishing the people who're trying to make good their mistakes in't the right way to go about making it so. You do understand that? It won't bring your dad back, neither.'

Joe nodded miserably. 'I know. But it made me feel better to see it. And to hear it. It's like I'm telling them how I feel, without having to look at them.'

'Well, now they'll know. So you can stop, can't you?'

'Do you have to tell Geordie it was me?' Joe asked, peering up at Bobby, who stared away into the distance and didn't answer. He didn't have to, and Joe sagged. Then a distraction struck him, in the form of a belated question. 'What were *you* doing there, anyway?'

Bobby tore his eyes away from the horizon, and gave him a crooked little smile. 'I was waiting for you, wasn't I?' Joe's eyes shot wide. 'Not you specific, like,' Bobby added. 'Just . . . whoever came along with a pocketful of rocks.' He nodded at Joe's coat. 'You can ditch those now, by the way.'

Joe let the rocks fall, one by one, into the mud at their feet. 'You were just waiting to see if anyone turned up?'

'Doidge went to see Sergeant Brewer about getting some kind of police guard at the pit, but there isn't enough constables for him to just put someone up there on the off chance. So he got his Watch onto it.'

Joe sat up straight. 'Watch? Like, spies?'

Bobby laughed. 'Nothing so fancy. We're his extra eyes and ears, when we're needed, that's all. But it's top secret.' He tapped the side of his nose and gave Joe a hard look. 'Got it?'

'No one knows? Not even Tory?'

'Definitely not. She'd likely give me a right hook for not telling her before.' Bobby's smile faded, as he returned to the serious matter that had brought them together today. 'What you did might have killed someone, Joe. Doidge told me you almost hit Tobias Able with one of your rocks.'

Joe swallowed past a hard lump in his throat. 'I never meant to hurt anyone.'

'Don't matter. If it came to court you'd have been condemned anyway.' Bobby linked his hands between his knees, and Joe watched his rough fingers working around each other, betraying an emotion that surprised him.

'I went through the war in a kind of daze,' Bobby went on,

seemingly going off on a track of his own. 'I never knew that what was happening over there was even going in, here,' he tapped his own temple, 'until I got home. Them tunnels, the noises, the closed-in feeling . . .' He shook his head. 'I eventually realised that if I got caught doing anything serious I'd be locked up. And I knew I'd never survive that. Not feeling the way I do now.' He fixed his steady gaze on Joe, who found it impossible to look away. 'I don't reckon, after what you went through in that landslide, that you'd fare any better. D'you understand?'

Joe did. He tried to imagine what it would be like, and even without ever having stepped inside a cell he knew he would wish himself gone rather than endure it. It was the most terrifying realisation he had ever had, and it left him dry-mouthed and trembling.

'I'll never do anything like it again,' he said, and while the words sounded almost trite, out here in the open air, he meant it. From the very roots of his soul, he meant it, and the regret hurt like a physical thing.

Bobby patted his knee. 'I know you won't, lad. And to answer your question: no, I'm not going to tell Geordie. You are.'

Joe's insides squirmed as he pictured Geordie's face; all that love and trust that had been growing between them, all blown away in the wind. 'Do you have to tell Mr Doidge and Sergeant Brewer, too?'

'I'll leave that to Geordie to decide. But you owe him the truth, after all he's done for you.'

Joe stared at the ground, misery creeping through him. Surely Geordie would have to let him go after this? He couldn't keep an apprentice he couldn't trust, one who was capable of violence and thoughtless behaviour. He took a few shallow breaths, trying not to let himself break into tears, and then prepared to climb down off the gate.

'You already know I've done some bad stuff,' Bobby said. 'Some when I was younger than you, but not all of it.'

Joe paused mid-turn and sat back down, waiting for Bobby to continue; anything to put off the moment when he would have to return to the forge, and destroy the only thing he had left that was even close to family. 'What have you done?' he prompted, when Bobby fell silent again.

'The smuggling thing you know about, I'm sure,' Bobby said. 'But there's other stuff too. I've nicked watches and tried to sell them on. You know Tommy Ash?' Joe nodded. 'Well, I did that to him before I knew him, and now we're pals. I've pinched fish off the catch and sold it myself in the market. I still get work on the boats, 'cause the skippers know me, but they watch me more closely now.'

Joe frowned. 'It sounds like you're trying to tell me it's all right to steal,' he said doubtfully.

'Then you're not listening properly. When I was a lad, I got a smaller kid, Eddie Scoble, to steal a bunch of tools off Priddy Farm. I sold them in Truro market and never gave him the proceeds. Him and me are all right, too. Not the best of friends, but we rub along and he eventually stopped wanting to hit me. Which is a good thing,' he added wryly, 'since he's grown-up now, and even if *he's* still a bit of a weed, his stepdad's a good size.' He grinned, a far-off look on his face as he fell back into the past for a moment. 'Tory knows what I've done, all of it, and she and I, well . . .' He shrugged. 'We're whatever we are. But whatever *that* is, the biggest part of it is that we're friends.'

Joe understood, then, and his heart filled up a little. 'I still like you, too,' he said quietly.

'Good. So you see? I've broken laws, for a hundred reasons and for a long, long time, but I've learned how to stop, and people know that now. And the people I . . . I *care about*, still care about me.'

'Because you've tried to change.'

'Yes.'

'And you're truthful.'

'Whatever else I might be,' Bobby agreed. He bumped Joe with his shoulder. 'Ready to go and talk to Geordie now?'

Joe nodded, and climbed off the gate. Bobby jumped down and landed beside him, and Joe looked up at him. 'What will you be doing, while I'm talking to Geordie?'

'I don't know, why? Do you want me to come with you?'

'No. He's out riding with Lynette, I'll tell him everything when he gets back. But if you haven't got anything planned, I think you should remember what you've just told me.'

Bobby raised an eyebrow. 'What do you mean?'

'I mean, it's time you came clean to Tory about the Watch.' Joe slung his leg over the seat of his bike, and as he free-wheeled down the hill he threw a quick look over his shoulder. 'Good luck!'

He left Bobby standing in the road, a bemused half-smile on his face, and his mind turned to Bobby's words: *The people I care about, still care about me.* He swallowed a tight knot of fear, and hoped with all his heart that Geordie Sargent would turn out to be more than just his boss. He would find out very soon.

CHAPTER TWENTY-THREE

Foggintor Quarry never seemed to get any closer. Daniel had broken out of the trees near the road, onto a slope that carried him up towards the horizon, and was now feeling more terrifyingly exposed with every step. Behind him he heard sirens and vehicles, shouts and whistles, and now and again a single gunshot split the air and his breath snagged. He tensed for the impact of a bullet, but it never came, and after a while he realised the shots were still coming from inside the prison.

He breasted the slope at last, to find Dartmoor spread out ahead of him, with no shelter between himself and the quarry. He hesitated, questioning whether to ignore Stephen's advice, but he didn't know the area well enough to find an alternative. So he set off across the exposed moorland, dropping every now and again to the sodden ground, not because he'd thought someone was pursuing him, but because all he could hear was his own rasping breath, whistling in and out of his lungs – there might have been twenty men and dogs after him, and the first he'd know would be canine teeth in the back of his leg. So he took advantage of every small collection of rocks, and small dip in the land, and lay there for a moment to get his breathing under control. And to listen.

He rose from one such break, sweat running into his eyes despite the chilly air, and legs trembling as they fought to support his weight. The quarry wasn't that far from Princetown, but the terrain was unpredictable, and it would only take a single misstep to send him straight back to Dartmoor with a broken ankle, and then back on the wing to face Newbury's hired man. Or worse; if men had died in the mutiny, Exeter, for a swift and certain cure. Either way he wouldn't live to reject another birthday.

He could see the sheer granite faces of the quarry now, and assumed there would be some form of flooded basin, but he had no idea if there were going to be any viable places to hide, where experienced prison officers wouldn't find him. This must be the first place any escapee would make for, after all. Once more he questioned Stephen's advice, but once more he pushed on, knowing there was nothing else for it now. He stumbled to a stop on ground peppered with rocks of all sizes; another moment and he would have been sliding down, and into the distinctive blue-green pool of a disused granite quarry. He glanced behind him, unable to believe he still hadn't been seen, but he knew the guard who'd shot Ray would have sounded the alarm that he'd escaped, and it was only a matter of time. The important thing now was to find cover, and to stay there until dark.

To his right he could see a long pathway leading from the track down to the pool, and he took a few steps towards it before realising it was too obvious. Instead, he struck away to his left, slipping and sliding over loose scree and kicking rocks that tumbled away out of sight and made an ominously heavy splash as they hit the water. He judged it must be particularly deep along here, and began to move more carefully, using his hands to steady himself, and eventually finding himself coming up against shallower ground.

He fumbled his way over the unpredictable rocky outcrops, and then doubled back until he was able to tuck himself into a crevice, and there he drew his knees up to his chest and allowed his head to fall onto his folded arms. The enormity of what he'd done finally began creeping in at the edges of his consciousness; the rock thrown at Alfred Dunn's car only the first link in a hideously long chain that had led him here. He didn't fight it, he let every illegal and immoral act play out in detail, forcing himself to accept the blame so he could throw off the luxury of feeling unfairly battered by fate. But, he reasoned, as he finally raised his head and looked around, accepting responsibility did not mean he deserved to die. *That* he would fight. Right up to his last breath.

He was sheltered from the wind here, but the air was still cold and, as the sun began to lose the little strength it had, the clammy chill began to seep through Daniel's clothes and into his bones. His stomach growled and ached, and he pulled his knees in tighter, as if he might be able to squeeze the emptiness away. He squinted up at the cloud-darkened sky, unable to make his mind work well enough to gauge the time of day.

He couldn't remember how long it had been since Stephen had appeared at his door, but he supposed it must be early afternoon now, taking into account the times he'd lain in hollows and behind rocks, getting his breath back and listening for pursuers. Which meant, on a cold January day, he might have three hours at best before the light became tricky and difficult to rely on; he would have to make his way out of the quarry before then, or he'd soon find himself back down here again, nursing injuries he could do without. For now though, he could rest, and there was a chance he might even snatch some sleep. He had to try, at least; tonight was apt to be a long and difficult one ... If he was lucky enough to make it that far.

He turned up the collar of his coat, and rested his arms on his knees again, pillowing his cheek. Then he closed his eyes, dragged in the deepest breath he could manage and feeling his lungs straining, then let it out slowly. The world could carry on without him, just for a while.

The wind woke him, changing direction and screaming as it was sliced by the edges of the rock behind which he'd taken shelter. It was still daylight, and he might have tried to doze away again if he hadn't heard a voice directly above him.

'You two! Check down there.'

Daniel's heart leapt into his throat, and he felt the frantic hammering of it through every pulse point. For one terrible moment he thought he was going to be sick, but knew there would be nothing there, and he breathed slowly and deeply in an effort to quash the feeling. He heard boots on the scree, sliding as he had done, voices cursing in the same breathless, grumbling way, and then kicking against stones as the two men in in question began scouting the area.

He listened for the sound of dogs and didn't hear any, but, he cautioned himself, that didn't mean they weren't right above his head now, straining at their leashes and panting to be set free to carry out the search themselves. There was no way of knowing how many men had broken out, or if any of them had yet been identified, and Daniel was reasonably sure that, to the prison officer who'd shot Ray, and taken aim at him, he'd have been nothing more than another man in an arrowed coat and too-big trousers.

He'd kept his head down, out of fear of being found by a bullet, so he clung to the thought that it would be some time yet, before he was named. If these men were searching for several escapees they probably wouldn't want to spend too long in one place.

He listened to the two men climbing over the abandoned quarry workings, shouting to one another and to whoever had remained at the top, and he squeezed ever tighter into his tiny crevice in the rocks. When the footsteps died away, in the direction of the path Daniel had ignored, he heard the man above him instruct them to search for freshly revealed earth where a rock might have been recently dislodged, and for more obvious signs such as the ones his sliding boots might have made. They were being more thorough than he'd liked, but he sent a brief prayer of thanks that he hadn't come down that way after all. Nor, it seemed, had anyone else, and the two men were eventually called back to continue the search across the moor instead.

Daniel waited an agonising half an hour longer, watching the sky begin to darken, before he felt safe to emerge from his cramped, chilly refuge. There was no sound now, except the wind, yet as he climbed the easy path this time he was unbearably tense; braced for a cry of triumph, and to discover his pursuers had lain low after all, waiting to catch him in the open. No one did.

He waited on the higher ground until daylight began to fade in earnest, then took his bearings once again and set off across the open moorland towards Peter Tavy. The moor undulated more steeply than it seemed from a distance, and many times he would fix his gaze on a drift of smoke against the sky, that looked as if another ten minutes would bring him right into the village, only to find himself breasting a rise that revealed another expanse of scrubland.

The sky had vanished now, and all Daniel could see were the rock-strewn gullies that stood between himself and the farm Stephen had marked on his rudimentary map. His energy, earlier fuelled by fear and the need to put as much land between himself and Princetown as possible, was almost depleted now, but finally he was able to see, just ahead, a lighter piece of ground; a winding track that looked as if it led to the main road.

With a little grunt of relief, he fixed his gaze on it and reached for his last reserves of speed. He stumbled forward, putting out a hand to brace himself on a rock as he negotiated a ditch, but a moment later the grass beneath his feet vanished and for a single breathless moment there was nothing, no sensation of touch beneath his hand, or the soles of his boots. Then, with a jarring impact that sent twin shrieks of pain up through his leg and along his arm, he struck solid ground again with his whole right side. His back erupted once more into a river of fire, and he cried out as he was momentarily back in that room with Ned Newbury.

His head bounced, thankfully on something softer than granite, but it took him a moment of stunned immobility to realise what had happened; the ditch had been far deeper than he'd realised, and he lay now with his right side completely immersed in ice-cold running water. He pushed himself back and away, and acknowledged the faint throb of a twisted ankle, but as he moved his right arm he hissed in pain and twisted it to get a better look.

The inside-out coat was ripped down the arm, and the shirt and jumper beneath were soaked, but also sticky. He swallowed a fresh surge of nausea, and clamped a hand around his upper arm, not wanting to look any more. It wouldn't achieve anything. Instead, he managed to climb to his feet and, limping for a few steps until his ankle accepted his weight without too much complaint, he managed to cross the stream and climb up the far side.

After that it was a mere few minutes until he reached the outskirts of the village. He pulled out Stephen's note, relieved he'd put it into the left pocket instead of the right; it would now be only so much soggy, unreadable paper otherwise. He smoothed it onto his bent knee and turned it so he could match up what he was seeing in front of him. The farm was on this side of the village, and, according to Stephen's drawing it should be away to his right once he reached the road. He put the note away again, and set off on what he fervently hoped was the last leg of his journey.

The rain was starting now, heavy drops that worked their way through the fibres of his clothes and froze the top of his head. He kept his eyes fixed carefully on the ground ahead of him, risking only the occasional look around, and finally came to a gate with a painted sign on a wooden slab attached to it. It was too dark to read it, but it had to be Cudlip Farm. Daniel wiped his face with his left sleeve, pressed his stinging right arm more firmly into his side, and pushed open the gate, wincing at the loud creaking noise it made.

Once it had clicked shut again the farmyard was quiet; rain plinked into puddles, but apart from that all Daniel could hear was the faint, contented murmur of hens settling down for the night in their nearby houses. The farmhouse itself was in darkness, and his spirits fell, but he knew there would be somewhere he could stay until the family returned. There was sure to be.

He looked around, feeling the dribble of chilly water creeping down his face and neck, and wiping the worst of it away again. He debated whether to risk just knocking at the door, but before he could do it the gate creaked again, and Daniel whirled to see the light of a torch which just about illuminated the figure who carried it. His mind spun for a moment, unable to decide whether to run for it or stand his ground and explain himself, but the man spoke.

'You'll be Pearce, then.'

'Wh . . . what?'

'The convict,' the man said, his voice amiable enough but with a guarded edge. 'The one they're lookin' for.' He shone his torch at Daniel's coat, and a faint grin touched his weathered features. 'Yeah, thought so.'

'I don't know what—'

'Stop it, lad. You think you're the first escaped prisoner we've had here? What did you do that got you put you in there?'

Daniel simply stared. It seemed his future might actually depend on whether or not this farmer approved of his conviction. 'Look, I'll go,' he said. 'Don't worry, I'm not a danger to you.'

'Danger?' The farmer gave a short laugh. 'Unless you've got some sort of weapon about you, you're no more danger to me than they bleddy chickens.' He flashed his torch towards the hen houses, then peered more closely at Daniel's arm. 'What've you done there?'

'I fell.'

The farmer gave a deep sigh. 'Come on then, best get you cleaned up.' He led the way around to the back of the house, where Daniel saw there was a light on after all, in a downstairs room.

'How did you know my name?' he asked.

'We've had them here already, lookin' for you,' the farmer said. 'Not an hour since. We're always one of the first places they come to.'

Daniel hung back, wary again. 'Don't they leave someone behind, just in case?'

242

'Think they've got men to spare for that, do you?'

'Well . . . If they come back, will you tell them I'm here?'

The farmer turned and regarded him for a minute. 'Not decided yet.' He turned to the door and twisted the handle. 'Come on, Gracie'll sort you out.'

'Gracie!' Daniel realised that, concentrating on the hand-drawn map, he'd forgotten about the note itself. He pulled it from his pocket again and thrust it at the farmer. 'Please, give her this so she knows not to be afraid.'

'Afraid!' This time the farmer's laugh was louder, and less mocking. He sounded genuinely amused. 'Don't you worry yourself about Gracie,' he said, still chuckling, but he held out his hand for the note. 'Give it here, then, and get on inside before we both catch our deaths.'

They stepped into a porch, where the farmer hung his coat on a peg and indicated Daniel should do the same, before leading him into a generously sized kitchen. Daniel was immediately enveloped in the warm, almost overwhelmingly rich smell of beef and vegetables, and a pain twisted in his empty stomach. He only vaguely took in the sharp gasp of a woman who stood beside a cooking range, ladle in hand, and the farmer's hasty explanations washed over him, as he became acutely aware of every bruise, every ache and, more than anything else, the tiredness that was creeping through him. It eclipsed even the hunger, as the farmer guided him to sit at the table and then went to close the heavy curtain to block anyone from looking in.

When he looked at the woman again she was reading the letter, and her defensive stance had softened somewhat. But she remained cautious as she echoed the farmer's question.

'Why were you there in the first place?'

He told her, in a low, mumbling voice, how he had seen red and thrown the rock at Alfred Dunn's car. She looked unconvinced. 'Why does it say your life depends on you getting away, then? You don't get the rope for smashing up a car. Not even for the side of a house.'

Daniel shook his head. 'I ... there was ...' He stopped as the kitchen door opened, and a girl of around five or six came in, wrapped in a woolly house coat and clutching a stuffed lamb. She stopped as her gaze lit on Daniel, her dark eyes wide and interested.

'Who are *you*?'

'Tilly!' The farmer's wife flapped a hand at her. 'Seen and not heard, child.'

The girl was followed by a young woman with dark-red hair and bright-blue eyes, and a dusting of freckles that made her look younger than she probably was. Daniel realised who this must be, and he tried to stand but his exhausted and trembling legs wouldn't let him.

'Stay sat, boy,' the farmer said quickly. 'Gracie, fetch the doin's, would you? He's got a cut needs seein' to.'

Doin's. Daniel's mother used that word, to describe anything for which she had no immediate name. It made him smile, but at the same time a little flutter of fear re-awoke in him at the thought of her; the police were sure to go straight to her, expecting him to have made a beeline for the safety of home. He prayed they would treat her kindly, quickly realise she knew nothing of what had happened, and not turn the small house upside-down searching for him. She would be distraught.

Gracie's look of curiosity had vanished, and she left the room quickly, leaving the little girl, Tilly, still regarding him with huge, solemn eyes. Daniel gave her as friendly a smile as he could manage, and she took it as an invitation, climbing onto the chair directly opposite him, placing her lamb carefully on the table beside her, and propping her chin on her hands to keep her eyes focused on Daniel. He grew uncomfortable under that steady gaze, and he couldn't help finding that absurd, given all he'd endured in the past few months; he wished the farmer or his wife would intervene, but they had stepped out into the hall and were talking quietly and intently, shooting him the odd glance through the open doorway. So, he just wrapped his hand around his injured arm, smiled once more at Tilly, and waited silently for Gracie to reappear.

CHAPTER TWENTY-FOUR

Pencarrack Moor lacked some of the striking natural landmarks of Dartmoor, and the deep valleys of Bodmin Moor; in fact most people believed it to be simply a continuation of Bodmin Moor, with the same profusion of disused engine houses and chimney stacks. But a band of densely packed trees, Pencarrack Woods, stretched from the back end of the clay pit out to the road from Bodmin; a neat line that separated them. This side of that line was high, mostly exposed ground, with gentle slopes and expanses of reasonably flat, solid grass that made it the perfect place to give horses their head and let them fly.

Geordie leaned low over Mack's neck, and, pushing everything that had been worrying him to the back of his mind, he concentrated on the drumming of the bay's hooves on the grass, and the wind burning his face and pulling at his clothes. But it was getting late now, darkness was just beginning to fall, and as Mack crested the hill and slowed to walk, those troubling thoughts crept back. He couldn't put it off any longer. He was finally going to take Joe aside and discuss what had been happening.

Not far behind him, Lynette was putting one of the newer

horses through her paces, and Geordie could hear them drawing closer as the slight rise flattened out. He pulled Mack to a halt and sat for a moment, looking out across the moor, as Lynette edged Bella up alongside him.

'She's doing well,' Geordie said, nodding at the grey mare. He remembered her from her work at the clay pit; it was good to see how she'd fleshed out and grown in strength since the stables had taken her on.

'She is, physically, but she's still quite nervy. I have to be careful with her.' Lynette patted Bella's neck, and studied Geordie closely for a moment. 'Are you all right? You've been ... distant. For a while, actually. Is it still that business about Marion? Because I promise you—'

'No,' he said quickly. 'It's nothing to do with her, or with you.'

'You're still worried about Stephen.'

The blunt observation was a distraction from thinking about Joe, so he nodded. 'That disturbance showed me something I don't like to think about. The way Stephen was keeping his eye on this Davis bloke right from the start. And when it all started he was pulled right out of the way. It was ...' He shrugged. 'Just *strange*.' He nudged Mack forwards with his knees, and they began to pick their way down the slope.

'Did the guard think Stephen was a ringleader?' Lynette asked.

'No, that's just the thing. It looked as if he'd been waiting for something to start, and then pulled Stephen away for his own good.' He paused for a moment. 'I saw weapons changing hands between visitors and prisoners. I *knew* I had to report it.'

'But you didn't,' Lynette guessed.

'How did you know?' He twisted in the saddle to see her studying him, and she gave him a faint smile.

'Your face. You look as if you think you deserve to be back there in chains.'

'Maybe I do. Let's stop here for a minute.'

They dismounted, and sat side by side on a mound of granite. Lynette shivered, and Geordie opened his coat to let her move against his side. She put an arm around his waist, then withdrew it and sat up straight again, looking concerned.

'You're still losing weight.'

'I've been busy.' He shrugged. 'I keep forgetting to eat my dinner.' He gestured again with his coat, and she snuggled beneath it.

'You can't go without meals,' she said, sounding like a stern parent, which made him smile. She plucked at the flapping end of his belt. 'You've put another hole in this, as well, haven't you?'

Geordie remembered how leaving his knife on the kitchen table had led to his discovery about Joe, and he quickly moved the subject back onto its former track, telling Lynette that Stephen's silent plea had stopped him from reporting what he'd seen at the prison.

'The moment word got out, Stephen would have been for it,' he said. 'God only knows what they'd have done to him.'

Lynette was silent while she digested this. 'What you saw wouldn't have been all of it though, would it?'

'How do you mean?'

'I mean, there will have been other weapons in the prison the whole time, wouldn't there?'

'Without a doubt.'

'And more being passed at different parts of the room.'

He nodded. 'Bound to have been.'

'And was it obvious to anyone else that Stephen was being protected from becoming involved? I mean *really* obvious?'

Geordie thought back to the way the guard had pinned Stephen against the wall, and shook his head. 'I think anyone else would have assumed he'd been all set to dive in, and was being held at bay.'

Lynette nodded. 'Then stop worrying,' she said gently. 'You got Gwenna out, and that's the main thing.'

'I wish to God there was something I could do to get *him* out, before whatever's going to happen, happens.' Speaking was hard, suddenly, so he stopped, and straightened his back, looking away across the moor. The horses were growing restless now, so he rolled his shoulders and stood up, then held out a hand to Lynette.

'Ready?'

'I'll say.' She accepted his hand and he pulled her to her feet. She gathered up Bella's reins. 'It's been too long since we've been able to do this. Pity it's getting dark.'

Geordie re-buttoned his coat, then swung up into the saddle and winced. 'I've not had enough practice at this lately, my backside feels like there's nothing between skin and bone.'

'I'll check for you later,' Lynette promised, and grinned when he adopted a mock maiden-aunt's look of disapproval.

His own smile faded as he recognised a figure coming out of a high, ornately wrought gate up ahead. The house to which the gate belonged was only just visible in the distance, but the man who now stood in the road was unmistakeably Jago Carne.

'What's he doing here?' Lynette muttered.

'Looks like he's working.' Geordie nodded at the wheelbarrow half-buried in the hedge. 'Someone's idiot enough to give him a job, that's their lookout, I suppose.'

'We can't really avoid him, can we?'

Geordie shook his head. The beaten pathway took them momentarily onto the road and right past the gate, on which he could now see a plaque with the house name inscribed on it: *Hazelmere*.

Lynette frowned. 'That's where that crooked flight trainer-turned-smuggler lives. Or lived.'

'Presumably that's how Carne got this job, then. They must have arranged it in prison.'

They were drawing too close to openly discuss the man now, and Carne, in turn, had recognised them and turned away. He made a show of fussing with the lock on the gate, until Geordie and Lynette had moved past the house and back onto the grassy moorland path.

'Well done,' Lynette said.

'For what?'

'For not getting under his skin, or letting him under yours. I hope that means you've both turned a corner, I don't want to have to worry any more about the two of you knocking seven bells out of one another.'

'Seven bells?' Geordie laughed. 'Where did *that* expression come from?'

'Tory.' Lynette smiled. 'Where else?'

'Well, you don't have to worry,' Geordie promised her. 'Seems as if we've both learned our lessons, one way and another.'

'I know your lesson was hideously painful,' Lynette said, 'but selfishly I still prefer it to his.'

'You and me both.' Geordie took her hand and they rode like that for a little while, their linked hands swinging between them, until the path narrowed and Lynette nudged Bella ahead. When the path widened again and Geordie didn't ride forward, she looked over her shoulder.

'Tired of holding my hand already, then?' she called. 'That didn't take long.'

'I'm just admiring the view,' he called back, letting his gaze travel with exaggerated appreciation over her form. He tried on a posh voice. 'What an absolutely *marvellous* seat you have, my dear!'

Lynette's shout of shocked laughter was a heartening reward, and he moved Mack up alongside her again. 'We'd better get these two back,' he said, patting Mack's neck. 'Joe'll need time to get ready for his lesson. Race you back to the road?'

Lynette gave a brief sigh of regret. 'I think Bella's had enough for today.'

'Oh.' Disappointed, Geordie released the reins he'd gathered in anticipation. 'All right, I'll . . . Oi!'

But he was shouting at the back view of an eager grey horse and her rider, as Lynette and Bella became a single shape dwindling into the distance. Lynette glanced back over her shoulder as Geordie kicked Mack into a canter, and her laughter was caught up by the wind and thrown back to him. He shouted again, but his own laughter turned it into only something he and Mack could hear, as they both leaned into the chase.

It was fully dark by the time he had cleaned and settled Mack for the night, and walked back to the forge. Usually on a Sunday night his thoughts would have turned to the next day's workload; orders, supplies, and how much time he could allow for droppers-in, but tonight all his thoughts were on how to broach the matter of the vandalism at the clay works. Perhaps he should put it aside until they were settled in for the night and could talk properly. Joe appeared in the doorway of the cottage, as Geordie latched the gate closed.

'You'll never guess who's working up at the posh place at Hazelmere,' Geordie called across the yard. 'Jago bloody Carne! Fancy giving that thug a key to your property.'

It was hard to interpret the boy's expression, but he looked torn. A little frightened, but with an air of resolve about him, and Geordie frowned. 'What is it?'

'Sergeant Brewer telephoned,' Joe said. 'He wants to see you. Urgent, like.'

Geordie's spirits dipped. Surely no one else knew about Joe. If so they'd have talked to the boy directly. This must be Watcher business then. 'Did he say why?' he asked, turning back to unlatch the gate again.

Joe shook his head. 'Just said to send you down there the minute you got back.'

'Right.' Geordie blew out a sigh that was at least half relief; he'd be forced now to put off his confrontation with Joe until tomorrow. 'You'd better get yourself off to bed, we've got a busy day tomorrow and I'll need you up early.'

He took the van down to Caernoweth, resenting the need to use fuel on something that wasn't connected to the forge, but it would have taken far too long to walk, and even longer in the dark. Brewer was on his feet staring at a wall map, as Geordie pushed open the office door uninvited.

He turned with a scowl, which faded when he saw who it was. 'Don't bother sitting down, lad,' he said grimly. 'You've got work to do.'

'What's happened?'

'There's been a riot at Dartmoor.'

Geordie's blood turned to slow-moving ice. 'Anyone hurt?'

'Several, but no fatalities reported as yet.' Brewer returned to

252

stand behind his desk. 'Make no mistake, though, this is serious. Crownhill Barracks sent two companies of infantry, and machine guns. People have been shot. There have been beatings, bad ones, and serious injuries from weapons brought in from outside.'

'Christ.' A painful stab of guilt brought heat to Geordie's face that he hoped would go unnoticed.

'The administration block was set on fire,' Brewer went on, sitting down. 'Most of the records have been destroyed.' He seemed oblivious to Geordie's horror, but then, Geordie reasoned, he had no way of knowing Geordie's brother was a Dartmoor inmate. He'd certainly regret impulsively enlisting Geordie's service as a Watcher once he found out.

'All efforts are on stopping an escaped convict from getting off English soil,' Brewer was saying. 'He's already been convicted of assault on a prison officer, unprovoked, and vicious. I'm setting you all on duty, watching as much of the coastline as you can, and looking out for anyone who fits the description.'

He pushed a sheet of paper across the desk, and Geordie picked it up and read it aloud.

'Daniel Evan Pearce. Age: twenty-seven. Dark hair. Unshaven at time of absconding. Blue eyes. Five feet eleven inches. Prison clothing at time of absconding. Naval tattoos: left shoulder: anchor, with *Plymouth* beneath; left forearm: small star with initials: EJP. 1914.' He looked up questioningly.

'Father's initials,' Brewer said. 'Deceased.'

'Is Pearce really likely to come here? Has he got family here?'

Brewer shrugged. 'Not as far as we know. His mother's in Plymouth, so most of the recovery effort's gone there, but all coastal constabularies are put on alert.' Brewer's instruction was brief, and clear. 'I've told Gale and Donithorn, now I'm telling you. This bloke is desperate, and that makes him dangerous. He's ex-navy, so he'll be trained and wily. Keep your wits and your whistles about you, and remember you're Watchers. You *watch*. You don't approach unless you have to, for instance if you believe he'll evade capture altogether unless you apprehend him. You report back to me, or, in a case like this, to any officer of the law that you can find. Got that?'

'And he's the only one to escape the prison?' Geordie pressed, his heart settling a little now. 'No one else tried it?'

'I'm sure plenty did. But Pearce was the only one to make it over.' Brewer sat back. 'Best get on then.' He nodded to the door, and Geordie left, his mind turning to Gwenna. If she'd heard anything about the riot she'd be relieved to know her father wasn't currently being chased across the moor by armed officers; for once, both he and Stephen could be considered to be in the safest place, if only he could be sure neither was among the wounded.

He jogged down to the Rosdews' shop, only to see the hand-written note added to the regular 'closed,' sign on the door: *Sorry for any inconvenience*. The van was missing from its usual spot next to the back gate, and the building was in complete darkness, leading Geordie to draw only one conclusion: Gwenna was on her way to Dartmoor, alone.

CHAPTER TWENTY-FIVE

When Gracie came back into the kitchen she had a small wicker box in one hand, and Stephen's note in the other. It had evidently been handed to her as she'd passed her mother in the hall, and she lifted her eyes from it, her expression fearful as she looked over at Daniel.

'He didn't do anything stupid, did he?'

'He knew better than to try and come with me,' Daniel said. 'He made sure I got out, and then, as far as I know, he kept his distance from it all.'

She seemed satisfied, but was still clearly worried as she put the letter aside on the table and set the box down. She lifted the lid to reveal a selection of bandages and ointments, then went to pour hot water into an enamel bowl, while Daniel pulled the box closer and eyed its contents nervously. She came back and sat down next to him, as her parents returned and her mother wordlessly spooned some of the rich-smelling stew into a dish which she placed at Daniel's left elbow. She added a spoon, and nodded at him to eat while Gracie took a pair of scissors to the sleeve of his shirt.

He gratefully abandoned himself to Gracie's mercies, picked

up the spoon awkwardly in his left hand, and dipped it into the thick stew. His stomach growled loudly in anticipation even before he'd lifted the spoon to his lips, and he saw Gracie's lips twitch in a kind of sympathetic amusement at the sound.

'You must be starving,' she said, as she peeled away the cut sides of the rough shirt. 'Eat as much as you can for now, but be careful. I know a bit about prison food from Stephen, and if you shovel something this rich down you you'll make yourself ill. We'll pack more food for you to take with you.'

'Why are you going away?' Tilly piped up. 'You can stay here.'

'No, he can't, love,' Gracie said. 'He's got to go, and *we've* got to pretend he was never here, all right?'

'I don't like to make the child lie,' Daniel mumbled, around a mouthful of the most deliciously flaking beef he could remember tasting. 'I'm sorry.'

'Don't give it a thought,' Gracie said. She dipped a cloth into the hot water, and indicated he should return his attention to his meal. 'If Stephen sent you, you're all right by us, which means we'll do whatever we have to. Geordie will be able to help you get away, I'm sure.'

Tilly sat upright, eyes widening again. 'My daddy's called Geordie. He gave me this, for Barney.' She picked up the lamb and flicked the bell on its collar.

'Mr Pearce is going to see your daddy,' Gracie said, flashing her a quick smile. 'We know he'll be able to help, don't we?'

'Can I go too?'

'Certainly not,' Mrs Martyn chipped in. 'You're all bathed and ready for bed. And please, for the love of all that's holy, stop jangling that blessed bell! I reckon your mother could hear that thing, all the way from your house!'

Tilly pulled a face but did as she was told. 'But I want to see Daddy. I haven't seen him for *years and years!*'

'You'll be able to visit him soon enough,' Gracie assured her, as Daniel smothered a smile at the child's theatrics. 'But Mrs Martyn's right, it's past your bedtime.'

'Can I stay up a bit later?' Tilly pleaded, her eyes still on Daniel.

Gracie exchanged a look with her mother, and relented. 'Just a little bit, then it's up you go, and no arguments. Your ma would have my hide.'

She began dabbing at Daniel's arm, and he jumped at the intense stinging sensation. He hadn't even looked at the damage yet, but the pain was worsening more as his other needs were satisfied, and he finally forced himself to look at what Gracie was doing. The bruising had not yet come out, but he knew from experience that most of his right arm, from mid-forearm to shoulder, would soon be a mass of purple and black. A gash, thankfully not too deep-looking, ran up from his elbow for around five inches, and it was this that Gracie was cleaning now, pulling threads of torn shirt free from clotting blood, and causing the whimper that broke loose before he could bite it back.

'What was your job, before?' Gracie asked him, another of those irritatingly sympathetic smiles just touching her eyes. He didn't want to say, particularly after that unmanly display, but he opted for the truth.

'I was a junior officer in the Royal Navy.'

She looked up, surprise on her face, then bit her lip. 'The navy.'

He sighed. 'It stings, all right?'

'Just finish your meal, sailor boy,' she said, openly grinning now. 'Let me do the difficult bit.'

'I don't know why Stephen spoke so highly of you,' Daniel grumbled, picking up his spoon again. 'Always said you were so sweet.'

Gracie's laughter spilled over. 'That just goes to show,' she said, tapping his wrist for emphasis, 'never trust a convicted criminal.'

He gave her a faint smile in return. After his flogging he should have been able to put this relatively minor wound in its proper place, but instead it was bringing the horror of it all back, and the last thing he wanted now was to draw attention to it. So he gladly accepted his role as the butt of the joke, and allowed himself to embrace the more hopeful situation in which he now found himself. He could feel his earlier tiredness slipping away again, replaced by an urgency to be on the move.

'Where did you say Stephen's brother lives?' he asked.

'Pencarrack, just this side of Caernoweth. The blacksmith's forge. You'll find it easily enough.'

Daniel started, hit suddenly by a cold realisation. 'You're not taking me?'

'*Taking* you?' Gracie had been about to start wrapping a clean bandage around his arm; now she stopped and sat back. 'Of course not! We've got a farm to run, we can't just drop everything. Not to mention the risk.' She resumed her work, and the bandage felt cool and tight against his skin, bringing instant relief. 'No, we'll lend you our car, but if you're caught we'll stay you've stolen it. Understand?' She met his gaze again, and this time her expression was one of cold warning. 'We'll deny ever having seen you, and ... Well, I suppose it won't matter much by then, but you'll have the theft added to your record if they catch you.'

Daniel nodded; of course he understood, now he thought about it, but that didn't help with the biggest problem of all. He waited until Gracie had finished and tied the bandage, then took a deep breath.

'I can't drive.'

The low murmur of conversation between Farmer Martyn and his wife stopped, and Gracie paused as she went to pick up the bowl of bloodied water. She returned her hands to her lap, and looked at them for a moment, before lifting her eyes once more to Daniel. She searched his face, as if she hoped he'd been joking, but must have seen the miserable truth there. The hesitant smile faded.

'Not even a little bit?'

'Not even that.' Daniel shrugged. 'I've never lived somewhere out of the way, like this, so I never needed to. And I could never have afforded a car anyway.'

Gracie looked at her father, then rose and wordlessly cleared the table of scraps of cloth and pinkish water. She clearly had no idea what to say now, and was leaving it to Farmer Martyn.

'*I* can't drive you, lad,' the farmer said in surprise. 'Nor can Gracie.'

'Can you teach me, then?'

'In the pitch dark?' The farmer looked at the curtained window. 'It'd be hard enough in daylight, in the short time you've got before the next lot of coppers comes knockin'.'

'Next lot?'

'Well, they ain't stupid. They know they're more likely to catch a convict on the second visit, when anyone who've been hidin' thinks the danger's passed.'

'Time for bed, Tilly,' Gracie said, holding out her hand. 'I'll read to you if you're good.'

'You won't,' the farmer said grimly. 'Your mother'll do that.

You can fetch the lad here some fresh clothes from my wardrobe, and get me the atlas from the sitting room. I'll have a look outside to see if the coast is clear.' He stood up and picked up his hat. 'Then you can teach him to drive.'

With an incredulous look at Daniel, as if it had been his idea, Gracie went to fetch the clothes. Her mother took Tilly off to bed; the little girl sent Daniel one more wistful look, and got midway through another request to accompany him before she was silenced and hurried up the stairs. Farmer Martyn went out into the night, torch in hand and face set in a scowl, and Daniel was left alone in the kitchen, wondering how long it would take him to walk to Pencarrack instead.

Mrs Martyn returned first. Evidently Tilly had been tired out by all the excitement, and refused a story after all, so there was time to go through the clothing Gracie brought down, and declare its suitability or otherwise. The trousers would have almost gone around his waist twice, but they would do, she said, with the addition of a belt. The shirt, she held up with a little frown and told Gracie to take back.

'This is your father's Sunday best,' she said. 'Fetch one from the laundry.' She looked at Daniel. 'Whatever you're wearing, we'll have to burn,' she said. 'We can't risk anyone finding it.' She pulled a face and sniffed, which said a hundred more words, but she settled for three. 'Good thing, too.'

'Get down to your vest then,' Gracie threw over her shoulder as she went into the little lean-to, off the kitchen.

Daniel hesitated, then, realising he wouldn't be able to avoid it after all, he moved his position so he stood with his back to the range, ostensibly keeping warm while he peeled off his own cut-up shirt and dropped it into the corner. Gracie came back carrying two freshly laundered but crumpled shirts, and let her mother choose which one she was prepared to sacrifice.

'I'll see you get it back,' Daniel promised, accepting the darker option; a green collarless shirt that needed patching on the elbow. He pushed his injured arm into the sleeve first, very carefully, and when Gracie took a step forward to help, he instinctively moved away and his back connected with the handle of the pot that lived on the range. Startled, he twisted away from it, and Gracie's raised hand fell back down. He already knew what he'd see when he looked at her, but he did it anyway.

She didn't say anything at first, just kept her eyes fixed on the raised welts and recently re-opened scabs that showed above the neckline of his grimy, blood-streaked vest. During the silence, Farmer Martyn came back in, bringing a chilly wind with him, and he too stopped dead and stared. Nobody moved for a long moment, then Gracie cleared her throat.

'I don't want to know what you did, to get that. I don't want to know anything, except ...' Her voice shook a little. 'Has this happened to Stephen too?'

'No,' Daniel said quietly.

'You swear?'

'On my mother's life.'

She nodded, and the tension around her mouth and eyes relaxed a little. She gestured to the star tattooed on his left forearm. 'Whose initials are those?'

'My dad's.'

'Nineteen-fourteen,' she read aloud. 'He died in the war, then?'

'No. He was blown up on the *Bulwark* while they were still in port. It was my tenth birthday.'

Gracie flinched in sympathy and stepped away to allow him to resume dressing. 'You never answered before. Why would your life have been in danger if you stayed?'

'I knocked a warder down. Which is also why I got the punishment.' He told her about Newbury, trying not to load his story with self-pity while at the same time trying to convey the singular attention Newbury had paid him, and why. He wasn't sure he succeeded.

'So your mother was sacked for stealing from this Dunn bloke?' Farmer Martyn put in, shrugging out of his coat. 'That seems quite—'

'She never stole,' Daniel snapped. 'She wouldn't have.'

'That's by the by,' Gracie said, glaring at her father. 'The point is, now Daniel's escaped there's more to worry about than some warder with a grudge. We've got to get him away before they come back looking for him. Is it clear out there, then?'

Martyn nodded. 'Far as I can see. You fit to make a move, boy?'

Daniel tucked the shirt into his borrowed trousers, and fastened the belt. 'Thank you all, for everything.'

'Oh, and get them boots off,' Martyn said, bending to loosen his own laces. 'These'll be a bit big on you, but them arrows won't do you no favours come daylight, out there in the mud.'

Daniel took off the prison boots, and pulled on the ones Martyn kicked across to him. His feet slid a little bit inside them, but the thickness of the socks helped. He flexed his feet a couple of times to get used to the feel, then nodded to show he was ready.

'Come on then,' Gracie said. She gave her mother a quick kiss on the cheek, and looked pointedly at her father, and then at the coat over his arm.

'Bloody hell,' Martyn sighed, and rummaged in the coat

pockets. He emptied them of two used handkerchiefs, a ball of string, and a tobacco tin, then handed the coat to a bemused but deeply grateful Daniel. 'Look after it!'

'I will.'

Daniel and Gracie made their way swiftly to the big, ungainly-looking Wolseley parked in the yard. It was mud-streaked, full of bits of hay, and on the back seat was an enormous, crumpled blanket that looked as if it had been there forever.

'For the dogs,' Gracie said, evidently reading his mind as she slipped off her knapsack and stashed it away behind the passenger seat. 'You might want to sleep under it if you get tired later. Though,' she added with a faint grin, 'it's not been washed in a while, so choose wisely.' She indicated he should get into the passenger seat, and she herself got in behind the wheel. 'I'll take us up into one of the fields at the back. We'll need a decent amount of space since we won't be using the lights once we're there.'

'Won't be ...' Daniel took a deep breath and tried to calm the shakiness when he let it out. Of course they wouldn't be. 'All right.'

'You just keep a look out.'

The car made its slow, careful way out of the yard, and as Gracie negotiated the lane, with the car's headlights on low and barely illuminating a few feet ahead, Daniel peered out for any sign of torches on the moor that surrounded them. He saw nothing that alarmed him, and he began to relax, until they stopped, and Gracie sat still for a moment before opening her door. Daniel took the opportunity to voice what he'd been thinking about all the way up.

'Would you do me a favour?'

Gracie let out a surprised snort. 'Just the one?'

Daniel smiled in the darkness. 'Just one more,' he amended. 'Would you go and see my mother? I'll give you her address. I'm just ... I'm worried they'd have gone to her, told her stuff that's not true. Or just turned the place upside-down looking for me. She'd be so upset.'

Gracie reached out and patted his hand. 'I will. I promise. Though how I'm going to get there with no car, I have no idea.'

'Oh hell! I hadn't thought. Is there—'

'Stop it, you idiot,' Gracie said, and he heard the smile in her voice. 'There's a train. And, if all else fails, I'll take the tractor.'

He looked across at her to see if she was being serious, and although he could barely see her he knew she was holding back laughter. Stephen was a very lucky man, he decided, as she pushed open the door and climbed out, and the tragedy of it all, and the unfairness, became more poignant still.

He opened his own door, and as they passed one another in front of the car he looked out across the moor where, from their vantage point, he could see the faint gleam of Tavistock's lights in the distance. He climbed in and took hold of the steering wheel, and while he waited for Gracie to settle into the passenger side, he stared at the blanket of lights and what they represented, and contemplated the next part of this increasingly daunting adventure.

CHAPTER TWENTY-SIX

Lynette turned the radio off, and she and Tory sat and looked at one another in silence for a moment. The news report hadn't been very detailed, just that the prison riot had been extremely serious but there was general relief that only one prisoner had escaped, aided by a fellow convict who had been injured, and was also likely to see his sentence increased as a result. Neither prisoner had been named, but both Lynette and Tory could list several who would have plenty to blame them for, should they risk returning to the area.

'Carne's been out for weeks,' Lynette said eventually. 'If he was going to get his revenge he'd have done it by now.'

'Then there's Colin Damerel,' Tory said. 'If it weren't for us, his son would still be alive.'

'*We* didn't give him up,' Lynette pointed out. 'Emma Kessel was the one who worked out where they'd be hiding and sent the police there, and she's moved away, so she's safe.'

'What about Peter Bolitho? Dennis Haydock?'

'Either of those might risk coming back,' Lynette agreed. 'Though I shouldn't think that flight trainer-turned-smuggler of yours would be one to shin over walls, and evade police and dogs.'

'No, Hocking wouldn't last ten minutes out on the moors,' Tory said. 'Nor would Colin Damerel, to be honest.' Then she sighed. 'It's probably none of them, and anyway we can't spend all day worrying.'

'What if it's Stephen?' Lynette said suddenly. 'He's got very little to lose by trying, and he's young. Presumably reasonably healthy. If anyone deserves their freedom, it's him.'

'In which case here's hoping the police and the dogs are having a bad day.' Tory looked troubled as she stood up and stacked the breakfast plates by the sink. 'Come on, let's get started downstairs. I'll telephone Gwenna later, and see if she's heard. She's bound to be worried about her dad if she has.'

While Tory turned the horses into the field after their feed, Lynette busied herself replacing the straw on the floor of the stalls. She'd worked up a sweat clearing out the old straw, and was feeling good about the work she was doing, but her mind was occupied with images of desperate criminals on the run from police across the moors. Particularly those who had a grudge against their hometown residents—

A dark shape loomed at the half door at her back, throwing a shadow onto the bare stone floor of the stall, and Lynette turned, crying out in shock, and stumbled back. She planted the rake hard, to stop herself from falling, and her eyes adjusted to the square of bright daylight and the ominous-looking silhouette in its centre.

'Geordie!' She put a hand to her chest and let out a shaky laugh, still leaning on her rake. 'Don't do that, we're all on pins here!'

'Sorry,' he said, unlatching the door so she could come out. 'I didn't mean to make you jump, I was just . . .' He peered past her, into the stall. 'Have you seen Joe today?'

'No, were we expecting him?' Lynette's heart still raced, and she slowed her breathing as the shock wore off. 'Monday's your busiest day, isn't it? We wouldn't have booked him in for a riding lesson.'

'That's why I'm hoping he hasn't suddenly decided he needs one.' He looked past her into the stall, as if he expected a shirking boy to be lurking in the corner, though Joe was as far from a shirker as it was possible to get.

'Tory's in the field if you want to check with her,' Lynette said. 'Have you heard the news this morning?'

'The riot?' Geordie's expression shifted from irritation to concern. 'Yes. I wanted to talk to you about—'

'Geordie,' Tory called, closing the paddock gate. 'Have you heard about the prison?'

'We were just talking about it.'

Lynette voiced one of the worries that had settled on her as she worked. 'Do you think Stephen might have tried to escape?'

'No.' Geordie sounded firm on that. 'And I think I'd have heard by now if he was badly hurt, too. I'm his next of kin, so there would have been a telegram at least.'

Lynette relaxed a little, but only until he spoke again.

'I think Gwenna's gone up there though. The shop's closed and there's a note on the door.'

Lynette frowned. 'I don't like the idea of that, do you? It'll be chaos. Even dangerous.'

'She must have gone alone, her mother's away.' Tory glanced over at Lynette's car, her face reflecting Lynette's own concern.

'She'll be upset, too, and probably not thinking straight. Maybe one of us should go after her.'

Lynette nodded. 'Could Bobby stand in for you, if we both go?'

'He's … probably going to be busy,' Tory said. She looked a little uncomfortable, which was odd in itself, but Lynette's curiosity was further piqued to see a quick glance flash between her and Geordie.

'I really need to clear something up with Joe,' Geordie said, before she could address it. 'You're sure he's not been near here today?'

'Positive,' Tory said. 'When did you see him last?'

'I looked in on him when I came back from … when I went to bed, last night, but when I got up early this morning, there was no sign. I waited a while in case he'd gone for milk or bread, but he hasn't come back.'

'Well, he's not booked in for a riding lesson,' Tory said. 'Is it possible he's just gone for a walk?'

Geordie shook his head. 'Unlikely. He knows we've got a lot to do.' He took off his hat and ran a hand through his hair, a habit Lynette recognised as rising agitation.

'Tell us what it is you need to clear up with him,' she said. 'Maybe that'll help.'

'That's the trouble,' Geordie said. 'I think it might tell us *why* he's gone, but not where.' He blew out a harsh breath. 'You've heard about the vandalism at the clay pit?'

'Most people now reckon that's Carne,' Lynette said. Her heart sank. 'Are you saying it isn't?'

'Much as I'd like it to be him, it's not.'

He told them how he'd seen the blade tip on John Doidge's desk, then discovered Joe's broken knife. 'I've just not been able to put it to him,' he confessed. 'He's such a fragile boy.'

'He's a boy who misses his father,' Lynette corrected, and when it looked as if Geordie was about to automatically, but absently, agree, she said it again. 'A boy who misses his *father*, Geordie.'

Geordie frowned slightly. 'Yes, which is why I haven't—'

'He doesn't need a kindly uncle,' she clarified. 'Or even a firm-handed boss. Remember that, when you find him. He needs someone to guide him. To pull him up when he's taking his frustrations out in all the wrong ways.'

Geordie tugged at his wayward hair again, and sighed. 'You're saying I've been too easy on him.'

'Understandably,' Lynette said. She took his hand. 'But he's at an age when he's going to test himself, and the world, and how they fit together. He's frustrated at losing your attention to Tilly . . .' She held up a hand to silence the protest she could see coming. 'And he has a genuine grievance against the clay pit. Specifically the management.'

'But John wasn't captain back then,' Geordie argued. 'All Joe's doing is costing them money so they can't do right by the men. Men like his dad was!'

'That's the adult talking,' Lynette said gently. 'Joe's not fifteen yet. He's confused and upset, and doesn't know where to turn to let out his anger.'

'So you're saying I should let myself bear the brunt of it,' Geordie said, and Lynette smiled.

'Give him a target, yes. God knows he needs one, and you can take it. But it'll also tell him that you don't just think of him as someone to keep an eye on until he's old enough to leave. That you think of him as a son. You do, don't you?'

'Of course I do.' Geordie drew her against him and rested his chin on top of her head in his customary manner. 'You're right, I know you are. All I have to do now, then, is find him.'

Lynette allowed herself the comfort of his closeness for a moment, then remembered the cryptic, wordless question and answer that had passed between him and Tory, who was now filling a bucket from the water pump. 'What were you talking about earlier, when you said Bobby was busy?'

'Doesn't matter,' Geordie said, pulling back. 'I need to find Joe.'

'He's probably gone for a walk down by the harbour,' Tory said, coming over to them with her bucket sloshing water unheeded on her trousers. 'Him and his dad lived down in Caernoweth most of their lives, he'll be used to being by the sea.'

'What makes you both think Bobby's busy today, particularly?' Lynette persisted. 'Come on, I saw that look.'

To her intense frustration they shared another one. Then Tory seemed to come to a decision, and turned to Lynette.

'I've just found out that Bobby's a Watcher. A sort of . . . ranger, who helps Sergeant Brewer out now and again.'

'And so am I,' Geordie added. Tory looked as startled as Lynette, and they both listened in growing astonishment as he told them about the Nigel Stibson incident, and then what had happened in Brewer's office. 'I haven't had to do anything yet,' he said, 'but now I'll be expected to keep a lookout for anyone acting suspiciously around the coastal parts. That's all. There's no danger involved; Brewer just wants extra eyes he can trust, and he said not to tell anyone.'

Lynette pushed her hands into her pockets as she looked up at Geordie. 'And there's you giving *me* a dressing down for not telling you about Marion.'

'That's not the same,' he protested. 'Tilly is my daughter, what happens to Marion directly affects her.'

'It *is* the same!' Lynette looked up at him, incredulous. 'You've just told me you spent the night I got back chasing some unknown man through the village in the dark, not having *any* idea whether or not he was carrying a weapon. And you've kept that from me for over a month!' She looked away, shaking her head. Knowing that you might just as easily have been killed? Of course it affects me.'

'Are you saying you want me to give it up?'

'Would you?'

He only hesitated for a moment. 'Yes,' he said. 'For your peace of mind, I would.'

'But do you want to?'

This time the pause was longer, and he shook his head. 'I didn't want to do it, at first,' he said. 'But then I thought about Xander, and how Alec Damerel and his father nearly got away with everything they'd done. And then there was the extra money, I couldn't say no to that, either.' He sighed. 'I didn't intend to keep you in the dark, no matter what Brewer said. But the longer the weeks went on, the harder it was to tell you.'

'And why *did* he tell you to keep it to yourself, anyway?'

'Because he's an idiot, who thinks women talk too much.'

Lynette's lips twitched at that, and her stance softened. 'You shouldn't give it up,' she said. She was aware of Tory moving away into the stable to give them their privacy, and she took both of Geordie's hands in hers. 'I just wish you'd been honest with me.'

'So do I.'

'Well, now we both know, what do you have to do about this escaped prisoner?'

'Nothing, directly, just keep an eye out. He's probably headed

271

for Plymouth, anyway, since he's ex-navy.' He looked around them again. 'I'm more worried about Joe, just now.'

Something blinked into light in Lynette's mind. 'You said Joe told you about the telephone message, didn't you? The one telling you to go and see Brewer?'

'Yes, he was waiting for me when I got back after our ride.'

'Do you think he thought Brewer had found out it was him breaking the windows?'

'I thought that myself, at first,' Geordie said. 'Then I realised Brewer wouldn't have wasted time speaking to me first, he'd have pulled Joe up on it right away.'

'It's like I said before though,' Lynette said gently, 'that's the adult talking. Joe might easily have been convinced the game was up, and gone into hiding until things died down.'

'He did look a bit strange when he gave me the message,' Geordie admitted.

'Did you talk to him again that night?'

He shook his head. 'Like I said, I checked in on him, but he was asleep.'

'And gone first thing.' Lynette felt a little swell of worry. 'Do you always check on him?'

Geordie nodded. 'He's usually still awake though.' He sounded as if the realisation was just settling into place as he spoke, and Lynette squeezed his hands.

'He'd have expected you then, stayed put pretending to be asleep, and left before you got up this morning.'

'But where would he go?'

'Does he know about the room under the folly?'

'I don't know.' Geordie looked around him, as if he still hoped he might see the boy lurking somewhere in the yard.

'Maybe he's down at the Tinner's,' Lynette suggested. 'He'd know it well, if his dad used to work there. And there's likely to be food there, too.'

'I'll go down there now.' Geordie pulled his hat back on. 'Can I take Mack?'

'Of course, but you'll have to fetch him in.' Lynette started into the tack room to unhook Mack's halter. 'What can I do to help?'

'Maybe you could go over the forge and keep watch, in case he comes back.'

'All right.' Lynette tossed him the rope halter. 'I'll just finish up here and then go over.'

Lynette watched him cross to the paddock, seeing the tense set of his shoulders, then, accepting there was nothing she could do to help him, she turned back to her task. She should have thought to ask him to hook down a fresh bale of straw while he'd been right there, and she sighed as she picked up her rake to fetch it herself.

She went into the small barn, rake in hand, and climbed half-way up the ladder. There was a knack to it, snagging the rake's tines around the string of the nearest bale, then pulling sharply, swinging off the side of the ladder as the bale tumbled past to land on the barn floor. Lynette thrust the rake forward, blindly, and bounced it around in order to orientate herself with the straw bales, then thrust it ahead of her and heard a muffled yelp, which made her shout in shock for the second time that day, and almost lose her footing.

She froze, just for a moment and listened; had it really sounded the way she'd thought, or had her imagination played a trick on her, and it was actually the cat? She let go of the rake and climbed the ladder slowly, hoping she could trust her own senses. As her head drew level with the loft floor, she squinted into the shadows, then slid back down the ladder and went to the barn door.

'Geordie!' He looked up in surprise from where he was leading Mack out of the paddock. 'Put him back,' she called, and gestured to the hay loft. 'I've found something here that belongs to you.'

CHAPTER TWENTY-SEVEN

The Railway Inn, Dartmoor

Gwenna picked at her breakfast, knowing she should eat something but feeling too queasy. It was barely light outside, too early yet to go to the prison in the hope of being allowed to speak to someone, and she wished she'd been able to sleep better the night before; her eyes were grainy and sore, and she felt rumpled and unrested, yet impatient to get the day started. Whatever it might bring.

Around her, a few dogged and determined reporters had stayed overnight, in this and some of the other pubs near the prison. Gwenna listened for any snippets that might tell her exactly how bad the riot had been, but other than a news report that told of a single escapee, and a fire in the administration block, she'd been unable to glean anything useful. That it had been started, or at least heavily involved, a gang from London with a stupid name, didn't calm her fears at all; she knew, from bitter experience, what gang members were apt to do to one another when things went sour.

On the next table, two men were weighing up the prospects of staying one more day, in the vain hope of an exclusive, against the comforts of their own beds.

'We've got everything we're going to get,' the older one grumbled. 'We've telephoned it in, they're not going to give us anything else, surely?'

'You never know,' his companion argued. 'This is just the time when the real stuff starts trickling out. We might find out a bit more about the lag that legged it. Hey, that could be the headline!' He grinned, but the older man just rolled his eyes.

'All right, look. The day shift'll be coming on in ten minutes. If we catch them on the changeover we might get something halfway useful, but I'm going to be back on that road by nine, whether you're with me or not.'

Gwenna pushed her full plate away, and hurried back to her room to collect her coat and bag. She paid her bill, keenly aware of the time ticking away, and found herself leaving the pub at the same time as the two reporters. They were still arguing about the pointlessness, or otherwise, of questioning prison officers who'd be fed up to the back teeth of that by now, but perhaps she, as a lone female with a genuine concern, might have better luck than two pushy reporters with their cameras ready.

After a fast five-minute walk, she found herself at the top of the short slope into the prison, staring down at the archway through which Geordie had driven them less than a week before. She had looked up the meaning of those words carved on it – *parcere subjectis* – and found that the translation was *spare the vanquished*. It made her shiver; her father was one of the vanquished. Had he been spared, during the awful events of yesterday morning?

The place was by no means back to normal. A crowd milled around the entrance; reporters, including the two from the Railway Inn, were prowling, searching for a way to get closer to the gates beyond the archway; orders to retreat were barked, with, Gwenna was sure, more ferocity than usual. A group of four prison officers was coming towards the entrance from the direction of the village, and Gwenna could see they were already wary, casting sharp glances at everyone they passed, their hands unencumbered and ready to snatch up the batons at their hips.

One of them, a tall man with a taut expression, hesitated as his gaze passed over Gwenna, and she only just stopped herself from reaching out to catch his arm as he passed; judging from the tension in his frame he might have reacted in any number of ways.

'Please,' she called out, her voice almost drowned in the many shouts directed at the officers going on duty, 'Jonas Rosdew – is he all right?'

The officer slowed, and turned to look at her again. Seizing their chance, people began crowding close.

'Tom Bullows! I've heard nothing . . .'

'Ruby Sparks!' a reporter bellowed. 'He started it, didn't he?'

'What about Joseph Conning?'

'I need to know about Stephen Sargent!'

Gwenna started, and her heartbeat picked up as she searched the crowd. She found a slight, pretty girl with red hair and freckles, who didn't seem to fit the loud voice, yet shouted again and confirmed it.

'Sargent! Stephen! Just tell me if he's all right!'

The officer had also locked onto that shout over the others, and he turned back to Gwenna. 'Rosdew was all right last night when

I left.' He pointed at the girl. 'Tell her the same goes for Sargent. And don't go anywhere.'

Gwenna watched, baffled but relieved, as he rejoined his colleagues and they passed through the prison doors. She let the others crowd the doors, while she herself hung back near the entrance.

'What did he say to you?'

She turned to see the red-haired girl pushing towards her through the crowd, and she stepped forward to meet her. 'Are you Gracie Martyn?'

The woman nodded. 'What did he say?' she repeated, clearly too agitated to ask how Gwenna knew her.

'He told me that my father was safe as of last night. Said to tell you Stephen was, too.'

'Oh, thank God.' Gracie's shoulders dropped in relief, and she pushed her messy hair away from her eyes, as if only now allowing herself some concern at her appearance. 'I'm glad for your father, too,' she added. 'It's been a dreadful time wondering.'

'The officer said not to go anywhere,' Gwenna told her. 'I think he might be going to check, and then come and tell us if anything happened after he left.'

They were being buffeted now, by people who'd heard the brief exchange and were clamouring for explanations, and Gwenna's anxiety climbed again. Was she really cut out for a career of this nature, if a largely benign, medium-sized crowd could make her feel this tense?

Gracie snapped at everyone to *bugger off!* drawing surprised looks from several of them, but their responses were interrupted by the arrival of around seventy soldiers, the leading lieutenants of whom cut through the crowds with practised ease. In the ensuing scramble for information, Gwenna and Gracie withdrew to the road where they watched from a safe distance, thankful that the attention was no longer on them as the battalion was admitted to the prison.

'Where shall we wait?' Gracie asked, and Gwenna saw she was shivering. Whether it from standing around in the cold for hours, or a reaction to the hostility of the crowd, it was impossible to say for sure, but she tended towards the former explanation; Gracie didn't seem the type to frighten easily.

'I don't know,' she said, 'I'm not familiar with this place.'

'Where are you from?'

'Cornwall. Caernoweth, to be exact.'

'That's a long way to come. What's your father's name?'

'Jonas Rosdew.'

Gracie thought for a moment, then shook her head in apology. 'Stephen might have mentioned him, but I can't recall.'

'I came up here with Geordie, the day of the disturbance.'

A light flashed on behind Gracie's bright-blue eyes. 'Geordie *Sargent*?'

Gwenna nodded. 'That's how I knew who you were.'

'Oh!' Gracie seized Gwenna's arm, and gave a little jump of excitement. 'I'm so glad you're here!' She looked back at the prison again, where people were finally beginning to drift away. 'I suppose that officer remembered you from that day, and that's why he put us together.'

'I can't imagine he'd remember me, particularly,' Gwenna said, frowning. 'I spent most of the time at the corner table. I don't remember him at all.'

'Let's just get in behind this wall, out of the wind. He might be waiting for more people to leave before he comes back out.' Gracie

279

still had hold of Gwenna's arm, and now she pulled her into the shelter of the neat stone wall by the prison entrance.

They didn't have to wait long. The officer reappeared after only around twenty minutes, during which time Gwenna had explained her almost-friendship with Lynette, and her longer-standing one with Tory. Gracie had, in turn, explained how she, Marion, Geordie and Stephen had been inseparable as children. It was nice to hear the way she spoke of them all, and Gwenna would have liked to have heard more, especially about the Sargent brothers as boys. But she was even more eager to hear what the officer had to say.

He'd spotted them huddled against the wall, and, ignoring the shouts from those reporters who were still hoping for their exclusive scoop, he jerked his head minutely to indicate they should follow him. 'The convicts are all locked up today,' he muttered as he passed them. 'Some of us have had to take over their duties, so I volunteered to fetch milk from the farm.'

'What can you tell us?' Gracie asked, hurrying to keep up with him as he strode away from the prison and its surrounds.

'Not here.' He kept going, and they followed without further questions, until they came to a small gate that led into an area of densely packed trees. Gwenna hesitated, her heart creeping into a faster beat as the officer unlatched the gate and gestured them ahead of him.

'It's quite all right,' he assured them. 'I just need to make sure we're not in earshot of anyone on the road. What I'm going to tell you could lose me my career.'

Gwenna looked at Gracie, who shrugged. 'I'm tougher than I look,' she said. '*And* I've got a knife in my boot.'

Gwenna glanced at the officer, and his hastily smothered smile eased her mind somewhat. She allowed him to close the gate behind them, and he took the lead again, taking them through the trees to a small clearing with a couple of fallen trees across it.

'Sit down,' he said, gesturing to one of the logs. He took the other, and clasped his hands between his knees, leaning forward with an earnest look on his face. 'My name's Finegan,' he said. 'You can call me Paul, if you like.' He turned to Gracie. 'I know your name,' he said. 'Stephen's spoken of you a great deal.'

'You know him well?' Gracie's voice trembled a little, for the first time, and Gwenna realised how frightened for him she'd been, behind the bravado.

Finegan drew in a long, slow breath, and held it for a moment while he studied each of them in turn. 'I meant what I said,' he cautioned. 'If any of this gets back I'll lose my job. I might even end up inside. And that's no picnic for an ex-screw.'

'We won't say a word,' Gwenna assured him.

'If you've been decent to Stephen,' Gracie added, 'you've got my promise too.'

'I've tried to be.' Finegan turned back to Gwenna. 'They drafted in those of us who weren't on duty, so some of us weren't there at the start, but we saw some bloody stuff, I can tell you. All I know of your dad is that he wasn't part of what happened. He and a good many others, loyal prisoners they're calling them, kept well clear and even helped out where they could.' He looked tired, and a little sickened by the events. 'They're being taken care of.'

'Thank you,' Gwenna said quietly, her heart calming for the first time since she'd left Brewer's office. 'I'm glad to know it.'

'It's Stephen I need to talk about,' Finegan went on, turning back to Gracie. 'I've been doing my damnedest to keep him out of bother since he arrived. He should never have been put in there.'

281

'No,' Gracie said, her voice tight. 'He shouldn't.'

Gwenna reached out and squeezed her arm, surprising herself; she'd never been demonstrative before. But there was something desperately sad about seeing this spiky young woman, with all her talk of knives in her boot, fighting tears as she thought of the man she'd loved all her life.

'The reason I've kept a watchful eye over him,' Finegan said, 'is because I was at the Peter Tavy Inn, the night George Sargent the elder took the blow to the head that ended up killing him. I saw it all.'

'*You* were the witness!' Gracie sat up straight, her eyes wide.

'That's why no one ever reported my name. A prison officer could take a lot of stick.' Finegan shrugged. 'Anyway, I knew George, a bit. We weren't friends, I used to sit a few tables away, but I could hear everything he said. We all could, he wasn't the quietest. The night it happened, I heard his two boys saying they wanted to get off home. It was one of them's birthday, I think.'

'Stephen's.'

Finegan nodded. 'So anyway, George took it personal when they didn't want to stay, and when I went outside to . . .' he cleared his throat, 'to water the plants, I could hear him shouting at the older boy—'

'Geordie.'

'Right. Shouting that he was trying to come between him and Stephen. There was a tussle, the lad slipped in the mud, and his dad landed on top of him. Well, George had his hands around the lad's throat, and his knee on his chest, and I was about to stand in and pull him away, when Stephen came out of the pub.' Finegan stopped again, and when he continued, his voice was lower. 'I was relieved, truth to tell. All I could think about was my job, and

282

word getting back that I'd been in a fight. Stephen couldn't shift his dad though, and the other one, Geordie, he was starting to get weak, and stopped fighting. I went forward to pitch in, and that's when Stephen found the bit of granite and gave his dad a whack. Just like that. It wasn't a big piece, either.'

'And you told the police about it when Stephen pleaded guilty to murder?' Gracie said.

'When I saw in the paper that he was to go to the rope,' Finegan clarified. 'I couldn't believe it.'

'Well, thank God you did.'

'I couldn't do anything more for him. So when I saw how he'd changed from who I knew as this quiet, likeable lad, into some kind of thug, I had to do something to make up for what I lacked when it mattered.'

'You didn't lack anything,' Gwenna said, hearing the self-disgust in the officer's voice. 'You said yourself you were about to step in.'

'I should have done it sooner. Should have said something about George before, too.'

'What about George?' Gracie asked. She leaned forward, seeing something, perhaps, in Finegan's expression that Gwenna had missed. 'Said *what*, Paul?'

Finegan's hands began twisting together, and his voice was stilted. 'George put your young man in hospital, didn't he?'

'Did he?' Gracie's voice sharpened. 'When?'

'It was passed off as appendicitis, so Stephen tells me. He'd have been about twenty-one.'

'My dad had to drive him to hospital that night,' Gracie said slowly, frowning in memory. 'The Sargents didn't have a car, and Stephen woke up in the night in dreadful pain. He had a fever, and was . . .' She swallowed. 'Geordie said he was screaming. It was a ruptured appendix, they told us the day after.'

'Who told you?' Finegan looked at her steadily. 'The doctors?'

'Well, no, I wasn't with him. We weren't together then, we were just friends. Geordie told me though, and he was there.'

'Geordie likely only knew what his dad told him,' Finegan pointed out. 'It's not my place to give details, so don't ask me. I'll let Stephen do that, if he's willing.'

Gracie nodded, looking bemused and upset, but didn't press him on it. 'You promise he didn't get caught up in it all yesterday?' she asked instead.

Finegan hesitated, and Gwenna tensed again. 'What is it?'

Finegan didn't look at either of them. 'He did do *something* that would get him into trouble, if anyone found out. Deep trouble,' he added, more quietly. 'He helped someone escape.'

Gwenna started in dismay. Gracie's expression didn't change, but she shifted slightly on the log and she spoke with evidently hard-won control. 'Only one person escaped, I heard on the news. And they said that person was injured.'

'The bloke who was injured wasn't helping him, he was just with him. Stephen was the one who let the lad out of chokey, and he did it to save his life.' Finegan shook his head. 'I'm doing all I can to make sure it doesn't come out.'

'How did you find out?'

'Stephen told me.'

'Then he must trust you with his life,' Gracie said. 'It's one thing to tell you about his past, but *this*?'

'I told you, I've spent the past few years trying to keep him . . . well, to be blunt, keep him alive. He angered a lot of people before he mellowed again.'

'You're the one who pulled him away from that smaller riot, in the visitors hall,' Gwenna realised belatedly. 'You must have known something was coming, to have been ready.'

'Most of us knew,' Finegan said. 'We just didn't know when it would happen.'

'So.' Gracie sat forward, her eyes on the prison officer. 'What about this man who escaped? Do they know where he went?'

'Daniel Pearce.' Finegan shook his head. 'They're checking all the docks in Plymouth.' He seemed to be speaking very pointedly, and only to Gracie, and Gwenna frowned. Finegan seemed to decide he'd said enough, and he stood up.

'If I don't get back smartish with the milk they'll send someone after me to make sure I'm all right.' He waited for Gracie and Gwenna to move ahead of him, then spoke again. 'Have you got any messages for him, for when I go back?'

Gracie stopped at the gate, and her eyes were glistening. 'Only one thing, and I don't expect you to deliver it word for word.' She placed a hand on Finegan's shoulder and stretched up to place a kiss on the corner of his mouth. 'You can tell him that, but in your own words.'

'I'm sure I'll find a more appropriate turn of phrase,' he said, flushing, and smiled down at her. 'Come and see him when you can, love. I'll make sure you get a table somewhere at the side of the hall.'

'Thank you.' Gracie returned his smile, through the glimmer of tears Gwenna could see still trembling in her eyes. They watched him set off up the road towards the farm, looking lighter in spirit to have unburdened himself, and it had clearly eased Gracie's heart to know that Stephen wasn't alone in there after all.

'What do we do now then?' Gwenna asked, looking around

her and half-expecting to see the escaped convict lurking behind one of the stone walls.

Gracie blew out a relieved sigh. 'Now,' she said, 'you can go home knowing your dad's safe, and I go back to the farm, where we'll all go on pretending we never met Daniel Pearce, never taught him to drive, and *definitely* never gave him my dad's car to escape in.'

Gwenna stopped in the middle of the road. 'What?'

'I'll explain someday, if I see you again.' Gracie gestured with her thumb, over her shoulder. 'I have to go this way. It's a bit of a walk.'

'I'll drive you home,' Gwenna said at once. 'And you can tell me what you meant by what you just said.'

'It's quite a story,' Gracie warned. 'Tell you what, I'll explain it over a decent breakfast. I don't know about you, but I haven't eaten a thing since yesterday dinner time.'

'That sounds perfect.'

But when they arrived at Cudlip Farm, all thoughts of Daniel Pearce, Stephen Sargent, and even Jonas Rosdew, flew from Gwenna's mind. The first thing they saw, when they pulled into the yard, was a police car. The second thing was Gracie's mother, who ran from the house, her face white and her eyes red-rimmed but filled with wild hope.

'Oh, thank God you're home.' She bent and peered into the van, ignoring Gwenna entirely. 'Have you got Tilly with you?'

'Of course not.' Gracie was already climbing out, and she grabbed at the door frame and stared at her mother in dismay. 'You mean—'

'She's gone,' Mrs Martyn said in a cracked voice. 'Nobody's seen her since last night.'

CHAPTER TWENTY-EIGHT

Daniel was dreaming. It was the usual muddle of images and emotions, and there were noises too; doors, but not the clanging of iron ones, this time. Quieter, more sinister and secretive clicks and clunks. A creak, a rustle, and more clunks. In his dream he was passing through long corridors, hearing those strangely muffled doors open and close behind him but unable to turn around to see who was pursuing him. The stone throat of this corridor was shrinking around him; he felt stifled and hemmed in, and his arms raised to push at the walls, to force them to retreat, to allow him to breathe ...

He opened his eyes, still gasping, to complete darkness. A few blinks, and a frantic shove at the heavy coat over his head, brought some kind of weakly filtered light, and he lay very still for a moment. His mind was still in the depths of whichever strange prison it had taken him to as he'd slept, but he gradually became aware of his breath condensing in front of him, and of creeping aches as his limbs awoke. He slowly came to realise he was lying across the two front seats of a car, and as soon as that memory settled into place he drew in a deep draught of the icy air around him, and tried to sit up.

A flare of pain shot through his right arm, as he raised it to grasp the steering wheel and haul himself upright, and the now-familiar tightness of the developing scar tissue on his back made him grunt out a string of words he'd learned in the navy but rarely felt such a deep and unassailable need to use. They didn't help. He eased himself more slowly into a sitting position, which brought him behind the wheel and staring at a breath-fogged windscreen, with no clue as to what lay beyond it. It was daylight, just.

He remembered the sheer terror of driving through unfamiliar towns, across empty moorlands and up and down twisting country lanes; hedges he couldn't see, but which knocked their bare twigs against the car when he drifted too close, and made him jerk the wheel the other way in a panic. Whenever he'd come to a junction he'd prayed he wouldn't see any lights coming the other way, but on several of the few of occasions he'd had to stop, the car had jerked into sullen silence, throwing him painfully against the steering wheel. He'd had to sit calmly and think back, hearing Gracie Martyn's instructions echoing in his memory, and putting them into action. The engine had, thankfully, coughed back into life without too much coaxing, and he'd continued on his way with a good deal of muttering under his breath.

Every time another car had come the other way, thankfully not too often, he had slowed almost to a stop, convinced that alone would be enough to draw the wrong kind of attention. Gracie's waning patience had deeply instilled some of her snappier retorts, which at least made them memorable, and after he'd stopped to re-fill the tank from the can of petrol Farmer Martyn had left in the boot, the necessary motions seemed to come almost naturally when he started up again.

But as he'd come through Bodmin and started towards

Pencarrack, his eyes, grainy and dry, he had struggled to see through the dark; the car's lights picked out too little of the road ahead. His muscles had begun protesting all that had been required of them that long, long day, and, sitting still, but tense, as he nudged the car westwards, they'd begun to settle into all the wrong positions. He'd felt the ominous beginnings of what would no doubt turn into one of the worst headaches he'd ever had, and that had been the final straw; he'd found a gateway that looked overgrown enough, and parked the car. He'd got out into the dark night, urinated into the hedge for what felt like an hour, then got back behind the wheel and sat motionless for a long time.

Tiredness eventually overcame his need to play the day through in his mind, and he'd considered climbing into the back seat, pulling that stinking dogs' blanket over him, and letting the world go away for a while. But he realised he might be required to drive away, at speed and at a moment's notice, so instead he'd pulled Farmer Martyn's coat over as much of his head as he could, and lain down across the front seats. He couldn't remember thinking about anything after that, he must have fallen asleep in minutes, if not seconds.

Now his bones and muscles grated like some old, rusty mechanism as he leaned forward and wiped his sleeve across the windscreen, and he muttered another few choice words to distract himself while he cleared as much of the glass as he could. He wound down the window and let the frigid early morning air blow inside, shivering as he pulled his collar up around his ears again. As he waited for the glass to clear he took out the page Farmer Martyn had torn from his atlas, and studied the thick pencil mark that mapped his route. Last night he had made himself stop now and again, when he knew where he was, to put another mark along the line to show where he'd been. The most recent was at a spot just west of Bodmin, and indicated Daniel would need to veer off soon, to begin crossing Pencarrack Moor.

He considered getting something to eat from the knapsack Gracie had put in the back, but decided to wait until he was away from the main road and could relax further. He rubbed his cold hands together and reached out to start the motor, hoping he would remember everything Gracie had taught him, and after a jerky start he edged the car out of the gateway and back onto the road. He felt lighter this morning, even more so than when he'd landed on the other side of the prison wall. Perhaps it was because he was beyond where any police or soldiers heading towards Plymouth docks might see him by chance, and since no one knew he was coming this far down into Cornwall all the attention would be behind him now.

There was danger in complacency, he knew that; still he smiled to see the countryside emerging all around him as he turned off the main road and began following the smaller track indicated on the map. After two months staring at high walls and bars, every glimpse of a wide-open space was like a new breath of life; he couldn't begin to imagine how Stephen Sargent felt, knowing what he'd lost and would never regain. His gratitude and sympathy were so tightly entwined now that he couldn't separate them. All he could do was ensure the man's brother recognised that sacrifice and courage, and knew how deeply Daniel appreciated it.

He crested a slight hill and saw the vista open up in front of him, but even as he began to smile again, another shape came into focus, one which made him utter a loud curse and stamp on the brake. Something slid off the back seat behind him, as the car slewed to a stop, and landed with a soft thump, presumably the bag of food. But it didn't matter if the cake was smashed, the soup spilled from the flask, or the sandwiches were crushed; what mattered was the police car parked up ahead, on the very junction Daniel was supposed to take towards Pencarrack.

Daniel gripped the steering wheel, his panicked gaze moving from the police car to the surrounding terrain, searching for a different route. He quickly found the answer. To his left, the ground undulated a little more than to his right, and the scrubby grass disappeared into a group of trees that might or might not be the edge of a wood. Whatever it turned into further on, it was big enough here to conceal a man until the threat was gone, so Daniel released the handbrake and let the car roll onto the verge, then eased his door open and slipped out. He kept one eye on the junction, hoping the policeman's attention was elsewhere, as he sidled around the back of the car and crouched, preparing to run.

He gave some thought to the fallen bag of food, knowing he might have to lie low for hours, and weighed up the risk of delay against the benefit of provision. But even as he belatedly remembered that Gracie had actually stashed it safely in the footwell, and not on the back seat, the door beside his head popped open and he heard a small, accusatory voice.

'I bumped my head.'

Daniel stared in mute horror as the door opened wider and Tilly Sargent poked one booted foot awkwardly out, then the other, and dropped to the ground beside him. She rubbed at her forehead, which, he was relieved to see, didn't seem to have suffered too badly from her slide onto the floor.

'You stopped too fast,' she added, as if her earlier point had somehow been missed.

'What ...' He managed to stop himself from dragging up

some of those old favourite naval expressions, and put the back of his hand to his mouth to stop himself from shouting. 'You're in your nightwear,' was all he managed to whisper, and it sounded so incongruous a detail to focus on, that he almost laughed. For that moment, even the police car down the road had ceased to be important. 'Why are you here?'

'I wanted to see Daddy,' Tilly explained patiently. 'You're going to see him, so I borrowed you.' She spoke so matter-of-factly, that for a moment Daniel couldn't think of a single thing to argue with.

'Why did you stay hidden all this time?' He risked a look over the bonnet of the car, but there was no movement at the junction. He crouched back down and looked at Tilly with mounting exasperation. 'You could have told me you were hiding in the back.'

'Gracie's mum told me I had to go to bed,' Tilly said. She reached back into the car and pulled something off the back seat. Daniel saw it was her toy lamb. 'You would have tooken me back.'

'Taken,' Daniel corrected absently, his mind racing. 'Look, you can't come with—'

'Yes I can!' Tilly's voice had risen, and Daniel shushed her quickly. It was a still, cold morning, and he had no idea how well sound travelled out here, but there was nothing to mask the shrill voice of the now scowling little girl who squatted at his side.

'Wait a minute.' He bit his lip as he thought quickly. If he sent her to the police car, which was surely the safest thing for her, he would be caught within minutes. On the other hand, he couldn't possibly leave her here alone. The only thing he could do was to take her to her father.

The thought of carrying her across uneven grass, with any number of potential, unknown hazards, made him break out in a

292

sweat; he just wasn't strong enough. His legs were like unwieldy blocks of wood, from sitting in the car for so long following the punishment he'd put them through yesterday, his right arm throbbed from his fall, and his head was still pounding with fear and adrenaline.

'Can you run fast?' he asked, wondering what on Earth he was thinking.

'Really fast,' she confirmed. 'I can run faster than Billy in my class, and he's '

'All right,' Daniel said hurriedly. He pointed to the trees. 'We need to get to there, without anybody seeing us.'

'Why?'

'Because if anyone sees *us*, then *you* won't see your daddy.'

'Why?'

'Because ...' Daniel floundered, then opted for the truth. 'Because I'm a bad man, who's done bad things, and if the police catch me they'll lock me up again. And they'll think I stole you away,' he added, 'so they'll take you straight back to Gracie and not to Pencarrack.'

'Gracie doesn't think you're bad,' Tilly pointed out. 'Nor do her mum and dad. Otherwise they wouldn't help you.'

'No. Well.' Daniel sighed. 'The rest of it's true anyway. So, if you want to see Geordie you've got to do exactly as I tell you. Right?'

Tilly nodded, and took a firmer grip on her lamb. Daniel reached into the back and snagged the strap of the knapsack; even if he'd been prepared to go without food he'd have to keep the child fed, as well as out of sight. He hooked the bag over his shoulder, and eased the car door closed; the car would attract less attention from passers-by that way.

'When I tell you to go, you go,' he said firmly. 'Don't stop, and don't look back to see if I'm following. I will be,' he added, seeing the sudden uncertainty on her face. 'But I might have to lie low once or twice.'

'Do I have to, as well?'

'Not unless you hear me shout. Just run, as fast as you can.' Daniel took one more look at the stationary police car, then nodded. 'Go!'

Tilly, one hand pulling her nightie up over her knees, the other gripping her lamb, went. Daniel watched her crossing the ground at a surprising speed, and rose to a half-crouch in alarm as she disappeared abruptly, before realising she'd simply found one of the natural dips in the terrain. He made himself wait until he saw her dark head bobbing near the tree line, then began sprinting, almost doubled over, following roughly the same path. With every step he was braced for another fall, dreading the sounds that might be pulled from him before he was able to stop himself.

But he didn't fall, and, with his heart pounding terrifyingly hard, he launched himself beneath the shelter of the trees, where Tilly had disappeared just a few minutes ago. He crashed to his knees, breathing hard, his hands sweating where they clutched at the handle of the knapsack. 'Tilly?' he called in a low voice. 'You can come out now.'

There was no movement, and he called again, growing worried. 'Tilly! It's all right, it's me, Daniel.'

There was a rustle just up ahead, and Tilly crept out from behind a rotten tree stump. She came over to where Daniel knelt, and, to his surprise, she put her arms around his neck and hugged him tightly. He hugged her back, feeling a prickling at the back of his eyes. What had he done, bringing this child into his own uncertain world? He should have stayed away from the farm, and from Gracie and her family, and definitely away from Tilly.

'I'm going to get you somewhere safe,' he promised her, his word muffled against the lamb that was pressed against his face. 'Are you hungry?'

Tilly drew away, shaking her head. 'I need another wee though.'

'Another?' Daniel remembered his dream. Those odd-sounding doors behind him. 'Did you get out and have one while I was asleep?'

'I tried not to wake you up.'

'You didn't.' Daniel sighed, more resolved than ever that he had to get her to safety. If he'd been sleeping so deeply that he'd incorporated potential danger sounds into his dreams, anything might have happened. 'We need to find a telephone,' he said, 'so we can tell Gracie and her mum and dad that you're all right. And what about your mother?'

'She's not very well,' Tilly said at once. 'I'm not supposed to worry her.'

'Well, Gracie'll have probably told her you're missing, by now, so she'll already be worried.' Daniel pulled open the knapsack and took out a wax paper-wrapped package. 'Go and ... see to your doin's,' he said. 'Then come back and have something to eat. We'll have a long walk ahead of us.'

He unwrapped the package to reveal two thickly buttered beef sandwiches, with generous slatherings of mustard, which he wasn't sure Tilly would like. But then, Gracie hadn't packed them with a six-year-old in mind. He scraped most of the mustard away with the crust of his own sandwich, and when Tilly came

295

back she accepted it, and pulled only a mild grimace of dislike as she bit into it.

They ate without talking at first, then Daniel coaxed out of her the story of what had happened with her mother's fall, and the loss of Tilly's little brother or sister. He learned why Geordie had left them, or at least as much of it as Tilly understood, and in turn he told her all about her Uncle Stephen, and how he'd helped Daniel almost from the first day they'd met. The child was sweet, if a little bit persistent with her questions, and it was hard to break the conversation, to pack up, and face the difficult walk ahead of them. But it was time.

Daniel closed the buckles on the knapsack, and slung it over his shoulder again. He consulted the much folded and torn atlas page, and found the clump of trees marked there. Then he peered ahead through the trees themselves, and saw a faint path that looked as if it led through in a fairly direct route. He turned back to his new companion, and held out his hand.

'Come on then, Travelling Tilly,' he said. 'Let's go and find your dad.'

CHAPTER TWENTY-NINE

'Sir, over here!'

The young constable by the farmyard gate was peering at the ground, and his sergeant, who was talking to Gracie, clicked his tongue irritably.

'What?'

'Footprints, sarge.'

'It's a thoroughfare, lad,' the sergeant said in tones of strained patience. 'Of course there are footprints. Now,' he said, turning back to Gracie. 'Your father says his vehicle was here when he went to bed last night, but gone this morning. When did you last—'

'Sir!' The constable's shout grew more urgent, but seemed unwilling to expand on what he'd seen, in front of civilians. The sergeant closed his notebook and nodded to excuse himself. As he crossed to the gate, Gwenna was about to express her relief, but saw that Gracie's gaze had lit on something lying in the mud. The young woman's shoulders slumped, and at first Gwenna took the gesture as some kind of defeat, then she recognised that, on the contrary, it was the lifting of a great weight. Gracie's eyes rose to meet hers, and her expression of taut fear had vanished.

'She's gone with him,' she said in a low voice. 'The little horror hid in the bloody car and went with him!'

'What?' Gwenna tried to see what Gracie had been looking at, but was distracted by the return of the sergeant who was frowning deeply.

'Are you sure you didn't see anyone last night?' he asked, taking out his book again.

'No, I told you. My mother put Gracie to bed while I washed the dishes, Dad finished up in the barn, and then we all went to bed.' Her expression folded again, and she was a picture of miserable fear. 'Do you think someone took my friend's little girl?'

'No,' the sergeant said. 'That would hold him up. It wouldn't suit him at all.'

'Suit who?' Gwenna asked.

'The lag who broke out of the prison,' the sergeant said. 'We've seen his boot prints in the mud by your gate, pointing that way.' He gestured down the hill, towards the river. 'Clear as day, those arrows cut into the soles.' He shook his head, almost sympathetic. 'Idiot thinks he'll get away from us, but they never do.'

'He came through our *yard*?' Gracie's eyes were wide. 'Do you think he intended to steal from us?'

'Likely just lying low,' the sergeant said comfortingly. 'I don't think he took your car though, that's more likely some local thief who couldn't be bothered walkin' home.' He gestured for the constable to use the car radio to pass on the news to those involved in the manhunt, and returned to his questions about Tilly. He had a satisfied air about him now though, as if he were already receiving his due praise from his superior. Then he patted Gracie on the arm, and reiterated that she should inform them immediately if the little girl turned up.

'She's most likely broken something, and gone to hide somewhere,' he assured her. 'That's nearly always what's happened.'

'Perhaps she's gone home,' Gwenna said, as if she knew the family well. 'You know what she's like when anyone's cross with her. She always wants her mum.'

'Of course,' Gracie said, a smile reappearing. 'Do you know, I'll bet that's what she's done! I'll go and speak to her mother, Sergeant; you needn't trouble yourselves with that. I'm sure you ought to be following those boot prints; anyway. So sorry to have distracted you from your job.'

'Not at all, miss.' The officer gave her a benign smile. 'Be sure to call again if your friend's daughter doesn't turn up for dinner time. And meantime we'll keep a lookout for your dad's car.'

When the police had driven away, Gracie crossed to the spot where her father's car usually sat, easily identified by the heavy tread marks in the yard. She bent down, just as her mother came back out of the house, and as she stood up she slipped something smoothly into her pocket. She crossed to comfort her mother.

'I'm going across to Marion's,' she said. 'I think Tilly probably went there. She knows the way well enough by road.'

Her mother looked cautiously relieved, clearly wanting to believe it. 'Do you think so?'

'She was talking about her father last night,' Gracie said, 'so it's likely she's a bit homesick. I told the policeman I'd go and see Marion anyway, to let her know what's happened. Hopefully we'll get there and find there's no need to worry after all. I'll telephone you as soon as I know.' She looked at Gwenna. 'Would you mind giving me a lift into the village? It's not far.'

Gwenna watched her hopes of that decent breakfast march off into the distance, but nodded. She was intrigued to find out how

Gracie knew where Tilly had gone, and it was obvious she didn't want to discuss it in front of her mother.

They got back into the van, and Gracie pointed out the way. As they drove through the gate, Gwenna tried to see the arrowed footprints the policeman had talked about and saw that they did indeed point to Daniel Pearce having left a mucky trail through the field. Gracie gave a low chuckle.

'That'll have been my dad,' she said. 'They swapped boots last night. Dad must have laid a false trail down to the river, to keep the search parties busy if they came back. I'll bet he's left them in the river down there. Turn right here.'

Gwenna grinned as she nosed out onto the lane. 'And what about Tilly? How did you know she'd gone off with Daniel?'

'Oh, I found this.' Gracie rummaged in her coat pocket and withdrew a ragged-looking yellow ribbon. She flicked the bell that hung on it. 'It's hers. She's forever being told how noisy it is, so my guess is that she took it off before she got into the car. That way she could be as quiet as she needed to be.' She shook her head, part admiring, part exasperated. 'She's always had a talent for hide-and-seek; she must have been in there all the time I was teaching Daniel to drive, hiding under the dog's blanket.'

'Will she be safe though, when he finds her?' Gwenna asked, not sure how the girl could be so cheerful about the whole thing. 'He's an escaped convict, after all.'

'You wouldn't worry, if you'd met him. He'll see she's looked after.'

'You seem very sure.'

'Stephen trusts him,' Gracie said simply. 'And they're going to find Geordie. That's good enough for me.'

'Then why didn't you tell your mother?'

'Because, as much as she's always liked Stephen, she doesn't know him like I do. She was good to Daniel last night, but when it comes to Tilly it might be a different story. I didn't want her telephoning the police again.' Gracie leaned forward. 'There, up that little road by the trees. The house with the yellow curtains upstairs. You needn't wait,' she added, as Gwenna drew to a stop outside the house. 'I can cut back across the fields.'

She thanked Gwenna and got out of the car just as the front door jerked open and a young woman stood there, her face a mask of misery. 'Gracie! Something terrible's . . . just come, quickly!'

'She must know already,' Gracie said, as Gwenna opened her door to follow her.

Marion gave Gwenna a quick, curious glance, and Gracie quickly introduced her as someone she'd met at the prison. But the word only seemed to increase Marion's agitation as she ushered them into the house, and they quickly realised it wasn't news of Tilly's disappearance that had worried her.

'They came here,' she said, as she followed them into the dark little sitting room. 'Them from the prison. Guards, and police and what-not.'

'They always do, though,' Gracie said. 'You know that. And it's not like Stephen was the one who escaped.'

'No, but the lad who did, Pearce, his name is, was Stephen's cellmate, and this was Stephen's last address. They reckoned he must have told Pearce to come here for help.' Marion fretted, twisting the material of her dress tightly in her fingers. 'I could *brain* your Stephen! Why bring Geordie into it?'

Gracie stepped closer to her friend and put a comforting hand on her arm. 'But now they know Geordie doesn't live here any more, they'll have no way of knowing where Daniel's gone to find him. You didn't tell them, did you?' she asked suddenly, her eyes narrowing as Marion looked away.

'Of course not!'

'Then they're both safe,' Gwenna put in, hoping she sounded convincing. 'The police will never think to look for Daniel down in Cornwall, let alone somewhere like Pencarrack. The thing is . . .' She threw Gracie a quick, nervous glance. It was time.

'What is it?' Marion demanded, looking from Gwenna to Gracie.

'I think Tilly's gone with him,' Gracie said quietly.

Marion's expression froze, and she stopped the frantic twisting of her fingers. Shocked tears glistened in her eyes, as she stared at a spot on the rug rather than look at Gracie. 'What?' she whispered.

Gracie hesitantly told her what she believed to have happened, and then drew the muddy bell from her pocket by its ribbon. 'So, we know she's in good hands,' she finished quietly, but from her voice it was clear she knew how it sounded.

'Good hands?' Marion's voice was barely audible, at first. '*Good* hands?' she repeated, incredulousness melting into horror. 'She's six years old, and with a . . . an escaped . . .' She fell silent, her throat working, and her gaze going to a framed photograph on the mantelpiece. Gwenna winced as she saw the wide brown eyes staring solemnly back at her. Six really was so very, very young. But Gracie was sending a silent plea for her to echo the optimism, and Gwenna dutifully nodded.

'Stephen knows Daniel's a good man,' she said. 'And Gracie's family wouldn't have helped someone they believe to be in the wrong, either, would they?'

'I'm only glad the police don't know where Daniel's going,'

Gracie said. 'It'd be just like Geordie to want to help, if only for Stephen's sake, but it would be terrible for him to be caught doing it. Both Sargent brothers in prison together?' She shook her head. 'Bad business. Everyone would want to take their chances against them.'

Marion sank down onto the arm of the chair beside her. Her face was pasty-looking, and, remembering the awful incident from which she was still recovering, Gwenna was about to suggest she leave them to it when Marion put a hand to her chest and closed her eyes.

'They *do* know where he's going.' Her voice was hollow.

Gracie and Gwenna exchanged another look, this time of dismay. 'You said you didn't tell them,' Gracie said. 'You said that—'

'They went upstairs, into our room, and had a good old rummage around. Nothing left of Geordie's there. Then they went into Tilly's, and they found a letter. Well, an old envelope with a note written on it.'

'A note?' Gracie shook her head briefly. 'But still—'

'"Dear Father Christmas",' Marion said flatly. '"I've gone to stay with my daddy, please don't forget to come and see me." And the address of the Pencarrack forge, right there, plain as you like.'

Silence fell over the room, broken by the spitting of a log, which made Gwenna jump, and brought her back to her senses. 'We need to telephone Geordie, and warn him. He can't become involved in this.'

'But he needs to be, for Tilly's sake,' Gracie argued. 'Still, he should be warned not to let the police see him.'

'I don't have a telephone,' Marion said. 'Nearest one would be the box in the village.'

303

'Show me where,' Gwenna said to Gracie. She turned back to Marion. 'Try not to worry about Tilly, Mrs Sargent. We'll make sure Geordie knows she's on her way.'

Repeated calls placed to the forge went unanswered. Eventually Gwenna asked for the stables instead, and told Lynette what had happened. She replaced the receiver and went out to where Gracie was pacing the road, her arms folded tight against her chest, and passed on the news that Geordie was unreachable. Then she offered to drive Gracie back to the farm.

'No,' Gracie said, and took a deep breath. 'I promised Daniel I'd go to see his mother, and make sure she hasn't been treated badly by the search parties. I was going to take a train, but perhaps you wouldn't mind dropping me off there on your way home, instead?'

'Of course. Where does she live?'

'Daniel's given me her address,' Gracie called, already running back to where Gwenna had left the van. 'But I don't know that area so we'll have to ask someone when we get near.'

'We'll have to be careful who we speak to, though,' Gwenna said, following her. She slipped into the driver's seat, grasped the steering wheel, and let out her pent-up breath. 'Safe to say, I think, that today it's best *not* to ask a policeman.'

CHAPTER THIRTY

Lynette filled the new horses' hay nets after Geordie and Joe had left, thinking about the exchange that had occurred between the two of them. Geordie had clearly taken her parenting advice to heart, and Joe's face had been a picture of astonishment as Geordie had thundered on at him for a good few minutes about responsibility and thought for others, and that was even before he'd move on to the damage the boy had caused at the pit.

When the tirade was over, Geordie had fixed him with a hard glare and demanded, 'Well? What have you got to say, boy?'

Joe's face had clouded over, and Lynette had seen the sudden uncertainty cross Geordie's, but as soon as the boy had shouted, 'Nothing!' and turned to stalk away, she'd known it was all right.

Joe had slammed the gate and vanished down the lane, and Geordie had turned to her in alarm. 'Well, that wasn't a very good—'

'That,' Lynette had said, pointing in the direction Joe had taken, 'was the healthy response of a rightfully rebuked boy. He'll have gone back to the forge, and he'll throw a few things around, you can put your last penny on it. But he had the same look about him that Xander used to get when he'd been told off by our father.'

Geordie had remained unconvinced for a moment, then she saw that her words had filtered through his dismay, and his hesitant smile had appeared. 'Your father.'

'He'll sulk for ages though,' she warned him, resting her hands on his chest as his arms came around her. 'And I expect he'll be very good at it. He probably won't speak to you until teatime.'

He grinned. 'I'd better go back and give him someone to sulk at then.'

'I wouldn't mind betting he's feeling more loved, and more secure right now than he has in months.'

'Really?'

'He was terrified,' Lynette said. 'But I was watching him. The more you shouted, the more he relaxed. He probably thought you'd sack him, and that would mean he'd lost you as well as his job. You just need to make sure he knows that, even if you do have to let him go someday, he's still your family.'

'I will.' He dropped his usual kiss on her forehead. 'Thank you, O wisest of women. Come up for your dinner, see if that brings him back to himself a bit sooner.'

He'd left soon afterwards, not wanting to leave the boy at the forge for too long on his own, and Lynette and Tory had returned to their own work. At around ten o'clock Tory had gone inside to make hot drinks, and Lynette took a moment to talk to the newer horses, murmuring gently as she moved around them. They had calmed a great deal since Tory had been working with them, but Sally, the newest pony, from the foundry explosion, was still alarmingly skittish. Bella wasn't entirely herself yet either, and

Lynette planned to take her for a walk in the fresh air after their mid-morning break. She was putting a halter aside, ready, when Tory returned waving a note.

'I just found this in the corner by the door. It was wrapped around a key. Gwenna's asked if one of us wouldn't mind opening up the shop for her for an hour or so.'

'She must be frantic,' Lynette said. 'Poor girl. You don't think Jonas would have risked trying to escape, do you?'

Tory shook her head. 'He'd be mad to, Gwenna says they plan to let him out later this year. Still, it's a worry, and I don't blame her for driving up there when she heard the news.'

Lynette nodded. 'I'm not happy though, her going up there alone into goodness knows what.'

'Then the least we can do is just what she asks,' Tory said. 'I don't mind doing it for a bit, if you can work Sally before you take Bella out.' She nodded at the foundry pony. 'I've got paperwork to do later though, so perhaps we can swap after dinner?'

Lynette agreed to go down to the Caernoweth shop at two, and closed the gate behind Tory's car as it rumbled off down the lane. She went back to work, walking Sally slowly around the yard, leading her closer each time to the paddock fence, where Hercules stopped his usual grazing and watched them curiously. Sally shied the first time, but on the next circuit she only took a small side-step and gave Hercules a mistrustful look. The third time, Sally stopped, and the two ponies shuffled closer together; Hercules stretched his neck forward, and Sally did likewise, and the two of them huffed at one another for a moment before Sally decided she'd had enough, and ambled onward.

Lynette took her back to her stall, reflecting once again on how easily she might have missed out on all this. If she hadn't decided to visit Bertie last year instead of writing, such a seemingly small decision, she wouldn't be standing here now, part-owner of this wonderful place. Geordie wouldn't have had the means to buy the forge, and take on an apprentice, so goodness knew where he and Joe would be now. If it hadn't been for Xander's voice, pushing her to be brave and visit this place, she would never have known either of them, but with Geordie she'd discovered a capacity for love she'd never imagined – where would that love have gone otherwise?

That thought was the one that intrigued her the most; if she hadn't come here, would she still be sitting in her parents' drawing room in Brighton, sensing hopelessly that there was someone out there that her heart belonged to? Would she simply have pushed that notion away, or would she have accepted the first man she felt remotely comfortable with? Lived a mediocre but satisfactory life, never knowing what she could have known here in Cornwall? She smiled as she closed Sally's stall door and gave the pony one last rub between the ears. No, that wouldn't have happened. Some other event would have brought her here, and into Geordie's path, the Fates would have made sure of that.

She was growing unusually hungry, and remembered they'd been too distracted by Gwenna's note to take their morning break. She looked at her watch; Geordie wouldn't stop for his dinner until one o'clock, and it was only just after eleven. She closed up the hay loft and went up to the flat to find something to eat that would carry her for the next two hours, after which she would drive down to relieve Tory at the Rosdews' shop. She was pushing open the door when she heard the telephone already ringing, and she quickened her steps, worried the caller would ring off before she got there. The operator connected the call, and Lynette heard Gwenna's voice coming down the line, rushed and worried sounding.

'The escaped convict is coming to find Geordie, and he's got Tilly with him!'

Lynette listened in growing incredulity as Gwenna fell over her words trying to explain all she knew. Her heart faltered when she realised the danger Geordie would be in if he was caught helping a criminal to evade capture.

'I tried calling him,' Gwenna said, 'but there's no answer.'

'They'll be working,' Lynette said. 'They won't hear the telephone from out there.'

'You'll have to warn him,' Gwenna said, 'the police already know Pearce is coming to find him.'

'*What?* How?'

'They found the address of the forge at his old house here in Peter Tavy.'

'But how do they know he—'

'I'll explain later. I'm going to come home, now I know my dad's safe, but I have to take Gracie somewhere first. Go and warn Geordie, quickly!'

Lynette hung up, and spent a precious few minutes hunting for her car key, before accepting that it would be quicker to go on foot if she cut through the small wooded area at the edge of the stables. She plunged into the trees on the other side of the paddock, and had to slow down to watch her footing on the wet roots and fallen branches and twigs; each step took far too long, and her imagination leapt into every ridiculous, far-fetched and terrifying scenario possible. By the time she emerged onto the village road she was out of breath, and convinced that she would arrive to find Geordie already being bundled into a police car. She rounded the corner by Gwinn's Copse and saw the smoke curling up through the trees, but as she came within sight of the forge she saw a burly figure striding towards it. It wasn't Sergeant Brewer, she saw with relief, so perhaps it had nothing to do with what was happening. But she didn't believe that.

She quickened her pace again as she saw the man turn into the yard. He was carrying nothing that looked as if it might need repairing, but perhaps he was simply picking something up? She forced her mind to accept that premise, and her pace to a more natural walk, and took a couple of deep breaths to steady herself. The last thing she wanted was to show worry or guilt. The gate remained open, as usual, so she was able to cross the yard almost all the way to the forge before the man heard her and turned to look. She recognised him, vaguely, but couldn't place him at first, and she was more eager to signal to Geordie that she needed to speak to him. Her eyes scanned the area but saw only Joe and the newcomer. Joe was looking nervous and trapped, as the man ignored Lynette and stepped closer to him.

'Where's your boss?'

'He's not here.'

'I can see that, boy! I said where is he?'

Lynette spoke up, her tone business-like to hide her relief. 'Can I help you? Have you come to collect something? I can probably find—'

'David Donithorn,' the man said, throwing a quick look over his shoulder. 'I'm here on behalf of Sergeant Brewer, who needs to speak to Mr Sargent on an urgent matter.'

So, he's another Watcher? Lynette wondered how many more

Brewer had working for him, and felt a tremor of unease that she had no idea, or who they might be. 'Well, as Joe says, he's not here. Can I carry a message from you, in case I see him?'

Donithorn spoke to Joe again, his voice hard. 'Are you going to answer me, or no?'

Joe flung Lynette a questioning look, and she shook her head minutely, but Joe's obvious nervousness won out. 'He's gone down to Priddy Farm,' he said. 'Keir Garvey's had a wheel come off one of his carts.'

Donithorn gestured at Geordie's van, parked by the fence. 'Long way to go on foot.'

'Van's out of petrol, we couldn't afford it until some payments come in. Mr Garvey came and fetched him.'

Lynette found a polite smile. 'We'll send him to see the sergeant when he returns.'

'I'll go and find him myself,' Donithorn said, clearly annoyed. He pushed past Lynette on his way out of the yard, and she turned back to Joe, trying not to show her disappointment. He wasn't to know, after all.

'I have to get to him quickly,' she said, peering past the gate to make sure Donithorn wasn't still lurking in the road.

'Why, what's happened?' Joe picked up his hammer again, to continue work.

'I can't stop to talk just now.' Lynette saw Donithorn had emerged on the other side of the copse, and she started across the yard. 'I'm going to have to go back to the stables for my car, and try to beat Mr Donithorn down to the farm.'

'Oh, Geordie's not there,' Joe said blithely. 'I lied about that.'

Lynette blinked, pushed out a relieved sigh, and came back. 'Where is he then?'

'He's gone to the clay works.'

'What for?'

'What's *happened*?' he countered.

She told him about the escaped prisoner and his quest to find Geordie, adding that the police now had the address of the forge and would be delighted to find Geordie and the prisoner together. At the last moment, however, she decided to keep the news about Tilly to herself; it would likely send Geordie off on some lunatic hunt to find the man, and defeat the object completely. Not to mention reawakening Joe's resentment towards Tilly. 'So if he's caught helping a convict, he'll be jailed for sure,' she finished. 'Now, your turn. Why's he at the clay works?'

Joe blushed, and cast his eyes downward. 'He's gone to plead my case with Mr Doidge.' His face was set in miserable guilt now. 'He wants to pay him back for the damage, but he don't want no one else to see him there and guess it was me, so he's gone the back way; up the bridle path and out onto the lane down from Hazelmere.'

'But he often has legitimate business at the pit' Lynette pointed out. 'No one would think twice at seeing him, surely?'

'He says everyone's on the sharp look-out, and since it's all stopped now he thinks if anyone sees him they'll put two and two together. So he's going to sneak into the pit through the north entrance. No one's working up that end just now.'

Lynette looked over at the bicycle leaning on the wall, but Joe must have seen the apprehension on her face as she eyed the pedals dubiously. It had been a long time since she'd ridden a bicycle. She gave Joe a pleading look.

'All right. I'll go.' He untied his apron, draped it across the anvil, and set off, and Lynette took several deep breaths to settle her nerves. Then she shut the open kiln Joe had been using, dampened down the fire in the oven, and went into the cottage to await news. She'd done all she could, and so had Gwenna. Now it was up to Joe.

CHAPTER THIRTY-ONE

Geordie pulled his collar up and his hat down, and shoved his hands into his pockets. The back road was much longer and twistier than the open pathway from the village, and had too many hills for his liking, but it offered a more sheltered route and several alternative destinations; he had no wish to meet anyone who'd immediately question why he was anywhere near South Pencarrack, with no clear business at the store.

The necessary further conversation with Joe, back at the forge, had bounced wildly between sulkiness and defensive argument from him, and raised voices on both sides; Geordie had kept in mind Lynette's assertion that Joe was responding in a healthy way to a firm, fatherly hand, and had fought his own instinct to back down. To his relief they had eventually fallen into a calmer discussion, leading to Geordie's decision to come clean to the one man who might be able to lock all this away for good.

Thankfully, John, more like a father than a friend, reluctantly agreed to Geordie's terms, and, on being assured there would be no further breakages, to keeping young Joe's name out of any discoveries he might make. Geordie made his first payment for the repairs, silently bidding farewell to new tyres for the van as he did so, and made his way back to the worked-out and abandoned north end of the pit. He kept his eyes peeled but saw no one, as he climbed the locked gate and dropped down to the road again, and, with a deep sigh of relief, and a sense of things finally slipping back into a more settled groove, he started back towards the forge.

The road was quiet, but this far on the outskirts of the village it wasn't unusual to go miles without seeing anyone, since the surface of the new road was much kinder on motor vehicles, and flatter for walkers. There were few houses dotted around this area, and all of them sat a long way into their own grounds, so if an inhabitant fancied a walk there were doubtless much more preferable routes to take. The peace was, in fact quite soothing, and Geordie found himself relaxing into the walk, and enjoying exercising his legs instead of his back and shoulders for a change.

He checked his pocket watch and saw that he'd been enjoying it rather too much, dawdling and absorbing the peace. Letting his mind ramble and travel where it would. It was already past half past eleven, it had been a long morning, and a difficult one, and it would take him over an hour to reach the village again, especially with these hills. Remembering he'd invited Lynette for her dinner, he quickened his step in case she came early after all.

Away to his right, the black line that marked the edge of Pencarrack Woods disappeared as he descended one hill, then drifted back into view as he puffed his way up the other side. Eventually it was lost to the mist behind him, which meant that Hazelmere, and Jago Carne, were just around the corner. Instantly Geordie's mood darkened. Images of the brute standing over him in the rain, his booted foot drawn back for another kick, flickered in the shadows of his mind, and he heard the echo of the taunt that had started it. *It's no wonder your missus took up with a real man, you liquor-soaked, useless excuse for a father . . .*

He realised his hands were clenched in their pockets, and determinedly took them out and uncurled them, but the grim remembrances lasted until he was long past Hazelmere and the likelihood of running into Carne. Only then did he try to concentrate once again on what lay ahead instead of what had passed into history. He pictured Joe's relief, when he learned it was all over, and then Lynette's smile warming him across the table in the cottage, and his musings turned to how soon he could pay off his debt and ask her the question that had rarely been far from his mind lately. Skimping on meals hadn't helped nearly enough, and she'd already noticed he was losing weight; he'd have to think of something else, or they'd still be living apart when they were fifty.

When he was halfway home, and had just rounded a tight bend, he became aware that the wind had dropped. He pushed his hat back on his head to let the air get to his hot face and heard the scraping and knocking of boots on the road behind him. He stopped to listen, wondering how long it had been going on while he'd been huddled inside the leather of his hat and the rough wool of his coat collar. His first thought was that Carne had spotted him passing, and was intent on finishing the job he'd started last year now that he'd met Geordie alone, without witnesses.

His heartbeat picked up a faster pace, but he was ready this time. Rather than melt into the hedge, he stood in the middle of the lane and turned back, to face the corner he'd just rounded; if Carne thought he was going to make an ass of himself by running, he'd be surprised; hopefully startled enough to falter and give Geordie a chance at the first blow this time.

But it wasn't Jago Carne who came around the bend, it was a man of medium height, beardless, with a mass of dark hair falling over his brow and a look of trapped fear as he came almost face-to-face with Geordie in the road.

Age: twenty-seven. Dark hair ... Blue eyes. Five feet eleven inches. Prison clothing at time of absconding ... No prison clothing here, but what he was wearing was ill-fitting and clearly borrowed, which could easily have extended to a borrowed razor. The man slithered to a halt, and his eyes cast left and right, but the road was narrow, and the hedges high. He straightened, and fixed his eyes on Geordie's.

'Morning,' he said, his voice clear, his tone easy. When Geordie neither responded nor moved aside, he tried again. 'Pencarrack that way, is it?' He pointed. 'Have I got far to go?'

'Nice try,' Geordie said dryly. 'I've got someone who'd like to meet you, Mr Pearce.'

Pearce's shoulders dipped, but only slightly. 'Pearce? Don't know who that is. My name's Micky Frier.'

'Tripe,' Geordie said mildly. His blood was thrumming now, as he recalled Brewer saying that he should simply report the sighting. But this man had badly assaulted a prison officer. *Vicious*, was the word Brewer had used, and Pearce certainly looked as if he could do something like that; there was a hardness to his features, and his eyes were constantly moving, assessing, judging, gauging. 'I've got to take you in,' Geordie said, feeling in his coat pocket for the handcuffs Brewer had given him. 'Will you put up a fight?'

Pearce looked about to once again deny understanding, then he shook his head. 'No. But you've got me wrong,' he added, as Geordie took a step towards him. 'I can guess what you've been

317

told, but I'm not a violent man. You don't need those.' He nodded at the cuffs. 'I'll walk with you.'

'You'll understand if I don't want to take that risk,' Geordie said. Pearce's manner confused him; he'd been expecting some thug on Carne's level, if not his size. This young man seemed to realise he'd gone as far as he could, and despite what he'd learned of him, Geordie found himself hoping they'd go easy on him when they got him back to Dartmoor.

Pearce placed his wrists together and held them out for the cuffs. 'Just let me explain as we go. Will you do that much?'

Geordie nodded. 'Of course. It'll go better for you that you've—'

His words were cut off in a grunt, as Pearce swung his linked hands like a club, striking him on the shoulder and sending him sprawling against the dry-stone wall. He was on his feet again quickly enough, but Pearce had already taken off down the road, and Geordie uttered a heavy curse before lurching after him. Pearce ran awkwardly, as if his limbs were either too tired to hold him upright, or suffering from lack of use. He staggered sideways into one hedge, used his hands to shove himself back into the centre, and almost sent himself into the opposite side. Geordie caught up easily enough, but if he'd thought Pearce was going to give in easily, once he realised there was no choice, he soon changed his mind.

Pearce spun around in a full circle, lashing out and making Geordie hiss and duck out of the way to avoid a lucky blow. He didn't fight like a military man, nor like someone capable of attacking a fit and healthy prison warder; whatever harm he'd done to that man, he'd probably done by chance. However, he was agile, and Geordie's ribs had flared painfully when he'd hit the stone wall, making him slower than he wanted to be. It took

318

him a while to push Pearce against the hedge, and Pearce fought him every inch of the way, alternately growling out curses and begging Geordie to listen.

'You had your chance to talk,' Geordie said, annoyed at being caught off-guard, and he shoved Pearce harder into the wall while he fumbled with the unfamiliar handcuffs. Pearce wriggled, and lurched left to right, and Geordie had to resort to planting his knee in the back of the prisoner's thigh, making him cry out and sag on that side.

'I'm not what you think,' Pearce gasped. 'I'm not a bad . . . ow! Christ, man!'

'Did you attack a warder?'

'Yes, but—'

'Right, then.' Geordie finally snapped the cuffs closed, and, with a huff of relief, grabbed the back of Pearce's coat and yanked him upright. 'Let's go and tell Sergeant Brewer you're not a bad *ow*, shall we?'

'Are you a policeman?' Pearce asked, as Geordie pushed him into a walk.

'No.'

'Then why have you got—'

'Shut up,' Geordie grunted. 'I'm not in the mood.'

'What's your name?'

'I said shut *up*.' He was wondering what Brewer would say about him bringing Pearce in, instead of doing as he'd been told. But then, he reasoned, Brewer was the one who'd given him the cuffs, and he'd actually said not to approach *unless you have to*. And he'd had to.

Satisfied he'd done the right thing, Geordie stopped worrying and instead studied the man in front of him. With hunched shoulders and a way of favouring his right leg, he was a sorry-looking sight and about as far from military neatness as it was possible to get. He also kept convulsively straightening his back and working his shoulders, before slumping again.

'Are you injured?' Geordie asked.

Pearce glanced over his shoulder, then looked away again without answering.

Geordie tried again. 'Look, I had to do this, but if I've—'

'I was flogged,' Pearce said dully. 'All this probably opened up some of the cuts, that's all.'

Geordie recalled Stephen's story, and wondered if this was the cellmate he'd mentioned. 'You *probably* shouldn't have smacked me into the wall, then.'

'I'm not complaining, am I?' Pearce snapped, still facing ahead. 'You brought it up.'

'Were you flogged for what you did to the warder?'

'Why do you care?'

Geordie shrugged. 'I don't.'

'Then take your own advice, and shut up.'

They hadn't been walking for more than five minutes before a shout went up somewhere ahead, and Geordie peered around Pearce's shambling figure to see a small shape pedalling furiously but with supreme effort, up the hill towards them.

'Joe?' He pulled Pearce to a stop. 'Wait there, lad!' he shouted. 'Don't come any closer!'

'You think I'd attack a child?' Pearce sounded incredulous.

'I don't know you, do I?' Geordie pointed out. 'I'm not taking the chance.' He raised his voice again, so it would reach where Joe had stopped twenty yards or so down the hill and was rubbing his healing leg. 'What is it? Is anyone hurt?'

'No.' Joe peered more closely at Pearce, and as his eyes found the handcuffs, they widened and he looked back at Geordie. 'Is he the escaped prisoner?'

'It's all right,' Geordie assured him. 'He can't get away, I'm taking him to Sergeant Brewer.'

'The police already know he's come looking for you!' Joe said urgently. 'You'll have to give him up quickly, or they'll never believe you were going to turn him in.'

Pearce spun back to face Geordie. '*You're* Stephen's brother?'

'What?' Geordie stepped back as Pearce moved towards him.

'Geordie Sargent?' Pearce persisted. He hissed in frustration as his hands moved ineffectually against the cuffs when he tried to reach for his pocket. 'I've got a note, from Stephen to Gracie!' He raised his hands, offering access to his pocket, but Geordie didn't move; he wasn't about to get caught out twice. 'Read it,' Pearce urged. 'Please!'

Geordie kept his eyes on Pearce's, alert for any flicker in them as he reluctantly reached into the coat pocket and withdrew the tattered note. It had clearly been soaked and dried several times over, and the lines were blurred. There was a roughly drawn sketch, and scribbled directions. Below it was a neater passage. 'Please help Daniel to reach Geordie,' he read aloud, 'his life depends on it, and we depend on you. Forgive me for taking the coward's path in this. My heart is yours. S.' He looked up. 'This is from Stephen?'

Pearce nodded. 'I took it to the farm he drew on there, and Gracie Martyn lent me her father's car. And his clothes,' he added, indicating the outsized coat and boots. 'Please, don't give me up to the police. Stephen promised you wouldn't.'

Geordie felt anger stirring. How could his own brother put

him in this position? If anyone else had read this note he'd be implicated no matter what he tried to do here now. Though it might well be too late, he crumpled it in his fist and shoved it safely into his own pocket. There was only one thing he could do, and although it went against every ounce of trust he'd ever put in Stephen, he had to do it.

'I've got to take you in,' he said bluntly. 'I'm sorry for you, but I'm not going to prison for you.' From the corner of his eye, he saw the relief on Joe's face and knew he'd done the right thing. 'Go on back to the forge,' he told the boy. 'Keep working, so it all looks normal.'

'Lynette's there,' Joe said. 'She's the one who sent me to find you, after Miss Rosdew telephoned her to tell her about him.' He nodded at Pearce.

'Good. Tell her I've got him, and I'm taking him to Brewer.'

'Please!' Pearce took a step away as Geordie moved to grasp his arm. 'They'll kill me.' His blue eyes swam with desperate tears as he stared at Geordie. 'I mean it. I've never deliberately hurt anyone, but if I go back—'

'Explain it to Brewer.' Geordie felt wretched, but there was no help for it. 'I can't just let you go, not now they already think I'm waiting by to help you.'

'Not even for the sake of your daughter?' Pearce blurted, and Geordie stopped dead.

'What?'

'She stowed away in Farmer Martyn's car,' Pearce said. 'She came here with me.'

Geordie's stomach turned to ice. He couldn't speak for a moment, there were too many questions. Then the most important one broke free, hoarse and unsteady. 'Where is she?'

'It's all right,' Pearce said quickly. 'I left her with someone I trust, he'll look after her until you're ready to collect her.'

'Who?' Geordie didn't wait for a response, but grabbed Pearce's coat collar and shook it. 'Who?' he demanded again, his voice now raised to a shout.

'Someone I met in prison. I ran into him today by chance, and he offered to help.' Pearce's gaze went beyond Geordie, back towards the distant estate Geordie had passed by, blissfully oblivious, only minutes before. 'You might know him. He's called Jago Carne.'

CHAPTER THIRTY-TWO

Mrs Pearce lived in a long row of houses in the Keyham area of Plymouth, near the Dockyard. Several stops to ask for directions, combined with the address provided by Daniel, saw them turn up a steep side street just after midday, and pull up outside the house. Gwenna kept the engine running, and turned to say her farewells.

'Are you sure this is a good idea?' she asked, not for the first time. 'The police might be watching.'

'I should think they've long since been and gone,' Gracie said. 'And if they do ask me, I'll just say Stephen wrote to me from prison, and asked me to visit on Daniel's behalf. They know they were cellmates.' She put one hand on the door handle. 'Aren't you coming in?'

'I need to get back to Pencarrack,' Gwenna said. 'Anything might be going on there, and I don't know if Lynette's been able to warn Geordie. I might be able to help.'

'You can help more here,' Gracie said firmly. 'Come on. Mrs Pearce's son is putting his life in the hands of these people, and you know them. You can at least reassure her that they're good, and honest, and won't turn him in.'

'I can't promise that!' Gwenna saw the now-familiar steely light flash behind Gracie's eyes, but held her ground. 'Besides, you know Geordie better than I do.'

'You've known him more recently,' Gracie insisted, and Gwenna gave in and turned off the engine.

'I'll tell her what I can, but after that it's up to you to do what you have to. I need to get back.'

Gracie nodded and led the way up the short flight of stone steps, where she knocked without hesitation. A loud, demanding knock that demanded attention. Gwenna looked up and down the street and saw that several doors had opened, but the curious onlookers soon retreated, and curtains were already falling back into place.

'I'd imagine the police have been here already,' Gracie said, following her gaze. 'They'd have caused quite a stir.'

'The neighbours must be disappointed it's only us this time.' Gwenna turned back as the door handle twisted from the other side, and the door opened a crack.

'Who is it?' The voice was quiet and frightened sounding. Low-pitched, as if in an effort to control it.

'Mrs Pearce, my name's Gracie Martyn. I'm a . . . a friend of Daniel's.' Gracie looked back at Gwenna with the faintest of shrugs. 'Well, we got along all right,' she murmured, before returning to the crack in the door. 'Can I come in and talk to you for a minute?'

'*Daniel's* friend?' Mrs Pearce said doubtfully.

'Sort of. He gave me your address.' In a softer voice, and with her mouth close to the small gap in the doorway, she added, 'Please, people are watching, and probably listening.'

The door opened a little further, and Gwenna peered past

Gracie into the darkness of the house beyond it. She saw only a vague shape and a bowed head as she followed Gracie indoors, and nodded a polite *thank you* as she passed the woman in the hallway. Mrs Pearce closed the door and turned on the light, and Gwenna blinked in surprise. The voice, and the knowledge that this was the widowed mother of a grown man, had led her towards imagining a timid, cowed lady, possibly of advanced years, but Mrs Pearce was tall, proud-looking, and looked to be in her mid-forties at most. The next time she spoke, her voice came out clear and strong.

'You'll have to forgive me,' she said. 'The police and some prison officers came, and they upturned everything. Please, how is Daniel?'

Gwenna realised she was still frightened, but not of strangers at her door. Her fear was now only for her son, and she looked at them anxiously in turn, clearly not sure which of them had professed to be his friend.

'He was well when I last saw him,' Gracie began. 'That was quite late last night.'

Mrs Pearce let out a relieved sigh, and gestured to a door off the hall. 'Come and sit down,' she said. 'We can talk properly then.'

In the tidy little sitting room, Gracie made herself comfortable in one of the armchairs, while Gwenna perched on the edge of another, ready to leave as soon as she had said her piece. Gracie told Mrs Pearce, who insisted they call her Cathy, all she knew, and the woman's eyes first filled with tears, then closed briefly in thanks.

'I know you must be frantic, but believe me, he won't harm that little girl,' she assured them, wiping away the spilled tears. 'Daniel's not a violent or cruel man, despite when they say.'

Gwenna wanted to challenge that, by asking why he'd been convicted and sent to prison in the first place, but she stopped herself in time. 'I know you'll be worried about him,' she said, 'but if he finds the man he's looking for, he'll be quite safe.'

'You know this man?'

'I do. Quite well.' This was merely on the strength of their shared trip to the prison, but it had been an intense enough experience to tell her what she needed to know.

'He's the older brother of my fiancé,' Gracie put in. 'The one who helped him to escape.'

'It was good of you to let him have your father's car,' Cathy said doubtfully, and there was a faint frown on her face. 'But he—'

'Can't drive?' Gracie grinned, and the shadows lifted. 'He can now.'

Cathy was surprised into a laugh, despite her worry, and Gwenna saw that as her chance to leave. She stood up, and held out her hand.

'It was lovely to meet you, Cathy. I hope we've helped put your mind at rest about Daniel. As much as it can be, at least.'

'You're going home?' Cathy asked, shaking the proffered hand.

'It's a bit of a long drive,' Gwenna said. 'I have the family shop to run.'

'Take me with you,' Cathy said, and Gwenna blinked.

'Beg pardon?'

'Please, take me back to Cornwall so I can see Daniel. I haven't set eyes on him since November.'

'You haven't visited?'

Cathy's eyes glistened again. 'I've been kept away. Even after my visit was approved, when he'd been there some weeks, I was told I'd been refused by the governor.'

'Mrs Pearce ... Cathy,' Gracie said gently. 'Why did Alfred Dunn *really* sack you?'

Cathy looked at her warily. 'That's a strange question.'

'Daniel was convinced you would never have stolen anything, and, having met you, I have to say I'd be surprised too.'

'My boy has a lot of faith in his old mother,' Cathy said, with an uncomfortable little laugh. 'He's a good son.'

'Are you saying he's wrong?' Gracie asked, and motioned Gwenna to sit down again. Gwenna did so, still impatient to leave, but glad of the extra time to think about how she could turn down Cathy's reckless request.

'He's ...' Cathy sighed, and sank back down onto the settee. 'No, he's not wrong. I never stole from Mr Dunn when I worked for him, and that's the God's honest truth.'

'Then why?'

Cathy worked her fingers into the folds of her plain dress, and didn't respond for a minute; Gwenna was about to prompt her, when she looked up and smoothed the material over her knees.

'Alfred Dunn made ... advances to me,' she said. 'I was just a shop girl, a few years widowed and new to working, and he called me to his office after we'd shut. He said it was to talk about giving me some additional duties.' She gave a short, sharp laugh. 'Those kinds of duties weren't something I was interested in. Anyway, I turned him down flat. I expected my marching orders there and then, but he was playing a different game.'

'What kind of game?' Gwenna shifted forward in her seat again. She knew, all too well, how easy it was to become drawn into the clutches of someone with more power, and made to behave in ways that went against every instinct for decency. 'What did he do?'

'Nothing, for a long time. He stayed charming; leaving little gifts in my overall pocket, to find in the morning, offering me overtime before everyone else. That sort of thing.'

'Waiting for you to change your mind?' Gwenna asked.

Cathy nodded. 'But when I didn't, he called me back in and said I'd been accused of stealing, and it was up to me to prove I hadn't done it.'

'That's hardly fair!' Gracie looked appalled. 'What did he say had been stolen?'

'Things they couldn't prove. Things that get used up, like food, washing powder, that sort of thing.' Cathy's face grew paler as she went on. 'I could've been sacked for that, on its own. But the trouble was, I went up to his office out of hours, to talk to him. To ...' She snatched a breath that looked as if it hurt. 'Please, promise me you'll never tell Daniel?'

'You went to try and put it right,' Gwenna guessed. 'To take him up on his original offer.'

Cathy nodded. 'I couldn't think what else to do.' She squeezed her eyes shut, and a tear of humiliation crept onto her cheek. 'I waited until everyone else was gone, and I sprayed some of the perfume from a sample bottle on the fragrance counter, undid a button ...' Her fingers strayed near the tightly closed neck of her blouse. 'I brushed out my hair, and I walked as tall as I could, right up to his office door.' She opened her eyes again, as if the image she was painting was too vivid for its canvas.

'What happened?' Gracie asked, in a whisper.

'When I was outside the door preparing what to say and gathering the courage to say it, I heard him talking. I almost ran away, right there and then, but I realised he was on the telephone, so I told myself off for a frightened fool, and stayed put until he'd

329

finished. Did you know he's also a councillor?' They shook their heads. 'Well, it was clear he was talking about council business, so I didn't really listen.' She cleared her throat. 'Or I didn't until I heard him talking about payment. Some storage sheds down by the docks, the owner was trying to push an application through to get it turned into shops. Dunn was promising to get it approved.'

'At a price,' Gwenna guessed.

'There's others, too, I found out after. He's been taking bribes for years.'

Gwenna and Gracie exchanged a quick look. 'And did you go through with your plan to . . . to soften him up?' Gwenna asked.

'No, I couldn't bring myself to do it.' Cathy lowered her head, as if the admission was shameful. 'I tried to use what I knew against him, instead. I was such an idiot.'

'You weren't!' Gwenna reached for her hand. 'You kept your dignity, and you did what you could.'

'It wasn't enough! I had no proof, and Mr Dunn knew it. He came around here,' she added, looking around her. 'To this very house, one afternoon. Daniel was in work, but still doing part-time continuation day classes back then, so he was doing schoolwork upstairs. Mr Dunn didn't expect that, he never knew Daniel was home.' She let out a steadying breath. 'He told me he was going to put word about that I was a thief and couldn't be trusted, and so he did. I couldn't find shop work anywhere after that. I took in washing for a while though, and now I clean those same council offices where he still does his dirty deals.'

'No wonder Daniel lost his temper that night,' Gracie said. 'Still, if he hadn't been drunk—'

'It was his birthday,' Cathy said. 'He never celebrates them usually, not since his dad died. He'd have been dragged out

330

though, probably by his daft cousin Micky. They're in the same division ... *were*,' she corrected herself. 'Daniel was discharged.'

'If only he hadn't seen Dunn's car,' Gwenna mused. 'Life really does turn on a sixpence.'

'Daniel told me about the officer who'd been making his life a misery,' Gracie said. 'Ned Newbury.'

'That's the one.' Cathy sniffed, and patted her pocket for a handkerchief. 'Married to Alison Newbury, née Dunn. Alfred's daughter.'

Gwenna shook her head. 'And you think this Newbury was acting under Dunn's orders not to allow you visits?'

'I'm sure of it. There's no other reason. They're making sure I know all about what's happening, but that I can't prove it, nor stop it.'

'He knows he can control you through Daniel,' Gracie said, with an edge to her voice. 'Or he could, at least.'

Cathy gave Gwenna a pleading look. 'So, now you've heard the whole sorry tale, will you *please* take me with you? Daniel can't come here, it's too dangerous.'

'It's dangerous there too, now the police know where he's going,' Gwenna reminded her. 'If he finds Geordie he'll be safer, but they'll add kidnapping and stealing a car, if they do catch him.'

'You being in the town might draw attention to the place, as well,' Gracie added. 'You won't really be helping him at all.'

'Nobody down there needs to know who I am, do they?' Cathy's tone became somewhat stubborn. She lifted her chin. 'I could just get a train down, anyway.'

Gwenna and Gracie shared another long look, and eventually Gwenna nodded. 'All right,' she said. 'I'll take you, and you can stay at my house until my mum gets back. We'll try and arrange for you and Daniel to meet somewhere secret.'

Cathy slumped in relief. 'Thank you. I'll get my things together. I'll be quick, I promise.'

She left the room, and Gracie stood up. 'I'll get the train back to Princetown,' she said. 'Keyham station's just up the road.' She came over and hugged Gwenna goodbye. 'Take care of yourself, and of Cathy. Daniel too.' Her voice cracked a little. 'Wire news of my little Tilly monster, won't you?'

'Of course I will,' Gwenna said. 'From what you and Cathy have told me of Daniel I'm sure she'll be absolutely fine, but I'll send both you and Marion a telegram the minute I know anything.'

'It's Daniel I feel sorry for,' Gracie said, pulling back with a forced smile. 'That scamp will run rings around him, and make him wish he'd stayed behind bars.'

Gwenna gave a little laugh, hearing the pain and worry beneath the flippant words. 'I'll be in touch,' she promised again.

Then Gracie was gone, and soon afterwards Cathy came downstairs with a small bag, and clutching her house keys in her hand. They set off towards the Torpoint Ferry in silence, but as they passed from Devon to Cornwall, and the prison fell further and further behind them, Cathy began to talk. It took nothing more than a soft question, about the last time she had seen her son, to open the flood gates.

'When they took him down,' she said, her voice flat as she stared out of the window at the changing countryside, 'he had this look on his face, this . . . disbelief. All I wanted was to go to him and tell him everything would be all right. He's been the one solid thing in my life since his father died, and I couldn't be the same for him, the one time he really needed me.'

'He will have understood,' Gwenna ventured. She was assuming a lot though, she realised.

'It's my fault he was so filled with hate for Alfred Dunn,' Cathy fretted. 'I hated him so much myself, it's all Daniel saw, for a long, long time.' She was pulling her sleeves down and twisting her fingers into them, but she didn't take her eyes off the passing scenery; Gwenna guessed she was seeing none of it. 'What if . . .' Cathy's breath stuck and she swallowed hard to clear it. 'What if, when I get there, when I see him again, he . . . he blames me? Pushes me away? What if he can't bear to even see me?'

Gwenna wanted to reassure her, but how could she, when part of her shared that fear? Daniel might easily resent his mother for subjecting him to so much anger, for instilling it in him too, at such a young age. 'Tell me something about him,' she urged instead. 'Tell me something that will bring him to life for me.'

There was a long silence, and Gwenna let it roll on. She glanced sideways and saw that there was a new stillness about Cathy now; her mind had evidently taken her back to a calmer time, but one that still resonated with deep sadness.

'He was one thing I could rely on,' she said at last. 'He was never that good at his books, but worked hard at them, and he was wise beyond his years. He had to be, when we lost Evan that way. So sudden, and him not even left to join the fighting yet.'

'It must have been so hard for you both,' Gwenna said, imagining a ten-year-old boy on his birthday, waiting for the father who would never come home; the confusion, the shock, the cold realisation that everything must now change overnight.

'He got a job on the docks when he left school, at fourteen, but he'd done so poorly at school he wanted to make up for it, so he did those part-time lessons I told you about.' She sniffed, and took out a handkerchief. 'Then he joined the navy, and I thought that was it. He'd gone. But he sent every spare penny back to me, and kept hardly anything for himself. Oh, he was a lad,' she added, and a tiny laugh escaped her, 'and didn't we know it. Him and his pals, and especially his cousin, they could make me tear my hair out at times, and as he got older he had me wondering what on Earth he'd be up to next. But his heart . . . That's always been good. Steadfast. And he never once let me down, not even when he was sent to prison.' Her voice caught. 'I was the one who failed him.'

'No,' Gwenna said. She took her hand off the wheel to gently press Cathy's. 'You didn't. I'm going to take you to him, and leave you both alone so you can sit and talk to your hearts' content. Then my friends and I will work out how to help you both.'

She gripped the steering wheel more tightly, feeling the weight of great responsibility settle on her shoulders. As the van ate up the miles beneath them, she thought ahead to what might happen once they arrived, and could only pray that she wouldn't be the one letting anyone down.

CHAPTER THIRTY-THREE

Daniel had never seen such mingled panic and fury on another man's face. Geordie had pushed him away the moment Jago Carne's name had left his mouth, and turned to stare back up the road. There was clearly something dark that lay between the two men, though Carne had never hinted at it, and Daniel been so relieved to relinquish responsibility of the child, that he hadn't stopped to consider it.

He had been carrying Tilly for some time, responding to her pleas for a *piggy-back instead!* with an inward shudder and an outward promise of, 'Maybe later.' When they'd emerged from the woods, onto the land near the China clay pit, he had put her down to walk, but the going had been too slow and he'd soon given in and picked her up again. His injured arm had been screaming by then, and every step he took on his right leg was punishing him as well. That fall on the moors had more likely resulted in a sprained ankle than a twisted one, and working unfamiliar pedals with his feet, as he'd mastered the technique of driving, hadn't helped.

They'd approached the huge house with *Hazelmere* painted in swirling script on its iron gates, and Daniel's mind had taken an unexpected path. Maybe he could set the girl on the long driveway and tell her to run to the house and ask for help; by the time she found someone, and they got the story out of her, he would be long gone. Unless there was anyone lurking nearby in the grounds, of course. Daniel had put Tilly down again and told her to wait quietly until he came back. He'd stepped up to the gate and peered through, his heart sinking when he saw a wheelbarrow parked just off the driveway, half-filled and with a rake leaning against it. Then the workman had come into view, and there was no mistaking the man's height, burly frame, and distinctive beard. Daniel had closed his eyes in relief, put his curled finger and thumb to his mouth, and whistled, short and sharp.

Jago Carne's astonishment at seeing him had melted instantly into welcome, and then into respect when he learned that Daniel had not been officially released, as he'd assumed. He'd heard nothing of the riot, and Daniel quickly filled him in. Although they'd barely known one another a week, before Carne himself had been released, they'd spent that time working closely together and Daniel had trusted him instinctively from the start. He'd formed an instant opinion of the Cornishman as one who'd waste no time in standing up for himself, but who was equally ready to stand up for any smaller bloke who'd found himself on the wrong side of a fist-fight through no fault of his own. Daniel felt his trust had been vindicated, more than once, and if anyone was an innocent today, it was Tilly Sargent.

He'd gratefully accepted a drink from Carne's flask and then called Tilly over, introducing her only as the girl from the farm where he'd taken the car. That was true enough, but linking her to Stephen, should the police come knocking, would put his old cellmate and friend at serious risk of deeper investigation. It hadn't felt, at the time, as if he was holding Tilly hostage, but now he'd traded her whereabouts for his own escape, he understood that was exactly what he had done. Especially now, faced with the girl's father in this state of mingled fear and fury.

'Carne doesn't know who she is,' he said, but he could see this gave Geordie no comfort at all. 'I never said she was your daughter, but you going to get her will just prove—'

'If you don't think he'll work that out, you don't know him,' Geordie said grimly 'He's no fool, and anyway she's probably already told him herself.' He rubbed his hands over his face, and pointed to Joe. 'He'll take you somewhere you can hide until they give up looking for you. But the cuffs stay on.' He re-cuffed Daniel's hands in front of him, then threw the key to Joe, who caught it neatly. 'Make sure neither David Donithorn nor Bobby Gale sees him, all right? They'll already be watching for him.'

'Let me come with you,' Daniel said. 'I can talk to—'

'No! If Carne sees me, that's one thing, and he'll expect it. If I'm with *you* it'll make his day. He'll be on to the police faster than you can blink, and it'll put Stephen in the firing line too. You need to get out of sight. Now.' Geordie was already walking backwards up the hill as he spoke, and Daniel could see his eyes blazing even from this distance. 'I never want to see you again, Pearce. Unless anything's happened to my daughter, then you'd better hope I don't find you.' He turned and began to run, and Daniel heard the boy's voice behind him, flat and mistrustful, suddenly older.

'Come on, then.'

Joe walked behind Daniel, wheeling his bicycle and no doubt ready to jump onto it if Daniel should make a break for freedom. But Daniel had no intention of doing so.

'What's the history with him and Carne?' he asked Joe, who didn't respond. 'He seems like a decent enough bloke,' he persisted, 'but then so does Carne.'

'Carne's not fit to clean Geordie's boots,' Joe said shortly, but wouldn't be drawn any further.

'Where will you take me?'

'There's a place,' Joe said. 'A secret room, but I don't know how to get into it so I'm going to ask someone who does.'

'Stephen said Geordie would help me,' Daniel persisted. 'If he won't see me again, how can he help?' He looked over his shoulder in time to see Joe shrugging, and once again sized up his chances of escape. But he'd get nowhere with his hands cuffed, and if he tried to take the key from Joe someone might get hurt. He sighed and faced the front again, acknowledging that he had no choice for now.

Perhaps when they put him in this so-called secret room, they'd see fit to remove the restraints and he could take his chances then.

They came to the village down a short hill, and Joe told him to take the turning on the left, past a clump of bare trees. A short way down that road they came to a cottage with a large yard and an open-fronted forge. Daniel recalled Stephen telling him that his brother was a blacksmith.

'Is this a good idea, bringing me to Geordie's own place?' he asked, but again Joe ignored him, and gestured him through the gate ahead of him. He pushed in front as they reached the door, and led Daniel into a small, dimly lit room.

'Lynette!' he shouted, looking around, and a moment later a door at the far side of the room opened and a woman came in. She stopped and stared at Daniel, who found himself staring back, bemused by her elegant poise in a place like this. She was of average height, no more, but seemed taller and despite the working clothes she had the kind of presence that wouldn't have seemed out of place at a rear admiral's garden party. 'Who are you?'

'This is . . .' Joe stopped and looked at him. 'Pearce?'

'Daniel.' He tried to hold out his hand, and only looked stupidly down at it when he remembered he couldn't. 'Daniel Pearce.'

'The escaped convict?'

'Geordie caught him,' Joe explained, going over to warm his hands over the kettle that sat on the range.

'Where is he then? And where's Tilly?' Lynette demanded.

Joe's head whipped around and he stared accusingly at her. 'Did *you* know about her? Why didn't you tell me?'

'Because I didn't want Geordie rushing off to find him,' Lynette said. She caught Daniel's expression and shook her head. 'Much good that did, apparently. Where are they?'

'He's gone to get her,' Daniel said. 'I offered to go with him, but—'

'Mr Carne's got her!' Joe blurted, and Lynette's face turned pale.

'How?' she breathed.

Joe gave Daniel a look of such contempt it made him flinch. '*He* gave her to him.'

'I . . . I know him, a bit,' Daniel stammered. 'I had no idea there was ill feeling between him and Geordie. I would never have left her with him if I had.'

'God.' Lynette braced her hands on the back of the nearest chair, and bowed her head. Then she lifted it again and looked at Joe. 'What did Geordie say to do with him?'

339

'We're to find somewhere to hide him until the search is called off. I thought maybe the folly, but I don't know how to get in.'

'Come with me,' she said to Daniel, and took her coat down off the peg. 'Joe, stay here, and keep up with the story that Geordie's down with Mr Garvey.' She pulled on her coat and picked up her hat, then looked at Daniel thoughtfully. 'We'll have to get my car from the stables, which means you might be seen. I'm not leaving you here though, it's an even bigger risk. Joe, fetch Geordie's old hat, love, would you? And if those things have a key I'd better have that, too.' She pointed at the handcuffs, and Joe dug in his pocket.

Daniel's hungry eyes watched the key appear in the boy's hand, only to disappear once again, this time into Lynette's coat pocket. Part of him was appalled to find himself wondering how easy it would be to overpower her along the way, and he forced himself to remain patient. If she refused to release him, however, he would have to think again.

He pulled the leather hat on, smelling the wood smoke that lived in the cloth inside. He turned his collar up and lowered his face, and Lynette nodded. 'You'll do from a distance, come on.'

Before he followed her, Daniel turned to Joe. 'Look, lad, I'm sorry for everything I've laid at your door, truly.'

'You'll be sorrier if Geordie doesn't get my sister back,' Joe said, and Lynette stopped still in the doorway. She didn't look back, but Daniel saw from the set of her shoulders that she'd caught her breath, and was letting out in a long, slow sigh. He didn't know what that meant, whether it was a sigh of regret or not, but her voice was hoarse as she spoke.

'He's right, you know, Mr Pearce. You'd better tell me exactly what happened, as we go.'

Daniel followed her out of the yard and back past the little copse of trees, and as they walked he gave her a brief description of everything that had happened since he'd woken to find Tilly in the back of the car. When they reached the main road, Lynette checked in all directions, before linking her arm through his and telling him to lower his head.

'From a distance you'll look enough like Geordie,' she said, in answer to his startled look, and placed her other hand over his cuffed ones, in a display of affection that looked more or less natural.

In this manner they crossed the road, and Lynette helped him climb a stile that delivered them into a small but dense group of trees. Nothing like the extended woods that he and Tilly had come through earlier, but closely packed, and with leaves that dripped on them with every step. Daniel's bladder was growing uncomfortably full, after the water he'd taken from Jago Carne's flask, and by the time they emerged at the back of a field, his need had grown more pressing still.

'Is this where you live?' he asked.

'Never mind. It's where I work, and where my car is.'

'Is there a . . . a lavatory?'

Lynette stopped halfway through climbing over the paddock fence. 'Can you go against a tree?'

'Not really.' He gave her a pointed look, and she sighed.

'Come on, then. And I suppose I'll have to unlock your wrists.' She sat astride the fence, her eyes hard when they found his. 'Can I trust you?'

'I promise you can.' He meant it, at least for now. 'Will you leave them off, if I prove it to you?'

'I don't know, yet.' Lynette jumped down. 'Come on, then.'

She helped him steady himself on top of the fence, and stood back while he landed in the field next to her. He staggered slightly as he landed, and when she caught at his arm to steady him he felt an unexpected strength in her grip, and instantly re-evaluated his chances of easily overcoming her. He was doubly glad he'd dismissed the notion.

Lynette took him through a large, neat yard with a couple of outbuildings and a large stable, on top of which, replacing its own arched roof, was a dwelling with a set of steps leading to it. Lynette looked around the yard for a moment, then, seemingly satisfied they were alone, she led him up the steps and into an untidy but homely looking flat.

'The bathroom's down there.' She pointed to a hallway that led off the combined kitchen and sitting room. 'Last door on the left.' She beckoned him closer, and took the key from her pocket. 'I'm putting you on trust,' she said, staring hard into his eyes. 'For Stephen's sake, and for no other reason.'

'Joe wouldn't tell me,' Daniel said, wincing as the cuff came clear and a pain shot through his injured arm. 'Why are Geordie and Carne at such odds that Geordie would think Carne could hurt a child? He wasn't in prison for anything violent.'

'It'd take too long,' Lynette said, 'and it's no one's place to tell you but Geordie's.' She stepped back and nodded towards the bathroom. 'Go on.'

Daniel went, and when he'd made himself more comfortable he cupped his sore hands beneath the tap and splashed his face with cold water. He raised his eyes to the mirror over the sink, saw someone haunted and unknown staring back at him, and looked away quickly; he couldn't afford to lose any sense of his own identity now. The window had drawn his gaze the moment

342

he'd walked in, and did so again now. It was small, but not too small to wriggle through, though his injuries would make it an extremely painful exercise, and he shuddered to think of how it would feel if he scraped his back on the frame. He looked out, and down, to see that the walkway that ran around the sides of the flat also crossed here, at the back, and, scraped back notwithstanding, he could be around it and down the steps before Lynette realised he was gone.

His heartbeat picked up, and his fingers were on the latch, before he came to his senses and stopped. Lynette was going to take him, against her better judgement, no doubt, to somewhere safe where he could lie low until the search had died down or given up altogether. After that, he had no idea what would happen, but at this very moment he had one person he could trust, and he owed her the same in return.

He rubbed his face with the towel, and was just replacing it on the hook when he heard the sound of a motor, out in the yard, and his heart skittered sickeningly against his ribs. He stepped over to the window, but couldn't crane his neck far enough to see the main part of the yard, and couldn't risk opening the window for a better view. Instead he remained very still, listening to his own pulse pounding in his ears, and to the sounds of voices coming up the outside steps. He pressed his ear to the door.

'We're back!' A voice he didn't recognise. Female and cheery, accompanied by the sound of something metal landing on a table. 'I thought you'd be at Geordie's. I've closed up the shop for dinner, since my helper here's been called into public service.'

Lynette's reply came from disturbingly close to the bathroom door, making Daniel jump and thank his stars he hadn't meddled with the window catch after all. 'Geordie's . . . busy. Hello, Bobby.'

Daniel froze, remembering Geordie's warning to Joe: *Make sure neither David . . . somebody . . . nor Bobby Gale sees him.* Could this be that same Bobby? It was a common enough name. But the man spoke, and removed all doubt.

'That escaped prisoner's in the area, they found the car he stole parked up by the woods. I'm on Watcher duty now.'

'Are you both going to go and look for him then?' Lynette asked. 'Or perhaps Tory could just drive you out onto the moor.'

'I will,' the woman said, 'but we're having a bit of dinner here first. It could be a long day and night out there. Bobby? Bathroom's yours first, if you want it.'

Daniel's throat went dry and he stepped back into the middle of the room, sweat prickling along his hairline. *Now what?*

CHAPTER THIRTY-FOUR

By the time Geordie reached Hazelmere again his ribs were pulsing in painful echoes of his racing heart. He studied the locked gate in frustration and growing fear, then scanned the top of the stone wall either side; no sharp wire prevented access, so he picked a spot on the wall that offered the most handholds, and climbed up. Jumping down on the other side elicited one of his more colourful curses, and he stood still for a moment until the swell of nausea died down, all the while letting his gaze sweep the grounds for anywhere Carne might have hidden a small child.

A small child. *His* small child. His lively, inquisitive, and above all, trusting, little Tilly. Images of her, as he'd left her and her mother in their home back in Peter Tavy, rose, unwanted but impossible to banish. Her arm locked around her toy sheep, eyes on him in sleepy confusion, that hug ... Geordie shook his head, but although the picture remained, he couldn't allow it to paralyse him. Instead, he used it to push everything else aside, and set off towards the big house in the distance. There would be outhouses there, he reasoned. He'd seen groups of trees and shrubs here, near the gate, but nowhere that someone like Tilly could be contained … if she had a choice, that was. The thought stopped him in his tracks, but only for a second, then he walked on. Faster, and caring less with every step whether or not he was seen.

The house seemed to take an age to reach, but as he grew closer he saw a few small sheds, and one large garage. Would Carne risk keeping her there? Geordie had no idea if Mrs Hocking drove, but living out here it was likely she'd have a chauffeur at least, so the garage would be in daily use. He stopped near a walled-off orchard filled with small, twisted apple trees, and trained his gaze on the two sheds closest to him. Carne would have wanted to hide Tilly away as quickly as possible, so it was most likely she would, at this very moment, be locked away in one of these.

He couldn't let himself picture her frightened, so he deliberately imagined her playing the best game of hide-and-seek of her life. Stowing away in Gracie's father's car had been the start of it, and now she would be using all her best tricks to stay hidden: holding her nose to keep from sneezing; curling into a tight ball with her hands over her head; breathing slowly, and through her mouth, and … *ah, please God, don't let her be scared* …

There was no one in sight, anywhere. Geordie straightened his back, walked calmly across the open grass to the shed, and walked around it until he found a window. Inside there was nothing but a wheelbarrow and a rake, and a few other tools a gardener or groundsman might use. Nowhere to hide so much as an illicit bottle of beer, let alone a little girl. Geordie sagged against the wall, his heartbeat settling as the disappointment seeped through him. Had he really expected it to be that easy?

'Oi! You there!'

The voice brought Geordie bolt upright again, and he looked across the grounds to where a tall, thin man had come out of the garage. His mind battled, for a moment, for a reason he should be skulking against the wall of the shed, but he quickly decided he needed no excuse.

'I'm looking for Jago Carne,' he said. 'I think he might have my daughter with him.'

The man frowned as he came closer. 'Daughter? He din't have no one with him when I seen him, and I'm the gardener. I'd have known if there was someone here who didn't ought to be.'

'And when did you see him?'

'About half hour since. He's gone to the station to fetch new tablecloths off the train, for Mrs Hocking. Took the pony and cart.'

'Christ!' Geordie spun on his heels, as if he might find a means of transport behind him if he willed it strongly enough. 'Is there a car I can borrow?' The man stared for a moment, and his brief, incredulous laugh told Geordie all he needed to know. 'A telephone, then? It's urgent, man!'

'He was on his own,' the gardener insisted. 'And Mrs Hocking's away, I can't go letting strangers into the house.'

Geordie wanted to argue, but knew it was pointless. The question now was whether he should simply wait and watch for Carne's return, or to try to catch them on the road and take Tilly back by force. The thought of his daughter spending one minute longer than she had to in the company of that dangerous thug was enough to send him running back towards the gate.

'Get to the station faster if you cut through the orchard and take the path along the wall,' the gardener called out helpfully. 'The bridle path'll get you to the top of the village, on the Bodmin road.'

Geordie thanked him, and climbed over the orchard wall, this time not stopping to catch his breath when he landed, but sprinting forward the moment his boots touched the grass. He found the path along the wall, which led on a diagonal away from the road, and increased his pace, telling himself that every step was bringing him closer to snatching Tilly away from Carne, and into the safety and warmth of her family. He wasn't sure he dared believe it, but it propelled him onward.

He reached the point where Hazelmere land met bridle path, and which, while it exposed him to the icy, stiffening wind, also afforded him a view of the railway station in the distance. From his vantage point, and in the bright, early afternoon light, he could see the puffing of steam from the idling train while the branch line turntable moved into place. Vehicles of all kinds were moving about in the car park, but he was too far away to identify the Hazelmere cart, or Jago Carne, and in another few steps the view of the station was lost.

He positioned himself behind the low wall that marked the edge of the property, and tucked his hands beneath his armpits to ward off the cold from the wind that was growing more insistent with each passing minute. He'd need to be able to use them to swing up into the back of the cart as it passed by.

Finally, Geordie heard the sound of pony's hooves on the path, and he raised himself carefully, high enough to see over the wall. He'd told himself that he needn't do it; the chance of it being any other cart was extremely slim, but he couldn't fight the impulse to see the cart that carried his daughter, to know she was coming closer . . .

Carne was pressing one hand to his hat to keep it in place, his beard was tugged by the wind, and the very sight of him pushed Geordie's rage into a sphere he'd never known before. Not even after the South Pencarrack disaster. He dropped back down, teeth clenched painfully hard in his effort to stop himself running straight at the man down the middle of the path, and instead he got his feet ready beneath him. The cart slowed as it passed, and Geordie rose again, poised to jump, but to his dismay Carne pulled hard on the reins, jerking the pony to a halt. The man uttered a few choice words, and twisted in his seat to pull at a loose tarpaulin string that was now flapping in the wind. As he did so his eyes found Geordie, and widened in shock. His curse became a bellow, as Geordie caught at the side of the cart before he could grab the reins again.

Geordie had already thrown one booted foot over the tail gate when his gaze fell on the canvas-covered mound in the corner of the cart, and his heart cramping painfully; he almost lost his footing as Carne lunged over the back of his seat and scrambled to stand between them.

'Remember what I said, maid,' Carne growled, nudging the soft form beneath the canvas with the side of his boot.

'Get away from her,' Geordie gasped, dragging his other foot in, and finding his balance again. 'If you've hurt her, I'll—'

'Hurt who, Sargent?' Carne's voice was soft, but mocking, now that he was in charge again.

'Don't mind him, love. I'm here!' Geordie felt all his confidence, and any command he might have had, fall away as he prayed for movement beneath the tarpaulin. It remained still, but she couldn't be sleeping, and he couldn't bring himself to imagine any other reason, except that she must be too terrified to move; he dreaded to think what Carne had told her would happen if she did. Geordie's thoughts were spinning in all the wrong directions. He couldn't concentrate on anything, couldn't think of a single thing to say that would make Carne realise what he'd done, and give up his prize. It was all his fault: if he hadn't made fun of Carne every chance he got; hadn't needled him, provoked him, and taken a hand in destroying his livelihood; hadn't revelled in his arrest and disgrace . . .

'She's done nothing to you,' he said at last, low and helpless. 'She's just a little girl. Let her go, and we'll sort this out between us.'

'Again?' Carne grinned. 'I enjoyed the last time, I must admit.' He gave Geordie a shrewd look, then glanced again at the motionless form. 'She said Pearce was taking her to find you. Why's that, then?'

Geordie stepped forward, his eyes still on the tarpaulin, sickeningly certain now that Tilly must have been knocked unconscious. She'd certainly have moved if she'd heard his voice. 'Let her go,' he repeated, 'and I'll tell you.'

'Tell me, and I'll let her go,' Carne countered at once. He placed one boot on the edge of the loose canvas, pinning it down while he knelt to tie it up again. 'Come on, I know he shared a cell with your brother. You pair helping him get away, is that it? Working together?'

'She was just hiding in the car Pearce stole,' Geordie said tightly. 'That farm's the closest one to the prison, that's all. Look, Carne, just let me—'

'Stay where you are,' Carne said with deceptive mildness, as he stood up again. 'I'll give her back when I'm good and ready.'

Geordie heard more pleading words lining up in his mind, ready to cajole, to beg, to offer whatever Carne wanted, but a glance at Carne's face smothered them all. There was a look of gladness there, a hunger to see Geordie brought even lower than before, and not just physically this time. To think he would use

350

an innocent six-year-old to do it ignited the fury that had come to a rolling boil and, not aware he was going to do it, Geordie lowered his head and butted Carne in the chin. He felt the impact travel all the way down his spine and into his hips, and followed the charge with a punch to Carne's face that drove the bigger man back a couple of steps.

Carne's legs connected with the raised edge of the cart, his knees buckled, and as he slid sideways Geordie lurched past him, grasped the edge of the tarpaulin, and tugged. It only served to tighten the knot that now secured it to the rail on the cart's edge, and he gave a grunt of frustration. By now Carne had recovered enough to kick out and knock Geordie's hand away from the string, and he grasped Geordie's arm to pull him back.

Panic had now overtaken anger, and Geordie somehow resisted, dragging at the tarpaulin and pulling hard enough to feel the tendons in his neck straining. He shouted in triumph as the string snapped under the combined strength of both men, and sent them sprawling. He crawled forwards, and felt a pair of brawny arms encircle his waist and clench tight, cutting off his breath and sending a heavy pulse of pain through him as Carne pulled him away from his goal once again. He landed hard on his side, and turned his head to see what had been revealed as he'd pulled the tarpaulin back; at the same moment Carne stopped fighting him, and rolled away.

Geordie lay still, breathing hard, and staring in disbelief. Three or four empty sacks lay around a medium-sized wooden crate with *Dunn Homewares* stickers along the sides and top. Mrs Hocking's delivery. He twisted to stare at Carne. 'Where is she?'

Carne slowly, deliberately wiped the back of his hand across his bloodied mouth. 'That'd be telling.'

'You said you had her.'

'I said I *had* her,' Carne agreed. The split lip made him look even more thuggish than ever, but there was something about his face that made Geordie look again; none of the expressions seemed to settle. His eyes were fixed, and the smile seemed more frozen than sneering, but there was puzzlement in the brow, and now it slid into a genuine-looking panic.

'What have you done with her?' Geordie demanded, pulling himself to his feet.

Carne swallowed. 'I had to bring her,' he muttered, rubbing at his lip again and smearing the blood ghoulishly across his cheek. 'I couldn't leave her back in the shed, not with Ogden hanging—'

'I don't care about that!' Geordie grabbed at Carne's coat with both hands. 'Where is she *now*?'

'I don't bloody *know*, that's what I'm telling you! She was right there, next to that!' Carne gestured at the box of homewares, and stared at it as if he thought the little girl might reveal herself after all. Then he turned an uncharacteristically frightened look on Geordie, chilling enough, even before he spoke Geordie's worst fears aloud. 'She must've fell out. There's bumps and holes in the road, and the bloody string was loose ... She probably crawled out, and ... she could have fallen out anywhere. Or maybe she jumped out when I wasn't looking,' he added, with desperate-sounding hope, but little conviction.

Geordie also turned to look, and this time he saw something he'd missed the first time. He shoved Carne away from him and bent to retrieve it from where it lay peeking out from beneath a sack: a small woollen lamb, without a bell, and without a little girl to wrap her arms around it. Wherever Tilly was now, she had not chosen to jump off this cart.

CHAPTER THIRTY-FIVE

Lynette stepped thankfully into the flat and closed the door. She stood breathing slowly and quietly for a moment, letting her mind unravel everything that had happened in the past hour and put it back together, in a more orderly manner. She'd thought her heart would never start beating again when Tory had gestured Bobby towards the bathroom, but any ideas she might have reached for, to stop him using it, would be hopeless.

'Wait,' she'd said, holding up a hand as he'd taken a step forward. 'There's something you need to know.' She'd hesitated again, then made her decision. 'I'm putting myself, Geordie, and Joe in your hands now, as well as one or two others.'

She had told them all she knew, from Gwenna's telephone call right up to the moment Lynette had come back to collect her car. Tory had looked at her, incredulous, and then at the bathroom door. 'He's in there, isn't he?'

Lynette had nodded. 'If you hadn't come back right this moment you'd never have known we were here.' She had turned to Bobby. 'Please,' she'd said in a low voice. 'For the sake of all the times you've hoped people would turn a blind eye on something you've done. For my sake, and for Geordie's, *please* turn one now.'

He'd hesitated, and Tory had given him a mild, but meaningful look. Lynette could see him battling with his conscience, eventually relenting and agreeing to turn a blind eye. For now, at least.

'If he turns out to be something other than you think he is, I'll have him,' he'd cautioned. 'But for the minute, I'll go along with it. Now, if you'll excuse me?' He nodded at the bathroom. 'I've still got pressing matters to attend to.'

Now they were out on the moors somewhere, the two of them, putting on a fine show of searching for the man Lynette had just safely hidden away from the world. In return, she herself had promised to work doubly hard in the stables that afternoon, and she started by pulling down two bales of straw from the hay loft, and dragging them into the stable. She returned to rake away the last stray bits from the floor of the small barn, using the physical labour to calm her racing mind, and when the floor was clean once more, she put her rake aside and went out to the paddock to bring in Hercules.

As she crossed the yard, however, she was startled and horrified to see two police cars pull up to the gate and disgorge three policemen apiece. David Donithorn was also with them, and he pointed at Lynette and said something to the officer closest to him, who nodded. The next moment the gate was open, and the yard filled with demanding voices and policemen pointing to the various buildings.

Lynette stood in stunned shock as six of the men swarmed to the stables and the tack room, and the seventh approached her with firm steps and a determined look on his face. She didn't recognise him.

'Miss Nicholls?' he said. 'Sergeant Clare, Bodmin Police. I'm here to conduct a search. You've heard about the escaped criminal, I assume?'

'Well, something on the news,' Lynette said, hoping she sounded baffled rather than worried. 'But why are you looking here?'

'He's known to have a connection to the blacksmith from Pencarrack.'

'To Geordie? But he's not—'

'His brother was in prison with the fugitive, miss. And the escape vehicle was seen in the area. Constable!' He gestured to the flat. 'Take Cardew and check the house.'

Lynette fought the urge to stop them, but it would only make things worse. She tried to think back, to anything that might betray the fact that Daniel had been here, but he hadn't changed any of his clothes, or even eaten or drunk anything. He hadn't shaved either, or left any other traces of himself, and she couldn't bring herself to think what would have happened if the police had arrived a couple of hours ago.

'You won't find him in there,' she called instead. 'I've been here all morning and no one's been here except those who belong here.'

'And what about Mr Sargent?' Clare asked her, taking out his notebook. 'Has he been here today?'

'No, he's working at his forge.'

'Bit of a troublemaker, as I recall.'

'Not at all,' Lynette said, allowing her annoyance to show now. 'How do you know him, anyway?'

355

'Last year, miss. I met him at the clay pit, before the riot down by the town hall.'

'Hardly a riot.' Lynette scowled. 'He was trying to stop it, anyway.'

'His reputation stands against him. And with a brother in the same prison, let alone the same prison cell as the fugitive, well.' Clare set off up the steps after his constables. 'And he's not at the forge, by the way,' he added over his shoulder. 'We've already searched it.'

Poor Joe. Lynette watched, with a rising but helpless anger, as the policemen first searched the barn and the hay loft, then moved among the horses, opening and closing the stalls doors with little or no regard for the nervous animals inside. Mack stood stoically steady throughout the invasion, Sally trembled in the corner, and Hercules was still in the paddock, but Bella's recovery had clearly been set back weeks, and the other new horses were stamping, rearing as far as their tethers would allow, and making enough noise to wake the dead. The air was filled with panicked neighing and the thumping of hooves on the wooden walls, and Lynette moved from one horse to the next, trying desperately to calm them down. She took a certain satisfaction from a human cry of pain, which told her just how much she'd changed since she'd come to live here, but she still didn't move to help; the police weren't her priority, and if they weren't being careful around the horses, and were being kicked or bitten for it, that was their lookout.

She desperately wanted to run up to the flat and keep an eye on what they were doing up there, but she had to wait, holding on to Bella's mane and stroking her repeatedly, until Clare and his constables returned. The sergeant called his officers to him, and they all said the same thing: no sign. Clare nodded, and gestured them back to the two cars outside the gate, and turned to Lynette.

'Thank you for your time, miss. And sorry if we caused the animals any distress.'

'*If?*' Lynette could barely spit the word out.

'I'm sorry,' he repeated, and while he actually seemed to mean it, Lynette could cheerfully have pushed him face down into the water trough.

'Where are you going to check next?' she asked. 'The Widows' Guild? Or perhaps you'll go straight for the old lady who lives above the sweet shop? I mean, I'm sure this escaped convict of yours must have eaten an aniseed ball at some point in his life.'

Sergeant Clare just looked at her for a moment, reproach touching his expression. 'I'm going to liaise with Sergeant Brewer,' he said calmly. 'I expect he'll know the area better than we do.'

He rejoined his waiting men, and as the sound of their motors died on the air Lynette pondered the inevitability of Brewer pointing to the folly, and the room beneath it. Before she could dwell on this further, however, she saw a tall figure emerge from the trees on the far side of the paddock, and climb over the fence. Geordie. As she went to meet him she saw with alarm that he was too pale, and looked sick with panic.

'Tilly,' he said, moving past her towards the yard. 'She's missing.'

Lynette went cold. 'But Joe told me she was with—'

'She's not, and he doesn't know where she is either.'

'Tory and Bobby have gone out already, pretending to look for Daniel. Maybe they'll find her.'

'Bloody Daniel!' Geordie tore his hat off and scrubbed at his hair before putting it back on, not breaking his stride. 'I could kill him myself.'

'The police were here looking for him.'

'I know, I waited until they'd gone. I wish they'd found him. I came here to borrow your car.'

They had reached the yard, but Lynette shook her head and started towards the tack room. 'The car will limit us to the roads. We should take the horses so we can go cross-country.'

They seized what they needed to tack up Mack and Bella, but Lynette was unsure about Bella's temperament after the invasion of her stall by the unknown intruders. She spent a few minutes calming her, then, when Geordie led the tacked up Mack out into the yard she realised the luxury of time had run out and she had to move quickly now. Bella stood remarkably steady, while Lynette carefully tacked her up, and Lynette mounted her with a sense of relief and joined Geordie by the gate.

Geordie told her everything as they rode, from when he'd run into Daniel near Hazelmere, to the moment he and Jago Carne had parted ways to begin their search. He reached into his coat pocket as they turned off the road and onto the heath, and showed her the battered-looking Barney, and Lynette's heart clenched painfully.

'She'd never go anywhere without it,' she agreed. 'What was Carne going to do with her, anyway?'

'Probably use her to force me into the open.' Geordie stuffed the lamb back into his pocket. 'He'd want nothing better than to see me locked up with Stephen.'

'She can't have fallen out, though,' Lynette said, frowning. 'You said she'd been kept right at the back of the cart, behind Carne.'

'She was, and the canvas should have been tied down. Carne only stopped when the string hit him in the back of the head, and he realised it was loose, otherwise we wouldn't have got into a fight. He thinks she'd crawled out already, he'd hit a bump, and she'd slipped off the back without him being any the wiser.'

'Or maybe she climbed out when he was at the station? After he'd put the box in there, but before he drove away? She might have been frightened enough to leave Barney, and even more scared to go back for it when she realised.'

'That's what I was hoping,' Geordie said. 'Carne's gone back to ask, since he was the one they'd remember being there. Someone will have seen her, if she got out there, a little girl on her own would stand out.' He gave her a bemused look. 'Carne was bloody terrified, I've never seen anything like it. So I reckon I can trust him on this one.'

Lynette eased Bella into a trot, as the ground flattened. 'I hope she didn't get onto the train to hide. That one meets up with the Cornish Riviera Express when it gets to Plymouth. Goes straight to Paddington, non-stop.'

She looked across at Geordie's face and realised she'd said the wrong thing. 'Actually,' she said quickly, 'it's *more* likely someone would find her if she did that.'

'Not if she got into the cargo carriage,' Geordie said grimly. 'I'll search out here, you go back and telephone the railway station in Plymouth. Bella still looks a bit unsettled anyway.'

Lynette had to agree; the horse was sidestepping too often. Why hadn't those stupid policemen given Lynette a chance to move the horses out before they'd begun their search?

She moved up alongside Geordie, and reached for his hand. She could feel the tension there, and the way it travelled up his forearm as he turned his hand to accept her touch. It was running through him like quivering steel, and she wished she could absorb some of his anguish. 'We'll find her,' she said softly.

'It's so cold out here,' he said, and his voice shook. 'We need to get everyone in on this search, this is no time for keeping secrets.'

'I'll send whoever I see on the way,' she promised.

'Brewer, too,' he stressed. 'It doesn't matter what happens, or if the story about me helping Daniel comes out … I just need her safe.'

Lynette squeezed his wrist and let him go, and they parted ways at the junction, with Lynette taking the faster way by road, and Geordie wheeling Mack's head so they faced the moorland path. She heard him bellowing his daughter's name in equal despair and hope, and images of the child, shivering in the January wind, alone and terrified, kept rising in front of her until she could see and think of nothing else.

CHAPTER THIRTY-SIX

Gwenna parked outside the shop, hoping her friends had found the time to step in for a few hours that morning, though it was definitely closed now. She would telephone the forge as soon as they got inside, and ask about Daniel. If he'd managed to win Geordie over, there was a good chance they would have taken him to Tyndall's Folly, so she planned to take Cathy out there too, as soon as evening fell. In the meantime, it had been a long drive, and a longer time since she'd eaten, and she was starting to feel a little light-headed from it all.

'I'll go and unlock the door,' she said to Cathy. 'But first I want to make sure Mum hasn't come back. It's best if you wait here until I call you.'

She went through the side gate and into the yard, pulling her key from her pocket as she went. There were no lights on, which was a good sign; she really couldn't face explaining everything to her mother today. She just wanted to light the fire, get warm, and find something to eat before she was required to traipse across the moor to the folly. The sooner all this was over, the better.

She slid the key into the lock and shoved at the door, which had a habit of sticking when the wood got damp. It squeaked open, and she had only taken a single step into the kitchen when she heard something that stopped her where she stood. From beyond the door on the other side of the room had come a scraping sound. The shop lay that way, but it had been shuttered when she'd looked from the road.

'Mum?' she called, her voice sounding thin and hesitant; if her mother had indeed come home early, it would have been to a cold and empty house, so wouldn't her first act have been to open the flue on the range? Put water on to boil for tea? There was nothing on the table, it was as clear and clean as Gwenna had left it last night. No bag, key, or hat had been dropped here. And there was no answering shout.

Gwenna's heart speeded up. An intruder then? Someone in the darkened shop, taking advantage it being closed on a Monday afternoon? Her mind took her back to New Year's Eve, and Nigel Stibson's vain attempt to steal the money from the till, only to be thwarted and resort to petty vandalism instead. What if he had been harbouring resentment ever since, and had returned for another go? But the sound had not come again, and the bell on the shop door would have rung if someone had gone out that way. So perhaps she had imagined it after all; heard an echo of her own squeaking, shuffling arrival and allowed her tight nerves and her memories to misinterpret it. Unconvinced by her own reasoning, she crossed the kitchen and eased open the door. Ahead of her was another door, leading into the rear of the shop; to her left lay a short hallway, the stairs, and the storeroom.

Gwenna stood very still, listening. The only sound was the

grandfather clock ticking at the foot of the stairs, and after a moment she shook her head and stepped back into the kitchen, to open up the flue and let some of the warmth from the stove flow back into the house. Before she had taken two steps, however, the sound came again, and this time she didn't stop to think. Her gaze lit on the short poker that stood propped against the stove, and she snatched it up and strode back into the passage, holding it out in front of her like a sword. She pushed open the shop door, about to shout Stibson's name, but stopped as she saw a note was propped between the buttons on the till; her friends must have stepped in for a couple of hours as requested, and left what was probably a list of sales, but there was nothing out of place here that she could see.

She walked carefully around the few low sets of shelves, satisfied herself that she was alone, and then retreated from the shop telling herself she was jumping at shadows. But, looking down the hall she saw the storeroom door wasn't tightly closed, as it had been when she'd left it yesterday morning after the inventory check. She took a firmer grip on the poker, and crept down the hall. 'Who's there?' she called. 'Mum? Tory?'

No answer.

'Stibson?' She pushed open the door, poised to swing the poker if she saw an intruder, but the room was still and silent. Heart hammering, she turned on the light and saw only boxes and crates, and the stacks of old newspapers used for insulation and lighting fires. She lowered the poker with a little sigh of relief, and switched the light off again, ready to go out and beckon Cathy in. As she did so, she caught a movement from the corner of her eye, and gave a wordless, panicked shout, swinging the poker blindly, unthinkingly, in a wide circle.

It connected; she heard a shout, and a second later, before she could turn to see what – or who – she'd hit, the poker was jerked violently from her grasp. She gave another shout, this time of rage, surprising herself, and slapped at the wall for the light switch again. But before she found it she heard the poker clang to the floor, and the hands that had seized it now grabbed her arms, instead.

'Wait!'

She didn't recognise the voice, so she kicked out, and the hands released her, allowing her to find the switch and flood the room with light once again. The intruder had been behind the door, flattened against the wall; a tall-ish young man, with tangled dark hair and wearing a coat several sizes too big for him. He was clutching his right leg and squeezing it, as if rubbing would hurt too much, and it took only a second for Gwenna to realise who this must be. She bent swiftly to pick up the poker, in case he wasn't the friendly, put-upon man that everyone seemed so sure he was.

'Daniel Pearce?' she demanded, bringing the poker up like a sword again. She prodded it against his coat, prompting him to raise his hands to shoulder height, to prove he was unarmed.

He nodded, looking up at her with a mixture of wariness and annoyance, and now she could see, beyond the tightly drawn features and emerging stubble, that in fact he wasn't much older than she was. 'There was no need for that,' he grumbled.

'No need? You broke into my shop!'

'I didn't! And anyway, I tried to talk to you, but you didn't listen. And you can put that down.' He nodded at the poker.'

Gwenna ignored him, her mind had just caught up. 'You *didn't* break in?'

364

'No.' Daniel stood up straight, still scowling. 'Your friend said you wouldn't mind. She left you a note in the shop, she said that's the first place you'd go.' He straightened his rumpled coat. 'I heard you go in there, so I thought you'd already know who I was.'

'Tory hid you here?'

'No, the other one. Lynette.'

'But . . . I assumed they'd take you to the folly,' Gwenna said, frowning.

'She said your friendly local copper knew all about that place, so once he knew I was on the way, it would be a mistake for me to hide there. But she reckoned he wouldn't think to look for me here. Now *please* put down the poker.'

Gwenna looked at it, and then back at him. 'Where did I hit you?'

'On the arm. Luckily not my bad one. The kick was something I could've done without though.' He squeezed his leg again. 'Look, I'm sorry I gave you a shock, but—'

'Oh!' Gwenna belatedly remembered Cathy, waiting out in the van. She kept her distance, still not wholly sure of him, but, finding his own wary annoyance oddly amusing, she trusted her instincts. 'Wait here. Promise me?' she added, as she moved past him into the hall.

'I promise,' he said. 'Frankly I'm scared not to.'

When she glared at him he offered her a faint, conciliatory smile. She decided, as she left him looking speculatively after her, that she quite liked it.

Cathy followed her into the kitchen, her bag clutched to herself like some kind of protective talisman and this time Gwenna closed and locked the back door, rattling it in its frame to be sure the new locks were doing their work.

'This is nice,' Cathy said dutifully. But her expression was pinched with tiredness and worry as she put her bag on the floor beside the sink.

'Bring that with you,' Gwenna said. 'You can put it out here.'

Cathy nodded, picked it up again and followed her out into the hall, where Gwenna knocked on the storeroom door.

'It's me,' she called, and pushed it open.

Daniel was standing at the back of the room this time, and the light was still on. His expression froze as he saw his mother, then disintegrated; he took a faltering half-step forward, and then Cathy was there, pulling him close and weeping into his shoulder.

Gwenna watched the reunion for a moment, seeing the tightness with which Cathy's hands grasped at her son's ragged and too-big coat, as if she could pass all the love and relief she felt into his soul, just by the strength of it. Neither spoke, and Gwenna understood, from when she'd seen her father again, that words were both pointless and inadequate. Daniel's bent head didn't move, but she saw his shoulders shaking, and she turned away, tears prickling at the back of her own eyes.

She left them alone, and went into the shop where she'd seen the note on the till. She plucked it free, and read it with a little groan; if she'd done this to begin with she'd have saved herself, and Daniel, a lot of trouble. Not to mention one or two extra bruises.

Gwenna,
    Stray Devonshire dog is in the storeroom. He is friendly and will not bite. Telephone the stables when you get in.
    L.

Gwenna smiled at the image of Daniel as a dog; he'd certainly looked ready to bite when she'd kicked out at him, but once the folly was ruled out as a hiding place Gwenna understood the reasoning behind bringing him here. There might be a faint connection with her father having been in prison alongside Daniel, but it was unlikely he'd risk jeopardising his early release by offering to help an escapee, and they'd realise that. Geordie was always going to be the most likely connection, so the forge would have been the worst choice of all.

She crossed the hall to the kitchen, listening to them talking, and relaxed into the knowledge that she had played her part, at least. She looked up as Cathy came in, with Daniel behind her looking warily out through the window at the gathering darkness.

'I'm going upstairs to wash and change.' Gwenna pointed to the kettle she'd moved to the centre of the range. 'That water should boil soon, if you'd like to put some tea in the pot.' Then she sighed in mild annoyance. 'I've left my bag in the van, I won't be a minute.' She could see Daniel's polite and instinctive response already bubbling up behind his lips, and laughed. 'No, you won't fetch it for me, you idiot.'

'No,' he agreed. 'Best not, now you mention it.' His smile was one of embarrassment this time, rather than conciliation, but she couldn't deny she found it equally appealing. She went out to the van, mulling this over. He was undeniably attractive, despite his gaunt appearance and scruffy, outsized clothes, and that smile looked enough of a rarity to be a challenge – not that she could blame him, after everything he'd been through. But he was either going to disappear soon, or go back to prison, so it was pointless to waste time examining her reaction to him. But react she had, and it had been a pleasant shock to discover she was capable of such an instant attraction, especially after Peter Bolitho. Daniel Pearce couldn't possibly have been more different to her former fiancé.

She opened the van door and reached in for her bag, but a conversation that was taking place on the pavement near the shop made her stop and listen. Anna Penhaligon and Alice Donithorn, David Donithorn's mother, were discussing something Alice had heard from her son.

'They're going to search everywhere,' Alice was saying, with unassailable authority. 'David said so. And he'd know,' she added, in a lower, more conspiratorial voice. Gwenna thought back to Bobby Gale's revelation, and wondered if David was a Watcher, as well. And if so, how many others were there?

'Surely not *everywhere*, though?' Anna protested, her Irish accent contrasting strongly with Alice's strong local one. 'I mean, what on Earth would they be thinking, that a stranger would risk taking him in?'

'Well, they've done everywhere between Pencarrack and here,' Alice said. 'They've done the stables, an' all, it's only a matter of time before they're knocking on Caernoweth doors, then right down through to Porthstennack I shouldn't be surprised. Watching the boats, you know.'

Gwenna backed slowly out of the van, her bag in her hand, and mumbled a greeting to the two women before returning to the house as casually as she could. Once inside, she abandoned any idea of washing and changing, and dropped the bag by the door. Daniel was already sipping tea from Gwenna's father's chunky china mug, and had removed his coat and hung it on his chair. His shirt was also too big for him, and his bagged trousers secured with a belt, to which a hole had been added a long way from the originals. He looked thin and pale, but relaxed, and even happy, until he looked at Gwenna's face.

'What?' he said, lowering his cup at once. 'What's wrong?'

'We've got to get you out of here,' she said. 'They're going to search the whole town, and even if they only find *you* here, Cathy, they'll know they're on the right path.'

Daniel half-rose, then sat down again, looking lost. 'Where can we go?'

'Somewhere that's already been searched,' Gwenna said, thinking as she spoke. Then she nodded. 'The stables. We'll go by the back roads, past Pencarrack House and through the Serth Valley. It's a hard slog that way, but we can't risk going by the main road, even in the van. They're probably stopping to search vehicles.'

Daniel stood and picked up his coat, and she saw him wince as he pulled it over his shoulders. He caught her looking, but the way his gaze slid quickly away discouraged her from asking about it. There was no time now, anyway.

'It'll be dark soon,' she said. 'This is the best time to go; it's shadowy, but we won't be needing flashlights yet, so it'll be easier to get there without being spotted.' She looked at Cathy. 'Are you going to be all right?' Cathy gave her an arched eyebrow look that spoke far louder than any words might have done, and Gwenna nodded. 'How about you?' she asked Daniel. 'You've done quite a lot of running in the past couple of days, will you be all right?'

'I'd have been better if someone hadn't given me a right hard kick in my dodgy leg,' he said dryly. 'But don't you worry about me.'

Gwenna was about to protest, but saw the corner of his mouth twitch. She kept her own face expressionless. 'Good. I won't.'

*

They left almost immediately, and Gwenna led them up through the fields at the backs of the houses. She was acutely aware of Daniel limping along at her side, and was about to tease him about playing to the gallery when she saw his face was pale, and his jaw set tight against grunts of pain as he struggled to find solid footholds in the muddy ground. She realised it was his mother he was hiding it from, not her, and she moved close to speak as quietly as she could.

'Are you sure you're going to be all right?'

He gave her a quick look, clearly about to throw her a careless affirmation, but there must have been something genuine showing in her eyes because he looked away again, and only nodded. Gwenna wasn't fooled.

'Look,' she said, keeping her voice low, 'stop if you have to.'

'Why are you being so nice?' He sounded almost angry, and Gwenna recoiled slightly.

'Because I'm a nice person,' she said tightly.

'Well, I'm not. You shouldn't be risking everything to help me.'

Gwenna looked across at Cathy, who seemed to be deliberately giving them space and was making her steady way up across the darkening field, her gaze fixed firmly ahead. She returned her attention to Daniel. 'Your mum thinks you're worth fighting for.' He gave an unexpectedly soft laugh, and Gwenna's heart reacted oddly, speeding up at the sound of it. 'I'm sure it can't all be bias,' she added, to disguise the jolt she felt. 'Tell me something you're proud of.'

He stopped. Looked at her. His eyes were shrouded in the gathering shadows, but she could see a new gleam in them that found its response in her own; her throat thickened. 'Tell me,' she said again, more softly.

'Nothing,' he said. The gleam intensified, and he swiped at his eyes angrily. 'Don't you understand that by now? My dad was blown up on my tenth birthday, and I followed him into the navy because I wanted to honour his memory, and to make him and Mum proud. And look at me.' He gestured to his ragged appearance and wild hair. 'On the run from prison, and likely to die if I go back. What is there to be proud of?'

Such self-loathing jarred with what Cathy had told Gwenna on their journey down, and Gwenna's heart hurt to hear it. She put her hand firmly on Daniel's shoulder, and gave him a gentle shake.

'You've cared for your mum since you were ten, in your own way. She told me so. She said that when you were old enough you gave her your wage, provided for you both, and kept a roof over her head. A fit of temper when you saw the man who'd tried to ruin you both was understandable, Daniel, believe me. Everything after that was just horrible luck.'

Daniel kept his eyes on her, she was glad of that, and even more so to see the tears hadn't fallen. The hint of a smile even appeared at the corner of his mouth. 'Horrible luck,' he repeated, and another soft laugh escaped into the night. 'I should have used that in court. It was just 'orrible luck, yer Honour.'

'Well, now your luck's changed,' Gwenna went on. 'You met Stephen, you met Lynette, and now you've met me.' She patted his shoulder, intending to convey a brisk, *come on then, let's go*, but he put his hand over hers, and held it there.

'Now I've met you,' he agreed. He shook his head, and his smile returned. Faint, but real. 'I'm still not sure what kind of luck that is.'

Gwenna grinned. 'Let's push on and find out, shall we?'

'Yes. Let's.' He held her gaze for a moment longer, and she felt the shift between them. The settling of something. She looked at where his hand still held hers pinned to his shoulder, and pointedly made no move to lift it; instead she pressed a little bit harder, and squeezed gently. Then she slid her hand down his arm, and their hands found each other's without comment or question as they set off again.

By the time they reached the far side of the Serth Valley, behind the enormous Pencarrack House, it was becoming hard to see easily. Even with eyes that had adjusted to the gradually creeping darkness, the three of them were stumbling and clutching at one another to prevent falls, and it was a relief to emerge onto the fields that backed onto the stables. But Gwenna, bending over to catch her breath, was startled to feel a hand gripping her harder than usual, and she looked up to see Cathy staring into the distance.

'Is *that* the stables?' Cathy pointed, and Gwenna was about to confirm the direction, when she realised the reason for Cathy's consternation, and her chest tightened in shock.

Against the night sky, a flash of orange came and went, followed by another, longer lasting flicker. Gwenna realised, as she stopped gasping in air and breathed through her nose instead, that the smell of smoke must have been there all along. Daniel uttered an oath and began to run, and a second later Gwenna and Cathy were running alongside him. As Gwenna's feet hit the grass she heard herself panting in rhythm: *no, no, no* ...

CHAPTER THIRTY-SEVEN

Joe Trevellick had always tried to do the right thing. Well, almost always. Chucking a few rocks was one thing, but he certainly hadn't wanted to make Geordie's life harder, just because he'd had nowhere to go after his dad died. The offer of home and work had saved him from an unknown fate, though Geordie was already stretched beyond his limits; Joe knew he'd never admit as much, however, not after Lynette had spent all her own money buying him the forge and the cottage. His and Joe's meals were taken separately lately, and Geordie said it was because they had to keep working, but Joe wasn't stupid; he knew Geordie was eating far less than he should be. So, to find out that he now had to pay for Joe's window-smashing spree made Joe feel thoroughly miserable, and wracked with guilt. He had to make it up, somehow.

The last thing Geordie needed now was a reputation for unfinished work, so when Lynette had taken that trouble-making prisoner away to hide him, Joe had kept at his tasks. But it hadn't been long before he'd grown restless and worried about what was going on back at Hazelmere. With a silent apology to his boss, he closed the fire damper and locked the gate, then set off on his bicycle, taking the road that would lead him across the moor and around the back of Hazelmere. His healing leg was sending out painful reminders that he'd already ridden too much today, but if he could help in some way, it would be worth it. Perhaps he could act as a decoy, attracting Carne's attention by messing about, as might be expected of a boy his age. That would leave Geordie free to search for Tilly.

He reached the junction near the railway station and prepared to tie his bicycle to the fence, in readiness for crossing the rough moorland, but before he'd got the string from his pocket, and untangled, he heard hoof beats in the grass on the bridle path. They were unhurried, and not particularly fast, and Joe couldn't yet see the horse or pony that was making them, but they were coming from the direction of Hazelmere. An uneasy feeling uncurled inside him, and without knowing precisely why, he shoved the string back into his pocket and wheeled his bicycle back out of sight.

He was relieved he'd done so, when he peeked out from behind the wall and saw Carne's bulky frame, dwarfing the seat of a small cart, and Carne driving the pony on with irritable sounding clicks and grunts. The cart passed by and turned towards the station, and Joe stared after it into the back of the cart, at a small, hunched shape covered with a tarpaulin. As he watched, the tarpaulin moved, and Joe's breath stopped. He left his bicycle behind the wall and followed the cart, which was thankfully forced to move slowly, down the hill and into the car park at the side of the station.

A train was just rounding the bend in the tracks up ahead, and Joe recognised it as the one he'd often been sent to meet, coming from Plymouth and carrying cargo as well as passengers. Geordie sometimes sent him here to collect tools and materials for his work, so he knew this engine would be turned around on the turntable and sent back, but it would wait here for a good while first while packages were loaded and unloaded. There would be plenty of time for Joe to get into the cart while Carne wasn't looking, and make sure his eyes had not been playing tricks.

He really wanted to draw attention to what was happening, and expose Jago Carne for the kidnapper he was; to put all this into the hands of a grown-up and get the police in to see justice done. But once the little girl explained who she was, it would all come back to Geordie; as soon as anyone found out he had played a part in helping an escaped criminal, he would be sent to prison himself, the forge's reputation destroyed, and Joe would be left alone again. He had to do this in secret if he could.

He started towards the cart, hiding between cars and vans as he waited for Carne to climb down and go to fetch his package, feeling sure his frantic heartbeat would give him away to anyone standing within a few feet. But no one spared him a second glance, except someone whose car he was standing too close to, and who threw him a dark, warning look. He gave them his best smile and an apologetic wave, and moved away.

To his consternation, Carne remained sitting in the cart while the train chuffed into place against the platform, and doors were opened all along its length. But the longer he waited, the more Joe was convinced it was because Tilly was hidden in the back. Sure enough, just before he eventually climbed down, Carne looked around him and then twisted his head to say something, in a voice too low for Joe to hear.

Joe readied himself, as Carne walked towards the freight carriage, a piece of paper in his hand ready to pick up whatever

375

his boss had sent him for. But he looked over his shoulder every minute or so and Joe realised, with sinking spirits, that it was going to be impossible to climb into the cart and take Tilly without being seen. He thought hard for a moment, then wound his way back through the bustle, and half-ran, half-limped, back up the hill, to a point where the tarmac looked particularly rough, and he thought the cart's wheels would make the most noise. There he stood in the hedgerow, feeling spikes of winter-hard bramble stems digging into his skin, and the tension snaking up through him until he could hardly breathe.

Cars came and went, carrying newly arrived passengers, and the occasional cart rumbled by. Joe was heartened to note that nobody seemed to take undue notice of a boy loitering beside the hedge, so hopefully Carne would be equally focused on the road, and not on the identities of people wandering past. At length the Hazelmere cart made its sluggish way back up the hill, and Joe braced himself to use his weakened limbs to their limits. The cart took up almost the entire road, and he pushed himself away from the wall, shoved his hands into his pockets, and scuffed his sulky way past. Playing, to the best of his ability, the reluctant messenger on his way to collect a parcel.

The moment the cart was past him his courage faltered, but he gave himself no time to change his mind. He turned, grabbed the rail, and scrambled aboard, lying flat and breathing hard. But Carne didn't look back, intent on urging his pony past the crumbled road surface and on towards the junction with the bridle path. Joe skittered sideways and set to work on the string that tied the tarpaulin down. His fingers fumbled, and he heard a faint moan coming from under the canvas, then the string was free. He kept hold of it tightly in one hand, aware that it was long enough to fly up and hit Carne in the back of the neck, and with the other he lifted the edge of the tarpaulin to see Tilly cowering against a box of home wares.

She was lying curled up on a pile of sacks, and was neither tied nor gagged, but something had kept her there, and Joe guessed it was threats alone. Her dark eyes flew wide at the sight of him, but there was no time to do anything except gesture frantically for her to hush. A glance at Carne showed he was still concentrating, and Joe reached for Tilly's hand and pulled, as hard as he could.

She slithered towards him as they reached the top of the hill, and the cart slowed once more to enable the pony to turn off the road. Then they were on the moor, and, while the cart was already rocking and uneven, there would never be a better opportunity; Joe dragged Tilly with him off the cart and onto the grass. He cushioned her fall as best he could, but to his great surprise and relief she didn't utter a sound, though it must still have hurt a great deal. He himself had to bite back a miserable yell as his bad leg erupted into a fireball of pain, but he pulled at Tilly's hand until they were back on the road.

Carne had urged his pony on, oblivious, towards Hazelmere, and Joe looked down at Tilly. She stared up at him trustingly, still silent, her eyes filled with tears but a faint smile trembling on her lips. He couldn't think of anything to say, and her silence was unnerving him, so he just pointed to where he'd hidden his bicycle.

'Can you hold on tight?' She nodded, and took the hand he held out. As they began to walk, he heard a hissing sound, and realised she'd whispered something. 'What did you say?'

Tilly looked around fearfully, then spoke up. 'I lost Barney.'

'Who's Barn . . . oh, your lamb. Is he in the cart?' She nodded, and he sighed. 'Then he's gone forever.' Her mouth puckered for the first time, and he scowled. 'Unless *you* want to go and get him back?' Her hair flew as she shook her head frantically. 'Right then,' he said, relenting and rubbing her arm. 'Come on, we'll take you to your dad's house.'

The forge was just as he'd left it. The cottage, however, was not. Joe assumed the police had been in searching for Pearce; several things in the kitchen had been upturned, for no reason since they were hardly likely to be concealing an escaped criminal. The bedroom doors were both wide open, as were the wardrobes, and there were wet boot prints on the stone flags in the back porch.

Tilly was becoming agitated now, and Joe wondered if Carne had discovered she was missing yet. He might come straight here, if so, especially if he knew Geordie wasn't here. The thought made him feel queasy, and he picked up his coat again and opened the door.

'Where are we going?' Tilly asked, her voice rising. Joe spotted the signs that another wail was coming, and spoke quickly.

'To the stables,' he said. 'Wouldn't you like to see Hercules and Boots again?'

The magic words. Tilly's smile only faltered when she automatically looked around for Barney and then remembered where she'd left him.

'Come on then,' he urged. 'Let's see if your daddy's there waiting for you.'

He didn't take the bicycle this time. The afternoon was drawing to its end, and the sun had dipped a long way since he'd set off to find Tilly; the roads were too uneven to risk spilling them both to the ground through poor visibility. She'd made no fuss about the scrape on her arm from falling off the cart, but that had been onto grass, and a fall onto hard tarmac, at any kind of speed, was another matter entirely.

Instead, he led her across the road, and into the same woods through which Lynette would have taken Pearce when she went to fetch her car. He came this way often when visiting the stables, and didn't need full daylight to see them safely through to the back of the paddock. Hercules was still out, and from the stable came the shuffle and impatient whicker of horses waiting for their evening feed, but, looking in as he passed, Joe saw at once that Mack and Bella were missing. Tory's van was gone, but Lynette's car was still there, so it seemed clear to him that Geordie had returned, and that he and Lynette had taken their familiar horses out. Perhaps to find Tilly. He wished he could get word to them that she was safe, but all he could do was make sure she remained so until they returned.

'I'm going to get you into a good hiding place,' he said. She'd been good at that game on Christmas Day, and would need to be now, too, if the police were still prowling about. He led her to the small barn, and ushered her in, closing the door behind them.

'It's too dark,' Tilly said, her voice tremulous again.

Joe felt her hand patting around until it found his, and he took it and gave it a quick squeeze. 'Stand still a minute, and your eyes will get used to it.'

She did, but he could tell that it would soon be too dark for him to be able to help, anyway, so he pushed the door open a crack. 'Get up the ladder—' he pointed '—and go right to the back. I'll light the paraffin lamp.'

She went, scrambling up as quickly and easily as she had at Christmas; she'd told him then, not that he'd been interested, that she spent a lot of time on her friends' farm, so she was clearly well used to this. He saw that the barn floor had recently been swept clean of straw, which at least saved him a job, and he carefully placed the lamp near the foot of the ladder before lighting it. He turned it down as low as it would go without stuttering out, then shouted up the ladder. 'I'll go and get some food.'

'No!' Tilly crawled back to the lip of the loft. 'Come up here with me!'

Joe sighed. 'We're both hungry,' he pointed out. 'Just lie very still, all right? Like you did at Christmas.'

'Like I did in the cart,' she said, with a resigned tone that Joe found deeply upsetting. 'All right.'

'Tilly—'

'Get cheese,' she said, vanishing back into the loft, and the matter was decided.

Joe pulled open the barn door and stepped out into the breezy yard. It was eerie in the gathering dark, with no one around, and the horses growing more impatient by the minute; surely Tory and Lynette would be back soon. But his stomach was growling in sympathy with the horses, and it would be easy enough to get in through the little bathroom window.

He levered it open and wriggled through, grunting as his bad leg flared again but was soon on his way down the short hallway to the kitchen. He hoped he'd see someone there after all, although he'd have some explaining to do, but the flat was empty and quiet. He found a half loaf of bread, some cheese, as promised, and a plate of thickly sliced ham, and, unable to negotiate the window again with his new burdens, he let himself out through the door.

It seemed darker than ever outside now, and he almost tripped more than once as he made his way back across the yard, glad when he elbowed the barn door open again and the light from the lamp showed him the foot of the ladder. He'd need at least one spare hand to climb, so he kicked the door closed again behind him, and re-arranged the plates in his hand, echoing one of Geordie's favourite curse words as a couple of slices of ham slid onto the floor.

Tilly appeared at the top of the ladder again and stretched out her hands to take the bread and the cheese, allowing him to climb up and flop down beside her with relief. 'Eat up,' he said. 'Your dad will be here soon.'

Tilly tore off some bread and a corner of the block of cheese, and Joe realised as he watched that it must have been a long time since she'd had anything to eat. He was doubly glad he'd taken the time to fetch this. He picked up a piece of the ham and ate it, keeping one eye on the barn door in case the police returned. A shape in the corner of the barn made him jump, as it loomed impossibly tall, then he gave a short laugh as he recognised Boots, a fraction the size of his shadow.

'You didn't half give me a start, you daft moggie.'

'Ooh, is it Boots?' Tilly lurched forward and Joe had to grab the back of her coat to stop her tumbling off the platform. 'Here, kitty kitty!'

Boots gave her a disinterested look, but his nose twitched and he came closer, his tail going up and his mood altering considerably as he saw the pieces of ham Joe had dropped by the foot of the ladder. Tilly yelped in delight when he snatched it up and began chewing, and when he'd finished she tossed a piece of cheese over.

'Don't,' Joe said. 'We need it, we might be up here for hours yet.'

'He's hungry, just like the horses are,' Tilly countered, and before Joe could stop her she had picked up another piece and dropped onto the floor below.

381

Boots pounced, his tail whipped sideways, and his haunches hit the paraffin lamp, knocking it against the foot of the ladder. It should have instantly gone out, but, to Joe's alarm, he heard the tinkle of glass, and the flame flared with the inrush of air, setting light to the paraffin spilled on the ladder.

'Come here,' he snapped to Tilly. 'Follow me down, quick!' He started to climb down, but as he looked between his feet he saw flames climbing hungrily towards him. Even if he jumped past them now, should his bad leg permit it, he would never be able to persuade Tilly to trust him and do the same. He climbed back up, already feeling heat on the backs of his legs, and turned ready to kick the burning ladder away. With one foot on the top rung, he tried to predict which way it would fall, and in the end panic dictated he should just kick as hard as he could, and hope it landed squarely on the stone floor.

He kicked. The ladder rose a few feet, then the bottom, already eaten away to a skeleton by the flames, gave way and it slid away from his control. It landed directly beneath the hay loft, sending sparks soaring upward to catch at the wood beneath them, and the straw that covered it.

Joe grabbed Tilly, his heart thumping in terror as he saw a flicker on the far side of the loft, followed by a wisp of smoke and, finally, a tongue of flame. He leaned over and stared at the floor of the barn, which suddenly seemed twice as far away as it had before, and tried to imagine landing on it; he felt sick at the pain he knew it would cause him, but he could endure it, he'd done it before. Tilly was one he had to convince.

'Come here,' he said hoarsely, and, trusting as ever, Tilly crawled over to him, her eyes fixed on the thick smoke that was now pouring from the straw bales. At the moment the smoke was worst of it, and was bad enough, but flames would soon take over as the heat dried the straw out, and that meant time was short.

'I'm going to dangle you over the edge, and you'll have to jump the rest of the way.' He tried to ignore the look of panic on her face, but what he couldn't ignore was the violent shaking of her head. 'You have to,' he urged. 'You'll fall a little way, but if you bend your legs you'll be all right.'

'It's too far!' she wailed. 'I'll be broken!'

'You'll be *burned* if you stay here!' He regretted the shout immediately, as she shrank back in terror, but he couldn't help it now. 'Come here.' He took a firm hold of her wrists, but she was surprisingly strong, and fought back hard; after catching one of her freed hands across his face, he eventually had to accept that it wasn't going to work. The flames danced their deadly way closer, and Joe watched them, sick with fear and wondering how long it would be before they ate everything in their path.

CHAPTER THIRTY-EIGHT

Daniel skidded to a halt in the middle of the yard, staring in horror at the flames that were eating through the highest part of the barn roof. A glance at the house on top of the stable showed him dark windows and no sign of life, but the stables themselves were a riot of panicking horses, who must have smelled the smoke. His first instinct was to go to them, until a high-pitched cry issued from the small barn, and his gut lurched.

'I'm coming!' he yelled, and shoved open the barn door. He was vaguely aware of Gwenna close behind him, and already knew better than to tell her to stay outside, so he just waved away the smoke and stared in dismay at the hay loft, ablaze and almost consumed.

A young voice bellowed, *'Now!'* and a short scream followed, but Daniel couldn't see who had made it, or why. Then he caught movement through the swirling smoke and a bright flicker away to his left; a child stumbled towards him and he put out his hands to prevent her falling, even as the three bales of straw on which she'd landed crackled into life, and became a miniature bonfire. She clasped him around the hips and buried her face in his coat, and he could feel her shaking all over as he clutched at her in relief.

'Tilly! Thank God.' His mother appeared in the doorway behind him, and he urged Tilly towards her. 'She'll take care of you. Go!'

'Joe's up there!' Tilly pointed behind her, but the breath she took, in order to add more, caught in her throat and she began coughing; Daniel's mother hurried forward and swept her up, then retreated to the cold night air outside. As the door swung all the way open Daniel heard a distant clanging sound, brought intermittently closer by the wind.

'Where's the ladder?' Gwenna gasped. 'We have to get him down!'

Daniel pressed the heels of his hands to his streaming eyes, then looked around to see the remains of the ladder, lying on the floor beneath the hay loft and now charred almost beyond recognition.

'Go and see if you can find another,' he managed, before breaking off to cough and spit. 'Joe? Where are you? Can you jump too?'

'No, there—' The boy retched, and his voice was tearful and frightened when he spoke again. 'There are no more bales . . .' he coughed again. 'All on fire.'

'Can't you just jump?' Even as he said it, Daniel realised it was too dangerous from such a height. But he breathed a little more easily as he heard the fire engine bells coming closer; help was on the way. He stepped forward to tell Joe as much, but his relief immediately died; that help was coming too late. The boy was cowering on a few feet of untouched floor; he'd created some kind of fire break, as best he could, after getting Tilly out of harm's way, but the last of the straw he'd used was even now being consumed by flames, and fire was taking hold of the bare floorboards. If the boy didn't get off that platform right now he would be taken down by the collapsing hay loft and probably killed, buried beneath a mountain of fire.

Daniel heard shouts, and the heavy motor of the fire engine idling outside the closed gate, and he paused in hope for just a second, but a pained scream from Joe propelled him into action. He leapt forward and kicked at the burning straw to scatter it, burying his face in the crook of his elbow and coughing anyway. He looked up to see Joe, one hand clutching at his cheek, eyes wide and frightened, leaning towards him as if urging him on to greater speed. And with good reason. Bits of burning straw floated in the air around him, one of which had presumably caused the scream as it touched his face, and he was beating them back, sobbing as he did so. There was absolutely no time to waste. Daniel steadied himself, and, with fire still crawling around his boots, he held out his arms.

'Jump,' he yelled, bracing himself; this was no six-year-old girl, after all.

'You'll get caught!'

'Just jump!'

Joe didn't hesitate a moment longer. He grasped the edge of the loft and swung himself over, dangling for a second with his feet waving above Daniel's waiting arms, then let go. He thudded against Daniel's chest, and somehow Daniel closed his arms around the boy's narrow frame, staggering back with the impact and losing his balance. He fell, with Joe's weight on top of him, and the back of his head connected with the stone floor with a sickening crack. Flares shot through his head and neck, and a dull, sick feeling spread through him; even the pain in his back faded to a faint stinging, and he was faintly conscious of Joe rolling off him, still sobbing.

'Daniel, you have to get away . . .' Gwenna's voice. Urgent, but seeming very far away.

Another shout, also distant, and Daniel realised it was the ringing in his head that was keeping them that way. This one was male, demanding but frantic, and he guessed Geordie had returned and was being held back, very much against his will. Daniel lay absolutely still, positive that, should he try to move, he would discover he was unable to, and that he might never do so again. The thought struck such a deep horror in him that he almost wished for death there and then.

The bells stopped. More shouts, unfamiliar voices, a hand on his arm. He knew he had to get out of sight, that he would be re-arrested as soon as he was found here, but then he'd known that even as he'd urged Joe to jump to safety. At least now he knew it had been worth it. He blinked slowly, his breath wheezing in and out, sounding even to himself like an old set of bellows that were past their best. There was different pain now, in various parts of his body, and he forced himself to welcome it all. It meant he hadn't broken his neck, despite how it felt. Perhaps the prison medic would go easy on him . . .

'Daniel, please!'

But it was too late. The doorway was filled with dark shapes, and he could hear the wooden wheels of the fire engine's turntable, moving the ladder into position. Strong hands grasped him under the arms and then he was moving. Dragged backwards out of the way to allow the firemen to do their job. His eyes closed as the bliss of fresh air blew across his face, and he found he'd stopped caring about going back to Dartmoor after all. He'd had his flogging, and survived it. If he was to endure another, he'd survive that, too. A few extra years on his sentence? Just look to Stephen for an example of stoic acceptance there.

A more familiar hand touched his face and he opened his eyes again. Smiled. Closed them. His mother would be all right; she had friends now who believed her. They'd help her get her justice, and he deserved his. All this, because of one stupid act of vengeance . . . He fleetingly, half-dreamily wondered where he would be right this minute, if he hadn't caved in to his cousin's determination to go out that night. Bizarrely he found he was smiling, though he didn't know if it was showing on his face. He'd *said* it was a bad idea to go out on his birthday. Next time, Micky Frier should bloody well listen to him.

He was lying on a bed in an unfamiliar room. The bitter smell of smoke in the air told him he was still at the stables, though there was no noise outside the window, so the firemen must have done their job and gone. Daniel found a moment to thank the prevailing winds for not blowing the flames towards the stable, and the house above it, then the door opened and let in some of the light from the hall. His mother's voice drifted through the semi-dark room.

'Daniel? Are you awake?'

Daniel tried to speak, but discovered his voice box had been replaced with a handful of glass while he'd been asleep. His mother held up a hand to discourage any attempt to talk, and picked up a cup of water from the bedside table. She slipped a hand behind Daniel's shoulders, easing him to a sitting position before she gave him the drink. Daniel sipped it, and handed it back with a grateful nod.

'The police are waiting to take you back,' she said quietly. 'I'm sorry, love, I tried to—'

'No,' he croaked, 'don't be sorry.'

'But it's my fault. All of it. If I hadn't been so sure I could get the better of Mr Dunn, he wouldn't have made that warder give you such a terrible time.'

'I was the one who threw the brick at his car,' he reminded her, still in a hoarse whisper, which hurt less than trying to talk. 'Nobody made me do that.' He tried to swallow. 'How are Joe and Tilly?'

'They're both very shaken up, but not badly hurt. And that's thanks to you.'

'And Joe's face?'

'A small-ish burn, not deep, so the doctor said. His hair is badly singed in a couple of places, another minute or two and . . . well.'

The door opened further, and Daniel stiffened as a uniformed police sergeant stepped into the room. This was it, then. He tried to sit up straighter, but the pain that radiated from his head to the base of his spine stopped him.

'I'm here to take you back, lad,' the officer said, and he sounded regretful but firm. 'I'm Sergeant Brewer.'

'He's not ready yet!' His mother stood up. 'The doctor wants to see him first.'

'Call her in, then,' Brewer said. 'I'll come back d'rectly. You—' he pointed at Daniel, leaving no room to misinterpret the look in his eyes '—will be here when I get back, or I'll be asking serious questions of all these kind people who've looked after you.'

'I will be,' Daniel promised hoarsely. 'You have my word.'

'Such as that is.' Brewer sniffed. 'I've got two Watchers out there, anyway, so don't try anything funny.'

Daniel looked down at his bed, then back at Brewer, in disbelief that the policeman had even thought the threat necessary, and Brewer shrugged. He backed out of the room, and a moment later a woman he'd never seen before came in, carrying a tray. It was so reminiscent of Gracie and her little basket of torture, that Daniel found himself looking pleadingly at his mother. She smiled, not without sympathy.

'This is Doctor Stuart; she saw you when they first brought you out of the barn.'

The doctor promised she'd be gentle, and that he'd be up and about in no time, but as soon as the door was closed the cheerful smile fell away, and she turned serious, light-blue eyes on Daniel. 'Take off that shirt,' she said gently, 'and lie on your front.'

'It's my head that hurts,' he began, but he could tell from the look on her face that she'd already seen what he hoped he'd hidden from his mother. He was grateful she hadn't said anything, but the sympathy on her face almost undid him. He unbuttoned Farmer Martyn's shirt and accepted her help to remove it, then he met her eyes once more before he turned over to lie on his stomach. She didn't draw a shocked gasp – he was listening for it – but she did rest a cool hand on the back of his neck, just once, in a gesture of comfort, before she set wordlessly to work.

A little later he was making grateful use of the washbowl and a ewer of hot water Tory had brought in for him, when he heard something of a commotion in the yard. An exclamation and raised voices came from the room beyond the little hallway, and he moved to the window and peered out. A horse and rider were outlined against the small patch of light by the tack room, the rider bending low over the horse's neck. A moment later the door banged, and there were thundering boots on the steps down to the yard. Daniel watched the woman dismount and turn, saw the gleam of reflected light on blonde hair, and then she was enveloped in a flurry of black as Geordie reached her and seized her in his arms. The horse pulled at the reins, now held loosely, and the two of them turned as one, to ease it with soothing pats and murmurs. Geordie's other hand did not let go of Lynette's, Daniel noted with a little smile, envious at their obvious love for one another.

His mind turned towards the stern, dark-haired girl who had first whacked him with a poker, and then kicked him, before abandoning her own comfort and safety to lead him and his mother here, through the darkness. Gwen-*na*, as she'd insisted, when he'd had the temerity to shorten her name in his mumbled thanks earlier. When they'd linked hands, after he'd almost broken down on their way up here, it had felt so unquestionably natural, that they'd gone several paces before he'd even realised it. She'd given him just enough belief in himself to keep going, and then stepped away while he'd carefully considered it before allowing himself to accept it. Every matelot needed a Gwenna Rosdew, he concluded, if only to take the half-brick out of his hand and lead him back to his barracks.

The smile returned, but it wasn't envy for Geordie and Lynette; it was regret that he and Gwenna had only met now, when it was already too late to explore what lay behind the beautiful, but aloof, head-girl manner, and the cool-headed determination. She had been exhausted and drained, and very pale in the harsh light that had flooded the storeroom, but even as she'd vented her fright, disguised ably as annoyance, he'd felt the pull of something warm and surprisingly intense between them. He thought she'd felt it too, and it was just too damned bad they'd never be able to explore it.

'Horrible luck, yer Honour,' he murmured now, and his sighing breath fogged the windowpane, blocking out the touching scene in the yard below.

He continued washing the worst of the smoke from his skin, and pulled on the clothes Tory had left on the bed. Bobby's, evidently, and although they were rough and patched, they were clean, and fit much better than Mr Martyn's. He spared a moment's regret for the mess he'd made of the farmer's coat, after promising he'd look after it, and he hoped it could be saved. Then he eased open the door, uncertain of his reception and who would be there to deliver it, but relaxed when he saw his mother sitting next to Gwenna on the settee. Gwenna looked up, and a fleeting smile touched her eyes before she looked away again, as if she'd given too much away. His heart responded with a little leap.

Geordie and Lynette had not yet come back in, but Tory and Bobby were there, and Tory jumped up when she saw him.

'Sit down,' she ordered. 'I'll make you some cocoa. I think you could probably do with a drop of something a bit stronger in it, too, couldn't you?'

He smiled, a bit weakly. 'How about the something stronger, with a drop of cocoa in it?' he suggested, and Tory nodded.

'Right you are.'

He noticed how she couldn't pass the window without looking out of it, and realised she was seeing the ruined barn rather than the return of her friend. 'How bad is the damage?'

'Oh.' She shrugged, pasting a smile on that didn't entirely convince him. 'It's not as bad as it might be, thanks to whoever spotted the flames and called the fire brigade.'

'And the children are safe,' Bobby put in. 'I've got a great fondness for them, young Joe in particular.' He held out his hand. 'I owe you a debt of gratitude.'

'The clothes are enough,' Daniel said, and accepted the solemn handshake with a nod and a slightly embarrassed smile.

'How are *you* feeling?' Gwenna asked.

'Sore,' he admitted, rubbing tentatively at the back of his head. 'Doctor Stuart says I might be concussed, so I'm to look out for certain things and tell the prison doctor.'

'You're definitely going back, then?' He didn't quite dare to hope she sounded upset, but he thought perhaps he wasn't imagining it, when he saw her lips tighten into a thin line as he nodded.

'Sergeant Brewer said he'll be back later,' Tory said, returning from the kitchen to press a warm cup into Daniel's hands. 'I'm not giving you anything too strong after all, in case you *are* concussed, sorry.'

Daniel sipped at the hot, chocolatey drink, tasting the tang of brandy in its depths. 'Perfect, thank you. Where are the children?'

'Asleep in Lynette's room,' Gwenna said. She opened her mouth to say more, but a knock at the door stopped everyone, and they all turned to look, as if it were possible to see through the wood to the visitor beyond. Daniel had a cold feeling he knew who it would be, though, and when Tory crossed the room and looked back at him, her expression said she knew it too.

CHAPTER THIRTY-NINE

Lynette gave Bella a final pat, and closed the stall door. She was still shaken by the way the horse had bolted, for no discernible reason at the time, though she realised now that it was the thick smell of smoke, exacerbating the horse's already nervous response to the police visit earlier. She'd fought to cling on, it was all she could do, since Bella wouldn't be stopped no matter what she tried to do. Tory could probably have done it, she reflected now, but as it was, Joe and Tilly had been left alone, and would have died if Daniel hadn't given everything up to bring them to safety.

'Looks like time's up for Daniel,' Geordie said as they watched Sergeant Brewer being admitted upstairs. 'Poor bugger.'

'Have you had time to speak to him?'

'Not yet. The doctor was with him at first, then she told us to let him sleep for a while. I don't know if he's awake again yet.' He put his arm around her shoulders and let out another long sigh as he rested his head against hers. 'I can't tell you how relieved I am you're back. I should never have let you go off alone.'

'We had to separate,' she said. 'But I shouldn't have taken Bella at all, and I think I knew that, deep down. She's been unsettled all day.'

'How far did she carry you?'

'I couldn't pull her up until we'd got halfway down to Porthstennack.' Lynette slipped her arm under his as they made their way to the flat, taking comfort from his closeness. 'I should have come back when she finally stopped, instead of just leading her along the cliff.'

'You were only trying to calm her down,' he said. 'Better that than get back on too quickly and risk her throwing you.'

'At least I'd already told Brewer about Tilly by that point.' Lynette stopped and looked up at him. 'Thank God she's all right.'

'Thank Joe,' he corrected her. 'The lad put himself at real risk, doing that for her.'

'He called her his sister,' Lynette said, with a wondering little laugh as she remembered. 'You could have knocked me over with a feather.'

'What he did for her today speaks even louder. Not to mention what Daniel did for him.' There was a world of feeling in the touch of his lips on her brow when he bent to kiss her. 'I owe him as much help as I can with Brewer, after that.'

They went up the steps and into the sitting room, where they saw Daniel had, indeed, woken and joined the others. He sat perched nervously on the edge of the seat nearest the window, a mug of cocoa clutched in his pale hands, while Sergeant Brewer had dragged over a chair from the kitchen table. Lynette noticed that Cathy, who'd been sitting next to Gwenna, had removed herself from the proceedings. Probably to protect Gwenna.

'Right, lad,' Brewer said, sitting down. 'Governor Roberts is keen to get you back on the moor, where you belong.'

Daniel nodded carefully. 'How long have I got?' He sounded awful, as if talking still hurt a great deal.

'As long as it takes me to question Mr Sargent here.' Brewer turned his gaze on Geordie, sending a small shock through Lynette. She should have expected it, and he clearly had; he faced Brewer calmly, as if he knew he was on borrowed time here now.

'What have you got to say, Sargent?'

'About what?'

'About you detaining me, I should think,' Daniel said, before Brewer could reply.

Brewer frowned. 'He was *harbouring* you, Mr Pearce, and encouraging these people to do the same.'

'No, he caught me,' Daniel insisted. 'On the road to Hazelmere. You can ask young Joe, he was there, too. Sargent was going to bring me straight to you, before I told him about Tilly.'

'Ah yes, your daughter.' Brewer turned to Geordie again. 'Good of your friend here to bring her down to you. I did hear you and your wife had disagreements about her not letting you see her.'

'Can I ask who told you that?' Geordie asked, his tone still polite, but Lynette felt the tension lock his frame tight. 'Or shall I just guess?'

'It doesn't matter,' Brewer said. 'But the fact that she's here, and that she arrived with our young convict—'

'Wait, Geordie didn't know about that,' Daniel protested. 'She stowed away in the car I . . . I stole.'

'And anyway, the information you've been given is out of date,' Lynette put in, before Daniel could tangle himself up. 'Geordie and Marion are on good terms, and Geordie can see Tilly anytime now. She even stayed all over Christmas.'

'Geordie *was* bringing me to you, sir, before he found out I'd left her with Jago Carne,' Daniel said. His tone and manner were both respectful and earnest. 'He had no intention of helping me. Why would he?'

'You'll have to see it from our point of view, lad,' Brewer said. 'You shared a cell with his brother, and here you are in the house of his ... lady friend.' He threw Lynette a quick, embarrassed look, then returned to Daniel. 'Even you would find it hard to discount that coincidence.'

'Just a minute though,' Gwenna broke in, and as all gazes swept to her, she seemed to shrink back, but only for a second. 'You're only here because you searched *Stephen's* last address, and you only found the address of the forge, because Geordie's wife happens to live there now. You had no reason to think Daniel knew anything at all about Geordie, you're just guessing!'

'Yet here he is,' Brewer said again, but they could all see the uncertainty flickering in his expression now.

'In the home of *my* friends,' Gwenna said, 'not just Geordie's.'

Brewer leapt on that, and gave her a thin smile. 'And your father's in Dartmoor as well, isn't he?'

Lynette tensed, but Gwenna shook her head and gave Brewer a pitying look. 'As if my dad would risk the chance of getting out early, just for the sake of someone he barely knows. I'll bet if you ask anyone at the prison you'll find they barely spoke two words.'

'Who *is* your dad?' Daniel asked her. He seemed genuinely surprised.

'Jonas Rosdew.'

He frowned and shook his head, as Gracie had done. 'Sorry. Doesn't ring any bells.'

'Exactly. And he never mentions you either.'

He gave her faint smile. 'I'm sure you meant that in a good way.'

The exchange between them seemed so natural that even Lynette didn't question it. 'Anyway,' she said, 'Geordie's address is the forge, and you didn't find Daniel there, did you?'

'No, we found him out in *your* barn, with the child he abducted!' Brewer scowled, clearly sensing things were getting away from him.

'I'm not denying it,' Daniel said quietly. 'Although it's true she did sneak into the car, and she'll tell you the same thing. But that doesn't mean her father knew about it, or was helping me. I told you, he was going to bring me to you.'

'So, you're admitting you stole the car.'

'I've already said so,' Daniel said. 'Listen. I broke out without anyone's help, except the Elephant and Castle gang, who unlocked my cell. I stole the car from the farm I came to when I was running away. The girl was hiding in the back; apparently she likes to play hide and seek.' He sat back, and rubbed his hands over his face tiredly, then went on. 'I saw a police car up on the junction, and didn't want to drive past it. That's when I found Tilly in the car. I couldn't risk her giving me away, so I took her through the woods, and when we came out we were near a place called Hazelmere. I thought it best if I left Tilly with someone safe. That's when I realised Jago Carne, who I *did* know in prison, was the handyman. I trusted him, so I left her there and went on.' He looked at Geordie. 'I'm sorry,' he said quietly. 'I wouldn't have done if it I'd known.'

'And that's when you met Mr Sargent here,' Brewer pressed. 'Who said he was bringing you in.'

'Yes. He put handcuffs on me, so I wasn't in a position to try and escape.'

'And you didn't offer to exchange your freedom for his daughter's whereabouts?'

Lynette held her breath; Geordie's future depended on Daniel being convincing now. She could feel Geordie standing very still beside her but didn't dare look at him. She looked only at Daniel, who fixed his calm gaze on Sergeant Brewer, and spoke without hesitation.

'No, I did not. I told him where she was, and he put me in the custody of young Joe.'

'To do what?'

'To bring me straight to you.'

'And why didn't he?'

Daniel lowered his face. 'I pushed him over and grabbed the handcuff key,' he said, his voice rich with self-disgust. 'Then I cut through the trees, and ended up here.'

'In time to help the lad you'd *just* knocked over, escape a fire that had *already* destroyed half a barn.' Brewer's gaze was hard as it lingered on Daniel's bowed head. 'H.G. Wells lend you his time machine, did he?'

Daniel gave him a look of reproach, that Lynette thought probably worked better than a sigh and a roll of the eyes would have done. 'I hid in the trees for a long time,' he said. 'I don't know the area, so I ... I didn't come out until I smelled the smoke.' Daniel looked up again. 'That's when I realised it was more important to save the boy than to stay hidden.'

'Very commendable, I'm sure,' Brewer said dryly. But his expression had softened slightly, and Lynette allowed herself to breathe again. She looked across at Gwenna, who was studying Daniel with an unexpected intensity. There was no hope that he would be spared being taken back to Dartmoor, but he had at least taken Geordie's name out of Brewer's circle of suspicion, and, added to his act of courage in standing among the burning straw bales to catch Joe, perhaps it might help reduce the likelihood that his sentence would be extended by too much.

As Brewer continued writing in his notebook, with everyone silently awaiting the moment he would have to take Daniel away, Lynette's bedroom door opened and a tousled head appeared around it, peering down the hall and into the sitting room. The dark eyes lit on Geordie, and with an exclamation of delight, Tilly came running in, dressed in one of Lynette's blouses as a makeshift nightshirt. She flung herself on her father, and he picked her up, squeezing her tightly and burying his face in her curls.

'I found someone who's been missing you,' he said, and put her down again so he could reach into his coat pocket. 'Who do you think?'

Tilly clasped her hands together and stared up at him with wide-eyed hope. 'Barney?'

'Ba-a-a-arney!' he agreed, laughing, and pulled the lamb out of his pocket with a flourish. As he did so, something else flicked out and landed on the floor next to Brewer's chair; a screwed-up piece of paper. Daniel's eyes followed it, and they widened with dismay. As did Geordie's, Lynette saw, as she looked back up at him. His breath seemed to have stopped, and his hand convulsively clutched at the lamb Tilly was trying to take from him, ignoring his daughter's bewildered little grunts of frustration.

Brewer gave the crumpled note a casual glance, then bent and picked it up, ready to hand back. But he looked more closely, and his gaze went to Daniel and then to Geordie as he smoothed it out on his notepad. Lynette was able to see the crest on the top, and the lettering: *His Majesty's Convict Prison, Dartmoor.*

CHAPTER FORTY

Daniel's eyes fixed on Brewer as he read the note. All the fire and fight had finally seeped out of him, and he knew, that, not only was he going back, he was probably taking Geordie with him.

Brewer pushed out a deep sigh of regret, and read aloud: 'When dark go northwest to Peter Tavy. Cudlip Farm. Show this letter to Gracie. Will help you.' He looked at Daniel. 'Is this Gracie the one whose car you, uh, *stole*?' When Daniel didn't answer, he shrugged. 'We've heard they found your boot prints heading down towards the river, so I have to assume she refused your help, and you came back for the car later.'

Daniel was still trying to absorb the news that his distinctive arrowed boot prints showed him going somewhere he'd never been. Then he realised how far Farmer Martyn had gone, in order to help him, a complete stranger, and he felt an ache in his throat. 'Yes,' he managed.

'I was there when they found those footprints,' Gwenna said, and Daniel blinked in surprise. 'I met Gracie at the prison when I was enquiring after my dad. She invited me back for breakfast.'

Brewer nodded and made a note in his book. 'I see. So, Pearce,

Miss Martyn of Cudlip Farm refused to help, and that's how come the young miss here—' he pointed at Tilly, who'd at last managed to wrest Barney from her father's hand '—came to be hiding in the back, is it? Heard you two … um, *arguing* about where you were going, and came to find her dad?'

Daniel realised Brewer was trying to construct a story that would exonerate the Martyns from suspicion. The man had a heart, then. He nodded, relieved. 'That's exactly it.'

'I did hear them talking,' Tilly piped up, and Daniel's heart skipped; if she mentioned they'd been indoors at the time, and not at all at loggerheads, all Brewer's efforts, and his own, would be wasted. 'I sneaked out after bedtime. I told Mrs Martyn I didn't want a story so she'd leave me alone.' She beamed up at her father for his approval, but he was staring fixedly at the note.

'And who wrote this?' Brewer asked, his eyes boring into Daniel's as he abandoned his cosy tone. 'Your cellmate. Come on, lad, I can help Miss Martyn but I can't help a bloke who's aided and abetted an escaped convict.'

'What would happen to someone who might have done such a thing?' Lynette asked.

'I don't know, miss. I'm not a magistrate, nor a judge. But I'd suppose they might just add time onto his sentence. Provided he didn't actually help the prisoner over the wall, or unlock his cell.' He turned back to Daniel, who shook his head.

'It was the lags from the Elephant and Castle gang who unlocked the doors down in chokey, ask anyone. Nobody helped me, I found the ladder leaning against the wall by the governor's office.'

'You do realise there'll be a full criminal trial about this mutiny,' Brewer said. 'Are you prepared for that?'

'I am. I stole clothes from the Martyns' wash house, and the car from the yard. Miss Martyn couldn't stop me, and I told her she mustn't tell anyone, or else I'd be caught. And then it would be the worst for Stephen once I got back inside,' he added. 'That's what the note was about. What he meant by the coward's way.'

'Path,' Brewer corrected, looking at the note again.

'Yes.'

'Not that he was being a coward for not trying to escape?'

Daniel shook his head firmly. 'No. I told him to point me at someone who could get me away, or I'd ...' He faltered, going against everything in his nature. 'I'd use a chiv on him.'

Brewer folded the note and tucked it into his own pocket. 'I see. And you've threatened Mr Sargent's friends here the same, I assume? That you'd hurt his brother if they turned you in?'

Daniel looked up to see Geordie's eyes on him as he nodded. 'Yes. That's about it.'

'Then I'm left with no alternative now, but to re-arrest you, awaiting transport back to Dartmoor.' Brewer stood up, and Daniel rose too, his hands held out before him to receive the cuffs.

Geordie spoke up. 'Will he be put anywhere near Stephen?'

'I can't say. But I'll let them know what he's said.' Brewer fastened the cuffs, and took Daniel by the elbow.

'Will I ...' Daniel faltered now. 'Will I be flogged again?'

'Again?' Brewer frowned. 'I didn't realise. How long since?'

'Almost three weeks.' Daniel was aware of the shock on Gwenna's face, but deliberately didn't allow himself to catch her eye. The fear was crawling through him like a live thing, as he recalled the A frame, the chemical smells, and the sounds, even before the first stroke had landed. Had he really kept trying to tell himself he could endure it again?

'It's not my decision, lad,' Brewer said, but he sounded troubled. 'If it's of any help, I could tell them how you risked your safety, and gave yourself up, to save Geordie's apprentice.'

'Joe's more than that,' Geordie snapped. 'And what Daniel did deserves proper recognition. I'll plead his case myself, if I have to.'

'Shouldn't be necessary,' Brewer said, leading Daniel across the room. 'I'll make it for him.'

'If Councillor Dunn is still manipulating the officers, it won't make a difference!'

All eyes went to Gwenna, who'd stood up now too, and was moving quickly to block the doorway. 'Sergeant Brewer, you can't let him go back there until this is all sorted out.'

Brewer looked from her to Daniel, and back again. 'What in the world are you prattling about, miss? Who's Councillor Dunn when he's at home?'

'He's on the Plymouth city council,' Gwenna said. She took a deep breath and called down the corridor. 'Cathy, you'd better come out now.'

Daniel groaned as his mother appeared; she had come so close to escaping the attention of the police, and now Gwenna had ruined everything. Gwenna gave him a look that was somehow both apologetic and stubborn at the same time, and he shook his head in frustration, but she ignored him.

'Please sit down, Sergeant, and hear what Mrs Pearce has to say.'

Brewer seemed about to refuse, but there was something about the way Daniel's mother held herself that evidently convinced him to listen.

They sat in silence while the whole nasty story spilled out, and Daniel watched his mother's face as she told it, familiarity allowing him to read the emotions beneath the outward calm. As the details revealed themselves, those he'd never known and those he had, he felt himself grow still more tense, his hatred for both Dunn and Newbury intensified to what felt like dangerous levels, but his sorrow for the way his mother had felt the need to keep the worst of it to herself, robbed him of the words he needed to express it.

'And have you any proof of what's been going on?' Brewer asked at length. 'I'm not saying I disb'lieve you,' he added hurriedly, as Gwenna opened her mouth ready to argue. 'But something like this . . . well. It's hard to prove.'

'I clean the offices where he works,' Cathy said. 'I've seen letters, to and from the owners of the storage sheds that got made into shops, and how they were rushed through planning. But Dunn's name isn't on any of them; he's just the whispering mouth in the right ear, when the time comes.'

'And the right bank account,' Gwenna added, her voice hard. 'Cathy says this has been going on for years, sergeant. And he has that prison guard waiting to set his dogs onto Daniel the minute he goes back in. With Dunn on his side, he can promise all kinds of things in return for Daniel's life.'

'It's the only reason I left,' Daniel said quietly. 'I was in no fit state, not really, but when . . . when Davis unlocked my door, I realised that if I stayed, especially with everyone running riot, I'd be dead before dinnertime.' It was only a half-lie, but he still daren't implicate Stephen any further in this, even if Brewer did seem to be softening. 'Please, look into this, and keep me somewhere else until you have. Stephen was right.' He nodded at Brewer's pocket, where the note now lay. 'My life does depend on it.'

Brewer looked torn. 'I'll have to notify Devon that you've been found, so the search can be called off. I can't answer as to whether they'll come and fetch you, or whether they'll listen to anything I have to say on the matter.'

Daniel tried not to let his fear show, but he knew it must. 'I understand.'

'Please,' Gwenna urged. 'Do your best.'

'I'll take you back to the station for now,' Brewer said. 'On your honour that you won't try to make a break for it. You'll only be hurting yourself if you do.'

'I won't.'

'Sargent, with me. You can watch over him while I make the telephone call.'

Geordie nodded, and squeezed Lynette's arm. 'I won't be long.'

Later it seemed everything had happened in the space of a few minutes, but when Daniel thought about it he realised it must have been a good deal longer. He and Geordie had climbed into Sergeant Brewer's car, squashed into the back seat shoulder-to-shoulder, and travelled the short distance down to Caernoweth in silence. There was no question of making any kind of escape attempt; his breathing still rasped from the smoke he had taken in, and his head pounded sickening with every pulse beat. It was relentless. He'd have got precisely nowhere, even if he'd been left alone in the car and Brewer had left the door wide open.

Geordie's presence was making him nervous as well; his earlier support notwithstanding, the blacksmith's parting words in the lane still rang loud and clear: *You'd better hope I don't find you …* Daniel might have saved Joe's life, but Joe was not his son. Tilly, on the other hand, he had given to the one man who knew what the loss of her would do to her father. It was only thanks to Joe that she was even alive, let alone safe.

At the Caernoweth police house they had sat in the anteroom, while Brewer went to make his telephone call. Daniel sat with his arms braced on his thighs, his head low, wishing desperately that the nausea would pass, and that his courage would return. Geordie still did not speak. He sat next to Daniel, upright and prepared for any move that Daniel might make, his face a hard, unreadable mask.

Brewer came out of his office, and cleared his throat. 'You're to stay in the station tonight. Tomorrow they'll send a van for you.' He must have seen the look of fear pass across Daniel's face, because his voice softened. 'You're going to Exeter, lad.'

It had the opposite effect than he'd evidently expected; Exeter prison meant only one thing to Daniel. His heart crashed, and he started to his feet, but Brewer's eyes widened in realisation. 'Only for the time being! 'Til things settle down at Dartmoor.'

'Christ!' Daniel slumped back into his seat, letting his breath out in a shaky sigh.

'What about Alfred Dunn?' Geordie asked. It was the first time he had spoken since they'd left the stables. 'Will they investigate him?'

'Can't say. Not my force. But as I said, Pearce, there's going to be a criminal trial of all the prisoners who took an active part in the mutiny. You'll have your chance to tell your tale then. In the meantime—' he switched his attention back to Geordie '—anything you can gather together, to support Mrs Pearce's version of events, can't hurt.'

Geordie nodded, and as he stood he held out his hand to Daniel. 'Good luck.'

Daniel raised his cuffed wrists and awkwardly shook the hand. 'I'm sorry,' he said, and was dismayed to hear his voice cracking. He didn't know whether it was relief, fear, delayed shock, or a combination of all three; he certainly felt them all.

'You saved my boy,' Geordie said. 'And about Tilly, well, you trusted Carne. Which makes you an idiot,' he added, 'but I can't punch you for being an idiot. Unfortunately.' A faint smile appeared, and it changed his face completely. 'I wish you all the best, Pearce. If you're good enough for Stephen, you're good enough for me.'

Daniel had left Caernoweth and Pencarrack the next morning, early, in the back of a van that bumped its ungainly way all the way up to Exeter Prison. There he had remained for several weeks, but he had been spared another flogging, and he'd even enjoyed a certain respect for escaping the notorious prison on the moor. But he knew it wouldn't last, and sure enough, in early March he was taken back to Dartmoor. This time he considered himself lucky to be confined to chokey once again, and although he was dismayed to learn that Ray Beatty had been denied medical treatment for his bullet wound until days later, he was glad to see his old friend in good spirits, as he was led down to the punishment block.

Daniel's case, along with around thirty others, was to be heard at a special assize in the Duchy Hall, in Princetown. The main trial was conducted first, with all the prisoners giving their testimonies over, and the jury later finding their verdict in just five hours. Ten were found not guilty, but Davis had been given an additional twelve years on his sentence, for his part in the attack on Officer Birch. Other sentences were similarly extended, and

Daniel knew he was in for a rough ride at his own, separate trial, for the significantly more serious indictment.

He stood in the dock, which had, he learned with a heavy sense of irony, been built for these trials by his fellow prisoners, and tried not to look at anyone directly as the case began. He'd hurt no one, at least that anyone could ascertain, but to have escaped, and evaded capture by means of theft and deception, was something nobody could deny, and his barrister did not even try. Instead, he pleaded mitigation, and listed the appalling treatment by Ned Newbury under the orders of Alfred Dunn.

But the jury, many of whom no doubt held Dunn in high regard, listened impassively, while Daniel's hopes gradually sank. One or two were outwardly disgusted by the accusations, until, to Daniel's puzzlement, his barrister called a witness he hadn't previously known about: Mrs Alison Newbury. His startled gaze flew around the hall, to see if this was as much of a surprise to everyone else, and, for the first time since the trial began, he saw her: Gwenna. Sitting in the public space, her eyes on him, steady and clear. Had she been there the whole time? He couldn't have said, even if his life had depended on it. But she was there now, and he felt his trembling heart settle into a slow, steady rhythm again. She lifted her chin a fraction, as their eyes met and held, making Daniel's own shoulders come up so he stood square and strong in the dock.

It was hard to turn away from her, but Mrs Newbury had stepped into the witness box now, and she too looked around the hall, her pale face creased with worry. She spoke up clearly though, when it was time, and told a sordid tale of secret meetings, overheard telephone calls, and laughter-filled de-briefing sessions in her father's library. She'd been more or less invisible, she said, as had her mother, and the two of them had often speculated on the identities of the prisoners singled out for special attention, but there was little they could do about it.

'But this one was different,' Alison said. She turned pleading eyes on Daniel. 'He was going to have you killed, you know.'

'Please direct your comments to myself or to Justice Finlay,' Daniel's barrister prompted gently. 'Are you sure about this?'

'I'm sure. He was going to get Thomas Davis to do it.' Alison looked at the judge, and raised her voice so it rang clearly through the hall. 'My husband was going to have Mr Pearce killed, and my father told him to do it.'

Daniel was led down to the punishment block once again; but it held little fear for him now; Newbury wouldn't dare try anything while he was being scrutinised so closely, and his cell down here felt familiar, secluded, and almost like home. The uproar that had followed Mrs Newbury's testimony had left him stunned, but, as he'd been hustled through the crowd on the way back to the van, his barrister had caught up with him, and assured him that all steps would be taken to have these new claims investigated. Daniel had been able to give him Gwenna's name, and the barrister had agreed, as the van door closed, to go and speak to her. Daniel's sentence had, in the meantime, been been extended by two years, but there was to be no further punishment. No flogging. The relief had almost brought him to tears.

'Well done, boy,' Ray called, ignoring the repeated orders to shut up, as always. 'Sorry to see you back. Grand news about your mate, though, innit?'

'What?' Daniel stopped dead. 'Who?' He resisted the pull on

his arms long enough for Beatty to deliver the best news Daniel could have hoped for.

'Sargent, who else? Apparently saved Warder Finegan's life in the riot, got his sentence reduced, and with time served, they've let him go! Not a pardon, like, he'll still have the record, but he's out. Gone!'

His voice faded, as Daniel allowed himself once more to be pulled along the corridor, but the words danced and sang in the air and in his heart, and, as the door to his solitary cell clanged shut behind him, he raised his face to the dirty, greasy ceiling, and laughed.

EPILOGUE

25 May 1932

Gwenna closed the shop for the night, and picked up the newspaper to read the latest news about the investigation into Alfred Dunn and Ned Newbury. The article was written by a young female reporter, whose name jumped off the page the moment Gwenna opened the paper. Emma Kessel had lived here in town until last year, had broken the real story of Lynette's brother's death, and was now writing for the *Western Evening Herald*. Gwenna envied the girl her exciting new life, but her own time would come; her mother needed her for now, at least until her father came home next month.

The trip she and Cathy had made to Alison Newbury's house, before the trial had begun, had been worth all the worry and the secrecy. The woman had been stand-offish to the point of rudeness, at first, even threatening to call the police. But it had only taken one or two probing questions from Cathy, for her to break down, and they had realised that her distance, and refusal to listen, had been born of fear. Once they had broken through,

Alison had collapsed in relieved tears and told them all she knew, and, after some persuading, agreed to be a witness for Daniel's defence.

As the story had emerged in the newspapers, following Alison's surprise revelations in the Duchy Hall, more people had come forward with their own stories. Dunn was arrested, charged, and convicted of fraud, and Newbury of attempted murder. For his own safety, Newbury was removed to Parkhurst Prison, on the Isle of Wight, but Alfred Dunn was currently occupying a cell in Dartmoor, and enjoying a much more frugal existence than he was used to.

Gwenna had known most of this already, but as her eyes travelled down the small rows of text, looking for something new, she sat up straight with a little cry.

> Daniel Pearce's original sentence has consequently been reduced to twelve months, with mitigating circumstances, to run concurrently with his sentence of two years for absconding during the prison mutiny on 24 January.

He would be out in a little over a year and a half. Possibly sooner if he, like her father, kept his head down and gave no trouble. Gwenna's heart thumped a little harder. She'd been to visit him twice, and each time they had grown more relaxed, and warmer with one another, and, as she'd left the last time, he had caught at her hand and given her that same speculative little smile she'd first seen in the storeroom. She had answered it with one of her own, and left with the memory of it settling in her heart. Who would have guessed she'd fall for an escaped convict, and one she'd hit with a poker before they'd even spoken? More to the point, who would have guessed he could return her feelings?

Gwenna ran downstairs, her spirits flying, and took down her coat. A brisk walk would help settle her down, or she'd never sleep. She called goodbye to her mother, and stepped out into the rapidly falling dusk, enjoying the feel of the late spring breeze in her hair. She wanted desperately to talk to someone who would understand her sudden happiness, but Geordie and Lynette were up in Devon, explaining their recent engagement to Marion and Tilly, and Tory would just be putting Hercules into his stable for the night.

Gwenna decided to go and visit Bertie at the air training base, and had just set off up the hill, when her attention was caught by a movement across the road outside Penhaligon's Attic. She prepared to wave, assuming it to be Anna or her husband Matthew, but when she looked properly she realised it was neither. The way the figure moved was instantly familiar, slipping like oil around the corner of the shop, and moving furtively towards the back yard. Gwenna felt a bright flash of anger, and before she realised what she was doing she was crossing the road at a run, and following the same path.

The figure was easing open the back gate as Gwenna reached him, and he turned with an exclamation of annoyance. But Gwenna wasn't interested in his feelings; she launched herself at him, spun him around, and pinned him against the wall.

'Nigel *bloody* Stibson,' she hissed, pulling his arms up behind him until he yelped. 'I've had about enough of you! Come with me.' She yanked him backwards, keeping his fists up behind his shoulder blades so he couldn't pull free, and marched him back out to the main road and up to the police house. He was so

414

stunned, he had put up no protest – at least after the first time, when she'd seized his ear with her free hand and twisted.

Sergeant Brewer met her in the short hallway, his eyes round with astonishment. 'What's this?'

'I caught him sneaking into the back of the Penhaligons' place,' Gwenna said. 'He wants a good hard lesson, don't you think?' She pushed him towards Brewer, who pulled a pair of handcuffs from his pocket and secured the furious Stibson to a short segment of a bar that ran along the hall.

'Did you catch him by yourself?' he asked. He was studying Gwenna, his eyes narrowed slightly.

'Of course. Little weed like him, it didn't take much.'

'Hmm. Come into the office a minute.'

Gwenna followed him, remembering what Bobby had told her after the incident with the Christmas Fair takings. Surely Brewer wouldn't ask a woman though; his reservations about the abilities of the fair sex were well documented.

He gestured to the chair. 'Sit down, Miss Rosdew.' She did so, and he studied her again, over steepled hands. 'May I call you Gwen?' She almost corrected him, but in the end she just nodded, in case he thought her rude. 'This isn't the first time I've had reason to commend you for your quick and courageous action, is it?' he asked.

'No.'

So he *was* going to ask her. And when he did, it would just be the beginning. Gwenna looked around the room, at the photographs of the constabulary, smartly turned out in their uniforms, and with such proud looks on their faces. From watcher to constable, from constable to sergeant ... Her future might be here in this town after all, but not as a shop assistant. She turned back to Brewer, in time to see him reach into his desk drawer and pull out a pair of handcuffs and a whistle. He laid them on the desk between them, and fixed her with a grave look.

'Have you ever heard of the Watchers?'

She suppressed a smile of triumph and excitement, and instead gave him an innocently puzzled look. 'No.'

'Good.'

Emerging from his office a little later, listening to Nigel Stibson protesting after her departing back, Gwenna opened the front door and looked up at the darkening sky to see the moon riding low over the trees: waning gibbous, just like New Year's Eve. A time for letting go. The threads that had tied her to her old life, and her old fears, were snapping one by one, and as she stood in the doorway she felt the unfamiliar weight of the handcuffs in her coat pocket. The excitement was still there, but now there was a sense of deep contentment too; a quiet happiness she'd forgotten she could feel.

Peter Bolitho, her bullish former fiancé, was out of her life, and so was her crooked flight instructor; under her own steam, she had eventually moved beyond their control. Even her father, as much as she loved him, would no longer hold her happiness and sense of worth in his hands. She pictured Daniel, smiling at her from across the scarred tabletop in the prison visitors' hall, and she wondered how tightly their futures were entwined; she certainly hoped there was something there for them, but whatever happened, it wouldn't stop her from following her own path through it all. She was happy to give him her heart, if he wanted it, and her soul, should he prove he deserved it, but there was only one person she would allow to be in charge of her life now—

'Gwen!' Brewer had appeared in the doorway of his office. 'Don't forget this.'

'Thank you.' She went back, and took the whistle that dangled from his fingers on its chain. 'Oh, Sergeant Brewer?'

'Yes?'

She put the whistle in her pocket, and strode down the path, turning at the gate to send him a broad smile. 'It's Gwen-*na*.'

HISTORICAL NOTE

I drew extensively on first-hand accounts for knowledge of prison life in 1930s, and in particular the Dartmoor Mutiny of January 1932. I apologise for any (minor) liberties I have taken, in the interests of my own narrative, but would like to mention that many things that might look like set dressing, or even convenience, are in fact true: the positioning of the houses beyond the prison wall, onto which Daniel escaped; the wrecked fire engine; the ladder up the wall by the governor's office . . . even the catalyst of ruined porridge, which fuelled the riot.

Many real-life prisoners and officers are named: Sparks, Davis – including his prison number – Greenhow, Cosgrave . . . and there's special guest appearance by Conning's 'spiv' hat, stolen and worn during the riot. Warder Tucker was real, as were Officer Birch, and the Elephant and Castle Gang. I took much of my information from the memoir of real-life Parkhurst prisoner W.F.R. Macartney, whose incredible book: *Walls Have Mouths* gave me a lot of the details I needed to flesh out the realities of prison life in this era. Descriptions of the riot itself have come from several sources, including Simon Dell's fantastic: *Mutiny on the Moor.* The eventual trial: its location, the judge's name, and prisoners' outcomes, are also historical fact. Although, of course, no such separate trial existed for Daniel Pearce, who is entirely my own creation.

ACKNOWLEDGEMENTS

I have so many people to thank for their help (knowingly or otherwise!) in the research of this book. Firstly, I would like to extend my gratitude to **Simon Dell**, whose published work was invaluable, and whose offers of advice have been gratefully received. I'd like to thank the **Dartmoor Prison Museum**, and in particular the deeply knowledgeable and generous **Paul Finegan**, who gave up his time to show me around personally, let me loose on a treasure-trove of documents and memorabilia, and who, as a big 'thank you,' became the hero of the hour in this novel. I could have written so much more into this book, but it wasn't fair on Daniel to keep him in prison any longer, just so I could play!

Thank you to **GH Bennett (Harry)**; historian, lecturer, and all-round good egg, who has guided me towards some brilliant research material, and to **Iain Channing**; lecturer in Criminology at the University of Plymouth, who did the same thing for me when I asked his advice about some of the historical aspects of prison life.

I also owe thanks – and new shoes – to my mum: **Anne Deegan**, who *never* rolls her eyes when I drag her along on a research outing! To everyone who has read my work and continues to support me; to the writing community on Facebook, who have kept my fingers moving on the keyboard during times of self-doubt; and to the wonderful editorial team at **Piatkus Books**, especially **Rebekah West** and **Donna Hillyer,** thank you all.